GOING FOR THE LOT!

Le sombre Anglais, même dans ses
amours, veut raisonner toujours. On
est plus raisonable en France.

[Voltaire]

Ross Wallis   Lagardelle, le 13 août '95.

ROSS WALLIS

MINERVA PRESS
MONTREUX LONDON WASHINGTON

GOING FOR THE LOT!
Copyright © Ross Wallis 1994

Front cover design by the author.

All Rights Reserved

ISBN 1 85863 378 8

First Published 1994 by
MINERVA PRESS
10 Cromwell Place
London SW7 2JN

Printed in Great Britain
Martins the Printers Ltd., Berwick Upon Tweed

GOING FOR
THE LOT!

To Liz, my dear wife, who helped me through the adventure of writing my first novel. It started as a diversion, developed into a love affair, and finally became an obsession; enough to test any partnership!

To my readers, with no encouragement to heed the saying that, when a new book appears, they should read an old one.

And to the only real characters from true life in this story: Jacob, Fosbury, and Yentl, our aristocats.

———

About the Author

Ross Wallis was educated in Australia, India, and Germany, before winning scholarships to Marlborough and Oxford, where he read Modern Languages at Lincoln College.

He served briefly in no less than three British cavalry regiments, none of which forced him to ride a horse. Subsequently he upset European industry to such an extent that he became an eminent management consultant. Even the *Financial Times* and the international management media have surprisingly accepted his occasional contributions.

In 1985, having resigned directorships, he went 'into Africa' to work in Zambia where, among other activities, he learned to fly light aircraft and travelled extensively in East and Southern Africa. He returned to France in 1990 and lives in the Lot with his wife, Liz, and their three cats.

He speaks fluent French and German, essential ingredients for his hobbies of big game viewing, flying, and admiring women of intellect and beauty. His first novel "Going for the Lot!", is to be followed by "Bwana Lot!" and "That's Yer Lot!"

————————

Author's Note

All the central characters in this novel are entirely imaginary. No resemblance whatsoever is intended between them and any persons, living or dead. The bustling town of Borinac in the Dordogne does not exist, nor do the tiny hamlet of Pisenhaut, the commune of Saint Juste, and the market town of Montcarmel in the Lot. This novel is offered as a work of fiction throughout, with deep affection for France, all the nations of Africa, and even Great Britain.

PART ONE

"Les vrais voyageurs sont ceux-là seuls,
qui partent pour partir."

Baudelaire: *"Les Fleurs du Mal"*

Chapter One

"I really don't believe Paul Hattersley has any idea what he's doing," said Diana, as she closed the lid of one of the two large suitcases which they had brought with them. "We spelled out to him exactly the specifications of the house we want. We told him what we are prepared to pay. And what has he done?"

She paused, expecting some reaction and, when there was none, she continued, as if thinking aloud to herself.

"He's shown us ruin after ruin. He's shown us dark, damp, isolated piles of stone in the wrong price range, on which we would anyway have to spend a fortune to get them into reasonable shape. In one of them — that frightful old mill — expensive French electricity would be on all day, it was so dark. All the windows were ridiculously small! *That's* what I miss, coming from the light and space of Africa."

She shrugged, flicked at some dust on the mantlepiece, and turned to leave the room.

"The bare truth is that we've nothing to show for almost three weeks' effort... Except non-starters."

James Wyllis looked up from the sofa on which he was sprawled, and watched his wife's slim, tanned legs as they disappeared into the small kitchen of the rented cottage. He thought, not for the first time, how lucky he was to have such a good-looking woman in his life. What did they say, he mused, about love being better the second time around?

"You're right, of course," he conceded, folding up the *Serie Bleue* map of the Bordeaux-Périgueux area, part of which they had come to know quite well. "The only one which might have been a possible runner," he continued, "was the one near Verteillac with the spiral staircase. That was until we saw that group of bloody *chasseurs* with their hounds, pounding all over the woods and shooting at anything and everything that looked as if it might move."

"That would have been great!" she called from the other room. "Just ideal for our cats! And we've only eight days left before our flight back to Zambia."

James pulled himself out of the sofa and walked slowly across the sparsely furnished room to the large double window. The Dronne, the small river which winds its lazy way across the Dordogne from Brantôme to Coutras, bore witness to the exceptionally long, hot summer which the region had enjoyed. You could wade across that, he thought, without even getting your knees wet.

"About the only good news," he said, "has been the weather." He took a deep breath and smiled. "Just fabulous! It should be a damn good year for wine, '89. Plenty of hot September sun. That's when it's so critical for the vines."

She came back into the room and joined him by the open window to watch a small, dead branch float by in what remained of the river. She took his hand, a wistful look touching her face.

"More than a bit different to the hippos and crocodiles in the Luangwa river," she sighed. "Almost as hot, though. It's hard to believe it's nearly the beginning of October."

"Let's have a drink," he suggested, "before we go out and find somewhere for supper"

He put a generous measure of *Ricard* into the two tumblers and watched the golden liquid turn to a misty white as he added water and ice.

"Good drink, this *Pastis*, when it's hot like this."

He took a large sip, letting the aniseed clear his palate before he swallowed it. I've had too many cigarettes today, he thought. He grimaced, putting it down to the stress of ineffective house-hunting.

They took their drinks outside. The ice tinkled in the glasses, as they went down the worn stone steps leading to the small garden. He glanced at the thermometer on the wall. It was registering 35°C in the shade.

Bloody good, he thought, for six o'clock in the evening. They made their way over to a small, round table made of local stone, which was placed in the shade of a pair of plane trees.

"I wish I hadn't brought so many sweaters," Diana muttered as they sat down. "And as for you! Whatever made you bring *three* suits?"

"Where shall we eat tonight?" he asked, ignoring the question. *"J'ai une faim du loup!* I'm ravenous!" He was surprised at how easily his knowledge of the language had revived itself in such a short period of time.

"We could try that small restaurant," she suggested. "You know, the one in the side street behind the main car park in Borinac. It looks as if it has a nice, cool *terrasse* in the garden at the back. We could eat outside. It probably won't be crowded. Most of the tourists seem to have gone back to wherever they live."

He winced at the thought of all those caravans, some of which even had TV aerials.

"Let's do that," he agreed. "Let's hope they have gone back, particularly the Brits. Back to their days working under neon lights and their evenings in smoke-filled pubs. Back to making money for next year's holiday with their families. Poor buggers! It's not too bad if they're Dutch or Swedish; at least you can't understand them, so you don't have to listen. But the Brits..."

"Remember, darling," Diana laughed, cutting short his words, "*we're* Brits as well."

*

As they drove down the winding river valley towards Borinac James smiled and thought that he had done well to change his mind about the hire car which they had initially collected at Paris-Orly. Temperatures during the drive south had been in the high thirties. The black limousine, with no sun-roof, had been like a silent sauna, its soft suspension making Diana feel sick. At Poitiers they had found a branch office and exchanged it for a soft-top Suzuki jeep, similar to the one in which they had had so many adventures in Africa. Now, with the hood down, the warm, scented air came at them from all sides. Even the crickets and tree frogs could be heard, and they caught an occasional remark from the ever-curious French, snatched away on the wind as they passed. They turned into the car park at Borinac. Rather than secure the hood, he removed the jeep's papers, his camera, and the rotor arm — the latter an old African habit to deter theft. He noticed some, not many, British registered cars, but gave no more thought to them as they walked down the alleyway to *Chez Françoise*.

As they entered the restaurant a middle-aged woman with a large, drooping bust came out from behind a small bar. She wiped the back of her hand, first across her forehead and then up and down her stained apron.

"*Bonsoir, Madame,*" James said politely. "*Nous aimerions bien dîner.* We would like supper. A table outside on the *terrasse,* if possible. *Avec un apéritif, s'il vous plaît. Deux gins et Schweppes, sans glaçon.*" Diana grinned, as always, at the '*sans glaçon',* no ice. It was one of his most inflexible rules: never take ice with a drink in a public place. This policy had been applied rigidly for many years, ever since he had caught a waiter relieving himself on the blocks of ice outside the kitchens of a Nairobi hotel. The woman tried to smile, but the corners of her mouth refused to lift. The effort visibly faltered, then failed. They started to make for the rear garden, but stopped when the woman repeated their order in a strong accent from somewhere near Luton.

"Two is it, my luv? And double G-and-T's, no ice, and on the patio. Right, my darlings, comin' up soon. But, seein' as 'ow we're very busy tonight, we won't mind a little wait, will we?"

Some thirty faces, their mouths full, looked up from their food. Diana could almost feel the hairs bristle on the back of James's neck. Then came a remark from a large, pink-bosomed woman with bleached, ash-blonde hair and a badly peeling cleavage, who was sitting at a table by the door.

"Jack," she said in a loud voice, "them's what I saw last week in the *Cave de la Tour,* buying all that expensive red wine." As she spoke, bits of *cassoulet* and chopped mushrooms in sauce sprayed from her bulging mouth, landing on her partner's glasses and the front of his striped T-shirt. The man, who had to be Jack, patted them away with a resigned gesture and wiped his glasses without a pause in his rate of eating. He looked straight at James, and then at Diana.

"Give over, Iris, and keep bloody voice down!" he said in a dour Yorkshire accent. "They might be English. I doubt it though, dressed like that. From the state of him it looks like he's been dragged out of the African bush backwards!"

They had a long-standing, personal code word for any form of disaster.

"Bagshot! Sounds painful!" said Diana.

The droopy-busted apron lady offered an 'I'm-just-coming-my-darlings', as they walked towards the exit.

"We've just remembered something terribly important," James explained to her. "We've forgotten to lock in our cats. One can't be too careful with the *chasseurs* at this time of the year. Terribly sorry! Maybe we'll come again another time, eh? Maybe, perhaps even, next year! *Bonne soirée à tous!*"

Their exit thus managed and, once outside, James let out an uncharacteristically restrained *"Merde!"*. In the car park once more, what they had not seen, and what would have sent out a warning signal had they noticed it, was evidence of a more permanent Anglo-Saxon presence. It was true that there were a few cars proudly bearing British number plates; the rest were demonstrably registered in France. However, on closer examination, they also bore little, telltale stickers, proclaiming 'GB', or 'We've seen the Lions of Longleat', or 'Windsurfers do it standing up', or 'Dodo Cricket Supporters' Club'.

"No bloody wonder!" James hissed. "Just look at that! How do the French stand for it? These are the local British expats. It's like a replay of the *invasion Britannique.*"

Irritation and stress were beginning to show, heightened by the pangs of hunger and brought on by the frustrated desire for a good meal.

"Come on, darling. Let's go to Gaston's at Tocane-Saint-Apré. We'll see if he can do as well as he did last week."

*

The evening turned out to be one of sheer delight. Not one detail could be faulted, even by a serious gourmet. From the very first moment they arrived, there was that special ambience which combines genuine bonhomie with serious, determined cuisine. As they approached, the heavy oak door was swung open by Monsieur Gaston Larroque, *Diplôme des Arts de la Table* and a *Seigneur des Vins*.

"*M'sieur, 'dame, bonsoir et bienvenue!*" he greeted them with a slight bow. "*Mais c'est vous, Monsieur Wyllis, n'est-ce pas?* You were here last week, weren't you? *Bienvenue,* once again!" And then, giving Diana that appreciative look, which a Frenchman does without causing offence, he went on, *"Oui, oui! Je me souviens de votre charmante épouse.* I remember your charming wife."

He made a discreet sign towards the desk, from behind which a young, pretty girl emerged. She was dressed in black, with a diminutive white lace apron covering her flat stomach.

"Brigitte," he beckoned, *"la table au fond à gauche.* The table at the back on the left."

The girl led the way between the other diners, swaying in the way French girls do so well when they know a man is enjoying watching them.

"Bonsoir, Monsieur, Madame!" she said with an attractive smile. *"Vous voilà de retour.* Here you are again. *Vous prenez un apéritif?"*

James started to ask for two glasses of *Kir Royale,* but before he could finish there was Gaston with an ice bucket, inside which stood a bottle of *Mercier Brut* champagne.

"C'est à vous! Un tout petit cadeau de ma part. A tiny present from me to you. *Tchin, Tchin!"*

With the faintest suggestion of a flourish, Gaston handed over the menus and the wine list. The other diners paid them no attention other than, as they entered the room, the usual *"Monsieur, Madame"*, with which they politely greet even complete strangers in public places. Hushed conversations were being conducted at each of the tables. There was an occasional burst of controlled laughter from a young group seated on the other side of the vaulted room. Candles flickered, reflected in the crystal glass and silver, which made each table a work of art in itself. A delighted *'O-là-là, là-là!'* greeted one of the dishes as it appeared on a neighbouring table. They ordered from the *menu gastronomique,* starting with *Médaillons de Langouste* and *Asperges Sauce Mornay,* shaped morsels of crayfish and asparagus in a white, cheese-flavoured sauce. This was followed by *Terrine de Chevreuil* and *Salade aux Lardons,* a rough venison pâté and salad mixed with small strips of hot bacon. Diana then enjoyed a magnificent *Truite Grillée aux Champignons,* a grilled trout garnished with mushrooms, while James contented himself with what he thought would be a small helping of slivers of *Magret garni,* thin slices of duck breast. However, when it arrived, the garnish included tiny onions, smeared lightly in a mouth-watering sauce, quails' eggs, and the tiny breast of smoked snipe.

At this stage they were both beginning to give up, but the combination of Gaston's watchful eye and the experience of the true professional sensed, if not felt, that battle must now be joined as a matter of honour. He turned to the girl and whispered some instructions. Then, like a noble battleship, he advanced towards their table.

"*Tout va bien, M'sieu?*" he asked solicitously. "You are ready soon for the main course, no? *C'est superbe!*" He was not going to be swayed by any protestations that they had eaten enough, and that the coffee should now follow.

"*Mais, ce n'est pas tellement grave!* It's not all that serious! You can rest a little. *Reculez un peu!* Have a short break! Some lime sorbet will, how you say, clean the palate. *Et puis, il vous faut continuer jusqu'au bout!* Then you must go right through to the very end!"

As if on a perfectly rehearsed cue, Brigitte arrived with a tray of sorbets. Small beads of condensation lay on the outside of the silver goblets, inside each of which were three *boules* of the pale, iced water. Gaston returned to the table with a large bottle, on which there was a label in finely penned, copperplate script. As he poured a tiny measure of the amber liquid over each sorbet, James saw the words '*Calvados, Réserve du Patron*' written across the top of the bottle.

"*C'est mon oncle qui le m'a donné après la guerre.* A present from my uncle after the war. *Allez, mes amis! Soyons courageux! Bon appétit!*"

The sorbets were a masterful solution, exquisitely cold and refreshing. There followed *Filets de Charollais,* beef fillets from the famous herd of Burgundy, a basket which groaned with fresh fruits, the *Plateau de Fromages,* and as much black coffee as they wanted. The sigh of relief, tinged with some pride that justice had been done to a truly special meal, was heard all over the room. Smiles of approval beamed from all sides. The elderly, distinguished-looking gentleman at the next table offered a polite "*Bravo!*", just as if it had been his honour that had been saved. When James paid the bill, the *Mercier Brut,* an '86 *Gaillac Perlé* from *Domaine de Labarthe,* a *Volnay '85,* and a *Fleurie '79* stood empty on the table. As from all great meals in

France, they emerged as if they had experienced a sensitively produced play in five acts, performed by a cast of distinguished actors in a well-known theatre.

The night air was still warm for the short journey back to the cottage. The moon, wheat-coloured in the slight haze caused by the heat of the day, was just climbing above the level of the tree tops. Wisps of mist lay over the river valley. A nightjar darted across the beam from the headlights.

"That was *formidable*! *Superbe!*" sighed Diana as they entered the cottage. James tugged at his cravat, and pulled it free from his neck.

"A nightcap, darling?" he asked. "Would you like a wet whisky, or something else?"

"No thanks, James. I've had more than enough to eat and drink for one week." She smiled, touched the back of his neck, and blew a whisper into his ear. "But I'll have something else, if you like."

"*Ouais! D'ac, chérie!*" he mimicked the local slang as best he could. "*T'as le sang chaud et les cuisses légères, mais je t'aime.* You're hot-blooded and very forward, but I love you!"

He gave the door of the refrigerator a wide berth, locked the door of the cottage, and followed her into the bedroom.

Chapter Two

When they woke up, the sun was already climbing into a clear, blue sky. The outbuildings around the cottage were bathed in almost painfully bright sunshine, contrasted here and there with dark, purple shadows. The old stonework threw back the still heat. On the steps up to the door of the cottage, which they had left open during the night in an attempt to create a through draft, the hydrangea in its medium-sized, terracotta pot was already beginning to wilt, its leaves limp and visibly suffering. There was no wind at all. Complete silence had fallen on the valley. Even the water birds, normally busy and active along the river bank at this hour, had decided to conserve their energy. It was going to be very hot.

James took a sip from the bowl of café au lait which Diana set before him.

"I think," he announced, "I must have a word with Paul. We must not continue to rely solely on him. This is too important and time is running out. We'll have to try our luck with the estate agents in the town. He'll just have to lump it if he doesn't collect his commission on a sale. But I would rather clear the way. Better to be out in the open and legitimate than to sneak off behind his back to other sources without telling him."

"Good. I agree," she said emphatically. "Do just that. It'll be so much more simple if we do our own thing."

He finished his coffee and glanced at the kitchen clock. It was just after ten. He dressed quickly, pulled on his bush boots, and went outside. The heat came at him from all directions. The thermometer was already just over 30°C. He looked across at the farmhouse fifty yards up the lane. All the shutters were firmly closed. There was no sign of life. He returned to the kitchen, poured himself a second bowl of coffee, and went through into the bedroom. Diana was already dressed, looking fresh and cool.

"It looks as if the lazy sod is still in bed. Shit! What a way to win a war! We'll never find a house at this rate." He paused, wondering what to do next, but it was Diana who made up his mind.

"In that case," she suggested, "I think we should just go."

They looked in the windows of three estate agents in Borinac. The glare on the glass made it difficult to see inside easily. Another couple, obviously English, were looking at a photograph of a stone barn. Most of its roof was missing, and it looked as if it was surrounded by tall weeds and obsolete farm equipment. A horse-drawn plough appeared to be the focal point of the picture, the colours of which had faded almost to a monochrome, suggesting that it had been in the window for some time.

"That's not bad," the man said. "It's only two hundred thousand francs, with over three hectares."

"How long would it take you to fix it up then?" asked the woman.

"About a year, luv, give or take a month or two. Piece of cake, I should think. We'll call in this afternoon for details, if you want. We can probably get at least twenty percent knocked off that price."

"Oh! Should we? You're not being serious, are you, Gordon?"

"Put your money in bricks and mortar, that's what I say. You can't go wrong over here nowadays. Good investment, I should think."

"But that barn's made of stone, not bricks, Gordon."

"Don't be daft, Sheila. Manner of speaking, it is."

Bloody idiots, thought James. He could not comprehend the masochism which drove people to live among rubble and dust for months, sometimes for years, in pursuit of restoration.

James felt stupid standing against the window, shielding his eyes in his attempt to see inside. He looked at Diana, who nodded, and they walked back to the first office which they had seen that morning. From the outside it appeared to have a greater selection of properties to offer than the other two. He opened the door and followed her inside. A short man, less than five feet tall, in his late twenties, dressed in shirt sleeves and baggy trousers, was struggling to replace a file on a shelf almost beyond his reach. He managed to push it halfway into its intended space. As he turned to face them the file fell off the shelf, emptying most of its contents on the floor

"Merde!" he swore softly, his embarrassment evident as he scooped up photographs, maps, and assorted papers, dumping them in an untidy pile on top of the nearest filing cabinet.

"Bonjour, Monsieur, Madame," he said, shaking hands with them. *"Je m'excuse."* He waved his hand at the mess which he had just

created. He did not introduce himself.

The agent indicated the two chairs facing his desk, remaining standing until they sat down. He's even shorter than I am, thought Diana, who mistrusted all small men. She thought that she caught a shifty look in his eye as he sat down and almost disappeared from view behind the desk. Gradually his composure returned and, to their surprise, he started talking confidently in passable English, with only a slight trace of an accent.

"You are house-hunting, like so many of your compatriots. This is the largest and most successful estate agency here. I am sure we can fix you up. Let me show you a sample of the properties we have." He asked no questions. "Here. Have a look at some of these," he resumed. "Take your time. The price range is shown on the file cover. Try this one first. All these are in the lowest price bracket we handle." He pushed a loose-leaf folder across the desk. "All our prices are inclusive of agency fees," he explained. "Here, in this part of France, it is normal that the vendor adds agency fees to the asking price of the property. I can assure you that there are no hidden extras."

James, always interested in languages, praised his excellent English. "My father is Welsh. He is a property developer, nothing to do with this business which is run by my mother, who is Corsican. I went to the London School of Economics."

"Right. Well, that explains it," James commented vaguely, not at all sure what it was that had been explained. Most of what he had heard about the LSE had not been all that good. They opened the first file, which contained only colour photographs. Each was marked in the right-hand top corner with a reference number and the asking price. External views of between forty and fifty houses and barns were portrayed. They flipped through them quickly. Some of the pictures were faded. Most of the buildings themselves were dilapidated ruins. None took their fancy.

"Another file?" It was the first question the young man had asked them. "Have a go with this one."

The price bracket had increased significantly.

"These are too expensive," Diana said firmly. "Have you any, which are nearer to the price of the last lot?"

"Certainly, Madam. But, like the file you just looked at, I think you will find that nearly all of them need some structural alterations done to them."

He placed another thick file on the desk. He was right. Lack of maintenance, and the need for rather more than just cosmetic repairs stared back at them from almost every page.

"Some good profits for the building trade in that file," Diana muttered. "And for the demolition gangs," James added, as he shut the folder and passed it back to the agent.

Flicking through a third file, Diana stopped James as he was about to ignore a view of a neat, small, stone house. It had a tiny *pigeonnier,* and the corner of a swimming-pool could just be seen in the picture. The price was well within their range.

"What is the accommodation in this house? Diana asked.

"And where is it?" added James.

The young agent stood up, came out from behind his desk, and walked over to a large-scale map on the wall.

"It's here. A really nice spot." He took a pointer and indicated a green map pin. "The people selling are in a hurry. They will drop their asking price, of that I'm certain. They've bought a flat in Biarritz, and are now saddled with a bridging loan. It must be costing them a small fortune, with interest rates as high as they are."

James wondered about the probity of telling strangers such confidential information. I wouldn't ask him to sell a house for us, he thought.

The agent crossed to the filing cabinet, on top of which he had piled the contents of the file which had fallen out of the shelf. He continued talking as he extracted a slim folder which was marked *'Madame Grandet, Moulinac'.*

"Three bedrooms, if I remember correctly, one large reception, kitchen, bathroom, useful outbuildings. I think she was breeding dogs. Two-and-a-half hectares, with a good field, well-fenced, and some woodland." He had the folder open now, and was checking its contents. "Ah, yes," he resumed. "How stupid of me to forget! A nice swimming-pool, not too large, an orchard with fruit trees, and a row of superb vines. That's about it. A well-maintained, small property, in excellent condition throughout. I can strongly recommend it." He returned to the map on the wall. "The nearest town," he continued, "with sensible shopping is Moulinac, situated on this river. It's about six kilometres from the property. I believe there is a *boulangerie* and a small *épicerie* in Belmont, which will be your nearest village." He paused, wondering what else he might mention to persuade his clients to view this problematic property. "It's an altogether delightful area," he added lamely.

Diana noticed the slight emphasis which he had placed on the words *'your nearest village'*.

"It looks a bit near that railway line and this main road," James grunted, putting on his glasses to take a closer look at the map. He measured the distance roughly with his finger, and checked it against the scale of the map. "About two kilometres, I should say. Certainly no more than three. Too bloody close for my liking!"

"In fact," said the agent, "you cannot hear or see the road or the railway at all from the property. The land rises there, towards the north, and there is this large area of woodland. It's a bit difficult to see from the map, but the woods act as a barrier long before you get anywhere near the railway line, which is down in the valley."

Diana did not react. Map-reading was not one of her strong points. They looked through the rest of the file and saw nothing else of interest in it.

James was not filled with great enthusiasm. It was much too small, he thought.

"I suppose we could go and have a look at it," he mumbled reluctantly.

"Certainly! But you must, if you think you might be interested. The picture does not do justice to the place. The owner's name is Grandet. The husband will be at work, but *Madame* Grandet is at home most of the time. I'll give her a ring now."

He picked up the telephone on his desk and rapidly tapped out the eight-figure number. Diana glanced at James, who was taking a second, closer look at the map on the wall. She had the strangest feeling, that the agent had called the same number on many previous occasions, although she could not think why.

She could just hear the metallic sound of a woman's voice coming from the receiver.

"*Allô, oui! J'écoute.*"

"*Madame Grandet? Bonjour! C'est moi, Monsieur Martin.*"

He pronounced his name 'Marteing', and it was the first time he had used it thus far during the interview.

"You are there this afternoon?" he asked. "*Ah, bon! J'ai des clients, Monsieur et Madame... Un moment, Madame Grandet. Ne quittez pas!*" He stopped and held his hand over the mouthpiece, his embarrassment showing as he realized that he did not know their name.

"*Comment vous vous appelez, Madame?*" he asked, looking at Diana.

"Wyllis."

"*Madame Grandet? Monsieur et Madame Wyllis... Ce sont des Anglais. Oui, oui! Mais oui! Bien sûr! Vers trois heures cet après-midi? Impeccable! Au revoir, Madame.*"

Monsieur Martin pushed the file to one side of his desk, and turned back to his clients.

"*Madame* Grandet will be expecting you at around three this afternoon," he explained. "You have a map? Good. I will mark it for you. I'm sure you will like the place. She's very house-proud, *Madame* Grandet. The house is like a new pin."

They thanked Monsieur Martin, left his office, and emerged on to the crowded pavement.

"It's probably a very long shot," James observed languidly.

A pram, pushed by a fat lady in a hurry, crashed into the back of his legs.

"Sorry, dear," she shouted, as she disappeared round a corner.

"*Merde!*" James gasped. "That bloody hurt!"

He limped a few paces, looking at Diana for sympathy.

"I really want to get out of here, and fast."

"I know," she replied. "So do I."

As they walked back to the jeep they could hear English being spoken on all sides. He looked at the map in the jeep.

"It's about sixty kilometres away. Worth a try, I suppose."

"At any rate," Diana sighed, "it's well within our price range."

*

They found a small restaurant in St-Vincent-de-Connezac, where they chose the sixty francs menu: *potage, salade de tomates, dinde farcie,* stuffed breast of turkey, followed by *fromages.* The bill arrived just as they were finishing the carafe of red *vin du pays.* With plenty of time to spare, they stopped in Moulinac to look around. They noticed the picture of Madame Grandet's house in the windows of the two Moulinac estate agents. One of them was showing a figure lower than the original asking price. Whether intentionally or not, the old price had not been erased properly.

"Well, well!" Diana remarked. "See that? She's dropped twenty-five thousand francs. At least *Monsieur* bloody 'Marteing' was right about one thing. I didn't like him, though. He struck me as a thoroughly shifty character."

"That's because you don't like short-arses."

"No, it isn't. It's my woman's intuition. I'm usually right, as you know. It wouldn't surprise me one little bit if he turns out to be a slippery one."

They were not at all impressed by Moulinac. The town had a tired, seedy aura, seemingly exhausted, as if it had given up any remaining zest for life that it may have had at some time in the past. James made a mental note that, if the Grandet place was a possible buy, they would return to the rented cottage via Vaupont to see if that was any better. The map suggested that both towns were about equidistant from the Grandet property, which was exactly where Monsieur Martin had marked it on the map. This rather surprised James, who tended to view with suspicion anyone else's ability to read a map. In their usual way they spent some time viewing the property and its surroundings from a distance. It all seemed very peaceful, almost idyllic. Neither trains nor traffic could be heard from the valley below. No cars raced down the lane in front of the house. However, as they sat in the jeep, they both agreed that it looked somewhat artificial, giving them a too-good-to-be-true feeling, certainly not natural.

Everything appeared to be spotlessly tidy, manicured, well-scrubbed, polished — depending upon which detail or aspect was being assessed. The swimming-pool, larger than they were expecting to find, was an inviting splotch of blue, the water ruffled by a light breeze and reflecting the afternoon sun. Garden furniture was carefully arranged on the paving around it. The row of vines looked, indeed was, very well tended; there appeared to be three or four varieties of grape among its deep green foliage. The woods, which bordered the far side of the field, both of which Monsieur Martin had mentioned, would be an effective windbreak against anything winter might throw from the north at the house. Plenty of firewood, too, he thought.

"It was a great location," he conceded. "Just as Martin said it was."

He was starting to feel a little enthusiasm for the first time in three weeks. It was nearly three o'clock.

"Let's go and meet *Madame* Grandet," he suggested.

*

There were only about seven yards between the gate on the lane and the front door. Diana made a quick mental calculation: that's about three seconds, she thought, before the cats will be out on the road. They rang the bell; it was a curiously charming arrangement. A toggle at the gate was connected by a thin rope through a small pulley to an old, weather-beaten, ship's bell, which was hanging in the porch. As soon as it rang, Madame Grandet appeared. She was a small, grey-haired woman in her sixties. Her housecoat was gleaming white. It looked as if she had put it on just before their arrival. They introduced themselves and went inside.

"Tout est propre! Tout est propre!" she repeated. "All is clean," as if the Swiss Army Hygiene Inspectorate had suddenly invaded her domaine.

She led them from one spotlessly tidy room to the next, lifting the lavatory seat, picking up the plug in the basin, and pointing to the shining kitchen sink.

"Tout est propre!" she repeated endlessly.

Indeed, just as Monsieur Martin had predicted, it was like a new pin. It did not look as if anything had ever been touched, let alone used in normal, everyday life. However, the amount of space was very restricted, apart from the large main *salon*, off which were a cramped kitchen, a diminutive bathroom, and three bedrooms, two of which were small.

It was the outbuildings which may have started to sway their opinion. Here was security for the cats. There was even the possibility of breeding litter after litter of very expensive, pedigree Burmese kittens. The problem posed by the close proximity of the front door to the gate on the lane started to recede in importance. The grounds were superb. The sun was beating down on the trio as they went twice round the whole piece. Madame Grandet was becoming visibly more and more anxious. As they took their final turn up the line of vines James turned to the Frenchwoman to explore the basis for an agreement.

"*Madame* Grandet," he began. "*Monsieur* Martin instructed us with one selling price. In one of the two estate agencies in Moulinac that figure has been reduced by twenty-five thousand francs."

He paused, trying to see whether the old lady understood the importance of his preamble.

"Yes, *Monsieur*. That's perfectly correct," she replied, confirming the lower figure. She was following his line of thought with total clarity. "*Monsieur* Martin is a greedy imbecile who ignores instructions."

"Well, then. If you were to agree, *Madame*," he continued, "that a fair price for your property would involve a reduction of a further twenty thousand francs, it is just possible that you may have a sale. We like the place, but my wife and I need to discuss a few points."

He stopped, trying to read the change of mood which was appearing on her face. She's going to refuse point-blank, he thought. He was wrong. "*Ce n'est pas vrai!* It's not true!" she shrieked. "You want to buy?"

Disbelief was written all over her face. "That's why I have always loved the English. They are so decisive!" Little beads of perspiration were beginning to appear on her upper lip. "*D'accord! D'accord!*" she cried, giving each of them three kisses: left, right, and left again.

"Just let me discuss a few details with Diana."

*

There were, they agreed, several drawbacks. Most had to do with the chronic lack of space. The place could not possibly be a long-term proposition. The only question, therefore, was whether or not it would serve them as an adequate, temporary solution. Two advantages emerged during their short discussion. Firstly, there was no need to spend any money at all to make the place instantly habitable. Indeed, and most unusual in France, Madame Grandet had included in the price all the fixed electrical appliances. This was an additional bonus, which they had neither requested, nor expected. They had heard tales of kitchens being stripped and fixtures removed, such as the kitchen sink, which normal people would regard as part of the fabric of a house. Here, they could move in their goods and chattels and, so to speak, start living immediately.

As a result, the second advantage was that the house could undoubtedly be let profitably, if their time in Zambia was extended or even prolonged. They had not given much previous thought to this idea.

"But what about all our furniture?" Diana asked. "Our rugs, pictures, china, and all the things in store in England — they'll never fit in. There just isn't the space. There aren't enough cupboards for my china and glass. The kitchen is minuscule. And then, eventually, what about all our Zambian and African stuff that we've accumulated? There's quite a lot of it, you know."

"Well," he suggested, "some of the UK kit could come out here, stuff like some of the beds, sofas, chairs, and so on. Some, but not much, might have to stay in store if we want to keep it for later on, such as our big dining-room table and chairs. And the rest, for which we have no present or future use, can be sold. The good pieces can be sent to London. The rest can go in a local sale in, say, Camberley or Wimbledon. As for the Zambian end, when people are clearing off, they simply have a house sale, although I agree that there may be a little freight coming back." He grinned, and then added, "Like the three cats."

Diana pouted, her irritation testing her patience and the anxiety which she was experiencing at that moment.

"Stop being silly! It won't be a joke, you know. You forget just how many possessions we have. So do I, sometimes. For instance, just think of the pictures. There must be about ninety in England. I know, because I had to supervise their packing and removal after you had left for Africa. And I should think that there must be another fifty or so at the other end. Where on earth are we going to put all that? I think it's quite impractical."

He agreed, and then went on to suggest that they could use some of the outbuildings for storage space. They appeared to be in good repair, and he thought that nothing would become damp or be damaged.

"Dare I ask," he said, changing the subject, "how you feel about cat security?" He was surprised that she had not mentioned this earlier.

"Well, in one word: dodgy! I reckon Fosbury will need just three unattended seconds to reach the lane from the front door if it's left open. Still, we can always lock it. He'll just have to take his chances."

They both fell silent, looking at each other. James shrugged his shoulders and walked a few paces along the vines. He turned and went back to her, just as she was lighting a cigarette.

"Is there anything else," he asked, "that we haven't considered?"

"I don't think so," she said quietly.

"In that case, my dearest one, it's make-your-mind-up time, as they say. How do you really feel about it?" As he asked the question he felt the unfairness of it, adding, "I know it's a really unfair question. In real life, people don't go about buying unsurveyed houses on the spur of the moment. That is, not unless they are maniacs or fools with more money than sense. And we're neither, are we?"

"I don't think so," Diana murmured. "Although there are times when I begin to wonder about you." She was trying desperately to be rational and unemotional. "We wouldn't.... We *couldn't* lose money when we sell, could we? It's got to be a good investment. It broadens our risk base, or whatever you call it. It might even produce a reasonable income from letting. I think.... Yes! I think we should go for it!"

"D'accord! Agreed! Bloody good!"

He bent down, picked a bunch of the deep purple grapes and then, tucking his arm around her waist, they walked back up to the house.

*

Madame Grandet was waiting in her *salon*. A bottle of Martell brandy and an empty glass stood on the table.

"Shame!" Diana whispered in English. "She's got herself into a state. Perhaps *Monsieur* Martin was right after all. She must be under severe pressure to sell up on account of that bridging loan. I wonder how long the place has been on the market."

"*Madame* Grandet," said James, taking one of her small hands. "You are an extremely good saleswoman, and I shall tell your husband so when we meet him. Subject to the normal processes of your legal system, you have sold your house. *Nous allons l'acheter!* We shall buy it through *Monsieur* Martin's agency, for forty-five thousand francs less than the price shown in the prospectus. *D'accord?*"

She sat down.

"*D'accord, Monsieur,*" she agreed, bursting into tears.

Diana put her arm around her shoulders and comforted her gently.

"How do you say 'There, there' in French?" she asked.

"*Là là! Ne vous inquiétez pas, Madame!* Don't worry!" James said, trying to be helpful. He offered her his red, silk handkerchief. He knew he was no good with weeping women. Madame Grandet looked up at him from her chair. More tears were welling up in her eyes and spilling down her cheeks. She was now trying to smile and laugh at the same time, but the tears kept coming.

"*Je suis tellement heureuse!* I am so happy! We have waited so long to sell this place."

Diana shot a glance across the room at James, who could not read the message behind it. The Frenchwoman had started speaking again.

"He, that is, my husband, was getting quite ill over all the delays. He will also be more happy now. I will ring him at his shop. And you.... You are good people. You will not be changing your mind, will you? You, too, will be very happy here." She sniffed hard and wiped her eyes with the handkerchief. "But I am being just a silly, old, emotional woman! Come! Our custom on these occasions is a *vin d'honneur,* a bottle of champagne to celebrate."

She rose, went to the refrigerator, and reverently removed a bottle of *Heidsieck.* She passed it to James, who examined it with the respect it was due. Madame Grandet put three glasses on the table, as he took the wire off the cork.

"*O-là-là!*" he exclaimed, opening it with a practised flourish.

"*Attention! Soyez prudent!*" cried Madame Grandet, clapping her hands. "Don't spill any. It's supposed to bring bad luck, if you do."

He filled the glasses carefully, handing the first one to the Frenchwoman.

"*Tchin, tchin!*" she beamed, now well on the way to making a rapid recovery.

"*À votre santé, Madame!*" Diana returned the toast.

"*À la bonne vôtre!*" James gulped. As he looked down at his glass, which was already empty, he noticed two tiny drops of wine on the table. He gave them a surreptitious wipe with his sleeve. Neither of the two women noticed.

While they finished their champagne, which did not take long, they agreed that they would meet at Monsieur Martin's office at three o'clock the following afternoon. Monsieur Grandet would be present. They would have to sign the *Compromis de Vente*, a legally binding form of Statement of Intent to Purchase, to which there is no English equivalent. Once signed, there would be no going back, unless specific clauses were written in to the document to protect either or both parties. A *Notaire* would have to be instructed to handle subsequent transactions on behalf of the State.

With a cheerful "*À demain!* See you tomorrow!" Madame Grandet waved to them from the gate as they left. She disappeared into the house to telephone her husband, who would make all the arrangements for the next day.

"I hope we've done the right thing," said Diana softly. She had gone very quiet since drinking the champagne.

"Bloody good!" James pronounced, giving his thigh a hearty slap.

They made a brief tour of Vaupont on the way back. It was a pleasant, riverside town, bustling with activity. It had visibly won the contest with Moulinac for customers and trade. The sun was still shining as a clock somewhere struck six. They both felt good about the day's efforts.

Chapter Three

Paul Hattersley heard them when they returned to the cottage. He had been waiting for them since mid-morning. A big, tall man with unruly, red hair, he shambled over to greet them, a broad grin on his face. Diana noticed that he had on the same T-shirt and shorts which he had been wearing all week. He had not shaved, and she could smell the heavy garlic on his breath.

"I have good news for you," he announced cheerfully. "Which part would you like to hear first? The good, or the very good?"

"In that order, Paul," James replied, a note of irritation creeping into his voice.

"Well, whatever job you were after, James," he said pleasantly, holding out his hand, "it seems as if you must have landed it. Congratulations!" His handshake made James wince. "This fax came in just before lunch. It's what you've been waiting for, isn't it?"

"That's great news! Thank you very much."

He took the fax from Paul and, having read it quickly, he passed it to Diana. "What a relief! It's taken them long enough to make up their minds. And the other good news, Paul? Don't tell us you've found a wife!"

"No, no! Bachelor free, am I." Paul laughed. "No, this time I really do think I've found the perfect house for you. A seventeenth-century farmhouse. Quite stunning! The owners...."

"Hang on, Paul," James interrupted him. They were all still standing beside the jeep. "I tried to find you this morning to tell you that we were going to try a few estate agents. You weren't around. I couldn't find you. Your shutters were all closed. I assumed that you were still in bed. It was at about ten this morning, wasn't it, Diana?"

He looked at her for confirmation as she read the fax. She was smiling contentedly and looked excited.

"Yes... No. I don't know exactly. About then," she replied absent-mindedly. She was overjoyed at the prospect of the confirmed return to all her friends in Zambia.

"Well, anyway," James resumed, "that's *exactly* what we did, what we've been doing all day. I'm sorry to have to break it to you like this, Paul, but you're too late. We think we've found a house which will suit us well as a temporary base." He moved towards Diana. "In fact, with the news about the job, I think our mission in France is about to come to a successful conclusion. We have to be in Martin's office in Borinac at three tomorrow afternoon to do the necessary."

Paul did not appear in the least put out, but his face took on a serious look.

"I see," he shrugged. "But watch it with the Martins. Did you deal with the Corsican mother or her frightful son, Claude?"

"I presume it was the son. Why?"

"Crooked as bent sixpences, the pair of them!"

Paul's damning remark sounded neither like sour grapes, nor as if it was prompted through professional jealousy. He had said it as if he really meant it. He looked genuinely concerned.

"Whereabouts is this property?" he asked James. "Come over to my office in the farmhouse and show me on the map. We can have an *apéritif* while you tell me about it. Diana excused herself. She was reading the fax again, as she climbed the steps into the cottage. The two men strolled up the lane to the farmhouse

*

In Paul's office there were papers, maps, files, and books everywhere. Ashtrays had not been emptied and several dirty glasses were perched wherever they had last been used and put down. Paul found his map. He appeared to James to be oblivious of the air of disorganization and chaos in the room.

"Show me where," he said, as he spread the map over the clutter of files on his desk.

"There! Just there! In fact, that tiny, black dot is the house."

"Merde! Just what I was beginning to fear, I'm afraid. James, I'm sorry. I should have warned you, but I forgot. It gives me no pleasure to tell you this. I bet neither that little runt, Claude, nor the desperate owners said anything to you about the projected motorway down there." James felt as if a hand grenade, loaded with icy shards, had exploded in the room. He sat down on top of a heap of books, which

had been thrown in one of the two armchairs.

"Shit! You're not being serious?"

"Never more so, I'm afraid. Look, have a drink, and I'll tell you what little I've picked up on the grapevine. Red wine or whisky?"

"Whisky will do me more good at the moment. Thanks."

They sat, facing each other as Paul started to explain with carefully chosen words.

"For some few years now, a new autoroute has been under continuous and active consideration. It will run from Switzerland, right through to Spain when it is eventually completed, and it will connect, among other places, Lyon with Bordeaux. That means it will have to pass through the Dordogne. All sorts of pressure groups, cranks, various hotheads, genuine environmentalists, the *vignerons,* and so on have put up a long, expensive, and well-orchestrated campaign of active resistance. If my sources are correct, it appears they have lost. To cut a long story short, my latest information is that it's now going to go ahead. The only matter to be settled is a final decision on which of three alternative routes is preferred — that is to say, the one deemed to be the least objectionable. The government is determined to drive it through. They have swingeing powers, you know, if they are forced to apply them. My guess is that it's not a question of if, rather when, it will become an ugly fact of life."

Paul dragged his large frame out of the chair and shambled over to the sideboard. He poured James a second whisky and then continued his explanation.

"Coming closer to home, to your proposed home, I'm led to believe that the alternative routes all converge somewhere down here." His fingers brushed the map along the river valley, menacingly close to Moulinac and Vaupont.

"Merde! Bloody people! What a balls-up!"

"Did you by any chance sign anything today?"

James shook his head as he swallowed a mouthful of whisky.

"Well, in that case, you're not committed. Not yet. But you will be the moment you sign the *Compromis. "*

James slumped back in the chair, suddenly feeling weary, and wondering whether this fiasco would ever come to an end.

"Tell me, Paul. What action should we take now?"

"Right. The first thing you should do is to check my version. I haven't seen any plans, and I'm not absolutely sure where or when it will all start happening. There's only one place you can find out for certain. In that case, tomorrow morning, you must go down to Moulinac. Find the *Mairie,* the *Hôtel de Ville.* Remember, it will shut promptly at midday to allow the *hauts fonctionnaires,* the civil servants, their two hours for lunch. Ask in there if you can look at any plans, maps, drawings, or whatever, which have any bearing on the projected *péage.* They will have them; they can't refuse you. They're not allowed to deny access to the general public on such matters. See what you can find out. Speak to the *Secrétaire de Mairie*, if necessary. I'll be here tomorrow morning. Ring me if you need any help."

"Thanks, Paul. Thanks a hell of a lot! I'll do that."

James rose and turned to go and break the news to Diana, but Paul stopped him.

"I can see you're very disappointed," Paul continued in his strangely sympathetic manner. "I'm sorry about that, but these things happen, you know, particularly here in France. I know it too well. I've heard of cases where people have been well and truly screwed, and lost a lot of money. A new motorway, a new bypass, a bloody great electric pylon line, all these kinds of development affect immediately anything as sensitive as the property market. It's better to find out now, rather than later. I bet you that the property you looked at today has been on the market for months, if not a year or two. That's exactly why I don't bother to prospect down there — there are too many embuggeration factors! In that area," he pointed again at the map, "properties are sticking. In fact, they're stuck. And that little wimp, Claude, he knows it only too well. He hasn't got the ethics of a Marseilles docker with the clap. He'll screw anybody, or anything. He would never give you a proper briefing and run the risk of aborting a sale. Terrible reputation he has. Nasty, sawn-off bit of Corsican *merde!* What he needs is someone to give him a good fucking!"

James was thinking of Madame Grandet's exhibition of tears of relief and elation.

"I feel sorry for the owner," he muttered. "She was so over the moon. If we have to back out, I think it might kill her. Still, *'Il faut cultiver notre jardin'* is what Voltaire's Candide said, wasn't it? Anyway, thanks again for the advice. You've been most helpful, and I really mean that. Thanks also for the whisky. I'll be in touch tomorrow."

"Yes. Tomorrow is another day," Paul sighed. "Oh! By the way, James, have a look at this. Just in case. You never know."

He handed James a folder and reached for his red wine. On his way back to the cottage, James looked to see what Paul had given him. It was a prospectus. The headline read: "A delightful, seventeenth-century farmhouse in exquisite surroundings, offering..."

*

In the small kitchen, Diana had prepared a cold supper. She had showered, and was looking fresh and happy after the long day. On the table were *rillettes pur porc,* a mixed salad, cheese, and fruit. Beside the small gas cooker were the ingredients for the *crêpes* which would follow. He opened one of the cupboards and took out a bottle of Cahors *Château Nozières,* which he had found several days previously in a local supermarket. A small, gold medallion was stamped on the label, with the words: *'Médaille d'Or, 1985. Concours de Qualité des Vins de France, Foire Internationale de Paris'.*

"Everything all right?" she enquired, as he came through the door.

"Great," he lied, having finally decided, as he was walking back from the farmhouse, not to tell her at this stage about Paul's ominous news.

"You're pleased about the Zambian contract, aren't you?" he asked, trying to sound cheerful.

"Yes. A great relief. Well done, my darling," she replied, bending down to kiss him. "It's exactly what I wanted to happen."

He pulled the cork and emptied the dark red wine into a decanter. Let it breathe a bit, he thought. He felt as if he had been winched backwards through a mangle.

"I've got a *truc* on one of my toes." He became aware that she was talking. "If you don't mind, I'll try to find a chiropodist tomorrow and get it fixed. It's hurting me to walk. I want to have a look at the shops, too. I haven't had a chance since we arrived. But don't you come too. You hate trailing around after me. And you'll just get bad-tempered and in my way. Have a lie-in tomorrow. We've done what we set out to do. We've found a house. So take the morning off. You look completely bushed."

"No, darling. There's something I have to do. I'll drop you in the town tomorrow morning. You can find a taxi to get you back here when you've finished your shopping. I'm going back to Moulinac to check on something. We'll meet here sometime before lunch, around midday." She gave him a puzzled look, but said nothing.

*

James was awake earlier than he had intended. He had not realized the previous night just how tired he had been, until he had climbed into bed. The combination of success at the Grandet property, his elation tinged with relief about his job, and angry frustration over the probable deception perpetrated by Monsieur Martin had left no room for further rational thinking. Drained of all emotion, he had fallen almost immediately into a deep, dreamless sleep. Now, as he lay fully awake in bed, he was able to consider his next course of action. Diana, her back turned to him, was curled up and fast asleep. She had thrown back her duvet so that it only covered her legs. He noticed, as he had often seen before, that both her fists were tightly clenched. He wondered whether he had been wise to shield her from Paul's information and its implications. She was bound to have an opinion. If there were to be a crisis, she would wish to share it and to make a contribution to its resolution.

On the other hand, Paul may have been exaggerating. He had been vague about the alleged motorway routes. In fact, he had said that he was not at all sure about their precise location. Perhaps it would all turn out to be a false alarm. He made up his mind. He would stick to his plan, and find out as much as he could in Moulinac that morning. There was no point in worrying Diana at this stage. Decisions should not be made without all the relevant facts. Knowledge allows choices to be made. He would not reveal the purpose of his mission. Later perhaps, he thought, but not yet.

*

He dropped Diana in Borinac, and was walking up the steps of the *Mairie* in Moulinac as the clock in the square struck ten. The information desk was opposite the main entrance, inside a wide, dimly-lit hall. An old man with a floppy, black beret was shuffling away from the desk towards the door, which led out to the street. Arthritis had claimed yet another defenceless victim. He was heavily lined, and several days' growth of silvery stubble covered his weather-beaten face. The girl behind the desk was shaking her head sympathetically as the old man's bent back disappeared from view. The big, heavy door, caught by a sudden gust of wind from the street, closed with a bang. The sound echoed around the hall.

James approached the desk. A portrait of the President, flanked by two tricolours, stared down at him. The girl smiled. It was the kind of smile which says, "Yes, I know you think I'm pretty, and I am."

"Bonjour, Monsieur."

He could see that she wore no ring on her left hand.

"Bonjour, M'mselle."

He explained what he wanted. The girl nodded confidently, came out from behind the desk with a *"Suivez-moi, Monsieur,"* and led him through a side-door which was marked *'Salle de Lecture'* in faded letters. The reading room was dark. The competing odours of stale cigarette smoke, leather-bound books, newspapers, dusty files, and faded, velvet curtains filled the room, in the middle of which stood a long, oak table with a desk lamp at one end. She switched on the lamp, which cast its harsh light on to a thick document folder. It had been left lying open at a map. This is it, he thought. Now we can find out what the hell is happening around here.

"Voilà, Monsieur!" she pointed, and smiled again. *"Servez-vous.* Help yourself."

The map showed the river valley, with Moulinac, Vaupont, the railway line, and the main road. Three broad lines, superimposed in blue, red, and green ink, cut a swathe east to west across the area. The legend confirmed their significance: *'PROJECTED ALTERNATIVE MOTORWAY ROUTES'*. The red line was the preferred option. He put on his glasses and examined the details on the map. All three possible routes converged just on the north-eastern side of Belmont, before they cascaded down to the valley to track alongside the path of the main road. He took his small, pilot's ruler out of his bag, and carefully measured the distance between the Grandet house and the nearest point on the path of the projected motorway. He checked it against the scale. It was exactly nine hundred metres.

"Fuck that!" he said aloud.

He did not look at anything else in the folder. There was no need to do so — the evidence was damningly clear. Even if construction was delayed for another five years, the threat implied by the three obscene lines on the map would hang over the area like a black cloud. Property sales would continue to stagnate and prices would fall. He slammed the folder shut, its heavy cover throwing a cloud of dust into the light from the lamp.

The girl at the desk was engrossed in a copy of *Elle* magazine. She glanced up as she heard his footsteps.

"*Vous avez trouvé, ce que vous cherchiez?*" she asked pleasantly. "Did you find what you wanted?"

"*Malheureusement, oui!*" he replied. "Unfortunately, yes! Do you know when all that *merde* in there is going to happen? What do the local people think about it?"

"*En principe,*" she shrugged, "*on dit l'année prochaine.* In theory, they say next year. The people here are very worried." She handed him a neat, threefold brochure. On the front cover, in red, white and blue, were the unambiguous words: '*NON À L'AUTOROUTE!*'

"Could you please let me have two photocopies of the map?" She reached into a drawer in her desk.

"*Voilà! Trois francs, s'il vous plaît, Monsieur.*"

"*Merci bien, M'mselle. Allez! Au revoir, et bonne journée!*"

"*Au revoir! De même!* You, too," the girl said politely.

He knew it was not going to be a good day for him. As he went down the steps of the *Mairie* he looked across at the clock. It had taken less than ten minutes to confirm both Paul's worst predictions and the attempted deception by Monsieur Martin.

"*Monsieur* bloody Martin," he hissed aloud. "I'm going to screw you, you bastard! I'm going to hang your balls up outside your office door!" A passing *gendarme* stopped and gave him a quizzical took as he hurried to the jeep.

*

Shortly after he had finished telling Paul the outcome of his visit to

Moulinac, James was sitting at the kitchen table in the cottage, when Diana entered. He had been studying closely the new *Série Bleue* map which he had bought that morning in Moulinac. He looked up, feeling a little guilty.

"Get your toe fixed?" he asked.

"Yes. Very efficient, but it cost a bomb!"

She put a large plastic bag on the table. Splashed across it in English was the banal slogan: *"I do my shopping in Borinac!"*

"Merde!" he moaned. "Look at that! Bloody Boring-ac makes me puke!"

"I know," she nodded. "Isn't it bloody awful! But nice shops, damned expensive, and crawling with Brits. I didn't have to speak French once during the whole morning."

She rummaged inside the plastic bag, and pulled out a cotton shirt. It was a sludge green colour, with breast pockets and long sleeves ending in double cuffs. With a light kiss she handed it to him.

"Here. A present for you for being so patient with our house-hunting and for finding our new, temporary home."

"O-là-là, là-là! That's sexy!" He kissed her, this time a little less gently.

"I bought this too," she continued, opening the wrapping paper and holding up a thick, crew-neck jumper. It was woollen and soft grey. The front had on it the silhouettes of three black cats, set against a background of a full moon rising over the roof of a house.

"This is for me," she announced with a twirl.

"I'm glad you said that," he quipped. And then quickly added, in case his remark might be misinterpreted, *"Mais, que c'est superbe! Bravo, Madame!"*

"It was terribly, terribly expensive. Otherwise, all I bought were these postcards. I must send them off today."

He picked up the map which he had been studying, and put it away. It was time for an *apéritif*, he thought. He poured out two gins, making his own at least a double measure.

"Something's wrong, Jamie," she said quietly, as he added the slices of lemon and the tonic water. "I can tell. What is it?"

"T'as raison, chérie, comme toujours," he replied. "Here, sit down. You might need this." He pushed her drink across the table and

slumped into one of the wicker chairs.

"Bad news, I'm afraid. We can't possibly buy the Grandet place. Look at this." He placed on the table the photocopy of the map which he had collected from the *Mairie* in Moulinac.

"What are those thick black lines?" she asked.

"Those, my love, are the three alternative routes for what, at some time in the future, is going to be one of France's busiest and, no doubt, bloodiest motorways."

He pointed silently at the map, following slowly the projected red route.

"Look. That's where they converge," he explained. "There is Belmont. And here, that little, black dot, is *Madame* Grandet's house. It really doesn't matter which of the three options is chosen, although apparently the preferred route is this one." He pointed at the map again. "The distance between the house and that point of convergence is nine hundred metres, rather less than a mile."

At first, she said nothing. She just stared at the map and then at him. Slowly, her dazed look changed from one of total bewilderment, through disbelief, and then to full comprehension.

"What on earth are you saying? Do you mean to say...? It can't be true! I bloody well don't believe it! That damned, short-arsed cheat! I *knew* he was a creep! I bloody *knew* it! I knew it from the moment he first looked at me! How did you find this out?"

"From the *Mairie* at Moulinac. This is a copy of their map on view to the general public. Paul put me on to it yesterday evening. I'm sorry I didn't tell you last night. I didn't want to worry you, perhaps unnecessarily. Paul was only feeding me hearsay. He wasn't sure of all his facts. He might have been wrong. I had to go and check it out. But, there it is. Paul was right, after all."

He described the previous evening's discussion with Paul, and then explained what he had discovered at Moulinac that morning. She listened intently.

"That's it," he said in a dry tone. "I'm sorry, my love."

"Don't be sorry. It's a blessing you found out!"

"Well, we can't proceed with the Grandet property. That's obvious now, isn't it? Paul is sure that we are in no way committed, since we haven't signed anything."

"That poor *Madame* Grandet. Surely she can't have known anything about all this, can she? She'll have a stroke, or something. How are we going to tell her? I bet it was that creep, Martin, in cahoots with *Monsieur* Grandet, who put her up to this. Poor woman! How could they do this to her? Bloody irresponsible, I say! They've just been playing around with her emotions."

"*Her* emotions! What about *ours*?" he retorted.

"You must ring her right now, and cancel this afternoon's meeting. It will be a waste of time, and it will only upset her again."

He did not react immediately. He had already considered an abrupt telephone call to terminate the messy affair, and had dismissed the idea.

"No," he said firmly. "I have a better game-plan. If they want to play silly buggers with us, then we'll do the same with them. We'll keep our appointment this afternoon, and we'll give that little runt, Claude Martin, a lovely big surprise. I'll try not to hurt *Madame* Grandet's feelings but, under the circumstances, that may be a little difficult. But that smart arse, *'Marteing'*, is long overdue to learn a fundamental business lesson. I'm going to enjoy taking him apart!"

Chapter Four

The heat of the afternoon had melted the tarmac in places. Even at three o'clock in the afternoon the sun was baking the main street in Borinac. Tradesmen without the benefit of any air-conditioning had kept shut the doors to their shops in an attempt to conserve some of the cooler, indoor air. Shutters to the higher windows and balconies were closed everywhere. The air stood still in a vacuum of sweltering brightness. The humidity was the highest they had thus far experienced during their stay in France. From the south came the distant rumble of thunder several miles away. It must be brewing up for a storm, thought James, as he closed the roof of the jeep.

"Just hang on a minute," he said to Diana, who was glancing at the shop windows as they passed.

He disappeared into a shop, displaying hunting jackets and cartridge belts in its window. She waited outside and admired an arrangement of baby clothes in the next shop, thinking of the grandchild, which she wanted so much. Shame! she thought. How lovely they all are, but what a pity they're so expensive! When James reappeared, she caught a fleeting glimpse of a small thin object being concealed in his coat pocket. She thought no more about it.

Monsieur Martin's office was air-conditioned. It was cold, in contrast to the humid heat outside. As they went in, James wedged the door open. Monsieur Martin was sitting at his desk, talking to Madame Grandet and a heavily-built man with a balding head. Diana noticed that this time the agent was sitting on two cushions, and he was wearing a lightweight suit. Unlike during their previous visit to the office, everybody was introduced to each other. It was done very formally and very correctly. When Monsieur Grandet stood up, he towered over them all, and his handshake was as strong as a vice. He sat down, one leg crossed over the other, trying to look relaxed. He was not succeeding.

While the agent shuffled some papers from one side of his desk to the other, James took the opportunity to ask Monsieur Grandet what he did for a living.

"I'm a b-b-butcher," he replied in a gravel voice with a slight stutter. "Thirty-eight years in M-M-Moulinac."

James was not certain about the origin of his accent; he thought that it sounded like Aquitaine.

"B-B-Business is really b-b-bad," the butcher grumbled. "I've never known anything like it b-b-before. P-P-People are saying every day that they just don't have any m-m-money any m-m-more."

As he spoke, he pulled continuously at the top of his left sock, exposing the calf of his leg. James noticed that he had bad varicose veins. The combined smell of *Calvados* and garlic on his breath was overwhelming. James made a mental note not to pursue the subject of the state of his business. He remembered the agent's inappropriate comments about the couple's bridging loan. He felt he was in danger of starting to feel sorry for them.

Monsieur Martin, on the other side of the desk, was looking smug and self-satisfied. He was thinking to himself, had he not, at last, brought to a successful and well-earned conclusion this long, seemingly endless saga of the sale of the Grandet property? It had been on their books, he recalled, for more than three years. His mother, for whom he felt little or no affection, might even agree to pay him the bonus which he was intent upon demanding as his reward. He owed money to the betting shop in Périgueux, the owner of which was pressing hard for repayment with high interest charges.

Madame Grandet was sitting demurely, her handbag on her lap. She was wearing a pale blue, cotton outfit. She looked very chic in it. Surprisingly, it was she who spoke next. She suddenly snapped open her bag, and took out a small package wrapped in tissue paper.

"Monsieur Wyllis," she said. *"C'est à vous.* This is yours. Thank you so much for lending it to me."

James unwrapped the tissue to find his red, silk handkerchief inside it. It had been cleaned and pressed with great care.

"Madame Grandet," he protested. *"Ce que vous êtes tellement aimable!* How very kind of you! You shouldn't have bothered to have had it dry-cleaned. It was quite unnecessary to..."

"Non, non, non, Monsieur!" she interrupted him. *"Tout est propre! Comme toujours!"*

Monsieur Martin leaned forward as far as he could from his raised perch behind his desk. Diana was suddenly reminded of an ugly hyena, waiting its turn to pick over the remains of a buffalo kill.

"Well," said the agent, "perhaps we should now begin. I understand that a price has been discussed. A reduction of twenty-five thousand? Is that correct? Are all the parties in agreement?"

Madame Grandet raised her hand in protest.

"Non! Monsieur Martin, vous avez tort encore une fois!" she answered determinedly. "You are wrong yet again. That is not correct. Yesterday I assured *Monsieur* and *Madame* Wyllis that a reduction of forty-five thousand francs would be entirely acceptable, if there were no complications in the transaction."

"Zut! Bahhh, M-M-Madeleine!" Monsieur Grandet growled.

"Tais-toi! Imbécile!" snapped his wife, revealing unexpectedly a new side to her character

"I see," said the agent.

"And are there any complications?" asked James, addressing the agent. "I'm not aware of any on our side. We have the money for the statutory deposit. It's in London, waiting to be transferred. We can pay our deposit to the *Notaire* as soon as you give us the go-ahead. The balance is readily accessible, on completion of all the formalities. We are entirely in your trusted hands, *Monsieur.*"

He gave Monsieur Martin a searching look. The corner of the agent's left eye twitched involuntarily. He sat back in his chair, momentarily taken aback. He ignored James's question.

Fifteen-Love! thought James.

"May I just return to the matter of the selling price?" the agent resumed, talking rapidly to the French couple. "Why was I not informed about this new price? Did you know this, *Monsieur* Grandet?" His speech was wild and excited, and he was waving his arms with exaggerated gestures.

"You have discussed it with your wife, no?" he continued. "You've agreed this new price, yes?"

The butcher was becoming flustered. James understood the gist, but by no means all, of what was being said.

"Elle m-m-m'a raconté tout ce qu'elle a dit à M-M-M'sieur Wyllis," Monsieur Grandet confessed. He was slurring his words and

looked dejected. "She told m-m-me when I got b-b-back home last night. *Ce n'est qu'une connerie!* It's a cock-up! *C'était déjà un f-f-fait accompli!"*

"You realize," said the agent, "that I am still entitled to keep the original, agreed fee."

Go on! James said to himself. Have a bloody good argument! It'll put you both in good shape for what's coming next.

Monsieur Grandet was now on his feet, looking contemptuously down at the diminutive agent. He was rubbing his large, right fist into the palm of his left hand.

"I wouldn't like to meet him alone at night on a dark corner," James whispered in English to Diana.

She did not react. She was concentrating on the rapid exchange of heated words between the two men.

"Vous avez une gueule, qui ne m-m-me revient pas!" Monsieur Grandet was shouting. "You've got a m-m-mouth I really don't like! *Vous m-m-me faites dégobiller! Salopard!* You make me want to puke! You bastard!"

"Mais, Monsieur!" whined the agent. *"Je vous en prie!"*

"Des clous! No way!" The butcher's face was livid. A vein on his temple was swelling as he became increasingly angry. *"Con!* You'll get your b-b-bloody p-p-percentage of the f-f-final selling p-p-price when, b-b-but only when, the house is sold. *Vous êtes un résidu de f-f-fausse couche, vous!* You puny, little runt!"

In one quick movement, Madame Grandet picked up her handbag and swung it hard and accurately against her husband's knee.

"Ça suffit les gros mots! Enough swearing!" she shrieked.

"La b-b-barbe! Tu m-m-me f-f-fais m-m-mal! That hurt!"

It couldn't happen to a nicer person, thought James. That's the way to do it! Divide the enemy forces before committing to the attack.

The burly butcher sat down, and the house agent wiped his face with a paper tissue, knowing that he had lost that rally.

"Thirty-Love, I make it," James said to Diana.

Monsieur Martin might speak good English, but he was most certainly not a tennis fan. He completely missed the point.

"What's the problem, *Monsieur* Martin?" James enquired. "I wasn't able to follow all that. You were both speaking too quickly."

"Non! Non! Pas de problème, je vous assure!"

"But *are* there any complications, as *Madame* Grandet mentioned earlier, in this very simple transaction? Is there something I really ought to know? In business, you know, we must be scrupulously fair and above board with each other, mustn't we? Otherwise, the ball always ends up back in your court."

"Mais non! It's all perfectly straightforward... Simple, as you put it. I think we had better move on to the *Compromis de Vente*. You are, it is my duty to ask you, quite familiar with this procedure?"

"Yes," James replied. "I have a very good lawyer in London, who also trained at the Sorbonne. She briefed me thoroughly and told me about the most common pitfalls. Alas also, about the dirty tricks some people may like to play."

The eye twitched again. Forty-Love!

Monsieur Martin breathed in deeply. He slid the documents across the desk, at the same time offering James his pen.

"Monsieur Grandet," James said politely, "you are the vendor. It is your prerogative to be the first to sign."

He moved the forms casually round the side of the desk to where the butcher was sitting. Monsieur Grandet wrote his signature with a flourish, and pushed the papers back to the agent, who promptly returned them to James.

"Excuse me, please," James said quietly, feigning discomfort and embarrassment. "May I use your toilet?"

"Mais bien sûr!" Monsieur Martin pointed to a door. *"Les toilettes sont là-bas, au bout du couloir.* They're there, at the end of the passage."

The door gave on to a corridor, off which there was a traditional *pissoir* with *toilettes à la turque*. It had no door and stank of urine. He did not need to use it. All he wanted was a tactical break. This is like the Centre Court at Wimbledon, he mused, when a player leaves the match for no valid reason. They say it breaks an opponent's concentration. He smiled to himself. It was all going very well, he judged. Let the crooked, little man sweat it out for a while. He leaned against the passage wall and lit a cigarette. Allowing a full five minutes to elapse, he then returned calmly to the office.

"Are you all right?" Diana asked solicitously.

"Never felt better," he replied as he resumed his seat.

Although he did not want another cigarette, he fumbled for his packet and waved it at the agent.

"Vous permettez?"

He did not wait for his answer, inhaled deeply and blew a cloud of pungent smoke into the Frenchman's face.

"Now, *Monsieur* Martin. Where were we?" he asked vaguely. "Are we all ready for match point?"

The pen was offered a second time. It was a cheap ball-point, which advertised *'Agence Immobilière Martin'* with two telephone numbers. James looked at it, put it down as if it had leprosy, and rolled it disdainfully across the desk towards the estate agent. He reached into his inside pocket and produced the fountain pen which Diana had given him for their seventh anniversary. It was a magnificent object, machined with precision by Schaeffer and finished in malachite. It had been much admired. Slowly, he unscrewed the top. The gold nib glinted in the artificial light of the office.

James pointed the pen like a revolver at Monsieur Martin. He held it steadily, aiming the nib at the agent's eyes.

"Pistols at dawn!" James made as if he was joking, and then asked casually for a piece of paper.

The agent was baffled. There was silence in the room.

"I just want to get the ink to run," he explained, "so that we can complete this formality. That's all."

"Le voici!" Monsieur Martin volunteered his note pad.

James carefully tore off the top sheet of paper, mimicking the sound gangsters do in films when they simulate cutting their latest victim's throat. Monsieur Martin recoiled involuntarily, leaning back in his chair. Shielding the blank piece of paper with his left hand, James printed in bold, capital letters: *'ET OÙ PASSERA L'AUTOROUTE?'* He put down his pen and pushed the piece of paper gently across the desk to the estate agent. The young man stared dumbly at the written question. Monsieur Grandet blinked twice stupidly.

"But *what* is the meaning of all this?" cried Monsieur Martin.

"That, *Monsieur*, is precisely what I want to know. Where is the projected motorway going to be?"

"Quel péage? Je ne vous comprends pas! What motorway? I don't follow you!"

"Come, come, Martin!" James had been speaking in French for the benefit of the Grandet couple, but he now switched deliberately into English. "I may have come out of Africa, but I didn't come up the Zambezi without a paddle. You know about this, don't you?"

"About what?" protested the Frenchman, choking out his words.

"Stop fooling around and wasting everyone's time. About this..."

He took the photocopy of the Moulinac map out of his pocket, unfolded it, and placed it on the desk. Again, there was total silence.

"I will ask you once more," James continued, reverting to French, "but only once more, in front of your clients. You didn't know anything at all about this?"

"Si! Si! Mais ce n'est qu'un projet illusoire! Yes, yes! But it's only a pipe dream. It's not important." He was evidently going to try to bluff his way out of the attempted deceit. "It will never happen, not in this century. It probably won't even be started in my lifetime."

It's your time, that's running out, thought James. He was back in English now.

"My information is different. I was told at the *Mairie* in Moulinac this very morning that the project in that area will start early next year. This is a copy of their map. They've already begun construction further up towards Lyon. The powerful Bordeaux lobby has won the fight, I am informed. The *péage* will pass exactly nine hundred metres from the Grandet house, a really nice, noisy neighbour! And you have the temerity to sit there and pretend that it's not important! Well, old chap, it takes two to tango! The deal is off! And it was you who well and truly fucked it! Don't ever try a dirty trick like this again!"

James stood up. He pulled a small hunting knife out of his coat pocket, and flicked it open. He licked his thumb, brushed it lightly along the razor-sharp edge of the blade, and honed it on the fleshy part of his hand. Monsieur Martin had turned a sickly grey. The Grandets sat silently, not moving, as if their predicament was not new to them.

"Salaud de Martin!" James was speaking to him in French once more. "If you were my employee, I would give you just thirty minutes to clear your desk and go. Here, have a present, you dirty, little

crook!" He gave the estate agent the knife, taking care to offer it to him bone handle first. "Look after this well. Put it in a glass case and keep it here in your office, where you can see it every day. It will help you to remember today. Otherwise, you're going to end up so sharp, one day you'll cut yourself!" He pushed the handle roughly into Monsieur Martin's trembling hand. *"Salopard! Faites gaffe, Marteing!"* he swore at him. *"Vous allez vous foutre parterre!* You bastard! You watch it, Martin! You'll fall flat on your face!"

James pointed disgustedly at Monsieur Martin, who was holding his head in his hands, elbows resting on his desk.

"Madame, Monsieur," he continued calmly, turning to address the Grandets. *"Nous sommes vraiment désolés!* We are really very sorry! *Demandez-lui des explications!* Ask him to explain himself. And change your agent, that's my advice to you! *Bonne fin de journée! Adieu!"*

"Game! Set! And Match!" he smiled at Diana. "Come, darling, it's high time to leave this dump."

She did not reply as they left the office. She had uttered only four words throughout the entire proceedings. James used them now.

"Are you all right?" he asked gently.

"Never felt better!" she replied.

Walking down the pavement, she stopped him and asked, "Where did you get that knife? I didn't know you had one."

"Oh! In this little shop with the hunting gear. I should really have given it to Paul as a thank-you present. He's into all that. Still, with a little bit of luck, that liar and cheat "Marteing" will forget to close the blade, stick it in his trouser pocket, and castrate himself."

He entered the hunting shop and bought a replica of the knife. The proprietor smiled in recognition and gave him an odd look. James sheepishly returned the smile.

"Ce n'est qu'un petit cadeau pour un ami. It's just a little present for a friend," he said casually, as he paid for it.

It was just starting to rain, as he rejoined Diana outside. They ran for the jeep but they were soaked before they reached it. Once inside, they began to laugh.

"I think we deserve some bubbly," he suggested. "We've got some back at the cottage. *Un petit vin d'honneur!"*

Chapter Five

While they sat enjoying the champagne, it started to rain harder. The force of the wind increased and soon it was lashing the cottage, the rain driving at the windows in sheets of water and obscuring the view out to the river. With no guttering to catch it, rainwater was cascading off the canal tiles, bringing down with it pieces of moss and the leaves of the previous autumn. The sky had turned dark grey, and jet-black thunderclouds were moving in from the south-west. Brilliant lightning lit up the room, as if a gigantic flashgun had been triggered. Angry rolls of thunder followed, at first some distance away. Then the intervals between flash and boom became shorter. Suddenly, there was a huge crash as lightning and thunder exploded in unison, seemingly overhead. There was the sound of wood being torn apart, branches falling, and a heavy thud shook the cottage.

The champagne was good. They felt cosy, ensconced in the cottage, safely protected from the phenomenal power of this display of enraged nature. They decided not to dine out, and settled instead for *baguette,* cheese, red wine, and nectarines. The evening fell away into a dark night, the storm gradually abating. At last they were able to open the windows again. The air was fresh, reminiscent of Africa in the rainy season. At some stage, he found another bottle of champagne, hidden in the back of the refrigerator. They took it into the bedroom. Eventually they made love, and it was good for both of them.

*

Afterwards, and most unusually, he did not fall into his normal, deep sleep. The room was warm, too warm, and pitch-black. He could just hear Diana breathing steadily by his side. He found his torch and slipped silently from the bed. A light sleeper, Diana turned over as he left the room, but she did not wake up. In the kitchen he poured himself a large whisky. His favourite brand was almost as difficult to find in France as in Zambia. As often happened as he went on a nocturnal walk-about, his mind started racing. What was the time? Nearly two o'clock. *Merde!* he thought, I can't stand another day in the bloody Dordogne! Seven more days and then we'll be back in Lusaka, without having found a house. Come on! Think positively! You're in the wrong area of France. It's obvious, isn't it? He rose from the kitchen table and found the new map, his thought processes continuing. We must go somewhere further south... With no more bloody tourists... Lower house prices... Much less synthetically beautiful... More *sauvage,* like Africa... And no more signs, offering 'Bed and Breakfast'.

Inside another hour and a whisky later, he had made up his mind. He crept back into the bedroom and eased himself into the bed. Sleep still did not come. A barn owl screeched from one of the plane trees. Outside, from below the open window, there was a clatter of what sounded like broken tiles and old tin cans. Somewhere a tomcat called. A mosquito was bombing the room, the bed, his left ear. Come on! he thought. Action! It's now or never!

"Are you awake?" he asked, gently nudging Diana.

"What time is it?" she asked sleepily, stretching her hand towards him.

"About four-thirty."

"Oh! I feel terrible, as if I've been up all night."

"Come on, intrepid traveller! We're going south, to the Lot. Get your pants on, grab enough things for two nights, and we'll be off. You do the packing. We'll breakfast on the way and aim to reach Cahors by nine."

He wrote a short note to let Paul know that they would be away for three days, telling him that they would probably return sometime late on Monday. Torch in hand, he walked quietly up to the farmhouse, and slipped it under the front door. A clear sky with the last of the stars heralded a fine Saturday morning. He went over to the jeep and folded down the hood. They both preferred to drive with the wind in their hair. He entered the cottage, found the cool-box, and filled it with some wine, gin, bottles of tonic water, a corkscrew, and a dishcloth in which he wrapped two sturdy tumblers. For good measure, he put the remaining nectarines carefully on top, and then clipped down the lid.

"Essential stores!" he grinned, as Diana emerged from the

bedroom. She was already dressed, and carrying two light travelling bags. He took the bags and the cool-box, and loaded them into the back of the jeep.

"It'll be a little fresh at first," he said, "until the sun comes up." He was locking the cottage door when he thought of something else.

"Damn! I've forgotten something," he called to her over his shoulder and disappeared into the cottage.

Climbing into the jeep, he placed his powerful game-viewing binoculars and a roll of toilet paper in the glove compartment.

"More essential stores," he said, squeezing her hand. "Right! Let's go!"

*

They drove quietly away from the cottage, the headlights picking out a large branch which had been torn from one of the plane trees by the storm. It had crashed on to the stone table and shattered it.

"Lucky that didn't land on the jeep," he commented dryly.

"What will Paul think of us, going off like this?" she asked. "He has probably found another two ruins and lined them up for us to view today."

"I don't really care what Paul thinks. *Je m'en fous!* He offered his services. He's failed to find us a suitable house. The Dordogne is a disaster area, as far as I am concerned. Definitely not for us. It just doesn't seem to me like France, as I knew it; it doesn't look like France; it doesn't smell like France; it certainly doesn't sound like France; and, except for Gaston's, it didn't even taste like France! We'll do better, I'm sure, if we're back in control. Anyway, I've left Paul a note saying we might be back late on Monday."

Once out of the village, he accelerated, concentrating on the long, unfamiliar journey ahead.

"Don't be too hard on him, darling," she shouted over the noise of the engine. "He did, after all, save our bacon yesterday."

"True. He's a nice enough fellow. But for now, my love, you and I are going to find a house and buy it in the next three days. Either it will be a stopgap, to which we can bale out, or, if we get lucky, it'll be something more permanent and substantial. Either way, it'll allow us to move our stuff out of storage in England, get our non-residential status acknowledged, and perhaps, most importantly, give us somewhere to come if, or as is more likely, when the economy in Zambia spells out the sheer folly of remaining there."

The jeep, with the hood down in the fresh, early morning air, took the smooth road at near to its maximum speed. There was no traffic so early on a Saturday morning. With the accelerator pressed against the floor, he pushed the sturdy vehicle round the bends, cutting through the corners. They were both wearing their light anoraks to beat the chill from the swirling wind. They made good time, first eastward to Périgueux and then across to the N20. They turned south on the new bypass at Brive. By the time they had climbed the hills to the south of the city, diving into the dripping, floodlit tunnels of the new road, the sun was rising, and the idea of coffee and whatever else might be on offer seemed an attractive proposition. It was just after seven o'clock.

They came to a sign which claimed that, down the next turning to the left, travellers were offered *restauration rapide* at all hours. Ten minutes later, on the doorstep of a typical Quercy house, they were confronted by an elegant, elderly lady. She was wearing what passes in France for a dressing-gown. She had bright, blue eyes and a shock of white hair. Her lined face was lively and alert, even at such an early hour of the day.

"*Bonjour, Madame,*" said James, returning her smile. "*J'espère que nous ne vous dérangeons pas.* I hope we're not disturbing you, but we saw your sign, and—"

"*Pas de problème, mes enfants. Bienvenue! Entrez! Entrez tout de suite, s'il vous plaît.*" She turned, and they followed the head of white hair into a small room. The tables were laid for breakfast. "*Je peux vous offrir du café noir, du café au lait, des croissants, des oeufs selon votre choix.* Eggs, as you like them. *Voilà! Je suis à votre service!*"

Suddenly a different look came to her face. She pursed her lips, concern in her eyes and embarrassment touching her cheeks.

"*Mais, vous êtes anglais, bien sûr! Vous avez voyagé pendant toute la nuit.* You are tired. You have driven all night from Calais, yes? *Eeh! Mes pauvres!* My poor dears, you need to sleep together and come to breakfast after you have refreshed each other in the shower. I have a bed for you. *C'est un vrai grand lit! Superbe! Venez!*"

She was about to charge upstairs to throw them into bed when

Diana intervened.

"Mais non, Madame! Vous êtes très aimable, mais ce n'est pas nécessaire. We must be at Cahors before nine o'clock. *Café au lait, des croissants, et de la confiture, ça suffira. "*

She's just like a little dove, thought Diana. The white hair bobbed out into the kitchen with that hint of a shrug, perfected by French men and women when, without saying a word, they wish to express that they are baffled and need to walk away from the situation.

*

Half an hour later and well refreshed, they set off again. They turned south on the main road, but it was not long before Diana announced that she had to stop. She was having a severe bout of hiccups.

"I won't be more than a minute or two," she promised, stepping out of the jeep.

James had seen this performance many times before. He lit a cigarette while he watched and waited. There, on the grass verge of the N20, to the astonishment and delight of the commuter traffic which was just starting, she underwent her infallible cure, standing on her head, bare brown legs pointing gracefully to the sky and her khaki dress falling down over her head. It was the pretty pair of pale green lace knickers that *tout le monde* admired, tooting merrily on their horns and shouting ribald remarks as they slowed down to get a better view.

The crisis passed, and they continued to make good time in spite of the bends in the road, almost all of which had been daubed with the slogan, *"Non à l'Autoroute!"* After a few more kilometres, they passed a sign which read, *"Vous Quittez la Dordogne! Merci de Votre Visite! Bonne Route!"*

"Thank God for that!" he shouted out. "*Never* again!"

"But we'll have to go back to get our things from the cottage, won't we?"

"Well, never again after that!"

A little further on, another sign proclaimed: *"Bienvenue dans le Lot! Une Surprise à Chaque Pas!"*

"And may all our surprises be nice ones, too," he said gleefully.

Pulling over to the verge, they climbed out of the jeep and took photographs of each other and the sign. In the background, on either side, there were stunning views in the direction of Rocamadour and Gourdon. Immense, rocky outcrops, on which the small scrub oaks somehow gallantly survive, loomed in the distance, the light from the early sun emphasizing their primeval contours. Returning to the jeep, he sat pensively behind the steering wheel, and then leaned across to her. *"Sais-tu ce que je sais, le sais-tu? C'est que je t'aime,"* he whispered. "Do you know, what I know, do you? It's that I love you!"

With a slight pause Diana looked back from the sign and the views beyond, and uttered the first prophetic statement of the day.

"And this, my darling, might well be your little Lot!"

*

Morale, by now, was rising. A destination, if not a destiny, was ahead and not far away. It was going to be another bright, hot day. They took the steep hairpin bends down into Souillac, always attractive but sadly overcrowded in the season. At the other end of the town, they crossed to the south side of the Dordogne river, which flows through part of the north-west corner of the Lot before it reaches the region to which it gives its name. Climbing out of the river valley, the countryside began to reveal itself — first in subtle changes, and then with dramatic, natural and man-made gestures which demanded attention.

Stretching away to the east and gaining in altitude, beyond a narrow belt of fertile land known as the Limargue, lay the hilly region of the Ségala, an area of streams, chestnut forests, and sombre gorges, which are deep and sinister with ancient rocks and caves from the palaeozoic period. The N20 crossed the arid, limestone plateaux and hills of Les Causses, with stone houses surrounded on all sides by the ubiquitous scrub oaks and juniper trees. As the warmth of the sun made itself felt and bounced back from the rocky terrain, the air carried to them that special aroma of burnt-brown, dry grass, wild flowers, heather, bracken, and occasional pine. Just as one catches the scent of lion or buffalo, so Diana thought that she sensed the presence of young buck, an old vixen or, perhaps, a family of *sanglier,* the wild boar of the region. She was beginning to warm to the prospect of investigating an area which neither of them knew.

This was the savage land across which the Albigensian Crusade and The Hundred Years War had been ruthlessly pursued. It was here also that Richard the Lion-Heart made treaty with Phillipe Auguste at the end of the twelfth century, taking the Quercy into English territory. Here, too, a short distance south of Frayssinet, they were reminded of twentieth-century man's inhumanity to man. On a prominent hilltop, a dramatically stark memorial bears homage to the courage of the Resistance fighters and to the plight of thousands of deportees, taken from their families and homes to suffer and, in many cases, to die brutally under the jackboots of the Nazis.

At the top of the hill above Cahors they stopped to take in the spectacular view. The principal administrative centre of the Lot, Cahors stands on an isthmus, where the Lot river makes a sweeping loop around the promontory on which the city is built. The river valley then widens to the west, as the river flows more sedately towards Puy-l'Évêque and beyond Villeneuve, before joining the Rivers Tarn and Garonne on their way to Bordeaux and the open sea of the Golfe de Gascogne. To the right, picked out in the early morning sun, they could see clearly the white stonework of the *Château de Mercuès,* miraculously perched on a sheer, limestone cliff above the river. On the far side of the river acre upon acre of manicured vineyards stretched away to the south-west.

Below their viewpoint the city was already coming to life. Cars and vans of all shapes and ages, loaded with local produce, jostled their way towards the centre, dominated by the Cathedral in the Place Jean-Jacques Chapou, so named after the Resistance leader known as Capitaine Phillipe. Venerated as the *'Créateur et Animateur du Maquis du Lot',* he had been the prime mover, the driving force, behind one of the largest and most effective resistance groups in the country until, at the age of forty-five, he was killed on the seventeenth of July, 1944. Now, in the square which honours him, the Saturday market was noisily getting itself into its usual full swing. Today, as for centuries gone by, vociferous bartering would give way to bargains being struck. Money would change hands, old friends and rivals would meet, and all would consume quantities of wine and *pastis,* before going home to tell their stories to anyone who might be willing to listen.

They might have sat in the jeep and spent more time enjoying the view below, as the sun climbed higher into the cloudless sky. When they heard the deep bell of the Cathedral booming out nine o'clock, it drew them out of their reverie and back to the reality of a busy day ahead.

"We had better get going," James sighed. "Let's see if we can find someone down there who is prepared to sell us a house."

Chapter Six

They drove down the hill and found their way to the top of the Boulevard Gambetta, which was already beginning to fill up. A short distance down on the right there was a parking space. On the opposite side the proprietor of a *brasserie* was adjusting the layout of green plastic tables and chairs on the pavement. It was a task which he had to perform every sunny day of his life. He did it like an automaton, but with heavy-handed haste. Yet, each time a friend, client, or acquaintance passed, he found time to greet them with a handshake or a kiss on each cheek, depending upon the degree of intimacy in their relationship. He was protesting about something to his wife, whose duty it was to sweep into the road the few autumnal leaves which were just starting to fall.

"I would love a coffee," Diana said, "before we do anything else."

They crossed the road to the *brasserie,* and sat at a table in the full sun, which already felt far from autumnal. There was no doubt that it was going to be hot.

Afterwards, they decided to walk down, rather than up, the steep boulevard. This may have been because they had now been awake for about five hours, with a drive of more than three hundred kilometres behind them. However, there was no logical reason why both of them, without exchanging a word or even a glance, turned down the next small street on the left. James glanced up at the wall, where a blue plaque informed strangers to the city that this was the Rue des Platanes. Most of the shops were smart *salons de beauté* and small boutiques selling expensive, designer clothes. They passed a unisex hairdresser, two health-food shops, and a stall offering T-shirts and sandals. An effeminate photographer lounged beside the glass door of his studio. Beyond the window they noticed an exhibition of his work which, from a distance, gave the impression of high quality imagery, mostly in black and white. Strategically placed next door was a picture-framer, and then an old-fashioned saddler selling collars and identity discs for dogs and cats.

"That might be useful to know," Diana observed, thinking of the three Burmese cats back in Lusaka.

James saw from her body language that her mind was drifting back to the real centre of her life.

"En avant!" he said gently. "Forward!"

And then, quite suddenly, they were there. Why he felt that way, or how he knew that this was where it was all going to start, was of little consequence. They were standing in front of tall, wrought iron railings, which closed off a pretty courtyard, full of ornamental shrubs. Curving over an impressive, double gate with a coat-of-arms, a sign in faded gold lettering announced that Number 46 was the *'Agence Immobilière Louisor, Père et Fille. Toutes Transactions'*. The well-proportioned town house, which had been converted into offices, was set back from the narrow street. Fixed to the railings on each side of the gate were two wide, glass-cased notice boards, with a selection of full-plate, colour photographs of properties for sale or rent in the region. Both exteriors and interiors were portrayed, with brief descriptions of their amenities.

"We'll try in here," he decided, pushing open the gate.

The front door of the house was locked but, under a security bell on the right, a small card suggested to callers, *"Sonnez svp"*. He pressed the bell and, a few moments later, the door was opened. Having established that they might be looking for a house to buy, a young secretary let them in and led them into a tastefully furnished office. The girl went through an adjoining door, closing it gently behind her. They heard her saying something, and then the sound of another woman's voice. Shortly afterwards the door opened again, and a well-dressed woman entered the office. She looked striking and had about her an air of competence, as well as a discreet perfume.

"Monsieur, Madame. Bonjour," she greeted them. *"Je suis Louisor."*

"Our name is Wyllis. This is my wife, Diana, and I am James."

They sat down at the desk. Madame Louisor explained that her husband was out of town with another client. He would be back later, perhaps by mid-morning. In the meantime, as the other senior partner of the firm, she would be delighted to help in any way.

"You are English, of course." It was not a question.

"Yes," James replied. "We've come from Zambia to buy a house, here perhaps, even in the Lot."

"*O-là-là, là-là! De la Zambie, alors! C'est très loin, non?* It is very far, no?"

"Yes it's a long way, and we hope you can make it worth our while."

"We shall do our very best." Madame Louisor smiled. It was a nice, genuine smile in an attractive face. She had natural blonde hair, cut and shaped into an elegant French bob.

She was now speaking in faltering English, concentration showing in her eyes. "But a moment, please. Is it that you will want someone 'ere now as — 'ow you say it? — as a translator? There is a lady, one of my good friends. I can to 'er give a call of telephone. She will be 'ere in some little minutes."

"*Mais non, Madame! Aucun problème. Ça ne sera pas nécessaire,*" James replied. "If you will kindly speak slowly, we will both understand." Nevertheless, he wondered what he had said incorrectly to prompt her to offer an interpreter. And why was it, he asked himself, that they always knew that he was not an ordinary Frenchman, let alone correctly place him, or both of them for that matter, as English? And how and why do they always speak so fast, particularly when you ask them to slow down?

As if to prove that very point, Madame Louisor reverted to her own tongue and was now speaking even faster than before.

"I can see that you are asking yourself how it is that I say you are English, yes?"

She tilted her head slightly as she asked the question. She was now leaning forward across the desk towards James, revealing rather more than just the lace border of her low-cut bra.

"We get many English people coming in here. But most do not buy. They just look. They like to spend their holidays looking in other people's houses. It is very strange. It is very, very curious indeed."

She tilted her head again. This time it was more of a shrug, which started at the neck instead of with the shoulders, ending with a raising of the chin as a gesture of confidence that she was mastering the situation.

Her speech was now accelerating dangerously near to a top speed, beyond which neither of them would be able to follow.

"Yes, we find this hobby quite extraordinary, *très bizarre*. It is, perhaps, one of the Anglo-Saxon obsessions, no? *Comme le bricolage,* the DIY, or like washing one's car? I lived for a short time on the outskirts of London, and everyone was washing their cars! Imagine! But, for us estate agents, the English are not the worst. It is the Dutch! Unimaginable! Do you know, they want to look inside *every* cupboard, turn on *all* the taps, try *all* the keys in *all* the locks, and even examine the *fosse septique*. It is sometimes *so* embarrassing! "Yes, we get all types. *En tout cas, ils gaspillent beaucoup de temps.* In any event, they waste a lot of time."

"Well, *Madame* Louisor," James said firmly, "I can assure you that we will waste neither your husband's time nor yours *if* you can come up with the house we want *and* at the right price. *Et moi, je déteste le bricolage!* I hate DIY! Nor do we want British neighbours, with all their friends and relations visiting endlessly, trying to pretend that they don't really want a free holiday this year, as well as next."

Listening patiently to James, Diana felt the almost prophetic impact of his final statements. Which, she asked herself, would turn out to be true or false? Madame Louisor saw her looking politely at her watch.

"*Bon!*" she said expressively, using one of the most useful words in her language which, dependent on intonation and context, can mean almost anything.

"*Bon!* Tell me, then, what else do you want or do not want, in your new property?"

She reached across the desk and picked up a small, hand-held dictaphone.

"My notebook," she explained, waving the tiny machine at them. "*Vous permettez?*" she asked and, without waiting for an answer, she pushed the button to record the interview, which was evidently now about to begin.

*

Old habits die hard, or so they say. In his earlier days as a management consultant, James had been trained in the techniques of how to take the lead in, and thus control, any interview. He had applied them — not without success, he thought modestly — whether confronted by a Chairman, Chief Executive, shop steward, or a weeping secretary; his approach was always the same. Now, faced across the desk by the chic Madame Louisor, he reverted to his former self. The little red light on the dictaphone was shining brightly, indicating that the proceedings would not be lost on anyone as decorative and intelligent as the creature sitting opposite him.

"*Madame* Louisor," he began, shifting himself discreetly into a more businesslike posture. "Perhaps you will permit me to give you some useful background information. I'm confident you will find what I have to tell you will be relevant and helpful. As I said earlier, we don't want to waste your time or ours."

He looked across at Diana for encouragement. Her face, he thought, seemed to be telling him to get on with it, although he could not think why. Madame Louisor waited and listened attentively, well trained to anticipate when something important was about to happen in this room, confident that this frequently indicated a serious buyer.

"*Mais continuez, Monsieur Wyllis! Je vous en prie!*"

"We have come here from Zambia. I am employed there as an *haut fonctionnaire,* a senior official, working for an International Organization. I am the only white man in the Office of the Prime Minister."

He made a deliberate pause to gauge the impact on her of his carefully worded introductory comments. Madame Louisor had shown no sign, thus far, that she was unimpressed. After all, she thought, *hauts fonctionnaires* are everywhere. One can find them even in the smallest of communes. Generally, they were regarded by her compatriots as an almost total waste of taxpayers' money.

Madame Louisor leaned casually forward, this time ensuring that it was her cornflower blue eyes which widened with respect and close interest.

"My assignment down there," he resumed, "that is to say, in Zambia, may end at any time, perhaps even abruptly, with little or no notice. That's life in those parts, you know. Elections are due to take place shortly. It would take just a change in the administration, or perhaps a military coup, to throw a spanner in the works And then, *pouff!* We'll be out on our ear on the next plane."

He paused again, pleased with himself that he had remembered the idiom: *'Mettre des bâtons dans les roues'*, and he was satisfied that his gesticulations which accompanied the *'pouff!'* had been physically dramatic and adequately Gallic. He looked at both women, seeking renewed confirmation that his words were making the desired, strong impact.

Diana, taking advantage of his brief silence, leaned across to him, squeezing his right elbow.

"Wood for the trees, darling," she said pointedly in English, a fixed smile on her face. "*Madame* Louisor is not interested in our life history and future prospects."

The Frenchwoman smiled sweetly at her. James thought that there was quite enough smiling going on. In fact, if anything, there was rather too much. He was determined not to smile. This is serious business, he decided, gritting his teeth.

"The point is, *Madame*," he continued, "we are here now on home leave, our *congé annuel*. We have only three days left before we go back to Zambia. In those three days we must find and buy a house. *Voilà! C'est tout simple.*"

It was a deliberate lie on his part to suggest a remaining interval of only three days, but he excused himself on the grounds that it was never wise to give a truthful deadline. After all, nobody did, either in Africa or in France.

"*Aïe! Aïe! O-là-là, là-là! Voilà votre problème!*" Madame Louisor reacted, wide-eyed with astonishment. "You are in a very big hurry. The English do everything in such a hurry. It must be something to do with their climate. It is nice here. The weather is excellent, no? Take your time! You must change your date of return. Buying a house is not a thing to be done with such haste. It is like making love: it is an emotional event. You *must* enjoy it. You will have to change your plans."

James edged forward on his chair, thinking that it was high time that he did something to impress his personality on the situation he was facing, lest he lose control. He had to admit that the interview was not following the precise path which he intended.

"I'm afraid that is quite out of the question, *Madame*," he said firmly. "I have to be back at my post when they expect me. That is my duty. That is how we won the—"

"But tomorrow is Sunday. We are closed," Madame Louisor interjected. "The grandchildren are visiting us. The next day is Monday, when you will find nearly everything is also closed."

She shrugged, sitting back in the soft leather of her swivel chair. The hem of her well-cut skirt edged fractionally above a slim, suntanned knee. She noticed how James had enjoyed glancing down at it. It was, just as she had thought, a serious opportunity. They were few and far between, in times that were becoming increasingly difficult.

Madame Louisor held up her hand and then smiled again at her clients.

"Mais, ce n'est pas grave," she said decisively. "I have a plan, *un bon plan,* since you cannot, or will not, change your schedule. What we will do is this: I will shortly ask you some questions. I need to know very clearly, what it is you want and what you do not want. Then I will get out the details and photos of those properties on our books which I judge may interest you. Next, you will select just five or six of the most promising ones. Do you understand? *Bon!* I will then mark on your map where they are..." She hesitated briefly, and then continued, "Perhaps my husband will be back in time to mark your map. I myself am not very good with maps. I find them so boring. They are really men's toys. When all this has been done, I will get my girl to telephone each of the owners to inform them that today, this very afternoon, you will be coming to establish the precise location of their property and that, at this stage, you wish only to view from the outside. We will tell them that they will not be disturbed. It is very short notice and more polite this way."

As if thinking of something else, she swivelled her chair towards the window, running her fingers through her hair. The dictaphone clicked, and the red light went out. She swung back to the desk and quickly turned over the tiny cassette. Pressing the record button again, she continued speaking, as if there had been no interruption to her line of thought.

"You are staying in Cahors? *Bon!* As we contact each owner we will make a preliminary schedule of visits for tomorrow, so that you can view the interiors, talk to the owners, ask any questions, and so on. You may not wish to see inside all of them. You can make that judgement during the course of this afternoon. Then, this evening, my husband will telephone you at your hotel to discuss and arrange an agreed, final programme for Sunday. *Voilà!* You have made a hotel reservation, yes?"

"No," James replied. "Not yet. We only just arrived—"

Madame Louisor cut him off, pressing a button under her desk. They could just hear the sound of the buzzer in the next room, and the girl entered with a notebook in her hand.

"Céline, telephone immediately the *Hôtel Château de Mercuès.* Make a reservation in the name of *Monsieur* and *Madame* Wyllis. Warn the hotel that they may be arriving quite late this evening. Tell them, nevertheless, that they will definitely want dinner in the hotel. Find out at what time they take the last orders. On Saturdays, I believe, it's not after eleven." Turning to Diana, she asked, "Do you want a double bed, *un grand lit,* or do you prefer to sleep in single beds?"

They both answered together.

"It doesn't really matter," said James.

"Un grand lit," Diana replied.

The agent promptly ended any further discussion of beds and settled the matter.

"Alors, Céline, un grand lit," she decided. "And please make sure that the hotel knows who it is, who is making the reservation."

She looked up pensively at the small chandelier above her desk. These English! she thought, they can't even agree on what sort of a bed is best for making love! She stretched her back in a catlike movement. As she did so, the skirt moved an inch or two higher, suggesting the inside of a pair of silky thighs. She smoothed the cuff of her sleeve, and turned back to face her two clients. James thought that the cut of her blazer did justice to her shapely figure.

"You will find that it is very comfortable there, I assure you," she said emphatically. *"C'est un très bon hôtel. La cuisine est excellente, vraiment superbe! Très bon, mais pas bon marché!"*

Diana wondered what the words *'pas bon marché'* might imply for dinner, bed and breakfast. Oh well, she thought, they were on holiday. Or at least, it was *supposed* to be a holiday.

Her attention was drawn back as Madame Louisor continued to take command of all the arrangements.

"Now, what else? Ah, yes!" she said, as if the thought had just occurred to her. "Do you, *Monsieur*, have a good, large scale map of these parts?"

"No. Not with me. I rather stupidly left mine in the Dordogne. I will have to—"

"*Bon! Il vous faut acheter la Série Bleue,*" she interrupted, without appearing to do so. "It shows almost every property and all the small lanes. It is indispensable. If I may, I suggest you go now to the shop on the corner of Boulevard Gambetta and buy one."

He made as if he was about to protest, but Diana quickly agreed.

"That's a very good idea. We'll need a map, anyway. Then *Monsieur* Louisor can mark it for us before we go out on our safari."

"*Madame Louisor, c'est pas vrai que vous avez des petits enfants?*" he asked from the door. "It's not true that you have grandchildren?"

"*Mais si! Si! Si! J'en ai trois: Lucien, Jean-Marie, et la petite Gabrielle. Ça y est!*"

Shaking his head in disbelief, he left the office. On the pavement, he pulled out a *Gauloises* and left it unlit, hanging from the corner of his mouth. Quite a woman, he thought. I *must* be getting old!

Meanwhile in the office, the two women sat facing each other across the desk.

"*Les hommes!*" smiled Madame Louisor. "Are they always so like children? The French are just the same. *Mais, ça y est!* But there it is! And we poor, simple girls, we need them all the time, don't we?"

Diana nodded, not paying attention to the other woman's small talk, other than to wonder what she might really be meaning by the use of the words, 'them' and 'all the time'. She was concentrating on the task ahead, determined not to underestimate the other woman's tactics. She was mindful of the skill with which Madame Louisor had manoeuvred James out of the office and into the street. That was pretty impressive, Madame Louisor, she conceded. She knows that it's the woman who makes the final choice of a house. The way she simulated that her gambit to distance James was nothing more than a sudden brainwave was well done. It's probably a standard ploy, she decided, taught by training schools for French estate agents. Still, watch it, Diana! she said to herself. She's good at her job, is this one!

"Shall we get down to it, then?" she asked and gave Madame Louisor one of her most searching smiles.

Chapter Seven

Diana and James were in acceptably broad agreement on the most important, the essential features of any property they might buy. It was only when the 'merely desirable' details were discussed that opinions tended to differ. A final choice was complicated by the two alternative, basic strategies on which, ironically, they were unanimous: *either* finding somewhere as a temporary, future base, from which they could prospect at a more leisurely and thorough pace when eventually they arrived to make a new life in France, *or* opting for a more permanent solution if, as James frequently put it, they 'got lucky', and found the 'right' place.

The first alternative would be the cheaper in the short term, but it implied in due course all the costs and nuisance of a further move. If possible, this was to be avoided, mainly because neither of them coped well with any form of unnecessary, self-inflicted complications. When similar decisions had been taken in the past, they had both preferred the easier, simpler route — usually this cost more. The second option, however, would involve a larger capital outlay.

As she sat in the Louisor office, Diana realized that they had not yet agreed on a definitive price limit. To put it bluntly, they had not decided how much they could reasonably afford if an ideal property could be found. In addition, it was basically unsound to pay out a larger sum of money for an asset which, if for any reason they were unable to let it, might be lying empty and idle for some unspecified period, over which they had little or no control. And then, there was the acute time factor.

These thoughts were tumbling around inside her head as Diana started to describe their requirements.
"I would like to cover our essential needs first," she began.
"D'accord," agreed Madame Louisor.
"We have animals. They are cats actually, who will be returning with us from Zambia."
Through force of habit, she used the word 'who', indicating the

special relationship which existed in this dimension of her life.

"*Ouille!* My dear, I hope they're not lions or tigers! That would make our task even more difficult!"

"*Non, Madame,*" Diana smiled politely. "There are no wild tigers in Africa. These are three pedigree Burmese cats, very precious to us. They're my babies: Jacob, Fosbury, and Yentl. And so, any house which is right in a village or near a road is completely out of the question. There must be, therefore, a little land, but not too much. My husband doesn't want to spend the rest of his days tending the soil like a peasant. Nor does he want to be rushing up and down behind a lawnmower four days a week. In short, our first two requirements are security for the cats, with privacy and peaceful surroundings for us."

The agent noted the curious order in which the first two priorities had surfaced.

"*Bon!*" she nodded. "We can certainly offer you some good choices to meet both those needs."

"Then," continued Diana, encouraged that her top priority might be met, "it is essential that you understand that we're not contemplating *une ruine.*" She used that delightful word to understate the decay and lack of maintenance which so characterize many of the properties on the market. They had seen enough of them in the Dordogne.

"As you heard my husband say," she continued, "he detests *le bricolage*. He can't even bang a nail in straight, let alone put up a permanent shelf. And so, we want somewhere which is immediately habitable, and which requires no major, structural changes. That is to say, when we do finally leave Africa, we want to be able to move into a place with the absolute minimum of that kind of problem. Apart from anything else, we will have quite enough on our plate, without having the additional headache of trying to control, from a great distance, major repairs and the increased costs which would be involved. Ideally, the property should be in sufficiently good shape so that we can let it while we remain in Zambia. Incidentally, I see you handle rentals and, subject to your terms of business, we could put that matter in your hands as well."

Diana looked down at her notes, pleased with her inspired afterthought to suggest that further business would come the Louisor way *if* they came up with a viable solution.

"Mais bien sûr! Je comprends. " The agent checked her dictaphone, reached into a drawer, and placed a spare cassette on her desk. "However, since you have raised the matter of costs, could you please give me some idea of how much you plan to spend on your purchase? Try, if you can, to be as precise as possible. It will help us to help you. And also, while we are on the disagreeable but necessary subject of money, are you perhaps a buyer for cash? Or will you be arranging to finance your project with a loan from some source or another? I ask because, in the case of some of the properties we have, an important pre-requisite is that the monies will be available immediately and without delay, on completion."

"We are cash buyers, *Madame*. We do not have to wait to sell another property. We are not involved in, what we call in England, a 'chain'. There will be no need for a bridging loan. Our funds are invested safely in London, and they are readily accessible."

So, mused Madame Louisor with satisfaction, I *was* right after all. This could well be serious... and profitable.

"Très bon!" she said, showing no sign of her anticipation. "And the price range, please?"

"Well, that depends. As I said, we're not looking for a tumbledown barn to convert, or anything like that. There are, therefore, just two possibilities. It could be, for example, either, somewhere temporary, cheaper, smaller, a pied-à-terre, to be used as a future base from which to look for a permanent home. Or else, perhaps, a more substantial property which, no doubt, would carry a higher price. But, *Madame*, I do assure you, the latter would have to meet all our essential requirements. And I really do mean all of them. It would also, I think, have to satisfy most of the desirable but not, strictly speaking, essential features we are seeking." She frowned, as she continued, "I am not at all confident that we have sufficient time on this visit to do proper justice to the second alternative I have described. I think that we may have left it too late."

"Excellent. Je vous suis parfaitement. I follow you well. I can see that you have considered your options very carefully. This always helps. But don't concern yourself, *Madame. On verra!* We shall see!"

Madame Louisor was beginning to wonder whether she would ever

70

extract from her client the financial information which she had already requested twice in vain. She resolved to try once more, otherwise she would have to wait for the Englishman's return from his errand to buy a map. She took a deep breath to conceal her irritation.

"However, *Madame* Wyllis, if we are to be of service to you and your husband, you must tell me the price range you are contemplating for each of your two alternative plans, otherwise we run the risk of wasting time." Over the last few months Diana had given more thought than James to the question of what they could realistically afford. She now told the estate agent her top spending limits for the two options facing them.

"And I am talking francs, of course," she added. *"Pas en livres anglaises!* Not in English pounds!"

"Eh bien! Enfin! Aucun problème! Now that we have crossed the worst bridge in this affair, let us begin to discuss exactly what you would like those sums of money to buy here in the Lot."

*

At that moment the security buzzer on the front door gave two sharp, impatient squawks. The secretary entered and crossed the office to answer it. James reappeared, the *Gauloises* still hanging unlit from the corner of his mouth. He was clutching a *Série Bleue* map, which he waved at the two women."

"Me voilà de retour!" he announced. "Here I am again! Mission accomplished!" He turned to Diana, and asked with a grin, *"Et bien, chérie. T'as déjà acheté une propriété, ou non?* Have you bought a house yet?"

"We were just dealing with the price ranges for the two options, which you and I have discussed so much." The grin faded from his face, to be replaced by a blank look. "You know," Diana continued. "Either the stopgap or the permanent."

"Oh, yes!" he addressed Madame Louisor. "Difficult to be absolutely precise, without seeing the target, isn't it? It depends." He mentioned one figure for the temporary solution and, misreading her reaction, he quickly added, "If, of course, you can offer us something really suitable as a permanent home, then you could, perhaps, double that figure. Then it really would have to be, as you said earlier, *une affaire de coeur,* a love affair, wouldn't it?"

Madame Louisor noted the considerable discrepancy between her two clients. Her quick, mental calculation suggested that the Englishman appeared to be prepared to spend somewhere between thirty and sixty percent more than his wife, depending upon which alternative could be sold. It would have to be, she resolved, the more expensive, the more profitable one.

"That's quite a bit more, my love," Diana said, with a note of caution in her voice, "than I have suggested to *Madame*—"

"Never mind," he said, breaking into what looked like developing into further tedious analysis of their finances. "It really does depend upon what is offered, doesn't it? Have you finished going through our checklist yet? If not, I have my own copy here."

"No, we were just about to start," Diana replied. "So far, we've covered cat security, our own privacy, and a little land, but not too much; it must not be a wreck, and preferably a property which we can let. And, for Heaven's sake, I wish you would take that cigarette out of your mouth. It makes you look almost French!"

James took the unintended compliment gracefully, and removed the offending *Gauloises* from his mouth, carefully replacing it, as he thought a Frenchman would, in its crumpled packet. He checked the time. It was already after ten o'clock. Pulling out his copy of the list, which they had constructed together and, facing Madame Louisor, he began to describe, in no particular order of priority, the kind of house and amenities for which he would be prepared, if necessary, to quit Africa.

"It would be rather nice if the house had a *pigeonnier*. We know...," he paused, looking at Diana, who had not failed to notice the royal 'we' he always used. "We know it's not a logical priority, but if we're going to settle in this lovely area, well then... It seems right that we should be in keeping with the..."

*

The discussion continued for some time. Monsieur Louisor returned to his office. He was a handsome, energetic individual, who was as competent as his wife in their business. The two partners adjourned to the adjacent office for several minutes. When they returned, it was Monsieur Louisor who took the lead.

"Thank you both," he said politely, "for entrusting our firm with your business. You will not regret it. My wife has made me au fait with your requirements. I am certain we have several appropriate properties to interest you. We will now show you their details."

In contrast to their one and only earlier encounter with Monsieur Martin, the estate agent in Borinac, the Louisor system was efficient, comprehensive, and helpful. In descending order of price, transparent folders were produced one after the other. What particularly pleased Diana was that they had taken the trouble to have the details translated into adequate English. Each folder contained at least a dozen postcard-sized photographs of every important aspect of the property. The pictures looked professional, giving general views of the outside from different angles, interiors showing the principal rooms, particular features given special emphasis in the descriptions, and some breathtaking views of the surrounding countryside.

When Diana complimented the Frenchman on the excellence of his presentation, he shrugged.
"C'est normal," he replied in a dry tone. "We always try not to waste anyone's time."
"That looks much more like it!" James said excitedly, looking at what was described as a *gentilhommière,* a country seat.
"Une très, très belle propriété," chipped in Madame Louisor. "It is a splendid manor house. *Tout est dans un état vraiment superbe!* All in truly superb order!"
"But very near to your price limit," added her husband. "The price has just been reduced by more than fifteen percent to attract a cash buyer."
"Don't be silly, darling," Diana laughed. "What on earth are we going to do with fourteen bedrooms and six bathrooms, set in parkland of over seventy hectares?"
"But look!" he protested. *"What* a bargain! In England that would cost in pounds the same figure they're asking here in francs!"
"Yes, darling," Diana said patiently. "But do try to remember that we're not going to live in England."
"How large is a hectare?" James asked.
"Rather more than twice the size of your acre," Monsieur Louisor answered without hesitation. He had been asked the same question

many times before. "If you wish to be precise, you must multiply acres by two point four seven one one to convert them to hectares."

The search went on, interspersed with discussion, questions and comments, some of which were practical, others not. After nearly two hours had elapsed, they had set aside the details and pictures of five properties to visit. It was just after midday, the time when France stops for lunch. Monsieur Louisor marked the map carefully. Meanwhile, his wife and the secretary shared the task of contacting the owners.

"You will do us the honour of joining us for lunch?"

The invitation was a clear hint that food and wine must now take priority over work.

"Oh! That's really a most kind suggestion, *Monsieur*," James replied. "But it won't be necessary. If I eat and drink too much now, I'll just want to fall asleep this afternoon. No, we have work to do, and time is the enemy. We'll grab something to eat on our way to the first property. *Une omelette, des frites, et du rosé* — that will do us fine. *Nous vous remercions quand même. Une autre fois, peut-être, quand nous ne serons pas aussi pressés.* Thanks all the same. Maybe another time, when we won't be in so much of a hurry."

The Frenchman's face revealed nothing about his opinion of chips, washed down with *rosé* wine.

"Comme vous voulez," Monsieur Louisor said pleasantly. "It is probably as well to make sure you have time to see all five places today. *Eh bien! Courage et bonne chance à vous deux!* I will be ringing you this evening at about ten o'clock to check progress. You will be able to tell me, I hope, which of the houses you want to see inside, and then we can confirm your programme for tomorrow."

They took their leave and retraced the way back to the jeep. A parking ticket was clipped under the windscreen wiper. He pulled it off angrily. *"Merde alors!"* he grunted.

A passing schoolboy grinned up at him and pulled a face. James smiled back at him. He walked round the jeep to a convenient litter bin. "My contribution to France's efforts to recycle paper!"

He let the parking ticket fall in on top of the rubbish.

Chapter Eight

In what remained of the day, they did not expect to locate, as well as view in any detail, all five properties on their short-list. Surprisingly, they managed to assess four of them, although, as had been arranged, this was only from the outside. One, the most expensive, was not where Monsieur Louisor had marked it on the map. After a quick snack lunch, they went in search of the first place. It was up a bumpy, overgrown track outside the village of Berganty, to the east of Cahors. The house was perched uncomfortably on very steep terrain, which fell away into a valley. The photograph of it had been taken with great care, masking the tumble of thorns, bracken, and shoulder-high weeds which purported to be the garden.

Diana knew that they were wasting their time there while James strolled up the track to get a better view.

"It's clever, what a good photographer can do," she commented patiently when he returned to the jeep.

"I'll never be able to clear all that," he said. "We would have to bring back with us a dozen Zambians with machetes, and put them up for a year, to even make a dent in that lot!"

"The windows are too small, as usual," she grumbled, wondering how many more times she would level the same criticism at French houses.

"And look at that dreadful roof! They've obviously just renewed it, but why didn't they use those nice, old canal tiles one sees everywhere?"

"It's perfectly dreadful," was Diana's final assessment.

James stepped out of the jeep and walked round to the passenger's side. "You drive now. I'll navigate."

The second property was down in the Lot valley itself. In fact, it was almost in the river. A rise in the water level of less than ten feet would bring the river up over the garden and into the house.

"We need not waste time here," he muttered. "One flash flood and we would all be swimming for our lives."

"Pity! Nice looking place, and a beautiful garden."

"Right. Turn in here and we'll go on to the third one."

They never found it, and they wasted precious time, which irritated him.

"I'm surprised at Louisor making a mistake like that," he commented, showing her the map. "Look. Here is Labastide-Marnhac, which we've just been through. "That's the little lane leading up to St-Rémy, and we turned left down here. Now, that house over there is patently *not* the one in this photograph, is it?"

"Even *I* can see that, darling."

It was an ugly, little bungalow, fairly new, with metal shutters. It was typical of the kind of house in which so many French yearn to spend their retirement: no leaking roof, no crumbling stonework, no wooden shutters to maintain and, above all, *pas de bricolage.* This one, however, boasted a large garden, mostly given over to lawn. Arranged on it, with eccentric care for detail, was a display of gnomes, donkeys, bright-coloured dogs, some sitting with their tongues hanging out, others standing with a fixed snarl menacing the gate, and a bright purple, ornate wishing well.

"Merde! Look at all that!" he gasped, his astonishment turning to laughter. "Those things aren't cheap, I'm told. That guy must have spent a lifetime, collecting and paying for that lot!"

"They're not doing anyone any harm," she said quietly, thinking of the pleasure they must bring to their owner.

"Damn! What a bloody waste of time!"

She could sense his frustration as he folded the map for the route to the fourth property.

"This one is also down here, just a bit further south. It's not very far away — about seven miles, I should think. Then it's some twenty miles through country lanes to the last one, which is there."

"You know I can't read a map," she reminded him, as she started the engine.

That's true, he thought. Once, believing the railway line on the map to be the road, she became hopelessly lost in deepest Buckinghamshire.

"You're the navigator," she said, turning the jeep round. "So which way do we go now? The next house is the one which interested us the most, isn't it?"

"Yes," he nodded. "But I'm afraid it might be too small. Go back the way we came, and take the first right after the village. That'll take us back up to the N20."

They found St-Paul-de-Loubressac with no problem. It was a charming, hilltop village with a few shops. The house was on high ground on the far side of the village. At first sight it looked like a large *pigeonnier,* on its own and nothing else. When they approached closer, it became clear that at some time it had been a free-standing tower. It was square in shape, huge, and very attractive. Money had been lavished on its restoration, which had been done tastefully and with thoughtful planning. The tower itself looked as if it provided three floors, all of which had sizeable, stone mullion windows. On the far side, they could make out a well-proportioned extension, which had been added sympathetically, using the local stone and old canal roof tiles. The garden was small and neat. Most of it was taken up by a swimming-pool, a changing hut, also constructed in local stone, and a *terrasse* with an area for barbecues. His first impression was of serenity in an unusual setting.

The small lane on which they were parked overlooked the property and curved to border the garden on two sides. Small conifers had been planted to provide a screen in due course, but they were only about three feet high. The views to the south-west were like a picture postcard.
"Just look at that!" she sighed, taking it all in. "Louisor claimed that you can see the Pyrenees on a clear day from here."
"Well, that's about as true as saying that you could see Salisbury Cathedral, if it were also visible from here!"
"James! Don't be so cynical all the time!"
"Well, I'm only being wary of raising our expectations. I'm coming to the conclusion that, in answer to almost every question, these people just say the first thing that comes into their tiny heads — a bit like our lovely Africans. You know, the French have spent a lot of time in Africa, at least as long as the British. A large part of Africa is French-speaking."

He fell silent briefly, a quizzical look on his face. After a few seconds he began to chuckle and then turned to her with a broad gin.

"Come to think of it," he announced, "that might explain quite a lot!"

"Now you're being racist!"

"No, I'm not," he argued. "You know, as well as I do, that the most misunderstood word in Africa is, 'Yes'. For example, you arrive at a friend's house. The gate is firmly locked. The guard is nowhere to be seen. He's probably asleep somewhere. Eventually you find him or wake him up. So you ask the guard, 'Is the *Bwana* not in?' The answer is, 'Yes'. So then you enquire, 'Your *Bwana* is not there?' The reply is, 'That is very true, *Bwana*. Yes.' It's bloody hot, and you're getting nowhere fast. So you try, 'Your *Bwana* is not at home now?', and he will say, 'Yes, *Bwana*. It is as you are saying.' Eventually, to tie him down, you go through it all again, telling him, 'What you are saying is that your *Bwana* is not at home and that he is out.' 'Yes, *Bwana*,' he will say, 'but that is also very true, and it is indeed what I am now telling you. The *Bwana*, he say to me, he is back in just a little three hours.' If you want to press the point, you might go on, 'And when did the *Bwana* say this to you?' You will get the standard response, 'Ah! *Bwana*, but I don't know, *Bwana*!' So nobody is really any the wiser about anything. And from whom do you think the Africans learned and developed that kind of logic? No prizes for guessing! I find this part of France delightfully African with its lazy logic."

She let him finish his little monologue, having heard it many times before.

"So what?" she retorted. "That's nice, don't you think?"

"Well, yes it is," he continued. "But don't underestimate the French. In their way, they're just as confusing and devious as the Africans. They have two forms of saying 'yes'. They will say *'Oui'*, and they will say *'Si'*. And, like our African friends, what they probably mean is 'I don't know', or 'Perhaps'. After all, it was the French who passed on their curious logic to roughly half of Africa. There is always a 'but' in both French and African thinking."

Diana was pondering on the linguistic task with which she was confronted in the country of their choice.

"Well," she confessed, "I must admit I am getting a bit confused with learning the language. But I didn't do too badly, when I was alone with *Madame* Louisor this morning. It's the genders of nouns that get me."

"Voilà!" he agreed, warming to his favourite subject. "Exactly! What's the gender of a car?"

"Masculine," she answered confidently.

"Wrong! *'La voiture'.* And make-up?"

"Well, that should be feminine."

"No, I'm sorry. You're wrong again. *'Le maquillage'.* Almost every noun ending in *'-age'* is masculine. What about a homosexual?"

"Masculine, I suppose."

"Three in a row," he laughed. *'Une pédale'. Ce mot est du féminin.* One more try. The classic one: the vagina?"

"That really *has* to be feminine," she replied. "It's obvious!"

"Even with the beautiful female body, you're wrong again. *'Le vagin'. Voilà!* It's just the same with *'le con'.* I don't have to tell you what that means, do I? They're just illogical; and yet they are conceited enough to claim that *'Tout ce qui n'est pas clair, ce n'est pas français'."*

"What difference does it make?" she asked. "Why divide things into masculine and feminine, young and old, black and white? There are too many divisions. No wonder the world has so many divisive factions, competing over issues in the name of race, religion, trade, or whatever. What do the French say when they're pissed off?"

"Tout ça m'emmerde!"

She had suffered quite enough linguistics for one day. "What about getting on with our house-hunting?" she asked. "What do you think of this *petit coin de paradis?"*

"I'm a bit suspicious about the bloody N20. It's only just the other side of the village. It is, after all, the main road to Toulouse from around here. After that frightful fiasco with Martin and the Grandets, we'll have to make damn sure that it's not going to be yet another motorway. That's if you want to take it any further and see inside this place tomorrow. Louisor is going to ring us—"

"I don't like this lane," she said suddenly, pointing from left to right. "It's on the border of the garden all the way from there to over there. Anyone passing can't help but look straight into the place." She hesitated, and then suggested, "Let's see where it leads to round that corner."

A woman in a towelling wrap came out of the house and walked towards the swimming pool, watching them as they passed.

"It's certainly open to prying eyes," he agreed. "But eventually those little trees will grow and solve that problem."

They turned the corner and drove a further two hundred yards up the lane. A long, low building confronted them. It was surrounded by a high, wire-mesh security fence with big double gates. Beyond the fence was an area of concrete hard-stand, on which some thirty refrigerator trucks were parked in two neat rows. A large hoarding announced proudly that these were the premises of a distributor of frozen foods, supplying the whole of the Midi-Pyrénées.

Dumbfounded, they both sat in the jeep with its engine still running, their astonishment stifling any appropriate comment. Then they started laughing.

"Oh, my God!" she cried. "Isn't that just too beautiful! Just what we've been looking for all this time! Imagine all those trucks, grinding down the lane at all hours of the day and night, about five feet away from the swimming-pool! It's only because it's Saturday afternoon and we're here at the weekend that we haven't already been forced off the lane into the ditch. Imagine! How does anyone ever sleep in that house?"

"But darling," he said in a mock serious tone, "this is just perfect. We won't have to buy a deep-freezer, and frozen cat food will fall off the back of those trucks five days a week if you make friends with one of the drivers. Think about it! You'll be able to do most of your shopping on foot with one of those trendy little baskets on wheels."

"I wouldn't mind if this was Lusaka, but Louisor can stuff his view of the mountains. *Allez! On y va!*"

"*Et baah, oui! Chacun à sa merde!* Four down and one to play. *Vas-y, chérie!*"

*

They drove down small lanes in a south-westerly direction, passing over narrow, stone bridges, each of which announced that they were crossing or recrossing the Lupte, which was no more than a small stream. They were in Castelnau-Montratier just before five o'clock, and stopped to have coffee in the pretty, cobbled *place*. They followed the signs towards Montcarmel and, as they penetrated further into the area known as Quercy Blanc, the landscape started to change again. The road wound its way up over three successive ridges of limestone rock. Down in each of the valleys the fertile soil was being exploited to the full. Wheat, barley, sunflower, and maize had already been harvested. Some fields of sorghum remained, standing ripe, waiting for the combine harvesters to process it into cattle fodder. Fields of stubble were being ploughed or undersown. In parts, some good grassland was evidence that dairy farming was also taking place.

Most, but not all, of the farms appeared to be quite small, probably owned by peasant farmers. Here and there, a more substantial house, surrounded by sprawling, stone outbuildings, suggested a more prosperous landowner. Sophisticated irrigation equipment stood in place, where it had last been used. The contrast was stark between the lushness of the valleys and the wild, craggy cols, which were covered with scrub oaks, stunted broom, heather, and long tufts of grass, parched yellow by the sun. Compared with the valleys, it became several degrees warmer as they approached the top of each ridge, the heat bouncing back at them from the impressive, bleached rock face.

Then they were descending into Montcarmel, its fifteenth-century church and Renaissance castle presiding over the small market town from its vantage point on the hillside. They did not stop in the town, catching only a fleeting glimpse of a small square with four café-restaurants, a war memorial with tricolours, old men playing *boules* under chestnut trees, and a deserted garage. The smell of freshly baked bread came to them from a *boulangerie* opposite *La Presse*. The tree-lined road took them down past an agricultural co-operative and on to the main road, where they turned north-east towards Cahors with the sun behind them.

Six kilometres later, they found the lane to Saint Juste. Tucked into a bowl of small fields, above which towered steep cliffs of rock and oak, the tiny hamlet baked in the late afternoon sunshine, shuttered, somnolent, and silent. Chestnut trees, their leaves brown and about to fall, cast their welcoming shade over a courtyard in front of a stone house with steep steps leading up to a door and well-maintained, grey shutters. A small sign announced discreetly that this was the *Mairie,* open on Sunday mornings from ten until midday, and on Wednesday afternoons from three to five. From somewhere a dog barked languidly. Behind the *Mairie,* there stood a small church, only the bell tower of which was visible from the lane.

They climbed the steep hill out on the north side of the hamlet. If they met a tractor here, someone would have to give way. It would probably not be the tractor. A small cottage on the right was being guarded by two Alsatian puppies and several families of ducks. At the top, they stopped to look back into the bowl and the valley beyond. They could see no movement below them — no cars, no caravans, no tractors, no people.

"You won't get much more tranquility than that," James said quietly.

They were now crossing high, stony ground on the top of the escarpment. The sun had turned the grass into an almost auburn colour, flecked here and there with white, where it had finally died back. Huge boulders lay, dark and solidly immovable, nature having heaved them into unimaginable positions many centuries ago. Surprisingly, on slightly lower ground to their left, they passed a long, narrow field with three neat rows of vines. The heavy bunches of purple grapes looked ready for *les vendanges,* which would be profitable for the *vigneron* who owned them. A pair of large buzzards circled above, their broad wings motionless, as they sought and then found a thermal, rising from the heated, rocky terrain below them. A dog, a majestic, blue-grey Weimaraner, suddenly leaped from behind a thorn bush into the small lane. Diana had to brake fiercely to avoid running it over.

"*Chien méchant!*" she scolded, as it disappeared with a flick of its short tail into the grasses on the right.

"My favourite dog," he murmured, looking across the open space to catch a last glimpse of it as it bounded away powerfully in a determined, straight line.

As she drove the jeep over the top of the ridge, Diana suddenly became aware of the distinct change in the surrounding landscape. James noticed that her knuckles were turning white with effort as she gripped the steering wheel.

"It's quite like Africa just here, don't you think?" she shouted happily, as they turned to approach the hamlet of Pisenhaut.

"It's a bit like that stretch between Kafue and Mazabuka, when you climb up from the river flats into the foothills."

"Yes, it is," she agreed. "I was just trying to think why it reminded me of somewhere. Yes, you've got it. It's like that outcrop near the memorial, below the spot where Livingstone is said to have first sighted the Kafue river."

He pointed towards a stony mound strewn with more boulders and thorny shrubs, on the top of which a solitary, twisted scrub oak, larger than most, offered some cover and shade.

"Leopards could live over there, among those rocks," he said wistfully.

Chapter Nine

As they approached Pisenhaut, there was a break in the trees lining the left-hand side of the road. A field of silvery white stubble sloped gently away to form the neck of a shallow valley. On the far side, a gravelled drive curved round two large, mature walnut trees which flanked what appeared to be an old, stone well. Through the foliage they could see a beautiful, square *pigeonnier* on the end of a stone house. The view of the garden was obscured, as they reached the end of the gap in the trees.

"I think that might have been it, down there on the left," he said.

"Do you want me to stop and reverse?"

"No, we'll go round to have a look from the entrance first. Take the next left."

The lane into which they turned went downhill to a sharp bend, on the corner of which was a house sign with the words, "Bon Porteau". It pointed up two hundred yards of driveway to the walnut trees, where it curved out of sight up and away to the left. The entrance to the drive was marked by two old millstones, and on the left there was an orchard. Beyond it, towards the house, which was hidden from view by oak and maple trees, they could just make out an area of lawn, a flat stone bench next to a blue cedar, and a privet hedge on the top of a grassy bank.

"Let's go back up there," he suggested. "Go into this field and drive across it, until we find a proper view of the house itself. This looks a bit more interesting. It's about time we saw something which might be worth investigating."

Diana turned the jeep, as the bells in the next village were ringing out. They parked and looked out over the small valley, which funnelled gradually up to the house. She switched off the engine. There was total silence, except for the ticking of the exhaust as it cooled. The sun was behind them, now yellow and orange as it started to dip in the early evening sky. James looked at his watch. It was exactly six o'clock. He climbed out of the jeep, pulled the cool-box out of the back and put it on the ground.

"Bar's open," he grinned. "We've got wine and plenty of gin."

"Gin and tonic, please," she said.

She remained sitting behind the steering wheel, glass in hand, looking through the windscreen. He stood outside, leaning against the driver's door. They both sipped their drinks and went on looking. Neither of them spoke for some time.

*

They watched the house for half an hour. There was no sign of life; nothing moved. The windows were all firmly shuttered. The valley was silent.

"Pass me the binoculars, will you?" he asked.

Diana, who was reading the agent's description of the property, reached into the glove compartment and handed them to him.

"It says here, among other things," she read out, "that there are four good bedrooms and two large reception, a big roof *terrasse* and a huge cellar."

He focussed the powerful binoculars on the house. "The main part of the house seems to be older," he observed. "It's built of lovely, old stone and, from the look of it, the roof is good. That lower section at the front seems to have been added at some time, probably the result of some fairly recent restoration. The bedrooms must be in there, I think, behind those four tall pairs of shutters at ground level."

"That's a nice idea, to be able to get up in the morning and walk straight out into the garden."

He adjusted the focus of the binoculars and looked again at the house.

"There are another two large pairs of shutters on the floor above. I should think they must give access from the two reception rooms on to that roof *terrasse* you mentioned... Yes, they do... I can see more clearly now. The *terrasse* is vast. It must be every bit of sixty feet long. It forms the roof of the bedroom area, and there's a small wall, a parapet around it."

"Let me have a look?"

She took the field-glasses, spent a few moments refocussing them, and then looked closely at the house for some minutes.

"What a magnificent *pigeonnier,* and there's another room, right at the top of it," she exclaimed. "It all looks quite splendid." She handed the glasses back to him.

"Did you know that the square *pigeonnier,* like this one, is catholic, and that the round ones are Protestant?" he asked.

"I presume you mean the original owners were."

He smiled and held up the glasses again, taking another sweep of the surrounding land and then back to the house itself.

"Those six pairs of tall shutters, behind which I imagine are big French windows, are all louvred. The rest seem to be the traditional, solid wood type. A bit of maintenance is needed on all those I can see from here. I don't like that shit-coloured varnish, or whatever it is. Still, that's only cosmetic. There's obviously nobody in. Let's walk down there and see if we can get up to the house that way. I want to take a took at the other side and at the outbuildings — in particular, that big, stone barn."

To the left of the drive, they had noticed a grassy track on the far side of the orchard. It was flanked by dry stone walls, and appeared to lead up to the other side of the house. They decided to explore it. There was another millstone in the centre of the entrance to the track.

"That, I presume," he commented, "is to prevent people from driving up there."

There was a metal notice nailed to a tree, on which were painted the faded words, *"Chasse Gardée. Défense d'Entrer sous Peine d'Amende!"*

"What *does* that mean?" she asked.

"Roughly translated: No shooting, and Trespassers will be Prosecuted."

"Good! I like that," she smiled, thinking of the three cats. "Pretty, isn't it?"

"Right," he agreed, taking her hand. "Let's go and do some trespassing."

Honeysuckles and lilies, which had died back some months before, were growing out of the walls on each side of the track. Overhead, box hedging had been allowed to grow to form a high arch about twenty-five yards long. Below it, in permanent shade, bright green mosses thrived with, here and there, cacti and rock plants in the stone walls. As they approached the house, they crossed a small area of grass with two large, mature clumps of bamboo growing to a height of over twelve feet, casting their long shadows across the north-facing wall of the house.

"That's a good sign," he said. "Every serious garden should have some bamboo growing in it."

Above a window on the upper floor, the date '1791' had been carved into its heavy, stone lintel.

"Well, whoever had this place built must have kept his head and preserved his *liberté, égalité et fraternité!*" Below, at ground level, under an archway, there was a heavy oak door, studded with nails.

"Probably the door to the cellars," he said.

A table and chairs were set in the shade of the trees near the edge of the grass.

They walked along the side of the house, which they had not been able to see from where the jeep was parked. Covering the whole of this side of the house, a luxuriant Virginia creeper, deep red in its full autumn glory, had been trained across supporting wires to form a thick, overhead canopy. In its shade, there were more chairs and a long trestle-table. To the left, a broad expanse of lawn sloped gently away to a field, bordered by maple and oak trees. More tables and chairs were grouped carefully to take advantage of the shade of the trees during the heat of the day.

"Just took at that magnificent colour!" Diana exclaimed.

The splash of the autumnal orange on the maple leaves was so vivid that it seemed almost unreal, as if nature had unwittingly exaggerated the mixing of her paints.

They came to a large, covered entrance porch, inside which were heavy oak beams and upright supports. Looking out through a gap in the creeper, a small table, a chair, and a bench stood to one side of double oak doors. A vase of roses was placed on the table with a carafe of water, an upturned glass placed over its neck. Beside the porch there was an attractive border of herbaceous plants and flowering shrubs. To the left, stone steps led down to a wide patio, paved in natural stone, off which another solid door provided a secondary entrance to the lower level of the house. On the patio, there was further evidence of life al fresco.

"They clearly like living outside," he grinned. "I make that the fifth outside eating area."

The patio continued all the way round the south side of the house, narrowing to form a pavement outside the bedrooms with their tall, double shutters. They looked at the stone barn and at the other two outbuildings. All three appeared at first glance to have been carefully restored and well maintained. Across another field of grass beyond the barn, the view stretched away to more fields, hills, copses, and isolated, rocky outcrops. Looking out in this direction, they could see only one small house about two miles away.

"It might well be a bit of Africa," she remarked.

*

They started to retrace their footsteps when a cacophony of car horns suddenly started blaring from the direction of Pisenhaut. Some moments later a convoy of cars, followed by a minibus, turned up the drive and parked noisily outside the house. Remnants of white tulle were tied to the aerials of each vehicle. Men, women, and children of all ages, laughing merrily, tumbled out on to the drive and, with difficulty, formed themselves into two erratic ranks flanking the steps up to the porch.

"A wedding party!" he whispered, peeping round the corner of the barn. "Fine time to view a house!"

A large, squat, vintage Citroën, of the kind used in Inspector Maigret films, drove slowly up the drive. It was festooned with white ribbons, and the driver kept his hand firmly on the loud horn, which echoed and reverberated around the narrow valley. Shouts and cheers greeted the bride and bridegroom as they stepped out of the car and ran between the two lines of excited relatives and friends. A scruffy dog hurled itself at full speed up the steps, in close pursuit of the newly-weds. Someone rang the large brass bell in the porch and went on ringing it. The ragged guard of honour roared and screamed its approval. The children broke ranks, to disappear in all directions into the garden. Backs were slapped as the adults followed into the house.

"Pity we don't have an invitation," Diana said quietly. "It looks as if there's going to be one hell of a party now."

"Come on. We had better creep away before we get arrested."

They skirted the field, keeping well away from the house and the gardens. The sun was now nearly down, and dusk was beginning to herald darkness. As they quickly crossed the orchard, James noticed the difference in temperature at the foot of the shallow valley. By the time they reached the jeep, all the shutters of the house had been thrown open and lights were on in every room. Two large lanterns floodlit the roof *terrasse,* where most of the guests were assembling. The unmistakeable sound of champagne corks exploding in rapid succession filled the otherwise still evening air. They sat and watched the revelry for a few minutes. Now and then the dog barked excitedly, accompanied by squeals of delight from the children. It was a joyous sight. The house, now bathed in artificial light, looked truly welcoming.

"Well?" He looked at her to ask the question, which she was expecting. "Would you like to live there?"

"I'll think about it," was her enigmatic reply.

As they drove out of the field, an accordion started to play.

*

They returned to Cahors at a leisurely pace. The *Hôtel Château de Mercuès* was expecting them. They were installed in a comfortably furnished bedroom, in which there were a king-size bed, a sofa and armchairs, a writing desk, and a television with a video channel. Double French windows opened on to an oval balcony which looked out in the direction of the river and the vineyards beyond.

"I bet there's a fabulous view from here," James said, turning his back on the dark night.

The telephone rang. He looked at his watch, expecting the caller to be Monsieur Louisor, but it was someone from the hotel. He was informed politely that dinner was now being served, and that a table had been reserved for them when they were ready to go down.

"I know it's Saturday night and all that," he said to Diana, "but I really don't feel up to wading through a four-star hotel's menu at this hour."

"Nor do I," she agreed, with a shake of her head. "Why don't you ring down for some paté, bread, cheese, and a bowl of fruit? If you sleep on a full stomach, you'll just have your dreaded nightmares and neither of us will get a good night's rest."

"Good idea. We can also try a different Cahors wine."

While Diana was in the bathroom, he gave their order to the same polite voice, adding a request for their wine list.

"I've been longing for a good bath for three weeks," she called over the sound of running water. "The shower in the cottage is fine, but with all the *calcaire* in the water and no oil, my skin's gone completely dry."

He sat on the edge of the bath, and enjoyed admiring his wife's figure as she lay back in the scented water.

"What's that pong?"

"Jasmine," she replied, handing him a small bottle of expensively packaged bath oil. "Courtesy of the hotel. It's lovely."

"I take it that when Louisor rings, I should arrange for a look inside Bon Porteau tomorrow?"

"It might be worthwhile," she said, looking inscrutable.

"He should be ringing at any time now. I'll try to get him to fix it up for tomorrow morning."

"The poor owners! The place will be like an absolute tip after that party. They won't have much chance to clean up."

"All the better for our viewing," he retorted. "We'll see it, *sans aucun astiquage,* without any spit and polish, although I don't believe they go in very much for that sort of thing here. From what we have seen, they really don't seem to give a damn either about their untidiness or the paintwork in their houses." He paused, then added, "With the exception of Grandet."

Some ten minutes later the telephone rang again. This time it was Monsieur Louisor.

"How did you get on this afternoon?" he asked.

"Fine," James replied. "We saw four out of the five places. We couldn't find the one near Labastide-Marnhac, but it didn't matter. There's only one we liked. We want to see inside it tomorrow, preferably in the morning. It's the one called Bon Porteau."

"Tomorrow is Sunday. It may be difficult to arrange. This morning, when my wife rang the owner, a *Madame* Gautier, to tell her that you would be looking at the property from the outside, the reaction was rather confused. She seemed quite flustered. She said something about a marriage party, and that there would be *du monde,* a lot of people there."

"We know," James explained. "We saw them return to the house after the wedding ceremony. When we left the place, it looked as if they were just warming up for a damn good party. But if she wants to sell her place, then I presume that she'll let us have a look around inside. See what you can arrange, *Monsieur.*"

Monsieur Louisor rang off, having promised to ring back as quickly as possible. Within another five minutes he was telling James that a slightly tipsy Madame Gautier would be enchanted to meet them and to show them round from eleven o'clock onwards the following morning.

"*Elle est très charmante et pleine de vie,*" Monsieur Louisor added. "Now, I will give you my personal number, so that you can contact me tomorrow at any time during or after your visit. I shall be in all day."

A little later, there was a knock on the door and a young waitress entered the room. She was pushing an old-fashioned, wooden trolley. She gave James the wine list and waited for him to make his choice. He thought the *Domaine de Boulbènes, '85* looked interesting. He had noticed the place on his map. It was only fifteen or, perhaps twenty, kilometres from Bon Porteau.

"*C'est bon?*" he asked the young woman.

"*Eh baah, oui! Bien sûr!*" came the confident reply. "*C'est mon oncle. Ce vin est impeccable!*"

"*Baah, bon! Nous le prenons,*" he decided. "We'll take it." As she left the room, he added a further "*Baah, bon!*" to her departing back.

"What's so "*Bon! Bon!*" then?" asked Diana, as she emerged from the bathroom.

"*C'est toi, ma chérie,*" he replied.

"You tell such awful lies, Jamie! But I like it!"

She stood in front of him, naked except for a towel which was wrapped round her head.

"What time will it be in Zambia now?" she asked.

"The same as here, although I can never understand how that can be possible."

"Good. I've just got time, before they bring supper, to ring

Fackson and check on my babies."

It was to impress this special relationship upon their loyal houseman that the three cats were always referred to in this way from the outset. "These are my babies," he recalled Diana telling Fackson, when they had first arrived. "They are, to me, like your children and babies are to you and Gertrude. They are not like any other cats, to be chased away with stones. They are very, very *special*! Do you understand?"

"Ah! But yes, Madam! These will always be now our babies," he had replied, looking a little bewildered at the red, blue and cream Burmese cats blinking up at him from their basket.

"The residence of *Bwana* Wyllis," she heard Fackson's voice answering the telephone, which he always enjoyed doing, once he had overcome his initial disbelief that anyone could possibly be on the other end of the line.

He was following the procedure which they had painstakingly explained to him over a period of several months.

"The Bwana, he is not at home. Now I take your name, your numbers, and your little message."

"Muli bwanji, Fackson! I greet you! Here we are calling from France."

"Ah! Ah! *Bwino bwanji,* greetings, Madam! It is really not you, from so far away in that cold place?"

"Yes, Fackson. The *Bwana* and I are still here in France, looking for a *shamba*. How are my babies?"

"Ah! They are just a little bit all right. Big man, Jacob, he is watching from the stoep every day to see you maybe will come. Silly man, Fozzy, he is just very okay also. I am doing his brushing now-now. And little baby girl, Yenties, she is just very fine indeed! And the rains are not yet coming and it is still very hot-hot."

"And how are your own babies and the family?"

"Ah! Now they are very much all well. Gertrude was bitten by a snake and has a little bit fever. Little Ruth, she drink a mug of bleach last night and was just sick, and then again well. The other children are very well indeed, and I am now very hard busy in the house."

"Ask him if he has now finished building his house in Kalingalinga," James whispered.

She was intent upon listening to the rest of Fackson's news, and after a few minutes she was able to speak again.

"Fackson, the *Bwana* would like to know if your house is finished yet."

"Ah! But no, Madam. There is no roofing material in Lusaka. But it is not a big problem. It is not raining yet. I am now renting it to four families, as well as to Phebian, who is there now with his wife and baby."

"And is Moses behaving himself? Is he guarding properly at night, or is he asleep!"

"Ah! Moses is not here now-now. He has a big problem. A prisoner escaped and ran into the garden, when Moses was leaving the gate open. The police, they very quickly have shot him dead."

"Who? Moses, or the prisoner?"

"Ah! Sorry-sorry! It is the prisoner who is dead. But Moses he has had to carry the body back to the police station, and he has not returned from giving out statements. I have locked the gate now. The children have the key."

"So, everything is all right now?"

"Yes, Madam. It is all very all right now. But Madam, please to say to *Bwana,* if he need help, I will come to France on one of my brothers' horses from the police."

"*Chabwino,* very good, Fackson. I think the *Bwana* can manage this time. The phone is *mningi* expensive, so I say sleep well. *Gonani bwino!*"

"*Zikomo, Madam. Gonani bwino!* Thank you and goodbye, and please to say goodnight, *"Lala salama"*, to the *Bwana*. We hope you are having a good safari when you return, and all the family is thinking of the presents which you are bringing with you."

They ate what proved to be more than just a snack supper. The wine was superb. James turned on the video channel and they enjoyed watching *"Manon des Sources"*, before falling into the luxurious bed. His dreams that night were a chaotic tumble of disjointed images and events involving house-hunting, planting a small vineyard, chasing *chasseurs* out of his woods, and Jacob being savaged by a fox. At some stage, Madame Louisor was stroking his hair, and then he was caught in a forest fire, ducking and weaving his way through a tangle of undergrowth to escape the flames.

"You were having a nightmare, darling," he heard Diana telling him, as she brushed his hair off his damp forehead. "You should not have eaten so much of that strong cheese with your wine. Are we going to be all right now?"

"Yes, my love," he mumbled, and immediately started dreaming about buying garden machinery. In the morning, he could not arrive at any logical explanation or interpretation for such strange, subconscious activity.

Chapter Ten

There are many differences between Sunday morning in the Lot and, for example, its counterpart in many areas of Britain. Milk bottles and thick wads of newspapers do not lie uncollected on doorsteps. Curtains are not left drawn closed across bedroom windows until someone bothers to get up to boil a kettle. Men are not wandering about with bleary eyes, recovering from a heavy night in the pub. No cars are being washed, with an excess of detergent spilling into the streets. In France there are no milk bottles. The Sunday newspapers are commendably thinner than the weekday editions. Neither milk bottles nor newspapers are delivered to the home. Solid, wooden shutters are preferred to unlined curtains. With the exception of a few unlikely copies, there are no pubs.

The French seldom use kettles, certainly not electric ones. They are viewed with deep suspicion. Not only are they invariably imported, but also they have a curious habit of blowing fuses. In the unlikely event of a fuse remaining intact, they consume excess electricity. They rapidly attract a tough deposit of *calcaire,* which causes them to operate inefficiently and thus use even more electricity. Who, they will ask, can possibly make good coffee with such a *truc*? And, anyway, they do not like mending fuses on Sunday mornings. They do not like mending fuses at all. Few waste their time washing their battered cars and vans. They have other priorities. Apart from anything else, Sunday morning, in the towns and villages of the Lot, is Market Day.

So it was, when they left the hotel the next day. It was agreed that their room would be kept available for them, provided that they telephoned either to confirm or to cancel before six o'clock in the evening. James had paid the bill, and now they had with them their overnight bags, thus allowing them to keep their options open.

"Merde!" he cursed as they went out to the jeep. "That cost an arm and a leg! Your short telephone call to Fackson in Nalikwanda Road came to more than the room for the night!"

They arrived in Montcarmel one hour before their appointment with Madame Gautier at Bon Porteau.

"Eh bien!" he said. "Let's have a quick look at the town."

Turning up the hill off the main road and approaching the *place*, they soon realized that every available parking space was occupied, whether legitimately or not. Cars and vans were everywhere: on the pavement, double parked on yellow lines, and even on part of the venerated *piste de boules* under the chestnut trees. Only a small area of the pitch had been roped off, thus allowing the suntanned old men to pursue their daily competitions. The latter paid no heed to the jeep, with its attractive female passenger, as it entered the one-way street system. It was by then no longer possible to turn back.

On the outer fringes of the square, the route through to a possible exit on the far side was obstructed by stalls of farm produce, cheeses, wine for *dégustation gratuite*, plants and flowers, clothes, hats, basketwork, pots and pans, *brocante,* and every shape and size of bread. Space not taken up by the stalls, which had been trading for some two hours, was filled with animated people, greeting and kissing each other. Young children were darting between the legs of adults, some of whom were struggling with carrier bags full of their bargains. Others, who appeared to outnumber those intent upon shopping, either stood in groups exchanging news and gossip gathered since the previous Sunday, or wandered on their own, scanning the crowd for a possible impromptu rendezvous. Almost all carried several long loaves of bread, using them to joust their way through the swarm of happy people.

All four cafés were doing a busy trade, their tables and chairs spread over that part of the pavement allotted to them. Their clientele sat and indulged their two favourite occupations: watching the world go by, or, if someone or something caught the eye, taking long, slow sips of coffee, beer, *pruneaux* or *pastis*. The younger, more shapely ladies were exploiting this weekly opportunity to parade their latest outfits. They swayed their hips as they passed, pretending not to notice the appreciative, sometimes critical, glances of the menfolk. James edged the jeep forward slowly between the mass of human and inanimate obstacles. A disinterested *gendarme* watched their lack of progress. Satisfied that the speed limit was not going to be exceeded, he turned to continue his conversation with an attractive girl standing close to him. A dog with suicidal tendencies squeezed under the almost stationary jeep, intent upon following an irresistible scent picked up from somewhere on the other side of the *place*.

"Something tells me," James said in an irritated tone, "that we should not be here."

It took almost an hour to navigate less than four hundred metres of the only road through the town and emerge on the other side. By then, there was no time left to explore, as James had earlier suggested.

"*Merde!*" he cursed. "Now we'll be late for *Madame* Gautier."

"I'm sure she won't mind," said Diana, thinking of all the mess, which Madame Gautier would have been clearing up in preparation for their tour of inspection.

They reached Bon Porteau a mere twenty minutes after their scheduled arrival time. As they drove slowly towards the house Diana noticed that all the bedroom shutters were ominously closed.

*

Madame Gautier heard the jeep. She was sitting on a chair in the shade of the porch when they arrived. Perhaps into her sixties, with slightly dishevelled, peroxide hair and a warm smile, she came forward to greet them. James made his apologies for being late, explaining the delay in the market place.

"*Mais, ce n'est pas grave, quelques petites vingt minutes!*" she reassured him. "It's not serious, some twenty little minutes! In fact, it gave me an opportunity to sit down for the first time since dinner last night!" She led them into the shade of the porch, where she slumped back into her chair, indicating that they should do likewise.

"*Installez-vous!* Please sit down!" she insisted. "*Installez-vous, je vous en prie!*" she repeated.

She appeared out of breath, as if she had been rushing about in the heat which was beginning to make itself felt. She pushed a wisp of hair away from her face and, using what looked like a napkin, she dabbed at the drops of perspiration forming on her forehead and neck.

"I owe an explanation to you both," she said in very correct French, which James judged must be of Parisian origin. "I don't speak a word of English! *Pas un mot!* Not a single word!"

The admission came out as if she was confessing to a cardinal sin, as opposed to the mutually accepted attitude of both nationalities, which care very little whether or not they speak each other's language.

"Ne vous inquiétez pas, Madame," he said. "Don't worry. We speak a bit of your beautiful language."

"O-là-là, là-là! Vous parlez bien français!" she cried with relief. Then, suddenly, she broke into uncontrolled, hysterical laughter, trying to stifle it with the back of one hand over her mouth. "And to think that I've been up all night," she continued with a friendly tap on Diana's arm, "worrying myself into a frenzy that I would not be able to explain anything at all to you! *Mais, Dieu merci! Enfin, vous parlez français."*

James was anxious to make up for lost time and was looking for an opportunity to interrupt the exchange of words which were taking place.

"Please excuse the short notice of our visit," he interjected as soon as she paused for breath. "You see, we leave to return to Zambia the day after tomorrow, and we have only two days remaining in this visit to your country. We hope it isn't too inconvenient, but we wanted to, indeed had to, come and see your house today."

"O-là-là, là-là!" clucked Madame Gautier, turning to Diana. *"Vous venez de la Zambie!* But is he always in such a hurry? There are times in life when it isn't at all good to hurry, particularly in this frightful heat. My husband died of hurrying, poor man..." She touched Diana on the arm again and asked, *"Mais, toi aussi, tu sais parler français?"* She used the *'tu'* form, as adults do when they are talking to a member of the family, a close friend, a child, or a pet.

"Je vous suis parfaitement," Diana replied. "I can follow you very well, if you will just be kind enough to speak a little more slowly.

"Voilà! Bon!" Madame Gautier separated the two words like a teacher of elocution, and let out a loud, deep sigh.

Shame! thought Diana. She's very tired, if not exhausted. She's not going to get out of that chair in a hurry. She wants to break the ice first with a chat.

"My name is Diana. My husband is called James."

"Diana! Que c'est vraiment un joli prénom!" She pronounced it,

'Dianne'. "A name fit for a princess, no doubt. I am Félicie. You must call me Félicie, please. *Nous n'avons pas besoin de faire des cérémonies ici.* We don't need to stand on ceremony here."

"We understand that you had a marriage party yesterday."

"Had! *O-là-là!* Still have!" she shrieked at the top of her voice. She quickly put her hand over her mouth. "If you will please keep your voices down." She pointed at the floor, and then went on in a conspiratorial whisper. "Do you know, there are twenty-eight people asleep down there in the bedrooms and in the passage!" She then waved a hand towards the roof. "And another eighteen up there, in the four little rooms in the loft space! Seventy-eight guests, I had! *O-là-là, là-là! Du monde! Du monde!* Such a crowd! I expected only twelve to stay overnight, but when the party ended at around five this morning, thirty-four people couldn't make it to their cars. *Dieu merci!* They would not have found the end of the drive, let alone safely reached their homes!"

She shook her wrist and elbow, miming copious drinking of alcohol.

James remembered the happy scene from the previous evening, when the wedding party arrived at the house to interrupt their exploration of the property.

"It was a good party, then?" he asked.

"Too much! Too much!" Félicie protested loudly, forgetting her own request not to disturb her guests. "The young, you know, they cannot hold their liquor, like we can. And the noise all night! *Quel bruit!* I should think it was heard in Toulouse! And," she sighed, trying to smother another yawn, "I have been up ever since, clearing the debris. No bed for me last night."

With visible effort, the Frenchwoman rose to her feet and, without saying anything, she disappeared into the house. They sat quietly in the porch, looking out through the gap in the Virginia creeper at the lawn and the enchanting orange colour of the maple leaves, which they admired so much the day before. When Félicie returned, she was carrying a tray on which were set an attractive coffee pot, two cups, a small glass, and an unlabelled, green bottle.

She offered them coffee, and then poured herself a good measure from the bottle, replacing the cork with care.

"This is *pruneaux*," she explained. "It's good for courage after a long night, and it settles the liver." She raised her glass, and its contents disappeared in one quick swallow. *"Eh bien. Enfin.... Nous avons un tout petit problème,"* she said, licking her lips.

"*What* problem?" enquired James.

"Well," she said, pointing downwards. "You cannot possibly view the bedrooms. Not yet. Neither," she paused, looking upwards, "can you see those nice little rooms in the roof space. There are people sleeping everywhere. Some are in sleeping bags, some fully dressed, others in less clothes, and still others... Well, they are in intimate postures. *O-là-là! Non!* We cannot disturb them. It could be awful for you... For me... And for them! Particularly, if they are..."

"Never mind," he said, wanting to make progress. He checked the time. "Perhaps they'll all be on the move soon, getting ready for a heavy, traditional Sunday lunch, no?"

Félicie was shaking her head vigorously. She raised both hands and started waving them at him.

"Not a chance!" she said firmly. "But I did tell them all that they had to be off and away by three o'clock this afternoon, because I have two important guests coming. I hope they will remember to do as I asked."

"What? More guests!" Diana exclaimed, admiring her stamina.

"Mais bien sûr, ma chérie! Ce sont vous deux! You two are my guests! We will now take an *apéritif*. Then you will go to lunch at one of my favourite restaurants. It's not far away. I will explain how to find it. They are expecting you shortly after midday. Afterwards, you will come back here at, say, about four this afternoon. While you are away, my daughter will be able to clean up the remaining rubbish from the party. And I invite you to dinner here and then to stay the night. That is, after I have shown you around this superb property. I feel, for some reason, that it will suit you both, and that you will fall in love with it. If you do like this place and... If you do decide to buy it, then..." She hesitated, her fatigue muddling her train of thought, but then she continued with an expansive wave of her arm, "Then, if you are half as happy as I have been here, you will have found yourselves with a real bargain on your hands! *Voilà! C'est tout! Un vrai petit coin de paradis!"*

James made as if he was about to refuse her two invitations, but Diana stopped him. She was thinking that Félicie had made her plan, so they might as well go along with it.

"That's a wonderful idea," Diana said enthusiastically. "But only if you're sure it won't be too much trouble."

"*Non, non, non! Pas du tout!*" Félicie reassured her. "Not at all. This house was built for guests and parties. All my friends from Paris say so. They must like it, because they keep coming! *Il y a toujours le va-et-vient!* There are always friends and guests coming and going, as well as my family. I love it. It keeps me busy and stops me feeling lonely."

A series of piercing bleeps from a telephone somewhere inside the house cut short any further discussion of her unexpected invitation. Félicie swore softly and struggled out of her chair.

"*J'arrive! Merde, j'arrive!*" she shouted at the top of her voice, as if to let her caller know that she was coming. She ran through the front door, and the bleeps ceased abruptly.

"*Allô! Oui?*"

From outside, under the porch, they could hear her strident voice.

"*Eh bien, chérie, c'est toi! Tu viens? Bon! Mais, oui! Oui, oui! Ils sont vraiment ici... Très sympa! Alors, à tout à l'heure!*"

They heard her put the telephone down noisily.

"I shouldn't think anyone is still asleep after all that," James said with a grin. Bottles and glasses were being removed noisily from a cupboard. A door was slammed shut.

"*Entrez, Diana! Entrez, James!*" Félicie called to them. As they went into the room she explained, "That was my daughter, Pascale. She lives in Cahors. She's coming, as planned." She waved an arm at the bottles and glasses on the small table in the centre of the room. "*Je vous en prie, servez-vous!* I will have the *Armagnac*, James, if you will be so kind."

While he poured the drinks, Diana looked around the large room: exposed stone walls, huge oak beams supporting a wooden ceiling, an open fireplace at least seven feet wide with a thick beam serving as a mantlepiece, and a nice quarry-tiled floor. There was a pretty, arched window with an attractive stone corner-bench beneath it. The doors were panelled, and light was flooding in through the tall, double

French windows, which opened on to the roof *terrasse*. Félicie's voice interrupted her brief survey.

"Let's take our *apéritifs* out on to the *terrasse*," she suggested. "It's such a nice day again, even if it is a trifle too hot. But then, coming from Africa, *on y est vraiment comme chez vous!* This must seem to you like home from home."

*

The *terrasse* over the bedroom area was even larger than it had appeared when they had first seen it from the other side of the valley.

"*Santé!*" they said in unison, raising their glasses.

At the far end of the *terrasse,* set under a canopy of more Virginia creeper, stood a long, rustic table and some chairs.

"It's big enough to have a game of short tennis here," James said, walking over to the low parapet.

While the two women sat beside the table, he looked out across the shallow valley towards the field of stubble where they had parked the jeep on the previous evening. His gaze gradually shifted back up the gentle slope to the lawn area between the drive and the house. He suddenly let out an involuntary gasp.

"What on earth is *that* down there?" he called across to Félicie.

"Don't make such a noise!" Diana warned him. "There are people trying to sleep up there and down below us."

Félicie was chuckling at the surprised look on his face. She rose and walked slowly over to join him by the low wall.

"*Ça,*" she started to explain, pointing down at the lawn, "*on l'a appelée 'La folie de Félicie'!* 'Félicie's folly' is what they call it locally."

Below them, at the bottom of the bank outside the bedrooms, was a large hole in the lawn. It was more like a pit, measuring some sixty square feet. It looked as if it was an abandoned project to build a swimming-pool, which had somehow gone very wrong. At some time, it had been lined with thick, black, plastic sheeting, which was now torn in many places. Tall weeds, dead thistles, and a few self-seeded, small trees were growing through the plastic fabric, which flapped gently here and there in the warm breeze.

"I didn't see that as we drove in!" he exclaimed in such a surprised tone that Diana jumped up to join them.

"Good Lord!" she said politely.

"Yes, but what *is* it? What *was* it?" he asked again.

Félicie was giggling quietly at the look of consternation on the faces of her two guests.

"When my grandchildren came last summer," she explained, trying to look serious, "I thought we should have some water to amuse them. They come every year for the whole of the month of August. Last year it was hot, like now. They are old enough not to be in danger in water. They all swim well. And so, I asked *Monsieur* Briand, Marcel, in the next hamlet to excavate a large hole about two metres deep. He has a big machine. Then we put in the black, double lining. It was very expensive! Next, of course, we filled it up with water. *C'était un succès fou!* It was a terrific success! Throughout August last year the children were always in the water. I so love to see them enjoying themselves!"

James was appalled at the eyesore and was making no attempt to conceal his feelings.

"But look at it now! It's a bloody shambles! A real mess!"

"James! Don't be so tactless!" Diana said in English.

"De rien! It's nothing!" Félicie smiled at Diana as she heard the word 'tact'. "But then," she continued, "I made *une petite erreur*, a little mistake. After the grandchildren had gone away, I thought it looked so very boring. An uncle had offered to pay for the construction of a proper swimming-pool. I will show you later where it ought to be. So there I am, left with a large, ridiculous, unimaginative square of water. What should I do? So..." She was giggling uncontrollably again. "So I decided to put in some water plants to make it all look beautiful. They were very expensive! And then I bought the fish. They were also very expensive! Finally, came the ducks!" She stopped, as if her explanation was complete. She waited for a reaction. When there was none, she cried out, *"Mais voilà! C'est tout!"*

James felt embarrassed by the frankness of her explanation, and decided to make amends for his earlier brusque reaction.

"Well, I think that's a really nice idea!" he said supportively. "If we buy this property, one of our projects must surely be to revive your wonderful idea!"

"A wonderful idea, but..." Félicie clicked her tongue several times and wrung her hands. *"Mais c'était un vrai désastre! Une catastrophe!* I was in danger of becoming *un objet de raillerie,* a laughing-stock. It was all so very, so terribly embarrassing!"

"Mais pourquoi?" James asked. "But why? What happened?"

"Aïe! Aïe! Aïe! Mon Dieu! First the ducks turned on the *plastique!* Whoever heard of ducks eating plastic? In one week, with their beaks and their feet, they scratched out the plastic. Of course, then the water went away. Next, all the fish died! What about the water plants, you ask, yes? The water plants withered in the dry heat and then they also died!" She stopped again, this time because she was unable to stem the tears of mirth, which were rolling down her ruddy cheeks. With a peel of laughter, she cried out, "And so did the ducks! We had to kill them and eat them!"

She looked down at the eyesore and blew her nose. Diana noticed the echo as the sound came back across the valley.

"Que j'ai été stupide! How stupid I was! *Voilà ! C'est la folie de Félicie!* And I'm not brave enough to ask Briand to come back and fill it in again!"

They had a second round of drinks, before leaving for lunch as Félicie had arranged.

"You will come back again this afternoon, won't you?" she asked, with a look of concern on her tear-stained face.

"Of course we shall," Diana reassured her. "At about four o'clock. And Félicie, you must try and get a little rest."

"O-là!" Félicie laughed, waving them away.

*

They found the *Auberge de la Tour* at Sauzet without difficulty. Over a good lunch they discussed Félicie, her *folie,* the *terrasse,* and the one large room which they had briefly seen.

"She's a scream," he said. "And what stamina!"

"She's also pretty switched on," warned Diana. "Even though it's obvious she likes a bit more than a social tipple, she knows what she's doing."

"Pity about *la folie*. Still, it's no big thing. It'll only take Marcel Briand an hour to fill it in and smooth it over. A little bit of grass seed, *et voilà!*"

"Imagine," she said, changing the subject, "how hot it must be out there on that *terrasse* at the height of summer. It was warm enough today."

He, too, wanted to change the subject. Seeing his opportunity, he asked the question which had been pre-occupying his mind. "You do like the place so far, don't you?"

"Yes, I do," she replied. "But, we haven't seen much of it yet, have we?"

There was a note of caution in the tone of her voice. "That big room. What did Félicie call it?"

"*La pièce à vivre,* the living-room."

"Yes. The living-room is nice. Bright and airy. I love that stone bench built into the corner, and that arched window above it. I can picture some of our things fitting in very well. But—"

"Yes, so can I," he agreed, interrupting her. "What a marvellous fireplace! Imagine two or three large logs, blazing away in there in the depth of winter!"

He found himself remembering the conversation with Madame Louisor on the subject of her compatriots' strong feelings about *le bricolage*, a dislike which he readily shared with the French.

"Did you notice," he asked, following his train of thought, "that there is nothing in that room, but nothing, which will ever need painting or decorating? In many respects, the French have some really good ideas."

"Yes, but there will be a lot of other work. Think of the fireplace... And all that ash all over the place... And the dust! There must be an awful lot of cleaning to do. I bet all that exposed stonework, attractive and authentic as it is, must be a nightmare of a dust trap."

"Well, I'm sure we can get some local peasant girl to help for a few *sous* as pocket money. Do you like the *rosé?*

"M'mm!" she nodded. "Delicious!"

He examined the label and made a note of the name of the vineyard.

On their way back to Bon Porteau they came to a crossroads. He slowed down and then stopped, putting the jeep into reverse gear.

"What's up?" she asked, suddenly alarmed at his behaviour.

"Telephone box, back there," he explained. "I must just tell the hotel that we won't be needing that room tonight." He started to climb out of the jeep and then, turning to face her with a smile on his face, he added, "You were a bit quick off the mark in taking up Félicie's offer of a bed for the night!"

"And supper, too!" she added. "Well, it saves us another expensive hotel night, doesn't it?"

"True. True, my darling," he agreed.

"Anyway, I thought it was a really kind, generous gesture," she said defensively. "Besides, there aren't many people, I imagine, who get the opportunity to spend a night in the house they're going to buy, are there?" She smiled at his reaction, as the full meaning of her words struck him.

"Well! Well!" he laughed. "Will you be wanting the measurements of all the windows before we leave tomorrow?"

Chapter Eleven

As they approached Bon Porteau, the last of Félicie's unexpected overnight guests were leaving. Their departure very nearly ended abruptly. A battered 2CV hurled itself into a corner on the wrong side of the lane. The young driver saw the jeep just in time, and veered back towards his verge, the tiny Citroën heeling over like a racing dinghy rounding a buoy in a strong wind. The occupants were all teenagers. They were laughing as they passed, their car lurching back to the centre of the narrow lane to speed away in a cloud of blue smoke.

Félicie's daughter, Pascale, had evidently arrived. A solitary car was now parked in the shade of the walnut trees. Félicie greeted them and asked them whether lunch had been satisfactory.

"Yes, it was very good, but too much," James replied, holding his stomach.

"The food is good there, isn't it?" she said, seeking confirmation of her choice of venue and warming to her favourite topic and occupation. "There is a superb cook. One day, we will go there and have the *menu gastronomique.* If we give them a little notice, they will get the most succulent lobsters and king-size prawns. And their wines! They have the best cellar around here, except for mine!"

She led the way into the *pièce à vivre,* the living-room.

"Pascale!" she called. *"Pascale, viens vite! Ils sont arrivés."*

They heard footsteps descending some stairs and then a taller version of Félicie entered the room, carrying an armful of bed linen and towels. They were introduced, Félicie using first names only. Pascale, her face flushed, started to talk rapidly to her mother, who put up her hand to stop her.

"Il faut parler lentement. You must speak slowly so that Diana can understand. *Alors,"* she smiled at Diana and asked, *"on va commencer la visite guidée?*

Pascale excused herself, indicating the pile of laundry, and promised that she would meet them either later in the afternoon or else certainly over dinner. They heard her clatter downstairs, as they followed Félicie into the second reception room which was dominated by a large, highly polished dining table. *"La salle à manger,"* she announced unnecessarily. The size and shape of the room was a replica of the living-room except that, in a recess in the far wall, there was a tall window looking out over the top of the two bamboo clumps to a view of the countryside beyond. That must be the window, thought James, with '1791' carved into the stone lintel outside. The tall French windows were open, and sunlight was streaming in from the *terrasse*. We could use this as our drawing-room, thought Diana. Our big sofa will fit in very nicely over there.

They returned to the *pièce à vivre*, off which there was a diminutive kitchen. James worked out that they were now at the middle level of the *pigeonnier*. The room was cramped, dark, and disorganized. The beautiful, old stonework of the original structure was covered in plaster, which was painted a lurid crimson. The sombre colour seemed to emphasize the gloominess of the room, neutralizing the effect of daylight from a recessed window at the far end of the room.

"Oh dear!" Diana remarked involuntarily.

"Sink, gas burners, and one electric plate up here," Félicie was saying, as she waved her arms about. "Dishwasher, oak cupboards, the same floor tiles throughout..." Her commentary faltered, and then she pointed to the dishwasher. *"Je ne connais pas vos moyens.* I don't know how well off you are, but I will sell you that as an extra. I do all my proper cooking *dans la cave au sous-sol là-bas*, in the cellar down there in the basement. Here, I just keep the prepared food warm and, of course, do the washing-up. *Ça marche!"* She indicated the dishwasher again. *"Ça marche très bien!* It works very well! *Et voilà!*

James peered at it. He thought that it had seen many better days.

Félicie continued without a break, *"Deux escaliers,* two staircases — one going up, the other down. *Suivez-moi!"*

Under no circumstances could they be described as staircases. The one, which led to the room above, was almost a ladder. It was lethally steep with rickety banisters. After three narrow steps it turned a right angle on a tiny landing, to continue almost vertically upwards to a hatch in the ceiling. She leaped up the steps, lifted the hatch with a butt of her head, and pushed it back against a retaining clip on the wall.

"Mais il faut monter!" she called down to them as she disappeared from view. "But you must come up."

Diana managed her ascent without much difficulty, but each step of the assault course took its toll on James's shins. Once aloft, they found themselves in a delightful, beamed, square room with two windows, which provided good, natural light. They were at the top of the *pigeonnier.* The original stone walls remained exposed, and had not been subjected to the same tasteless treatment as in the small kitchen below.

"I call this the 'top room'. I sleep in here in the winter months. The warmth from the big fireplace rises and I don't need to use the central heating. I don't know how well off you are, but heating oil is very expensive in France."

Diana noted her second reference to the cost of living and her thinly-disguised probe into their means. Maybe, she thought, Félicie is a bit short of cash.

An old oak door, which looked as if it was original, led into four partitioned rooms in the loft space. James found that he could stand easily in the centre under the main ridge of the roof, the under side of which was clad with attractive boarding.

"Behind all this wood," Félicie explained, "is thick insulation. It keeps the rooms warm in winter; and yet they're cool, as you can feel now, even when it is hot outside. The grandchildren love to sleep up here. It makes four nice, little bedrooms for young children. Do you have any grandchildren?"

"Not yet," Diana replied wistfully. "I have a daughter, called Kim. I live in hope."

Félicie looked momentarily puzzled by her response.

"But your daughter is married, yes?"

Diana nodded, thinking of her only child and Andrew, her husband.

"Et puis, ma chérie," Félicie beamed at her, "it's only a matter of timing and effort. Then you must plant a tree!" She saw the confused looks which greeted this unexpected advice. *"Mais dans le jardin!"* she cried. "You must plant a tree in the garden! I've planted one for each grandchild. I will show you them later."

Félicie ducked through the trapdoor and swooped down the steps, habit accurately guiding her tiny feet. Diana again managed her descent passably well, but James had to turn round, like a sailor on a steep companionway. Cautiously, he tried to lower the hatch, but its weight caught him by surprise, and it cracked down on the top of his head. He took an instant dislike to the arrangement.

"*Ça va?*" Félicie asked solicitously. "*On s'y habitue vite!* Are you all right? One gets used to it quickly!"

Navigating the steps from the kitchen to and from the 'top room' proved to be safe and simple, compared to the next stairway. Félicie disappeared down to the lower level of the house.

"*C'est une échelle meunière. Elle est vraiment jolie, n'est-ce pas?*" she called up to them. "It's a miller's ladder. Really pretty, isn't it? We kept the original one."

Fascinated by this new challenge, James thought that it may well be a thing of great beauty to some people, but not very practical for living. He started to go down, facing the almost vertical drop. This time, it was the calves of his legs, not his shins, which felt the sharp edge of each narrow step. Rather less than halfway down, he was confronted by a thick beam at chest height. He had no option. He decided to turn around and descend backwards. Midway, despite his caution, his suede, desert boots lost their grip. He took the fastest and most painful route downwards, barely managing to stay on his feet as he crashed to the bottom.

Had he been able to pause in his descent, as did Diana, he would have noticed from about halfway down the ladder that there was a magnificent, top-down view of a bright yellow hip-bath.

"Good Lord!" Diana said in English. "That's a bit pubic, isn't it?"

"It depends on who is in it," laughed James. "But honestly, Diana, we couldn't live with those bloody ladders. They're a health hazard! How on earth does she carry a tray of hot food up that?"

"And how can she put up with that kitchen?" she asked, raising her eyes to the ceiling.

Félicie, who had not followed the conversation, was explaining the history of the *pigeonnier*, oblivious that serious reservations about survival were being discussed.

"It is thought to be one of the most beautifully proportioned *pigeonniers* in this region," she continued, sounding like a tour guide.

"In fact, TV France came last year to make a documentary about it. I didn't see it, but my friends said it was very well done. It was a good thing we preserved the ladder. It was one of the highlights of the film."

She led the way through a small doorway, encouraging them to keep up with her. Diana went through first and, as James followed, there was a sickening thud as his forehead made contact with the stone lintel. He staggered, momentarily stunned, a thin line of blood appearing in the gash just below the line of his hair. He looked meanly at the heavy slab of offending stone. It had been in place over the doorway for almost two hundred years. It was not going to give way to a mere twentieth-century human skull. A smear of blood, particles of skin, and some of his precious hair combined to warn him not to attempt it again.

"*C'est l'ancienne porte*. It's the original doorway in the outer wall of the *pigeonnier*," Félicie commented, as if that were sufficient justification for the damage to his head. She gave the wound a cursory glance and clicked her tongue. "*Ce n'est pas mal*. It's not bad," she muttered, not very reassuringly.

They were standing in a small hall, off which a long passage led along almost the entire length of the house to the bedrooms and bathroom. In the passage, they stopped to admire three black and white, framed photographs of the original house before it had been restored and the bedrooms added.

"That little door there," Félicie pointed with a chuckle, "is where you just banged your head!"

"They must have been very small people at the time of the Revolution," he said mournfully.

"They were, once they had lost their heads!" Diana quipped.

"*O-là-là!*" was the only reaction from Félicie.

The four bedrooms were identical in size, each with neat, practical cupboard space and a double French window out to the garden. The bathroom passed inspection. Although it was small, it had everything in it, except a bath. This partly explained the bizarre arrangement of the yellow hip-bath at the foot of the miller's ladder. They followed her through a second doorway back through the original outer wall of the house. To his relief, James did not have to duck this time and they entered a long room with no windows.

"*La chaudière,*" she said, pointing to a large, oil-fired boiler, made in Germany. It looked new, with a complicated array of temperature gauges, time switches, and pumps. She reached up to pull a switch, and it fired immediately. It looked efficient, robust, and thirsty.

"It is now heating the hot water. After we have walked around the gardens and woods, you will want showers."

A large, antique cupboard, in which she stored her house linen, and a very large chest freezer were the only other objects in the room. James thought that it might make quite a useful indoor workshop.

James followed the two women through the next doorway. He was concentrating on avoiding another low lintel, bent forward while ducking low, missed the step downwards and, losing his balance, he almost fell into the cellar.

"*Attention à la marche!* Mind the step!" Félicie's warning came too late. Pascale was busy, folding sheets and putting them in a neat pile on a small table.

"*Voilà!*" she announced, beaming with obvious pride. "*C'est ma cave!* This is my cellar! This is where I spend most of my time. I have spent so many, many happy hours in here. This is where I taught all the children to cook — daughters and sons alike. *J'adore cette cave!*"

It was not necessary to ask how she occupied her time. A delicious smell filled the big room.

A double sink, a washing machine, and a large, old-fashioned cooking stove with an expanse of work surfaces stood the length of one of the walls. She approached the stove, opened the oven door with bare hands, and checked the casserole inside.

"*On va manger le boeuf bourguignon ce soir. C'est superbe!*" she said, as the aroma of slow-cooking beef escaped into the room with the heat from the oven.

Another wall was lined with shelves, stacked with assorted jars containing jams, pickles, fruit, and maturing homemade liqueurs. At the far end of the shelves there was an arrangement of racking, containing trays with wooden sides and bases of wire netting.

"These are drying trays from the *prunerie,* which I will show you later," she explained.

The racks stretched from just above the level of the floor almost to the ceiling. They contained walnuts, hazel nuts, plums, pears, and apples. Most of the third wall was dedicated to the efficient storage of wine.

"Do these come with the sale of the house?" James asked, trying to read the vintages of some of the dusty, faded labels.

"Mais, ce que tu peux dire comme bêtises!" Félicie scolded him with mock severity. "What nonsense you do talk!"

Down on this scene brooded ten huge oak beams, each over a foot in girth and spanning the width of the house, resting where craftsmen had positioned them with loving care nearly two centuries earlier. Félicie saw him looking up at them with awe.

"Oui! Ce sont de vraies poutres," she confirmed. "Those are real beams." A beam of that size and length, he thought, must have come from large, mature trees. That would make the actual wood at least three hundred years old! Feeling small, he followed the two women out through the cellar door to emerge on to the grass in the early evening sunshine. He forgot to duck, but this time luck was on his side, as he felt the top of his hair gently brush another immovable slab of stone. He gingerly put his hand up to feel the gash on his forehead, which was now beginning to develop a dull ache.

"Beautiful evening, isn't it?" he said, trying to sound cheerful, at the same time giving Diana a rueful smile.

"Fucking midgets!" he swore silently under his breath.

Chapter Twelve

The gardens had not been designed by some latter-day French Capability Brown. Much of their all-pervading charm owed itself to the fact that nature herself had created an elegant sculpture among the immense shelves of rock, banks, slopes, and the valley itself in front of the house. They walked slowly from one garden to the next, acknowledging the logic of their layout. The hand of man was evident only through the presence of the lawns and those trees and plants, which were not indigenous. Félicie indicated the trees which she had planted at the birth of each grandchild.

"I did not plant this one," she admitted, standing next to the blue cedar by the drive. "This is Pascale's tree. It was placed here by her grandfather. It is now forty-two years old."

They followed her to the millstone at the entrance to the track, where they had explored the previous day. Diana looked up again at the notice, which referred to trespassers.

"This used to be a *chemin rural* with, of course, a public right of way," she explained as they walked slowly between the dry stone walls. "Of course, since it passes directly behind the house, we were concerned to acquire it from the commune, which is not a simple matter. However, I know the Mayor of Saint Juste very well, and he owed me several favours. To cut a long story short, my negotiations were successful. To prevent access, I had this millstone put across its entrance."

Diana wondered briefly what she meant by 'favours', and then thought no more about it.

They scrambled down into a shady dell, surrounded by large oaks and another huge walnut tree. Despite the dryness of the summer, the ground was moist and the soil soft under their feet.

"It's very important in this area," she continued her commentary, "to have water on one's property. Many — in fact, most people — do not. Here, we are extremely fortunate. We have three *sources,* which are entirely private. There is also a deep well of good water, which I will show you on the way back. In addition, we have two separate water supplies to the house, which I must explain to you later."

Some of the memorable scenes in *'Manon des Sources'* flashed through James's mind.

"Go and look over there," she said, pointing to a corner of the wooded hollow. "But take care where you stand, and mind the nettles. I will wait for you here, while you see if you can find our *petit trésor.* It's over there, near that large dead branch you can see. Don't fall in, because I can't swim!"

They approached the area which Félicie had indicated, brushing aside tall nettles and suckers, working their way towards a patch of pale sunlight, which filtered down through the overhanging trees. They stopped before a small structure, its walls and arched roof built entirely in local stone. It was much the same size and shape of a wayside shrine of the kind most commonly found beside alpine tracks. At some time in the past, a gate or grille had been fitted to the front, but now only its rusty, hinged supports remained. Inside, the water was so limpid that it created the illusion that the white, sandy bottom of the stone trough was a mere six inches below its surface.

"It's beautiful," Diana called to Félicie.

"It's also pure. I have had it tested. It is the envy of the neighbours."

James dipped his arm as far as he could into the cold, clear water, and was unable to reach the sandy base of the trough.

"Does it ever run dry?" he asked.

"Never. Not in my lifetime. This is the most active of our springs. My grandfather built the shelter to protect the *source* from falling leaves and dead branches." She came noisily through the undergrowth to stand beside them. "See there, how it overflows down into that *bassin* behind you." On account of the nettles and brambles, they were unaware that they had been standing on the very lip of a wide, stone-clad pit behind them. It was full of deep water. "He built another one over there, but the stonework is now breaking up, and it needs repairing." She mopped her forehead and turned to leave, calling to them, "*Venez!* We'll go down to the big field and then back to the house through the woods. You have yet to see *les dépendances* — the barn and the outbuildings."

The field was big, at least seven acres of grass, along the far side of which thick woods climbed up a steep slope to the skyline.

"That's the beginning of your woods," she explained. "They start there, on that slope, and go right up to the top. Then they go down into a valley on the other side and up to the top of the next ridge. In all, there are almost seven hectares of mature oak trees. They need a bit of thinning out here and there, but I have not bothered. Also I haven't got the money needed to undertake the work. *Je ne sais pas si tu as les moyens de le faire.* I don't know if you can afford to do it. But there's more than enough wood up there to keep the house fire going for generations, let alone just during your lifetime. We'll walk across the field and climb through over there."

Their host plunged through a wall of nettles and couch-grass, beckoning them to follow her.

"Surely, Félicie," James suggested as they entered the field, "there must be some local woodsman or wood merchant who would get in there and sort it out for nothing if you let him keep half the wood he fells."

"*Tout à fait possible,*" she agreed. "*C'est une bonne idée.*" She made no further comment and so James dropped the subject.

"Who looks after the three fields? Do you rent them out?" he asked. "They must be worth *un peu d'argent de poche,* a little pocket money!"

"The local farmer, Griffoul, cuts and keeps the hay. There is supposed to be a nominal rent, but you must not collect it. In these parts, you don't put *anything* in writing, and you must not collect one cent, *pas un sou,* as rent. Otherwise you will have difficulty getting him off your land if you ever want to take it back for some other good purpose. Moreover, he will claim for the cost of all the fertilizers and weed killers which he has been using since the arrangement began. *C'est pénible,* it's tough, but that's how it is."

Crossing the big field, Félicie pointed out the third *source* on the property. This time the spring was no more than a simple, large hole in the ground, overgrown with brambles and long grass.

"*Il y a de l'eau là-bas?*" he asked. "Is there water down there?"

"*Mais bien sûr!*" Félicie replied emphatically. "*Mais il faut la nettoyer.* Of course, but it needs cleaning out. A little maintenance, that's all! *Un tout petit peu d'entretien, c'est tout!*"

They explored the woods, finding here and there a rare natural clearing. They followed paths, once serviceable tracks but now fallen into disuse. Some were edged with dry stone walls, most of which had crumbled or had been broken down, the stones left where they had fallen. In places, the trees themselves were growing too close together, preventing healthy growth. James thought that an expert woodsman would advise the immediate removal of at least two out of every five trees in the thickest parts.

To their surprise, they emerged from the woods into the field of grass at the far end of the lawn at the back of the house.

"Now," said Félicie, who was panting and flushed, "now you must see the barn, the *prunerie*, and *l'ancien four,* the old bakery." She led them under the maple trees and across the lawn, and then pointed to an area which was almost flat.

"That is the place for your swimming-pool," she announced decisively. "That was where Uncle Jules was going to put it. There are no rocks there, and excavation would be a bagatelle for Briand's big, noisy machine." She hesitated, as if wondering what else she might be able to say to persuade them to put a swimming-pool there, after they had become the legitimate owners of the property. "Just there," she continued. "It would be in the sun for most of the day. There are no overhanging trees to drop their leaves and twigs in the water all the time. I have a friend, who spends hours each week, picking leaves and other debris out of his pool. So boring! As if one hasn't already got enough to do each day!"

"How on earth do you manage to cut all this grass?" James asked. "There must be more than a hectare of lawns, not to mention keeping the banks tidy. Surely, you don't do it all yourself?"

"Oh! Don't worry about that," Félicie replied vaguely. "There is always plenty of local help."

They walked up to the stone barn which, Félicie explained, had been restored at the same time as the main house. Beneath a wide, arched entrance in one of the end walls, there were large, wooden double doors, into which a small stable door had been set. Inside, although there was only one long window at the far end, it was unexpectedly bright and airy. Nevertheless, Félicie pressed a switch by the door and four spotlights, one in each corner, flooded the whole area with artificial light.

"Electricity and water are connected," she explained. "But they are not metered separately from the main house system."

The underside of the attractive, old canal tiles was visible above the exposed joists and rafters. The inside of the walls had been left with rough pointing between the original stonework, and the cement floor had been rendered to a smooth surface. In a corner at the end of one of the walls stood a large, open fireplace, the inside of which was blackened by wood smoke, indicating that it had been in working order at some time. A big oak beam across its width served as an attractive mantlepiece.

In the far corner by the window, a single tap had been installed above a large, flat stone, the centre of which was hollowed out to a depth of about nine inches. James walked over to examine it.

"That stone is one of the original washing sinks from the old house. There is another larger one down by the house."

"This one is big enough! Amazing!" he exclaimed, turning on the tap. Water splashed into the trough-like stone and flowed out through a small hole in the wall. "And someone," he went on enthusiastically, "has done a first-class job on this floor. If one wanted to convert this place into a guest cottage, floor tiles could be laid with no problem directly on to this surface."

"All the stonework and pointing," Félicie said proudly, "was done by the local stonemason, supervised by my husband. It has all been done to the highest quality of workmanship."

Félicie picked up a rag and wiped some dust from one of the panes of glass in the wide window.

"Planning consent is not a problem here, provided that the request is reasonable," she continued. "I know *Monsieur le Maire* very well. He has been a close friend of mine for many years. You don't need a *Permis de Construire* to make internal alterations; only if you want to put in windows and doors, which will change the external appearance of a building."

"The Mayor of where?" Diana asked.

"Why! Of Saint Juste, of course! Did you not know that you will be living in one of the smallest communes in the Lot, with its own *Mairie* and just sixty-nine inhabitants. *Voilà!*"

Diana remembered stopping briefly to look at the *Mairie* the day before, when they had first found Bon Porteau.

They toured the outside of the barn, below which there was another *bassin* similar to the one they had seen beside the first *source*.

"This one is also always full of water," she commented. *"Mais il faut faire attention!* But you must take care, especially with young children, because it is very deep and quite near to the house. However, if it were pumped out and sealed, *a fosse septique* could easily be dropped into it to serve your proposed cottage."

Below the barn and sheltered by the pair of large walnut trees, they inspected the stone well. James picked up a stone, letting it fall into the dark opening. The interval between the stone hitting water and the sound echoing back up from the depths suggested that it was, indeed, very deep.

They next approached a smaller, stone building, standing alone under a maple tree and surrounded by its own small lawn. It had a big, wide chimney stack. Félicie explained that it was *l'ancien four,* the old bakery.

"In the old days, each of the larger domaines took its turn to bake bread for the people in the surrounding villages." She threw open the door. *"Voila!"* she said dramatically. "Go in and have a look. Mind your heads! There's a torch there on the left, so you can see inside the old bread oven." The opening into the bread oven itself was very restricted, its blackened stone lintel forming a low arch, through which perhaps a small child might just be able to squeeze through. James flashed the torch inside, revealing a low, semicircular dome of narrow firebricks, some the colour of terracotta, some black, and others, surprisingly, almost white. The brickwork was intricate, and had been constructed with great skill and precision.

"This is just incredible!" he exclaimed. "I've never seen anything like this before!"

"I've always wanted," Félicie said pensively, "to convert this one room into a garden study, perhaps into a TV room for the grandchildren, or even an extra bedroom for guests. All that needs doing are the floor, a proper window, electricity and, perhaps, water."

They progressed to the final outbuilding, one side of which was open, protected only by a lean-to roof. Here, logs for the fire, garden machinery, flower pots, plastic bags of peat and fertilizer, rusty metal containers of chemicals, a knapsack sprayer of unknown vintage and design, and old car tyres were piled together in a muddled heap. On the opposite side of the building, she opened a pair of blackened double doors, under which passed two narrow, steel girders, which looked as if they had been designed for some miniature railway track. She reached inside and rolled out a long, steel-framed trolley, its iron wheels running smoothly on the two rails. Trays, of the same design they had seen in the cellar, were neatly layered on the trolley, behind and below which was a profusion of cast-iron piping leading from the inside of a fire door at the back of the building.

She showed them the fire door from the other side, explaining that, with the furnace lit and the trays full of plums, the doors would then be closed tightly. After a set period of time, the plums would dry to form prunes which, if left later to mature in *eau-de-vie,* was the original way to make the liqueur known today as *pruneaux.*

"It's illegal now," Félicie announced, holding the trolley to prevent it from rolling back into its shed.

"What is?" asked James, who was looking in astonishment at the extraordinary Heath Robinson contraption and its array of pipe-work.

"To dry prunes, using this method," she replied. "It's because people used to make their own alcohol and sell it. It was a form of liqueur, but it was really alcohol. The State put an end to it, because neither quality nor quantity were being controlled. And so, of course, the practice became something of a health hazard but, more importantly for the *fonctionnaires,* they were losing tax revenue. However, we all still use them!"

On their way down to the house, Félicie pointed out the large, original stone sink, which she had mentioned in the barn. It stood on the corner of the patio, now serving as an outsize flower trough, planted with geraniums, busy lizzies, lobelia, and a small amount of lavender.

"*Allez!* You must shower, and we'll take our *apéritif* on the *terrasse* as soon as you are ready."

After taking their showers, they sat together on the edge of the soft, wide bed in the first bedroom they had seen several hours earlier.

"I'm quite tired," Diana yawned. "I don't know how Félicie does it. We must have walked nearly five miles this afternoon. And now she'll be cooking supper."

"While we're on our own and I'm still sober," he said, with a serious look on his face, "we had better discuss what we want to do about this little property. You make your points first, darling. Which do you think are the good ones, and which are the bad?"

"Well, we need not worry about the good things — they're obvious, and we don't have time to discuss them now. I'll just say that I'm very pleased with cat security. It's a really safe haven for them. But, as far as I'm concerned, the worst aspect is that dreadful upstairs kitchen. It's just far too small and dark. I couldn't poke around in there for long. The second problem is the absence of a proper bathroom. The two of us alone could live with that yellow job at the foot of the steps, but I don't think our guests — in particular, my girlfriends — would enjoy having you wandering past and eyeing them every two minutes!"

He felt that he had to explore any further reservations she may have about the property, and so he continued to listen to her silently.

"Yes. I think there's far too much land," she continued. "You will never cope with all this garden."

"That," he argued forcefully, "is certainly not going to be a problem. You heard Félicie say there's plenty of cheap, local labour."

"No, I'm afraid I did not. I heard her being rather vague, perhaps even evasive, about the subject. I certainly didn't hear her say anything about labour being cheap."

"Well, we'll leave that one," he said quickly. "I don't think it's a big problem."

He stood up and crossed the room to close the tall shutters, plunging the bedroom into temporary darkness. He fumbled for the light switch, found it, and turned it on. He looked down at his wife, and stroked her damp hair.

"From my point of view," he countered, choosing his words judiciously. "I really think it's all great but, I must admit, I couldn't put up with those bloody steps. Now, if we had them ripped out and a proper staircase designed into the *pigeonnier,* it would prevent me from breaking my neck and it would make the kitchen much larger, bringing more daylight down the stairs from the top room. Then, we would have to clear off all that dreadful, red plaster, take the walls back to their original stonework, and redesign the kitchen."

"It will still be far too small," she persisted. "I can't see any solution there. Our cats need a utility room as well, don't forget that."

The three cats had always enjoyed the luxury of their own bedroom, and he knew for certain that this could easily become a major issue, even a stumbling block.

"In that case," he ventured, "we could make the existing, small kitchen into the utility room, and take up a corner of the living-room as a kitchen area. That's quite common here, as we've often seen. The best corner would be the one nearest to the new utility room and next to the French windows leading out to the roof *terrasse.*"

"*That's* not a bad idea! I wouldn't be cut off from guests when I'm busy preparing a meal. But what about the bathrooms?"

He started to get dressed while he considered the most appropriate response.

"Demolish the yellow arrangement," he replied, as if he had given it all a great deal of careful thought. "You're absolutely right. The bath is no use there, and anyway it's far too small. We'll throw it out. That will give more latitude to the eventual positioning of the new stairs. Then we simply build an *en-suite* bathroom on to the end of the far bedroom, which would be ours. How about that?"

"Someone's been doing some plotting, haven't they? It sounds very much like major structural alterations to a property with far too much land. We'll be failing to meet two out of our four top priorities, with only cat security and our privacy being fully met."

"But, darling," he continued, "the house is well-built and very attractive. We'll be self-sufficient for firewood, which is very important. And if we convert the barn, it could certainly produce an income, although I haven't thought that one through yet."

"And have you any idea, my love, what the new kitchen, a new utility room, a new bathroom, new stairs, fixing the fireplace, the barn conversion, garden machinery and, no doubt, umpteen other things cost?"

"No. Not the remotest idea! Quite a lot, I imagine. But we wouldn't have to do it all at once." He thought he might be winning the debate. "The new kitchen arrangements," he added tactfully, "would have to be given the first priority, of course!"

"And what about that low door," she reminded him, "where you very nearly killed yourself?"

"Duck or grouse, as they say!" he replied glibly. "I'll just have to get used to it, won't I?"

They finished dressing, remembering that Félicie and Pascal would be waiting for them on the roof *terrasse*.

"We did agree, some years ago," she said quietly, "that we would never again buy a house with a flat roof. Do you remember?"

"Yes, my love," he admitted. "You're absolutely right. I had completely forgotten that fiasco in England. But this is different. This is the biggest, most solid, flat roof I've ever seen. It must be as safe as the Bank of England! Look at it another way. If this property is within our price range, we will be getting ten times more room and space for less than two-thirds of the price of the last house we bought in Surrey five years ago. There's bags of scope here. I could dream up a whole catalogue of profitable projects for this place. I mean, just imagine the potential of it all! And, you must admit, it's a superb area — infinitely better than the bloody Dordogne!" She frowned, trying to follow the logic of this new element of lateral thinking, and remained silent.

She was climbing carefully up the miller's ladder when she stopped and looked back down at him.

"Do we know by any chance," she whispered, "what might be her asking price?"

"Isn't it in the agent's details?" he asked hoarsely, bending almost double to avoid the midway beam.

"No, there's no mention of it at all. It could be important to find out, my clever darling, *before* we commit ourselves to anything."

"Then I'll have to ask her, before she gets too confident. But, Diana, one more question. Do you think we should go ahead and buy it?"

"Yes! Of course! You great maniac!"

Chapter Thirteen

Sunset was imminent, when they joined Félicie and Pascale out on the *terrasse*. The valley was cast in deep shadow, its cooler air drifting up towards the house. By contrast, they could feel the warmth retained by the walls of the house and the heat rising from the stone paving of the *terrasse,* which was still bathed in an orange glow from the setting sun. A tray of fluted champagne glasses was on the long table, together with a set of typical *Provençal* bowls, filled with walnuts, olives, thin slices of smoked sausage, and the ubiquitous prunes. While Félicie commented on the rigours of the past twenty-four hours in her life, Pascale fetched a bottle of champagne from the kitchen and handed it to James.

"O-là-là!" he exclaimed appreciatively, examining the *Duval-Leroy* label. *"Félicie, que vous êtes trop gentille! C'est superbe!"*

In fact, as he carefully filled each glass, he was thinking guiltily that he would much prefer a good, strong gin and tonic at that moment.

"Is this *le vin d'honneur* then?" he asked.

"That depends," Félicie replied with a coy smile. *"Tchin, tchin!"* she beamed at them, reaching out to feel the quality of the material in Diana's dress.

They all raised their glasses.

"Santé!" they toasted each other, their voices echoing back to them from among the deepening shadows on the other side of the valley.

"Listen!" Diana murmured. "Even the valley is toasting us all as well!" Their laughter was followed by a hush, while none of them spoke.

It was James who broke the silence. He was puzzled by Félicie's earlier cryptic reply.

"It depends on what?" James asked.

"On whether you want to buy Bon Porteau, of course!" Félicie replied, as she put two olives and a prune into her mouth.

"I'm glad you've raised the subject," he said, feeling a little embarrassed, "because there is one small, remaining detail. Rather stupidly, we don't seem to have been given any information about your asking price."

"You mean Louisor has not told you?" She spat out the pips, and threw them over the parapet. *"O-là-là, là-là!* How strange! Only last week I instructed him that I was prepared to reduce by eighteen thousand francs for the house, together with *all* the land." She emphasized the word 'all' and then quickly mentioned a figure.

James remained poker-faced as his heart leaped. He looked over towards Diana who, at that split second, was smiling with her eyes shut.

"I do not want to sell piecemeal," Félicie continued. "I will not sell the fields to Griffoul. I know he wants them, but my husband, if he were alive, would want to keep the property intact. So that's the price for all of it."

"Félicie, would you please allow me a few minutes on your telephone?" he asked.

"Volontiérs!" she replied at once. "Of course! I'll show you where it is." Following her into the living-room, he looked back at Diana. Her head gave an imperceptible nod.

"There it is," Félicie pointed and then disappeared towards the small kitchen.

He could hear Pascale and Diana talking animatedly to each other out on the roof *terrasse*, while Félicie busied herself with plates and cutlery, the clatter coming to him as he picked up the receiver. He took a piece of paper out of his pocket and dialled the number written on it. Waiting for a reply, he became aware that Félicie had stopped making any noise. He heard the door of the refrigerator open and close, and then there was silence in the small kitchen. He immediately recognized the voice on the other end of the line.

"Allô! Oui, j'écoute!"

"Monsieur Louisor, good evening... It's Wyllis speaking. I hope I'm not disturbing your dinner... Yes, I am speaking from Bon Porteau..." He gave the agent Félicie's telephone number. "I want you to confirm something for me." He stopped speaking, as he heard a faint sound coming from the direction of the kitchen. It was like the shuffle of feet. He resumed his telephone conversation. "Yes... I

know tomorrow is Monday and that most places will be shut... Yes...
Can you persuade *Monsieur le Maître, le Notaire,* to be in his office
by nine-thirty tomorrow morning...? Yes, that's what I said... We can
only manage tomorrow... Why? Because we want to buy Bon
Porteau!"

At that moment, the door from the kitchen burst open and Félicie
ran into the room, waving her arms excitedly and jumping up and
down. *"C'est vrai? C'est vrai!"* she shouted. *"O-là-là, là-là, là-là,
Pascale! Viens vite! Diana! James! Je l'ai su!* I knew it! *Je l'ai su!"*
   "Monsieur Louisor..." James was having to bellow into the
receiver to make himself heard. *"Un moment, s'il vous plaît. Ne
quittez pas!"* He put his hand over the mouthpiece. "Louisor says," he
shouted at Félicie, "that it will be impossible to get *Monsieur le
Maître* into his office tomorrow."
   "Give him to me! Give it to me!" cried Félicie, snatching the
instrument from him. *"Non! Non, Monsieur!* You leave the *Notaire* to
me. I know *Monsieur le Maître* very well. He is a very close, personal
friend of mine. *Non, non, non!* I will arrange it all! Yes, he will do as
I ask him! He owes me many favours. It's high time I collected one in
return... *Bien sûr!* And you, *Monsieur,* just make sure you are in his
office by nine-thirty at the latest. *D'accord? D'accord! À demain."*

   Smiling to herself, she quietly put down the receiver. She crossed
the room to where Diana was now standing and kissed her three times.
   "Pascale!" she shrieked. "Another bottle of champagne from the
fridge! And now, Diana and James, we will celebrate *le vin
d'honneur!* I am so pleased that this beautiful place is going to be
yours. I could never have sold it to any of those dreadful people
Louisor has sent here." She was now wringing her hands, either in
sorrow, joy, pain, or relief. "Do you know something?" she asked in a
low voice, as if she was about to disclose a State secret. "Nearly all of
them did not like my wonderful kitchens! Imagine! Such uncivilized
stupidity!"

*

   The sun was finally setting when they finished *le vin d'honneur.*
This time it was a bottle of *Gaspart Valentin* — it was exquisite.

Félicie was both excited and tired, her mood shifting from voluble euphoria to silent, inward contemplation. Now and then, a look of sadness, even of regret, crept into her clear, blue eyes.

"We will dine out here," she announced. "But soon it may be quite chilly, I think. So Diana and you James, you might be needing a wrap or a pullover. Pascale, would you please bring the casserole up from the cellar? And turn these outside lights on before you go down."

Pascale left the group and, a few moments later, the whole *terrasse* was bathed in bright light from the two large, wrought iron lanterns on the wall of the house

While Félicie and Diana prepared the table, James looked out across the valley at the last remaining glow in the sky. The meal was served with good-humoured panache, a short commentary accompanying each dish as it appeared on the table. Courgette soup was followed by a small pastry *feuilleton,* containing braised layers of thinly sliced, stuffed pork in a delicious sauce. On the table there was a delightful china jug, in the centre of which was a separate compartment, sealed with a wide cork. He lifted the cork to find crushed ice inside.

"What is this, Félicie?" he enquired politely.

"It's a jug, which keeps the *vin rosé* nice and cool," she explained. "The wine is poured into the jug, around the central container with the ice in it. We'll have it now, with the pork."

The main course was the *boeuf bourguignon.* It had been fired in brandy and served with miniature carrots, a few *haricots verts*, and *pommes lyonnaise.* The wine was a *Château Laur, '85,* deep red, with a rich, velvet bouquet. Next came the salad, with a hint of garlic and a mouth-watering dressing. They finished with profiteroles and strong, black coffee. During the meal the conversation flowed easily. Félicie told them about the rich harvest of mushrooms available on the property, which they would enjoy when they eventually took up residence.

"There are hundreds, if not thousands of them, down in the orchard, at the bottom of the main lawn, and even *cèpes,* those large, very rich mushrooms of the woods."

Pascale wanted to know what life was like in Zambia, listening eagerly and wide-eyed, while Diana described some of the events and people in that beautiful land. Between one of the courses, Félicie telephoned the *Notaire*, who agreed without hesitation to place his office at their disposal the following morning.

James discussed with their host the nature of the agreements with the farmer, Monsieur Griffoul, and the maintenance of the fields.

"When it becomes appropriate," he said, "please tell *Monsieur* Griffoul that we want his work on the fields of this property to continue, just as you have arranged it in the past." He was pleased with her assurance that it would remain unchanged. "After completion of the sale," he continued, "which I suppose will take a few months, we would like you to continue living here until further notice, or at least for the remainder of the winter. That is, of course, if you would like to do that."

"But that is marvellous," Félicie exclaimed. "You see, with the proceeds from the sale, I plan to build a small house in the town. But work cannot start until February next year at the earliest. Then I must allow between six and eight months for its construction. I would pay, of course, for my electricity and heating oil, as well as my share of the taxes on the property, while I continue to live here. There will also be the water charges, which I'll explain later. I cannot tell you how much your kind offer means to me. I was getting quite worried about it all. Now I can plan my retirement."

Pascale cleared the dishes and then excused herself, since she had to return to Cahors that night. It was becoming evident that lack of sleep was catching up on Félicie. When they left the table on the *terrasse,* she placed a decanter of whisky and a bottle of *Calvados* on the small table in the living-room.

"*Sers-toi, je t'en prie,*" she said, indicating the drinks on the table. "I'm going to go to bed now, up in the top room. Make yourselves at home. Have a look at everything again. There may be some items, which you would like to buy. Make a list, and we'll discuss it in the morning. I'm usually up and about by six-thirty but, after the last two days, I'm not too sure that I'll ever wake up. *Allez! Bonne nuit!*"

They thanked her for the meal and said goodnight. They heard her climb the steps, and then open and close the hatch behind her. They sat quietly drinking the whisky, while they noted some of the fittings which, they hoped, would be either for sale or else left in place. After a brief tour of the house, they decided to go to bed.

"Are you happy about it all?" he asked.

"Yes, my love. We've got much more than I ever expected. It's wonderful!"

"Well, I don't think there will be any more surprises."

Shortly afterwards, they were making love in the house which they would buy on the following day.

*

The notion that their lives on that Monday morning might somehow move at a more leisurely pace was quickly dispelled. James looked at his watch shortly after six o'clock, disturbed by noises which seemed to him to be coming either from the kitchen or the scullery of a rowdy African hotel. What was absent, he thought, was that rhythmic beat and incessant joking of the kitchen staff. As he regained his full senses, he realized that it must be Félicie in the cellar. A transistor radio at full volume was forecasting storms across the nation, warning drivers of wet roads and the possibility of fallen trees. Against this background, Félicie was clattering plates, glasses, cutlery and cooking pots, the latter like badly-tuned kettle drums. The sound of a bottle rolling and then breaking on the stone floor of the cellar was followed by a loud, *"Ah! Merde!"* The debris from the previous evening was being cleared none too quietly.

He decided to dress and refresh his memory of the layout of the fields and woods on the property. A stiff breeze was blowing up the valley from the south-west. A sharp line of cloud marked the rapid approach of a frontal system coming up from the Pyrenees. The sky would soon be overcast. Not a good day for flying, he thought. He walked briskly. Everything he saw made him feel happy with their acquisition. By half-past seven, he was back in the living-room and soon light rain was falling. He did not think that the rain would last long. Over a large bowl of café au lait and *croissants*, he discussed with Félicie the list of 'extras', as she called them, which she would sell or leave behind. She consented to all except two items: the old brass bell in the porch, and an attractive, outside lantern on the corner of the barn which, she politely insisted, were of sentimental value.

Diana came upstairs, just as they were completing the short inventory.

"We forgot," she said, sipping her bowl of coffee, "to put on our list that long table out on the *terrasse.*"

"I could not take that anyway," Félicie commented, amused by this request. "You need four strong men just to move it. No, it belongs to the house." She then changed the subject. "I haven't explained yet about the two different water supplies to the house. The first system is the normal town water. It is metered and very expensive. I use it only very rarely. There is a tap in one of the manholes. I haven't turned it on at all these last four years, except for yesterday's marriage party. When there are many people staying, taking lots of baths and showers, flushing the toilets, and so on, you need the stronger pressure of the town water. But on my own, or if there are just two or four people in the house, it's far more economical to use *la source du château.* It is very much cheaper."

They both looked perplexed, and Diana looked across to James for clarification.

"*La source du château?* Which *château* is that?" he asked.

"*Mais, c'est ici! Le Château de Pisenhaut!*" she retorted. "Did you not see it when you drove through the hamlet? No! No, of course you didn't. How very silly of me! You would have come in from the direction of Montcarmel. The *château* is at the other end of the village, a magnificent wreck now. Its twin towers are sadly *en ruine.* Nobody actually knows who has title to it. But its marble fireplaces, magnificent staircase, and all the *joliespierres* have been removed or sold. *Imaginez-vous!* Such a well-proportioned *château,* plundered so thoughtlessly! The government should wake up and do something about it. *Après tout, c'est notre patrimoine!* After all, it's our heritage! Anyway, there is a *source* in the valley below it, shared by six properties whose owners are perpetual members of a registered association. The association is responsible for the maintenance of the small pumping station, the delivery system, the pipes, the annual water test, and so on. The water is, of course, free; it is the property of the association. But there has to be a charge for its upkeep."

Her explanation stopped, while she refilled their coffee bowls and brought more hot *croissants* to the table.

"The fairest way to allocate those charges," she resumed, "is, like the town water, according to individual consumption. So there is a separate tap and meter in a second manhole. *Le Secrétaire de Mairie,* who is one of the members of the association, reads the meter twice a year. The charges are always insignificant. You will become members once you own this property. You will have to attend the formal meetings of the association, which are held twice a year in the *Mairie* at Saint Juste. At these meetings, a little wine is consumed, gossip is exchanged, the accounts are discussed, the bank balance and savings accounts are examined and, dependent upon cash flow, the price of water is adjusted either upwards or downwards. Or else it stays the same. Then, also, each year there is the election of the committee, to which you, James, will be elected. I will arrange it. It all works very well, very happily, and, I'm glad to say, very cheaply. Even with all my garden hoses and the sprinkler system, my account works out at about one-tenth of the cost of consuming an equivalent amount of the town water. *Voilà!* And yet, believe it or not, some of our neighbours have *no* running water at all! Imagine! We are very lucky indeed to have such a very valuable arrangement!"

For future reference, he quickly wrote a few notes to remind himself about the two water supplies to the house and the need to test the main *source* for purity.

"What an absolutely brilliant way to organize something as important as good water!" he exclaimed. "It's a bit different to Lusaka! And that's why your garden is so green, in comparison to almost everywhere else!"

"Yes," Félicie nodded. "And the water from the *source* is much better than town water, which is always full of chemicals. That's why the suppliers of bottled water are among some of the richest people in this country. But, what you must always remember is to ensure that one of those two taps is always turned off. If you forget and leave them both on, as I have done, then the town water with its higher pressure will flow through the pipes in the house and go back up through the system into the *château source.* Don't ask me how or why, but it's a costly mistake. You don't want *n'importe qui,* any Tom, Dick or Harry, using your expensive water! Nor, now that I think about it, do we want our *source* contaminated by town water!"

*

At nine-thirty, they were all sitting in the office of *Monsieur le Maître*. A small, marble plaque on the wall discreetly announced to clients that the purchased privilege of the town's only *Notaire* had been passed — as is normal since the privilege is hereditary — from father to legally qualified son some six years previously. However, it was the father, a distinguished-looking man in his seventies, who presided over the meeting, with his young daughter-in-law present in the capacity of personal secretary. She was petite, with large brown eyes, which did not smile once during the meeting.

James sought clarification on the absence of the incumbent *Notaire*. It was the father who explained that it was he who, over the years, had always handled Madame Gautier's affairs.

"In France, *Monsieur* Wyllis," he said in a slow, measured tone, "once a *Notaire,* always a *Notaire*. And so, today, it will be my privilege to act for the State, for *Madame* Gautier and, of course, for you and your wife."

The documents which they would be required to initial and, in due course, sign had all been prepared in the standard format of French property law. Together with Félicie, a further seven members of her family would be required to testify on completion that they were willing parties to the sale — a complex arrangement with its origins in the notorious rules of succession, which can only be affected marginally by a will made in France or, for that matter, in England. Adequately forewarned on this aspect, James required *Monsieur le Maître* to include in the deed of sale a clause which, in effect, would modify those entrenched rights of inheritance. As was to be expected, the *Notaire* commented that this was not normal, that the State viewed such clauses with some mistrust but that, under the special circumstances, he would accede to the request. The document was amended to a final version, which enshrined the following set of unambiguous words:

"In the event of the death of one of the two acquiring parties, the property will pass to the survivor, as if the other party had never existed, the latter and his or her heirs relinquishing all claims on the estate during the surviving partner's lifetime."

Having navigated this obstacle, the entire document was then read aloud, slowly moving page by page from the naming of the interested parties and their antecedents, through the complex origins of the property and the identification of no less than thirty-one separate parcels of land, and finally to the interests of the State and the price, at which the property would change ownership. On each of the eighteen pages, they both had to sign their initials, indicating that they had read and understood the text to which they were giving their consent.

"To this price," *Monsieur le Maître* said in his formal manner, "must be added both the statutory fee due through this office to the State, as well as the commission as may be due to *Monsieur* Louisor, which I am required also to collect today."

"I had the firm impression," James challenged, leaning forward across the desk, "that the price quoted was to include all sale commission due to the estate agent."

"That may be the case in some transactions," Monsieur Louisor countered. "But, in the case of this particular sale the price agreed is exclusive of the fees of my office."

James paled at the implication of his quick calculation, which took the purchase price marginally above their agreed spending limit. He tried not to show any surprise, but Diana could see that his hand was shaking as he took their London cheque book from his document case.

"In that case, gentlemen," he asked, his tone making it clear that he was acting under duress, "what sum should I write on my cheque and to whom should I make it payable?"

Monsieur Louisor handed *Monsieur le Maître* a note with a figure written on it. This was added to the statutory fees, and the information was passed across the desk to James.

"H'mm! I see," was his only reaction, looking straight at the estate agent, and then writing out his cheque.

"The balance of the purchase price," the *Notaire* concluded, "must be transferred to the account of this office by no later than the fifteenth of January next year. And that, ladies and gentlemen, terminates the business of this morning. I understand that *Monsieur* Louisor has invited us all to take lunch as his guests at the *Hôtel du Lac*, and I will join you there as soon as possible. *Alors! À bientôt!*"

*

Lunch was a disaster. It was badly cooked and pretentiously served. Most of it remained uneaten, an unexpected embarrassment to both Monsieur Louisor and his compatriots. Félicie, in particular, was mortified and could not comprehend how any cook could create such a catastrophe with a dish as simple as roast duck.

"The only thing they managed not to ruin," she complained in a loud voice, "was the wine."

As can and, from time to time, does occur in matters of such importance as poorly prepared food, it was agreed that the bill should not be paid. Thus, the estate agent's sales commission remained intact, and it was on this unsavoury note that they parted company with *Monsieur le Maître* and Monsieur Louisor in the car park of the hotel.

"That was perfectly dreadful," Félicie said firmly. "I'm never going to go in there again!"

"I don't think we will either," agreed Diana.

Félicie invited them back to Bon Porteau, suggesting that she should prepare a *casse-croûte* before they left.
"A snack is really not necessary," he declined politely, "but, since the weather seems to be lifting, we would like to follow you back up to the house and take some photographs to remind us of what we've bought." It was not difficult to choose which were the best aspects to capture on film. The house and gardens were so photogenic that each time he looked through the viewfinder, a superb picture presented itself. It was not long before he found that he had finished his last film.

They thanked Félicie for her hospitality, reassuring her that they would keep her informed of their plans. As they went slowly down the drive, she was standing up on the roof *terrasse,* vigorously waving goodbye to them with a dishcloth. A small, solitary figure, she was still standing there when they looked back through the gap in the trees on the lane, from where they had caught their first glimpse of Bon Porteau. It was hard to believe that less than forty-eight hours had elapsed since that moment. During the drive back to the rented cottage in the Dordogne, they discussed how they might spend their remaining three precious days before the return flight to Zambia. They decided that it would be best to leave the cottage the following morning. This would give them the opportunity to drive at a leisurely pace towards Paris.

When they arrived at the cottage, it was late and heavy rain was falling. Both the desire to quit the Dordogne as soon as possible and the prospect of exploring another region of France caused them to rise early the next day. After breakfast, while Diana completed the packing, James related the events of the previous two days to Paul, who appeared to be genuinely relieved that they were pleased with the acquisition of Bon Porteau. James gave him the hunting knife, which he had bought in Borinac, and they parted on good terms, with the promise that they would make contact again when they returned.

They stopped in Limoges to visit one of the porcelain factories, and James found Diana an attractive, miniature box to add to her collection. The further north they drove, the more the weather started to improve, and they spent the night outside Tours in an *hostellerie,* which was comfortable and good value. James had not revisited the *châteaux* on the Loire and the Cher rivers since his childhood, and they were a completely new experience for Diana, who fell in love with the romantic splendour of Chenonceau and Chambord. Their route took them through Orléans, where they found a good restaurant in the Place du Matroi, and then on to Chartres to stand in awe before the one hundred and sixty stained-glass windows of the thirteenth-century Cathedral. For their last night, they unashamedly chose the best hotel in Versailles, where they celebrated the overall success of their mission.

It was with mixed feelings that they boarded the UTA Boeing 747 early the following morning. Once seated in the spacious first-class compartment, they were served champagne before takeoff. The aircraft lumbered off the apron and was taxiing towards the threshold of the runway, when Diana turned to him with an excited smile.

"Tchin, tchin!" she laughed, mimicking Félicie and raising her glass. "I wonder how long it will be before we manage to return."

"We can return whenever we want," he replied pensively.

"By the way," she muttered, reaching over to touch his arm, "that was a nasty, little shock. I mean, the fuss between the *Notaire* and Louisor."

"Yes, wasn't it just!" he agreed. "I thought Louisor might be pulling a fast one on me. I didn't tell you, but his sales commission came to exactly the same amount by which Félicie had reduced her selling price! But I have complete confidence in that very experienced *Notaire,* so *we* must have got it wrong somewhere along the line. And just the night before, I remember saying something about no more surprises! It's only the language barrier, you know."

"Only..! Oh, well, my love," she said, holding firmly on to his hand as the aircraft became airborne, "we'll just have to stay a little longer in Africa and save a bit more, won't we? What do you think of that idea?"

"Not a lot," was his unexpected reply, as he admitted to himself that he would like to return to Bon Porteau as soon as possible. "You know me, my love," he continued quietly. "With me, it's all or nothing. The Lot will be enough for me!"

PART TWO

"Il faut cultiver notre jardin."

Voltaire: *"Candide ou l'Optimisme"*

Chapter Fourteen

It was, in fact, almost exactly a year later that they arrived back at Charles de Gaulle airport. During the intervening period, events in Zambia had moved at an unusually fast pace. Multi-party elections were looming for the first time in twenty-five years of post-colonial, independent rule. Those with whom James had been working were manoeuvring themselves into strategic positions, from which they might have a better chance to ease into new and more lucrative posts. Self-interest became the byword. The developmental work which James had nurtured carefully over nearly five years faltered, then lost momentum, and finally degenerated into a lost cause. Faced with the reality that he was wasting his own time and his employer's money, he resigned.

Navigating an exit from an African state is never simple. The clearances, the permits, the declarations, and the disposal of some of their personal effects, which were not to be included in their air freight, entailed a mass of paperwork Among the plethora of mandatory documentation, one of the most important was the licence for the exportation to France of Jacob and Fosbury, the two surviving Burmese cats, who would accompany them in due course in the cabin of the French-owned aircraft. Anticipating that space and weight would be important factors in this undertaking, James decided that they would travel first-class. They would depart in style and comfort, as much for the benefit of the cats as for themselves. He noted wryly that the cost of the air fares had trebled in twelve months, such was the impact of rampant inflation.

In the final event, when they boarded their flight shortly before midnight, the authorities at Lusaka International Airport were demonstrably uninterested in their departure. In fact, those few officials who were on duty were asleep. Thus, the dossier of vital papers, which had taken two months to assemble, remained unchecked in his briefcase. Only a tired baggage handler noticed their passage through emigration and customs, reacting with good-humoured amusement at the extent of their hand luggage, which included two special carrier bags provided for the cats by the airline. Most of the rest of their impedimenta was also dedicated to feline comfort, ready to cater for every eventuality which might occur on the long flight. As they struggled across the apron to the waiting aircraft, Fosbury let out a howl of disapproval, protesting loudly all the way up the steps to the aircraft and into the cabin.

Even travelling in the luxury of the first-class compartment, there was insufficient space in the luggage racks to stow the cats' tray, a bag of sand, which had a small tear in it and was leaking, two plastic containers of cat food, their bowls, some of their toys, two small blankets, and a collapsible cage. In due course, an attractive air hostess came to their rescue, removing some of their bags to another section of the cabin which, she informed them, would not be occupied during the flight. Out of breath, his arms feeling as is they had been pulled forcibly out of their sockets, he slumped into the seat beside his wife. Welcome relief came in the form of champagne, served by the same hostess, who handed a piece of paper to Diana. "Due to industrial action," it read, "the Captain regrets to inform you that there will be no in-flight meal service, until the aircraft has taken off from Libreville for Paris."

Diana said nothing and quietly handed the note to James, whose face assumed a look of outraged fury. The hostess tactfully refilled his empty champagne glass.

"I am so sorry," she simpered. "But there is plenty more of this." She left the bottle on the tray in front of him.

"How long will it be," he enquired, "before we are airborne out of Libreville?"

"We're going to Gaborone in Botswana first to refuel," she explained. "Then we can proceed to Libreville. It will be eight hours, I'm afraid."

"Merde!" he cursed.

Expecting that they would be given an excellent dinner, they had deliberately not eaten anything since a snack for lunch.

"Oh well!" he said in a resigned tone. "We really ought to know by now that Africa is full of surprises. Nobody even bothered to look at our luggage or documentation. We could have half the nation's emeralds on board with us! The other surprise is our freight. Did you notice it being loaded on board? All nine crates of it!"

"You're joking!" Diana exclaimed. "You mean on the *same* flight?"

"Yes," he replied. "Most people don't see their unaccompanied, heavy baggage for weeks, or even months! I couldn't believe my eyes!"

Before the aircraft took off, the air hostess retrieved the empty bottle of champagne and the glasses. James looked across at Diana, as the undercarriage rose above Africa. She was looking down through the window at the receding runway lights.

"We will come back again, won't we?" she asked bravely.

"There's an old saying," he replied, squeezing her hand. "Once you have tasted the waters of the Zambezi, they will flow through your veins for the rest of your life."

She looked back out of the window as the aircraft banked, the lights of the city coming into view. Her eyes were moist with tears. Somewhere down there was the house in Nalikwanda Road where, under the shade of the tall bougainvillaea hedge, lay the tiny body of Yentl, the third and youngest cat, unable to make the journey to her new home. She looked down at her two survivors. They were both curled up, happily asleep in their snug carrier bags by her feet. In spite of two takeoffs and landings, as well as a tedious delay at Libreville, they did not stir until the Captain announced twenty-seven hours later that he was beginning the descent for Paris.

There was no urgent need for them to disembark among all the other passengers, who were jostling each other impatiently in their scramble for the exits. It would be another three hours, before they could take their connecting flight south to Toulouse. When the cabins were empty, he collected their seven pieces of hand luggage, and Diana picked up Jacob and Fosbury. Only half of the sand remained in the bag; the other half would be somewhere in one of the luggage lockers. James braced himself for the physical effort of transferring it all into the airport.

"Perhaps there'll be some trolleys," he said hopefully.

"We must get the cats into a secure lounge first," she said single-mindedly. "The poor babies! They must be dying for a pee."

They found a deserted lounge, and James mounted guard on the entrance door, not so much to keep other people out, rather more as a precaution against either cat escaping into the airport. He had visions of Jacob running amok in the main concourse, searching for a way out into the busy traffic. Methodically, Diana filled the tray with some sand and, one at a time, the cats politely responded to the call of nature, each taking a full three minutes to bring an expression of relief to their wide-eyed faces. She then filled one of the bowls from a water dispenser in the corner of the lounge.

"They mustn't get dehydrated," she pronounced. "That's enough, Fosbury! Otherwise you'll want to go again on the next flight." Some twenty minutes passed, before the tray was discreetly tipped out into a lavatory, washed, and packed away again.

Having checked that all bags were present, they emerged into a corridor, the end of which disappeared out of sight round a corner. Mercifully, there was a passenger conveyor belt about fifty yards away. As they approached it, James' heart sank — the belt was not moving. There was not one trolley to be seen anywhere. He had no alternative but to carry it all, and he arrived at the far end of the corridor in an exhausted, ill-tempered mood.

"*Pourquoi est-ce que ce truc de merde ne marche pas?*" he shouted angrily at the first, unfortunate airport official he saw. "Why isn't this bloody thing working?"

"*Mais si, Monsieur! Ça marche très bien!*" the official replied, unable to repress his amusement when confronted by this irate and tousled Englishman who was just visible under the load of bags. "But it does, sir! *C'est de la plus haute technologie!* All you have to do is to step on to it. *Voilà!* Then it moves very well!"

"*Merde!*" he swore. "Let's go and find some breakfast."

The onward flight to Toulouse was a nightmare, although it lasted only fifty minutes. The boarding gate was at the furthest extremity of the airport complex. Nevertheless, armed with the new technology of how to activate the *trottoir roulant*, at least he was spared a repeat of the physical effort of their disembarkation. Neither Jacob nor Fosbury, however, appreciated the noisy, jolting movement of the conveyor belt, and they were both swearing like troopers. Once on board, James discovered that all domestic flights are classified *espace non-fumeur,* a non-smoking area.

"Never mind, darling," Diana said soothingly. "It's only a short hop, and you smoked far too much during the flight last night."

To add to his disgruntlement, the flight was fully booked. Every seat was taken and there was no first-class facility. Being a smaller aircraft, there was nowhere to stow most of their bags, and this time they were forced to sit in narrow, cramped seats, with the cats wedged on top of them. Since he had no realistic alternative, James acquiesced, but the cats had no intention of following his good example. Noticing the difference in their treatment and surroundings, they kept up a continuous, repetitive commentary, indicating that their patience was now exhausted. In the seat across the aisle, a middle-aged Frenchwoman sat bemused, holding tightly to her a nervous, miniature poodle. This was too much for Fosbury, adding to his frustration at having to be incarcerated in a dark, and now uncomfortable, little bag, in which he had already spent the last thirty hours.

Fosbury would not settle down. He spat and growled at the dog throughout the flight.

"Il n'est pas très gentil!" the lady remarked. "He's not very nice!"

"It's just that he can't stand small poodles," Diana explained.

"Nor can I," boomed a voice in English from the seat behind her. Diana turned and smiled, noticing the man's khaki shirt and deep tan. He had a monocle hanging round his neck on a black cord. She thought no more about his comment, and turned her attention back to the noisy cats.

"Hush, my babies!" she whispered. "We're nearly there now."

Toulouse airport was blanketed in a cold, steady drizzle when they landed. There were trolleys everywhere, but neither customs nor immigration officials were present.

"We could have brought a dozen lions with us," Diana commented.

Waiting for the conveyor belt to deliver their four large suitcases, she watched the suntanned, rakish man in the bush shirt, who had been on the same flight. He was tall and good-looking, standing beside a blonde woman, who, she thought, might perhaps be of Eastern

European origin. She was making a fuss of a mongrel dog on a short lead.

"That chap looks as if he's come in from Africa." she said, noticing the desert boots he was wearing.

"Yes. Even the dog looks a bit African," James agreed. *"Mais, merde!* It's freezing cold in here. The weather's very different to this time last year. I would have thought that Toulouse was far enough south. It should still be warm in mid-September. We shall need our big sweaters, once we can get at our suitcases."

They had arranged through the airline to rent a big estate car, pending collection of their new jeep which, if all went to plan, was to be available from a local dealer the following morning. With two fully loaded trolleys, they braved the rain and managed to locate the hire car, loading it in such a way as to leave the rearmost compartment clear for the cats. These were now transferred from their carrier bags into the more familiar surroundings of their collapsible cage, which was lined with their fleecy blanket. While Diana organized the use of the tray, James went to find a telephone to contact Monsieur Louisor, as had been arranged from Zambia several weeks before their departure. The estate agent was in his office, and informed him that he and Madame Gautier would expect to meet them outside the church in Montcarmel at three o'clock that afternoon. They would then drive up to Bon Porteau and see them into the house. This arrangement left them ample time for their car journey, with an unhurried stop for lunch somewhere *en route*.

It was not until they had passed Montauban that he realized they were not on the most direct road to Montcarmel. They had eaten a good lunch with a carafe of red wine, and he had then driven away on the wrong side of the road from the restaurant. Neither event, he claimed, had any bearing whatsoever on his map-reading error — a signpost, which he was expecting to find, must have been obscured, either by the heavy rain, with which the windscreen wipers were not coping adequately, or by the car's windows, from which the condensation would not clear.

"Never mind," he said. "There's plenty of time. We'll just have to do two sides of a triangle via Cahors. It'll only take about twenty minutes longer."

Once they reached the main road between Cahors and Montcarmel, he felt more confident and began to relax, feeling that everything was now going according to plan and was under control. Some minutes later they were coming up behind a large, green removal van, which was developing a dangerous list on each bend, its wheels crossing the continuous white line in the centre of the road.

"I bet his load is twice as heavy as it should be," he said. "Bloody dangerous! And if the police, *les flics*, catch him crossing that line, he'll be in for a hefty, on-the-spot fine."

"It's not a French van," Diana observed. "They would probably let him off with a warning."

"No, they would not!" he argued. "That solid white line in France is known as *le mur,* the wall. You are not allowed to cross it under any circumstances. If you do, they treat it as one of the worst traffic offences."

Twice he tried, and failed, to overtake the van, the heavy spray making visibility difficult. Then he caught a glimpse of the gold-painted sign on the side of the vehicle.

"But that's Chapman's from Bagshot!" he shouted excitedly. "That must be our stuff from England. *Merde!* They're a day early. I organized their delivery for tomorrow afternoon!"

"What an amazing coincidence!" she laughed. "I wonder what the odds are against driving down the wrong road, and then bumping into your removal van from England in the middle of the Lot on the wrong day!"

The rain was still making it difficult and dangerous to overtake. However, after a few more kilometres, there was a straight stretch of road. The van slowed down and he managed to pass, sounding the horn and waving at the driver to pull in and stop.

The driver lowered his window when James walked towards the cab through the rain.

"Hey! Monsewer! Is this the bleedin' road for Mont Caramel?" he asked in a truculent tone.

"Yes. Well done, young man!" James replied, looking up from the road at a tired, young face which was smeared with oil. "I think you must have our stuff on board."

"What's your name then?" the young man asked suspiciously.

"Wyllis, and soon you'll be trying to find the house. It's called Bon Porteau."

"That's right," the driver said with relief, as he checked his papers. "Cor, you got enough junk in here to sink the Ark, if it's all yours. You goin' into the second-hand game, then? And who drew this thing, this map?"

James saw him wave the map, which he had carefully prepared and posted from abroad, in order to help the removal firm to find the right house.

"Yes, that's right," he nodded. "That's the map *I* drew to help you."

"Can't make head nor tail of it, we can't!"

The sound of voices woke up the co-driver, who leaned over towards James. He was about the same age as his colleague.

"Blimey, Guv!" he shouted over the noise of the engine. "Are we pleased to see you! We've been on the road for two days in this godforsaken country! Nobody speaks no English! Only bleedin' French! We've had to sleep in the cab since we left the ferry. Couldn't get no hotel room! No birds, neither! What a dump!"

"That's right," the driver agreed. "No proper breakfasts, and stupid, little cups of black coffee, which wouldn't drown a fly and what cost the earth! Beer's like gnat's piss, as well! No wonder they all look so miserable and are always out on strike! We haven't had a wash nor a shower neither, since we left the ferry. And we had a stoppage somewhere near gay Paree. Fuckin' French fuzz jumpin' up and down like a yo-yo, tryin' to tell us to move this bleedin' wreck off the road! What a fuckin' performance! We just pretended we couldn't understand a word he was on about. Which, of course, we couldn't!"

The driver opened a stained Thermos flask and poured himself a mug of what might at some time have been tea.

"You've made very good time, even so," James said, imagining that a 'stoppage' was the current jargon for a breakdown. "In fact, you're a day earlier than I expected." He was beginning to get very wet, standing in the rain, so he went on quickly. "Look, Montcarmel is just up the road. It's not more than about ten minutes away. Don't turn off into the town. That's the wrong road, and you won't be able to turn this monster around up there. If you stop on this main road by the electric sub-station at the bottom of the hill, we'll be about another ten minutes and then we'll join you. We can drive in convoy up to the house."

"Right, Guv." The driver was smiling now. "Cor! That was a bit of luck, findin' you here, I must say! Are you thinking of livin' here, then?"

"That's right," James nodded with a grin. "We've just arrived from Africa." Walking back to the hire car, he could hear their laughter coming from the cab.

"And he's forgotten his bloomin' paddle. They must be fuckin' mad, Steve!"

Chapter Fifteen

A good dictionary should define a 'plan' as being, among other things, a carefully considered arrangement for carrying out a sequence of future activities, which can and frequently does go awry. Such was to be the case during their first weeks and months in France. However, James always believed that if you did not know where you were going, then your final arrival at the right destination or goal would be nothing more than a mere fluke. If you have a plan, which deviates from its expected course, then at least it can be modified. He referred to this as 'a change of emphasis'.

They drove into the town square, and almost the first person they saw was Félicie Gautier. She recognized them immediately and came running down the pavement, her umbrella bobbing through the rain. She was waving excitedly and greeted them as if they were old friends.

"I was waiting for you just there," she pointed across the square, "so that I could keep an eye on the church just around the corner. But that imbecile, Louisor, when he arranged the meeting place, he didn't know that there are three churches in the town, so I told him to climb the hill and wait outside the other one, in case you went there first. Please give four long blasts on your car horn. That's the signal that you've arrived. Hopefully he'll hear it. I'm not going all the way up there in this rain!"

Monsieur Louisor emerged from one of the small roads, carrying a diminutive umbrella which had afforded him little shelter from the weather. The lower half of his trouser legs were soaked. The four of them stood under the awning of the *Tabac,* the rain deluging off the canvas material and forming large puddles on the pavement and in the road.

"I thought," James remarked, "that it would be sunny and autumnal here by now."

"Ouf! Quel temps de merde!" swore the estate agent.

"Mais, ce n'est pas normal!" added Félicie.

Monsieur Louisor noticed the heavily-laden estate car, parked on the opposite side of the square.

"But that's not the car you wrote to me about from Lusaka," he said, waving his umbrella at the hire car. "I've ordered you the jeep you wanted. Immediately after your call to my office this morning, I rang the dealer to check that all was in order. They are ready, waiting for you to collect it."

James thanked him for the efficient way in which he had handled his unusual request.

"No. That's a hire car from Toulouse. But look, we must get on now. We've been travelling for over thirty hours and everyone is tired, including our cats. We will follow you up to Bon Porteau now. There is one small complication. Waiting for us at the bottom of the hill is our removal van from England. Believe it or not, we just found it on the road from Cahors! He will follow us to the house."

"Mais quel miracle d'organisation!" Félicie exclaimed, as if the event had been a scheduled part of their intricate plan for the move. *"Et bon Dieu! Tu as aussi les chats avec toi! O-là-là, là-là!"*

Some minutes later, the convoy of three cars with the pantechnicon was winding its way along the small lane leading to Pisenhaut, the tall van brushing against some of the overhanging branches of the trees.

"Félicie hasn't changed much, has she?" he said, as they progressed slowly in front of the overloaded van.

"No, but I wonder if she's bothered to turn on the central heating. My babies are cold and tired. Still, now that our English kit is here, we can find out from the inventory which of the boxes contains their electric bed. If we plug it in as soon as we arrive, it will be warming up by the time they finish their meal."

Félicie had gone on ahead, so that by the time they arrived at Bon Porteau the house and shutters were open.

"I've just turned on the heating," she said. "I've had the oil tank filled for you. We can deal with all the bills sometime tomorrow. But be careful of the boiler; it uses a lot of expensive oil very quickly. *Je ne connais pas vos moyens!* I don't know how well off you are! But take care!"

James remembered vaguely from their visit a year ago how Félicie had repeatedly commented upon the cost-of-living, the need to economize, and her ignorance of their financial status.

"You must be feeling the cold, my dear," she went on, putting out a hand to feel the thick wool of the sweater Diana was wearing. "Come inside and bring the cats. James can deal with the removal men."

The two cats were installed in the furthest bedroom, still locked in their cage to prevent their escape while the doors of the house remained open. In the meantime, having failed to climb the steep curve at the end of the drive, the removal van had reversed across the lawn to a position as near as possible to the house, leaving two ugly, deep furrows in the soft turf. Seeing that there was no further contribution that he could make, Monsieur Louisor left, expressing the hope that they would be happy in their new home, and that, shortly, he and his wife would invite them to lunch or dinner at their house on the outskirts of Cahors. His wife, he said, was particularly looking forward to seeing them again, and had offered to show Diana round the Cahors shops the next time she came into town.

Supervised by James, it took the two young removal men less than an hour to transfer the contents of the van to the house. He had forgotten completely that they had accumulated so much and, after the comparative austerity of their way of life in Zambia, he felt guilty about all their material possessions. He was joined by Diana and Félicie, the latter consumed with curiosity, as item after item was carried into the house.

"*Mais, quel beau canapé!*" she said in admiration, as the two men struggled with the heavy, four-seater sofa into the room, which used to be Félicie's dining-room. She fawned over the beds, examined the desks, stroked the Jacobean dining table, and then cried out in ecstasy when she saw the old, stone, garden bench and the Cotswold stone collection of plant troughs.

"*Aïe! Aïe! Aïe! Qu'ils sont vraiment superbes!*" she said in an almost reverent tone.

"It's very much easier to move house, if you're an African," James commented. "You just put your belongings on your head and simply go."

The man, whose name was Steve, put down the last of the heavy, stone troughs and hurried over to speak to James.

"Do you want us to unpack the tea-chests, Guv?" he asked.

"Oh! No, not now. We will do it gradually ourselves later in the week."

"You know you've paid Chapman's for the unpackin', don't you?" Steve said, repeating his offer. "Otherwise, if we leave them chests here, you'll only get a bill for them. I think they charge about a tenner for each, don't they, Roger?"

"Yeah," replied Roger. "Something bleedin' absorbent like that, I think."

"You can tell Jim Chapman to go jump in the Thames," James retorted, laughing at Roger's turn of phrase. He grinned at them, and went on, "Come on inside. You've both done bloody well. Bring in your washing things, and have a damn good, hot shower before you push off. That's if it works!"

"Brilliant!" Steve said enthusiastically. "You sure your Missus won't mind, Guv?"

"Come on in out of the rain and get cleaned up," he said firmly. "And that's an *order*!"

"Okay, Guv! We're on our way!"

About an hour later, the removal van was preparing to leave. Its crew was well scrubbed and a few pounds richer than when they had arrived.

"That's very generous of you," Steve shouted from his cab. "All the best then, Guv! Hope you both settle in well. Rather you than me though. Give me Blighty anytime."

"Yeah," Roger chipped in. "If this bleedin' dinky toy don't stop on us, we'll be on the ferry this time tomorrow, tuckin' in to tomato sauce, sausages, eggs and chips, with a few good pints of real ale. Cheers then!"

"Goodbye, and thanks!" James shouted, as the engine started noisily. "And remember not to drive over that solid white line!"

He watched the green giant lumber away down the drive, turning out on to the lane in the wrong direction and heading for the depths of the Lot countryside.

*

Diana and Félicie were sitting quietly in the living-room, surrounded by tea-chests, most of which the Frenchwoman had inspected. In fact, it was Félicie who eventually found the cats' electric bed, such was her thirst for knowledge about how the English move house, even if they do come from Africa.

"I've had to leave my logs for you, James," she explained. "They wanted to charge me more than they're worth, just to move them down to the town. And anyway, the apartment I am renting has no fireplace. You can get the big fire going now and you'll find that the house will soon be warm. Kindling wood is in the *prunerie*."

"Thanks, Félicie," he replied. "But I think I'll just leave all the radiators on for tonight. We're both very tired. Besides, I don't want a big, open fire in an empty house. We'll just settle down the cats, and then go to the hotel where we're booked for the night."

Félicie took the hint, and prepared to leave. She handed James a bag of large, heavy keys.

"Eh bien!" she beamed at them. "I'll ring you tomorrow and come and explain everything." She made as if to leave and then stopped at the front door. "Oh! That reminds me! Several of your friends have been ringing me, but I can't speak English. Since they don't speak French, they shout and scream at me and then hang up!"

"But how on earth do they know your new number?" Diana asked, looking confused. "We gave them our number — that is to say, the number which belongs to this house."

"Don't you know? When you move house within the same telephone area in France, you take your old number with you? So I still have my old number. Your new number is..." She walked over to the telephone and read it out.

James thought briefly about the simple logic of such a cost-effective system.

"What a sensible arrangement!" James said.

"Oh, my God!" Diana groaned. "Then we've given your present number on our change-of-address cards to every one of our friends, our relatives, to the banks... To everybody!"

She thought back to all the hours of painstaking work she had done, combing through their address books and files, to ensure that everyone knew how to contact them.

"Merde!" James cursed. "I hadn't thought of that!"

"Well," Félicie said grimly, "I hope they won't go on ringing for too much longer. It's a terrible nuisance, and some of them sound quite angry! They shout at me, as if I'm a half-wit!"

"We'll fix it as soon as we can," he said, trying to reassure her that not all their friends were irate and short-tempered. "Perhaps we can ask the telephone company to divert calls automatically, so that you are not disturbed too often and too late at night."

"I will find out if that's possible," Félicie said, as she left. *"À demain!* See you tomorrow!"

As soon as Félicie had gone they immediately unpacked the electrically-heated cat bed, and discovered two additional cat trays, about which they had both forgotten, and a bag of cat litter. The latter proved to be an unexpected bonus, because the last of the sand from the banks of the Zambezi had finally leaked away somewhere between Toulouse airport, the hire car, and its eventual transfer to the house. He picked up the bed and the cat litter.

"While you feed the cats," he volunteered, "I'll take this downstairs and plug it in next to the radiator."

Without at least one of his hands free, it was difficult to descend the miller's ladder to the basement of the *pigeonnier*, and it was with some relief that he safely reached the ground floor. Diana followed him down without difficulty.

"I don't know," he said over his shoulder to her, "how Félicie managed all those years with that contraption."

"Well, she's only about half your height. Mind your—"

The warning was in vain. Although he remembered the small, low doorway through to the passage and ducked to try and avoid it, he misjudged the height. There was a loud crack, as his head made contact with the solid, stone lintel.

This time he fell into the passage in a heap, dropping the bed and the paper bag of cat litter, which broke open, scattering half its contents across the floor.

"Darling, are you hurt?" she cried, as she knelt beside him. "Please try to be more careful."

"Merde!" he swore, holding his head and struggling to his feet. "That bloody little door! I tell you, it's going to be a race to see which

is changed first: either raising that lintel or revamping some adequate stairs."

"I thought you said that the new kitchen arrangements had to have first priority."

"Don't worry about it," he said, touching his wound to check that he was not losing too much blood. "We've got the rest of our lives to get all this lot straight. We don't have to go at it like a bull in a china shop."

"Good! And I hope you really mean what you say. Let's deal with the cats and find our hotel. I don't want any supper. I'm shattered."

The cats were finally installed. They appeared to be none the worse after their long journey. They ran around the bedroom, investigating everything and stretching themselves repeatedly. James toured the house to close all the shutters, counting up to twenty-seven by the time he had finished the task.

"There's more than just a little bit of *bricolage* needed on those shutters," he told her, as they prepared to shut the house. *"C'est chiant, ça!* It's a real pain in the arse!

He then remembered that he had not checked that the central heating switches were set to operate all night, and disappeared towards the boiler room. A few minutes later he was shutting the heavy front doors, finding it difficult to turn the large keys in the locks. He had just succeeded with the inner door when the telephone rang. He checked the time on his watch. It was almost seven o'clock.

"I'll have to put some oil in these locks," he was saying, as he heard the shrill bleep of the telephone. "Damn! I suppose I had better answer it. It might be important."

*

He wrenched open the door and hurried across to the corner of the living-room, where the instrument noisily insisted on a reply.

"Allô! Oui, bonsoir! Oui, oui, oui! C'est moi. C'est Monsieur Wyllis à l'appareil."

"Bonsoir, M'sieu! This is BAF International, speaking from Toulouse Airport. We are your freight-forwarding agent. Your boxes from Zambia have just come in on the late flight from Paris. They are now waiting for clearance by Customs. We have all your

documentation, but Customs will not pass your consignment unless you can provide us with a *Certificat de Domicile.* If you can furnish us with the certificate tomorrow morning, then we will try to arrange delivery tomorrow afternoon, if that's convenient."

He looked across at Diana, who was sitting patiently on a tea-chest. He suddenly felt very tired.

"Et qu'est-ce que c'est un Certificat de Domicile?" he asked with a sigh. "And where do I get one?"

"It's very simple," said the voice on the other end of the line. "All you have to do is go to your *Mairie,* and they will issue it to you as a bona-fide householder in their commune. From the address we have for you, that will be the *Mairie de Saint Juste.* May we expect to get the certificate from you as early as possible tomorrow morning?"

"Well... Yes, I suppose so," he replied not very confidently. "If not, I'll ring you first thing in the morning. You see, I'm not too sure about the opening hours of the *Mairie* here. It's only a very small commune."

"Non, Monsieur! C'est tout à fait simple," said the voice. "All you do is find *Monsieur le Secrétaire de Mairie.* Go to his home. Explain to him the urgency. He will do the rest... By the way, do you know that you gave the wrong telephone number on your papers?"

"Yes. Unfortunately, we've done the same to everyone!"

"O-là-là! Merde, hein! C'est pénible, ça! C'est de la vraie connerie!"

James noted their telephone number and sat down to think. Diana looked across at him, as if to find out what was happening.

"What was all that about?" she asked.

He told her about the urgent request from Toulouse, at the same time trying to establish in his mind how to reschedule his programme for the following morning.

"Oh, well. Leave it for now," she said. "We've done quite enough today. And anyway, we really don't want all our African stuff piling up here now. Where on earth can we put it? It can't stand out in all this rain. Leave it darling! Ring them in the morning, and tell them that we may be ready to accept it here by the end of next week."

"Hell, no!" he insisted. "Have you any idea of the cost of ten days' demurrage in an airport warehouse? They would hammer us with an enormous bill plus, of course, the delivery costs to here. No, this isn't Africa! They don't leave freight hanging about on the tarmac for weeks, until someone eventually decides that it might be moved. No, we must recover it as soon as possible."

Suddenly, he thought that Félicie would know what to do. He dialled her number and listened to the unanswered ringing tone. There was no reply.

"Perhaps I misdialled," he said, trying the number again.

"Or else," Diana commented wryly, "she thinks it could be one of our angry friends!"

This time she did reply. Without sounding as if he was in a panic, he explained what was required, stressing the need for urgency.

"Pas de probléme!" she assured him. "I will ring Gérard Tillet now. I'll ask him to be in his office at eight o'clock in the morning. He's the *Secrétaire,* the man you want. I will collect you from your hotel and we'll go in my car. We'll get him to issue the certificate without delay, and then I'll take you back to the hotel... No, I won't! I've just remembered. I have to go to market, and it will be quicker for me to drop you off at Bon Porteau. Diana can find her way by herself from the hotel to the house, can't she? And then you just take the piece of paper down to Toulouse. As I said, *aucun problème.*" She hesitated, and then added, "And I'll bring an electricity bill, just in case. They're always useful!"

"That will be fine, Félicie. Thanks very much. By the way, just one other question, if you will be so kind. When does the supermarket open in the morning?"

She told him, and he thanked her again for her help.

Diana was still sitting, slumped on one of the tea-chests. She felt near to exhaustion. He described how Félicie would solve the problem.

"So, I'll go to the *Mairie* with her," he explained. "With a bit of luck, we'll be through there by half-past eight and she'll drop me off at the house. If you can get over to the supermarket when it opens at nine to buy the most urgent things, then you might be back up at the house by nine-thirty. Then I'll take the hire car to Toulouse and clear our stuff through Customs. After that, I'll go and collect our jeep and hand in the hire car. With a bit of luck, I should think I'll be back for a snack lunch by one o'clock. It'll be nice to have a *baguette* and some *rillettes* again." He saw the look on her face. "Or anything simple," he suggested tactfully. "Perhaps an omelette."

Diana continued to look miserable and confused, her mind numbed by fatigue.

"All this mad rush!" she complained. "All right, but I thought you said that we were going to take things easy and wind down gently in the Lot. Instead, you're going to go charging about all day tomorrow, and you'll only get uptight. You'll be—"

"Don't worry, my love," he interrupted her in a tone of voice which he hoped was soothing. "It's just the tail-end of the administration of our move, that's all. We can't leave our stuff at the airport, and I'm committed to collecting the jeep tomorrow. It's got to be done. After this, I promise that everything will settle down into a nice, gentle routine with no nasty surprises. You'll see. You're very tired, my love."

He put his arm round her shoulder, and kissed her. "Come on, let's go."

He started to walk her gently towards the front door, but she halted abruptly, pulled away from him, and walked back towards the telephone.

"I've forgotten to do one important thing," she said hoarsely. He could feel the exhaustion in her voice. "Before we go to the hotel, I must ring Kim and tell her we've arrived safely."

She dialled her daughter's number. It was Andrew, her son-in-law, who answered. She spoke briefly to both of them, and promised to telephone the next day at about the same time.

"Right," said James, when she put down the receiver. "Let's go and get a good night's sleep."

For the second time, he wrestled with the huge locks and, when they arrived at the hotel, they went straight to bed.

"Are you glad to be back in France?" he asked, finishing his whisky while he sat up in bed.

She made no reply. She was already fast asleep.

"*À demain, chérie!*" he whispered, kissing the top of her head lightly. Before he turned out the light, he looked at his watch. Forty-five hours had elapsed since their departure from Nalikwanda Road.

Chapter Sixteen

Félicie was at the hotel before eight o'clock the next morning. She came running in through the rain, which had fallen ceaselessly throughout the night. Diana was still sleeping soundly. Before leaving, he put his head round the corner of the hotel office and told the hotelier that he would return to settle the account later in the day, at the same time asking for some coffee to be taken up to his wife in about half-an-hour.

"This is very good of you, Félicie," he said, once they were inside her car.

"De rien! De rien!" she said, searching for the windscreen wiper switch. "It's nothing! *Mais quel temps affreux!* What terrible weather!"

"Does it usually rain as long and as hard as this at this time of the year?"

"Non! Non! Non! Ce n'est pas du tout normal!" she shouted over the roar of the engine. "It's not at all normal. In fact, it's most unusual. You were both here this time last year. We had supper out on the roof *terrasse.* Don't you remember?"

She noisily found a gear, and the car lurched violently backwards into a solid stone bollard in the car park.

"Aaah! Merde!" she cursed. "I'm a good driver, but I don't always find the gears."

"You should try an automatic," he suggested politely, reaching for the seat-belt.

The little car bounded forward out of the car park and, with no apparent regard for any oncoming traffic, she turned right into the main road, racing down the centre line towards the turning up to Saint Juste. He was just beginning to wonder about her brakes, when they locked tightly in a skid on the wet road surface and they slewed round dangerously into the lane. He just had time to catch a glimpse of the small sign which read: *St Juste 1,7.*

"Do you think *Monsieur* Tillet will be there already?" he asked, breathing a sigh of relief that he would only have to endure less than another two kilometres which, he calculated, would take a little more than one minute at their present high speed. Involuntarily, he found that he was pushing his right foot down on an imaginary brake, willing her to slow down.

"J'espère que oui!" she replied firmly, driving even faster up the narrow, twisting lane. "I hope so! I must get to market before the best bargains are sold. You can save a lot of money and get the best quality if you get to market early, you know."

He thought that she would save more money on tyres and petrol, if she drove with a little less haste.

They turned abruptly into the small car park in front of the *Mairie,* and parked dangerously close to one of the chestnut trees.

"Quel con! Il n'est pas encore là!" she muttered. "What a fool! He's not there yet!"

He looked across at the trees, remembering the last time he had seen them. It had been hot and sunny, with the courtyard in deep shadow. Now the leaves were beginning to turn and rain was spilling down the steps from the door to the *Mairie.* Almost immediately, a small moped came noisily round the corner from the opposite direction, turned into the square, and parked with a squeak of brakes under a bicycle shelter.

"Ah bon! Le voilà enfin!" she cried, quickly opening the car door. "Good! There he is at last!"

A small figure, encased in oilskin jacket and trousers, a scarf over his nose and mouth, and a large, bright red crash helmet with a smoke-coloured visor, dismounted nimbly and ran up the steps through the rain.

"Bonjour, M'sieu, 'dame!" he shouted from behind his visor, his strong accent muffled by his protective wear. "Come quickly! *Venez vite!* Let's all get out of this rain! *Merde! C'est déprimant, hein?* It's depressing, eh?" He was fumbling in the deep pocket of his jacket. He pulled out a bunch of keys, unlocked the door, and led them into a short, dark passage off which, with the aid of a pencil torch, he opened the door to his office. He said nothing as he switched on the light, a bare bulb suspended from a thin, frayed wire of dubious quality. He then crossed to the one window in the room, and threw open the heavy shutters before closing the window again.

The room was not large. Bare floorboards, old beams across the ceiling, a huge cupboard, an electric fire, a small photocopier, a pair of worn slippers, and a scrubbed oblong table with eight plain wooden chairs. On each of the walls were pinned a variety of official notices and posters, the gaudiest of which encouraged callers at the *Mairie* to donate blood to the national transfusion service. *Monsieur le Secrétaire* stood under the light, water dripping off his oilskins and spreading in a puddle at his feet.

"Aïe! Aïe! Aïe!" Félicie shrieked gleefully, pointing at the pool of water which had formed. *"Regardez bien, Monsieur! Alors, vous faites pipi!"*

Monsieur Tillet laughed, as he removed his crash helmet and scarf and then struggled out of his waterproof clothing, which he placed carefully on a hook behind the door. He was wearing long, green gumboots which, judging from the way he stepped out of them, looked as if they were two or three sizes too big for his feet. He placed them neatly together, heels to the wall beside the photocopier, and, putting on the pair of slippers, he ducked down to switch on the electric fire, which started to glow immediately.

For a few moments the three of them huddled around the fire to feel its welcome warmth.

"Voilà! Je suis presque prêt maintenant," he said, pushing his glasses straight. "There! I'm nearly ready now. It's on wet mornings like this that I often wish I could drive a car, but I never bothered to learn. So now, each time I go out, I have to put on all that lot to keep dry."

He laughed as he spoke, a warm smile creasing up his leathery face. He was a wiry man, about five feet tall. James thought that he might be sixty years old. He was introduced by Félicie, and they both sat down at the small table facing Monsieur Tillet's empty chair.

"Eh baah! Vous êtes Monsieur Wyllis!" he smiled again, pronouncing the name *'Willie'*. *"Bienvenue à Saint Juste! Bienvenue!"* He came round the table and they shook hands. *"Nous vous attendons depuis presqu'une année, Monsieur. Bienvenue! Je suis toujours à votre service!* We've been expecting you for almost a year. Welcome! I am always at your service! *Et bon! Un moment, s'il vous plaît!"*

He shuffled back towards his chair, picked up his keys from the table, and opened the large cupboard, into the top half of which files and thick, brown envelopes had been stacked neatly. The lower half revealed two inner doors, above which were four drawers. He searched through the keys and unlocked the two smaller compartments, from which he methodically extracted a blotting pad, a circular stand holding an array of official rubber stamps, and an ink pad. He placed these precisely on the table, and then opened one of the drawers. He removed three pencils, a rubber, a paper knife, and two ballpoint pens, one red and the other black. These were arranged meticulously, like a table-setting, on each side of the blotting pad. He then closed the small cupboard, locked them, and shut the large outer doors. He checked each item on the table, ensuring that they were all correctly in place.

It was not until he was entirely satisfied with his preparations that he scooped up his chair and sat down to face them.

"Bon!" he announced, with almost military precision. "I understand that you come from Zambia, like your friends from Kenya. It's very strange that four whites from Africa should come together in the very same week in Saint Juste, one of the very smallest communes in the Lot. You know this other couple of course, yes?"

"No. No, not at all," James replied. "This is the first I've heard of them."

"Ah! Très étrange!" remarked the Secretary, as if he believed that everyone in Africa should know everybody else, as is the case among the inhabitants of Saint Juste. "Very strange! Well, they are most charming, too. I met them yesterday when they came to present themselves to the Mayor."

"It is I," Félicie proclaimed pompously, "who will introduce *Monsieur* Wyllis and his wife to *Monsieur le Maire*. We have been invited for an *apéritif* in his home tomorrow afternoon. Now, please! We must get on immediately because I have to go to market."

Monsieur Tillet sighed, adjusted his glasses again, and checked the points of his pencils.

"Alors, on va commencer. I understand that you wish to have a *Certificat de Résidence* for the Customs."

"Non! Non! Non, Monsieur le Secrétaire. On m'a demandé un Certificat de Domicile," James replied. "No, what they want is a

Certificat de Domicile."

"Please dispense with the formalities, *Monsieur*. My name is Tillet, Gérard. I live in Pisenhaut at the end of the hamlet... In fact, it's the very last house. You can't miss it. There is a large blue cedar on the grass at the front... *Ah! Pardon! Je m'écarte du sujet!* I digress. Yes, they are the same: *de Domicile ou de Résidence*. They are the same form."

He returned to the cupboard, opened the doors again, and reached for one of the less thick, brown envelopes, from which he pulled out two forms.

"The Customs department," he announced with contempt, "is a den of lazy bureaucracy. *Les Douanes, con!* Just to be sure, I am going to issue you with *two* forms: one for you, and one for your wife."

He sat down, adjusted the position of his chair, and filled in the two forms. Three separate rubber stamps were studiously selected from the stand on the table. Each was turned upside down for verification, then breathed upon heavily, and finally pressed silently on to the inkpad. He shifted the position of the first form, took careful aim and, with three crashes which shook the room, each form was brought into official existence.

"Et voilà!" he announced with satisfaction. "There! Now all we need is two photocopies of each: one set for you, and the other for this office."

He shuffled back in his chair, stood up, and went over to the photocopier. He found the power lead, and plugged it into a socket which, James noticed, was hanging loosely and had not been firmly attached to the wall. Félicie was becoming visibly impatient.

"Almost there now," Monsieur Tillet smiled patiently. "It takes just a few minutes to warm up, that's all."

He put the first form into the machine, which whirred and delivered a blank piece of paper.

"Aaah! Merde!" he cursed softly. "Wrong way round again!" He laughed, as he corrected his mistake. "I'm always doing that!"

The second and third attempts produced the desired results, which he examined carefully before handing James the two originals and his set of copies.

"Je vous dois combien?" James asked, reaching for his purse. "How much do I owe you?"

"Rien du tout!" came the unexpected reply. "Nothing at all! It's all part of the service!"

The business over, Félicie leaped to her feet, quickly thanked Monsieur Tillet, and was running out of the office towards her car.

"Come, James," she shouted over her shoulder. "Come! I'm late already! I'll drop you at the house."

James thanked Gérard Tillet for his help. They shook hands and wished each other a pleasant day, expressing the hope that they would meet again soon as neighbours.

"The opening hours of this office are shown on the front door, *Monsieur.* Don't hesitate to come with any problem. Good luck with those bureaucrats, that lot in Customs. *À bientôt!* See you soon!" As James left the room, Monsieur Tillet was whistling happily to himself, laboriously starting to put each item on the table back into its appointed place in the cupboard.

*

Félicie raced up the drive at breakneck speed, the wheels of her car spinning and spewing gravel on to the grass verge. James thought that it might be a wise idea to put a speed limit sign beside one of the millstones, otherwise he could imagine that he would be for ever picking stones out of the grass to avoid damage to the mowers he intended to buy. Following this train of thought, he noticed for the first time how the grass had been allowed to grow. There were sodden leaves and branches everywhere, and the privet hedge had a distinctly unkempt took about it, all suggesting to him that there was going to be a great deal of outside work to do. The rain had eased slightly, but a cold, easterly wind was blowing down the valley and swirling in the porch.

He went into the house, checked his watch, and realized that Diana would be arriving soon. He was already behind his ambitious schedule for the day. He found some old newspaper, and fetched the kindling wood from the *prunerie.* He then lit the fire, which promptly belched smoke into the living-room, before it started to draw properly. By the time he had brought in the first two large logs, it was well alight. He was about to go down the miller's ladder to the cats when he heard Diana drive up to the porch. He put the two large logs on the fire and opened the door, just as she was struggling up the steps with a box of provisions.

As she stepped through the doorway, a gust of wind hit the porch and a cloud of ash and smoke from the fireplace was blown across the room.

"Good grief!" she cried. "Look at that! Quick, shut the door, before it does it again!"

"*Bonjour, chérie!*" he greeted her with a kiss. He took the box from her, and put it on the table. "*Tout va bien?*"

"*Bonjour.* I'm a bit late, I'm afraid. There were quite a lot of people in the supermarket, and it was all a bit confusing. I feel as if I've never seen so many goodies. It's almost obscene." She looked around the room. "Did you see that," she went on, "when that bloody wind got to the fireplace? Look at all this filthy mess! I expect the chimney needs a damn good clean, like everything else! *Merde!*"

It was the first time he had heard her use the word.

Her assessment was correct. It was difficult to see across the room, and the smoke was hanging in a pall over the clutter of tea-chests and cardboard boxes which filled the room.

"I think it probably only does that with an easterly wind like today," he said, trying to reassure her. "It's coming down—"

"To hell with the wind direction!" She ran her hand over the top of the sideboard. It was thick with ash and dust. "We'll have to do something about that as well."

"I'll put it on the list, my love."

"Have you dealt with the cats yet?"

"No, I thought I would get the fire going first. I was just going down to—"

She turned purposefully and disappeared down the steps. He checked that he had the forms for the freight agent, enough money, and a map. "I'm off to Toulouse, then!" he shouted down to her. "I'll be back as soon as I can after I've collected the jeep!"

"Goodbye, love!" she called up to him. "Drive carefully on these wet roads."

*

He drove well, but not as skilfully as he did before learning to fly a light aircraft. A plane has no gears, he mused. They just fly themselves. All you have to do is take off, read the map, try to understand the radio, and then land. He was thinking back to the blue skies of Zambia. He was going to miss his flying. With his Piper Cherokee he could be overhead Toulouse-Blagnac airport in twenty minutes. He looked at his watch, and allowed himself an hour for the journey. He found BAF International on the cargo-handling side of the airport, and handed the two certificates to the young manager who was having a noisy argument with a burly driver of a fork-lift truck.

"Je m'excuse, Monsieur. Mais je suis extrêmement pressé," he interrupted them. "I am very pressed for time. It would be good if you can arrange delivery for this afternoon, but not before four o'clock."

"En principe, oui, Monsieur," the agent replied. "In theory, yes."

"Merci beaucoup, Monsieur. Allez! Au revoir!"

He drove back on to the autoroute, leaving it at Montauban. He was looking forward to sitting behind the wheel of a jeep again. The N20 northwards brought him to the jeep dealership just thirty minutes before they were due to close for their lunch break of two hours.

He was shown into the office of a young, plump girl with a pretty face, who spoke excellent English with a strong American accent.

"Good morning, Mr Wyllis," she said brightly. "I am Fifine, the Customer Relations Manager here. Well! Well! You're all the way from Zambia! How about that now! We have your jeep. It's all ready, with temporary number plates. Jean-Louis, the foreman, will show you where everything is. But, before that, *Madame* Bizat particularly asked to meet you. She owns this enterprise. I'll take you on over right now, and while you chat with her, I'll go call the insurance agent. He'll be over in about ten minutes."

Fifine came out from behind her desk, and he followed her into an adjoining office. A tall, severe-looking woman in an expensive suit was talking volubly to a short, youngish man, who was wearing a blazer and tight-fitting trousers. She stopped abruptly when they entered the room. James was introduced as the English gentleman who had ordered a jeep from the ex-British colony of Northern Rhodesia.

"Bienvenue, Monsieur Wyllis," Madame Bizat purred at him. She came forward to shake hands, smoothing down her short skirt. She

was not beautiful. In fact, he thought that she had one of the least attractive faces he had ever seen in France. It was long, lantern-jawed, and her skin looked leathery, despite the ample make-up she was wearing. The one redeeming feature in her appearance was her legs, which were long with narrow, slim feet in classic style shoes. He estimated that the gold she was carrying on her neck and wrists was probably worth more than twice the value of the new car he was about to collect.

He looked towards Fifine, who was just about to leave the room with the young man in the blazer.

"Fifine," he said in English. "Try and get the insurance man here as quickly as possible. I'm very pushed for time." Fifine nodded and gave him a telling smile, the reason for which was lost on him.

"I am so pleased that we have at last met," Madame Bizat greeted him less formally. Her voice was now husky, and she continued to hold his hand. "I remember when your order arrived. It caused quite a stir. *Monsieur* Louisor, from Cahors, came all the way here to pass the order to me personally. I bought him a very good lunch as his sales commission. It's not every day that we sell a car to such a remote place as Zambia!"

Her dark brown eyes were penetrating, as she overtly looked him up and down.

"I think there may be some misunderstanding, *Madame*," he said, managing to free his hand from her grasp. "As of yesterday, my wife and I now live here permanently. We've bought a house the other side of Montcarmel. I shall not be going back to Africa, except perhaps for a holiday."

"Please call me Brigitte," she murmured softly. She moved a step closer to him, nervously twisting one of her heavy, gold bangles as she spoke. She flicked a wisp of jet black hair off her face, and he caught the waft of a strong perfume which he did not recognize.

"But how *romantic*! A holiday in Africa! Will you take me with you next time, *chéri*? No, of course you won't!" She was now pressing herself close to him, her eyes looking intently at him. She sighed, and he felt her pelvis as it moved imperceptibly closer against his thigh. "But you will, *chéri,* when we get to know each other better, perhaps even intimately, yes? I was thinking that you could take me out for lunch now... And then, afterwards... Well, we could go to my apartment. *Un tout petit bisou, hein?* A little cuddle, eh? I have some very interesting..."

She broke away suddenly, looking over his shoulder towards the door. Fifine was standing there. She must have witnessed the final scene. "Yes, Fifine?" Brigitte Bizat snapped.

"The insurance agent is here for *Monsieur* Wyllis," she replied, her manner betraying no visible opinion of her employer's behaviour.

"*Madame* Bizat, it was a pleasure to meet you," he said politely, concealing his relief. He said goodbye, and felt one of her long fingernails dig sensuously into the palm of his hand. "I really do have a lot to do today," he said lamely and followed Fifine out of the room. Fifine was giggling as she led him back to her office.

"I bet she tried to proposition you, right?" she laughed openly. "She does it with most men, and some women, too! She told me once that, if she could have sex for every car we sell, it wouldn't be enough. And we sell, on average, seventy a month! I suppose she can't help being a goddam nympho! But it's bad news at work, hey? Thank God, I quit in two weeks' time!"

"H'm, very strange, indeed!" he said. "Anyway, thanks for the rescue. I thought she was going to have me on the spot, perhaps even right there on her desk! What a bloody performance!" They were laughing when the insurance agent knocked and entered the office.

The agent was efficient and helpful. Yes, he would organize the *carte grise*, the *immatriculation* to obtain permanent registration plates, and he offered a significant discount on the annual premium.

"All I need from you, *Monsieur*," he explained confidently, "are the following documents: a domestic bill from *Électricité de France*; written proof of no motor insurance claims over the last five years; and, of course, a cheque for the annual premium. Then I can arrange everything for you. All you have to do is to collect and pay for your *vignette*, once I have obtained your *carte grise*, which I will mail to you."

"Why on earth do you need an electricity bill?" James enquired, recalling vaguely that Félicie had mentioned how useful it could be on occasions.

"The authorities," Fifine replied, "feel that it is a simple way of proving that a vehicle comes from a particular *département*. Your new car will be registered in the Lot. The number plates will terminate with the figures '46' for ease of identification. That's how people can recognize immediately whether the car is from Paris, or the Lot, or any other *département*. And it helps *les flics* to trace stolen vehicles. It's a different system here. In England, it is the car and its particular drivers who are insured; here, it is the car, regardless of the driver, just as long as he or she has a valid *Permis de Conduire,* a driving licence. There aren't too many '46' cars, for example, running around Paris."

James was having difficulty following the logic of her explanation, but he was not prepared to question it.

"I see," he said vaguely. "And what is a *vignette,* and where do I get it?"

"The *vignette* is the road tax for the car," the agent explained. "It's the small coloured sticker on the windscreen. You cannot get one without producing your *carte grise*, the registration document of the vehicle. You buy your first *vignette* from the *Trésor Public,* and you have to do that within fifteen days from today. Subsequent renewals can be bought each year at your nearest *Tabac.*"

"You mean to say," James laughed, "that the cigarette shop sells road fund licences?"

"Yes, and lots more besides," Fifine added. "For example, if you get done by the cops for, say, a parking offence, you pay your fine at the *Tabac* in your nearest town or village."

"I don't believe it!" he exclaimed. "What an absolutely splendid system."

James was looking worried, and Fifine asked him if there were any problems arising from their discussion so far.

"Well, I don't know if you can get round it, but I haven't brought an electricity bill with me. I don't know whether we have any in our name. We only moved in yesterday. I'll check with the previous owner of the house. Perhaps the account name was in fact changed last January, when we actually bought the place. Also, I'll have to write to my English insurers for proof of no claims. But that might take weeks! And I need my insurance now!"

"No problem," said the agent. "You're British! Your word is as good as *la livre anglaise,* the pound sterling, which is never devalued. I'll accept your verbal statement that you have five years with no claims, but when that letter arrives, I must have it on my files. However, ironical though it may seem to you, I cannot wait for the electricity bill. You will have to bring it here tomorrow. Give it to Fifine, and that will save you the trouble of having to find my office in the next town. So, *Monsieur,* if you will give me your cheque now, I will issue you with temporary cover for the next two weeks."

James gave the agent his cheque, and as soon as he received the legal minimum of papers he rose to leave.

"Well, I'll be back off home now," he said, looking at his watch, which told him that it was already nearly one o'clock. "Sorry if I delayed your lunch. I'll try to get back here about the same time tomorrow." Then he remembered. "Damn! The hire car from Toulouse! I've got to get it to their local office in Cahors, which is twelve kilometres away. Won't it be shut by now? Can anyone here help me? I can't drive two cars. And anyway, I don't know where to go."

"If you follow me in," Fifine volunteered, offering to drive the hire car to Cahors, "then you can bring me back here. I don't take lunch. I've been putting on so much weight in France that I'm now on a slimming regime."

"What about the hire car office being closed?" he asked.

"Oh, don't worry about that. We can leave the car in the railway station car park and give the keys to the man in the ticket office. I'll ring the car hire office this afternoon. They can pick up the car from there. It's quite normal."

Fifine's plan worked perfectly, rather better than James had envisaged. Within twenty minutes he was delivering her back to her office. "By the way, Fifine," he asked, "how is it that you speak such excellent English?"

"Oh! Didn't I tell you? My father is American. I was brought up there. That's where I'm going next month. I can't stand it here. It's far too provincial for me. I can't wait to get back to New York." She paused and then suddenly leaned over towards him, lightly brushing her lips on his cheek. "That was nice," she whispered. "Here, take my card. I've written on the back the ex-directory telephone number of my flat. If you ever want to come and see me on a lonely evening, give me a call. Didn't your Dad ever tell you that it's the girls with a bit of meat on them, who perform the best? Don't go near that six-foot, oversexed, half-Belgian Crazy Horse who owns this dump. *I* can show you a thing or two!"

She climbed out of the jeep and leaned in through the window. He noticed for the first time that only one of her eyes was blue, the other was brown. In a strange way he felt a strong attraction to her. A frisson of repressed lust was turning his mouth dry. How extraordinary! he thought, and started the engine.

"Why!" she exclaimed coyly. "You're just the nicest man to come out of the African bush this year! See you tomorrow, I hope!"

"Merde! You and Brigitte!" he laughed again. *"Qui se ressemble s'assemble!* Birds of a feather flock together! And I always thought a car was supposed to be an important sex symbol for men!"

She waved at him, smiled prettily again, and strolled away towards the offices, her overweight thighs putting a severe strain on her badly tailored uniform. Feeling his age, he tucked the card in the glove compartment and set off to return to the comparative normality of Bon Porteau.

Chapter Seventeen

In the past, whenever he had taken delivery of a new car, he had always made a brief effort to conserve it as a non-smoking zone. So it was on this occasion, as he drove back towards Bon Porteau. To strengthen his resolve he removed the ashtray and cigarette lighter, and placed them determinedly in the glove compartment. This time he reinforced his decision by tossing his packet of Gauloises on to the back seat, where they would be safely out of reach. Although he had eaten no breakfast and it was now lunchtime, he was not at all hungry. There was plenty of time to spare if everything went according to plan. The next major event would be the delivery of their heavy freight from Toulouse sometime after four o'clock. He drove the new jeep carefully, studying the switches and investigating the performance of the radio. The jeep handled well, its high technology diesel engine barely audible, unlike the grinding of the gears, which at first he found difficult to manage. He wondered if he should have bought the model with an automatic gearbox, and then recalled that the manufacturer did not offer that option.

He was passing the hotel where they had spent the night when he remembered that he had not paid the bill. He stopped and went in search of the proprietor, who assured him that Madame Wyllis had settled the account. She had paid *en espèces,* in cash, and he produced the hotel's copy of their bill for his verification.

"*Il ne faut pas payer deux fois, Monsieur!*" the hotelier said, laughing in a friendly way. "You don't have to pay twice! Even in France! You don't mind me asking, I hope, but have you come to live near here?"

"Yes," he replied. "We've just arrived from Africa, and we've bought Bon Porteau at Pisenhaut. We shall be living there permanently now."

"*O-là-là, là-là!*" the owner exclaimed. "I know now. You've bought *Madame* Gautier's house, the one with the beautiful *pigeonnier* which was shown on television last year. Lovely place! *Bonne chance, Monsieur... Et du courage!*"

James puzzled briefly over his reference to keeping one's chin up, but then gave it no more thought.

When he reached the turning to Saint Juste, he decided to investigate quickly Gérard Tillet's reference to the arrival of a couple from Kenya. He pulled over on to the verge to look at the map. He soon identified the lane, which follows the cliff top round the eastern side of Saint Juste. He thought that their house must be there. He found the lane with no difficulty, and after less than a quarter of a mile the tarmac ceased. The lane turned into a reasonably firm, stony drive, but its condition deteriorated rapidly as he followed it. When it entered an area of straggly wood, it became a muddy track, with deep potholes full of water. He was beginning to regret his decision, as the mud and water squelched and splashed under the new car. There was nowhere to turn round safely. He had no alternative but to persevere. Although he was driving cautiously, he misjudged the depth of one of the potholes, and thick, brown water sprayed up over the bonnet and on to the windscreen.

He stopped, cursing his folly and wondering whether to attempt to reverse all the way back. Then he caught sight of a small, wooden notice, nailed to a tree. He was just able to read the badly painted words: *'Attention aux Chevaux! Merci!'* He engaged four-wheel drive to follow the track down a slippery incline, at the end of which was a dilapidated barn and an attractive, cottage-style, stone house. Two large, open fields lay to either side of the track, but he saw no sign of the horses, to which the scruffy notice had referred. The jeep slithered to a halt in front of the barn, and a dog rushed out from the cover of a box hedge, where it had been sheltering from the rain. It wagged its tail energetically, barking and circling round him as he walked down to the house, trying to avoid the worst of the thick mud, which seemed to be everywhere.

He knew he had found the right house, because the dog was the same mongrel which they had seen the day before at Toulouse airport. He patted it cautiously on the head, encouraging it to calm down. The front door was opened before he reached it, and he recognized immediately the man who stood framed in the doorway. He was dressed in the same clothes which he had been wearing the previous day, except that two thick sweaters and a scarf wound round his neck concealed his bush shirt.

"You can't be a Frenchman," his voice boomed out. "Otherwise Satan would have bitten you by now!" He roared with laughter. "She's seen off three of them already!" he continued, laughing and holding out his hand. "Hullo! I'm Iain Drummond-Delaire. Come on in out of this shitty weather."

They went inside the house and, as Iain shut the door, he turned towards James and waved his arms vaguely.

"Sit down somewhere," he said, indicating a bed and a chair. "Let me get you something to drink." He paused, and then continued talking. "You were at the airport yesterday, weren't you? You've got that pretty, young wife with the cats, right? She *is* your wife, I suppose? Sorry, I didn't catch your name."

"I'm James Wyllis," he replied and, to avoid any possible future misrepresentation, he added, "And my wife is called Diana."

"Hell's bloody bells!" Iain growled. "Look at this bloody rain! My cellar's full up, you know."

"Oh? Where did you decide to buy your wine?"

"It's not full up with wine! No, I wish it was. It's swimming in bloody water! Dirty, filthy, cold, French rainwater! At least in Kenya the rain is mostly warm."

"Yes, we heard from Tillet, the Mayor's Secretary, that you're both from Kenya. He couldn't get over the strange fact that four whites have bowled up from out of Africa into his tiny commune. I understand it's one of the smallest communes in the Lot. It's a small world, isn't it?"

"Not small enough for me. What part are you from?"

"Zambia. I only spent about five years there, but Diana was there for some time before I met her."

"I have some friends down there, and in Zimbabwe too. I wonder when this place is going to warm up again. This is unbelievable for late September!"

He crossed the room to the fireplace and threw some wet wood on to the dismal fire, which was filling the room with smoke.

"Look, I'm sorry! I haven't got you a drink yet. What are you having? There's wine, gin, vodka, or beer? Like you, we're just moving in, so I can't offer you any ice, but it's so bloody cold we won't need any!"

"I once caught a waiter peeing on the blocks of ice outside the kitchens of a Nairobi hotel," James said absent-mindedly, accepting the offer of a drink. "It's rather put me off the stuff anyway."

"Ah! So you've been to Kenya, then? Which hotel was that?"

James told him, and added, "I've never had ice in a drink in any public place since then. And that applies to Africa and Europe."

"Bloody awful hotel, that one," Iain commented, going into the next room to find the gin and tonic which James had requested. "What on earth were you doing in a dump like that?"

"Funny you should say that. Diana felt that way about it as well. And I thought it was an up-market knocking shop full of European whores."

The room was dark, with small windows and a tiled floor. The sodden logs were smoking badly in the huge fireplace. There was a small occasional table, one chair, and an unmade, narrow, double bed, on to which had been thrown coats, towels, and a dog basket. Beside the bed, some partly unpacked suitcases were propped against the wall. A crude, unfinished staircase of bare wood took up one corner of the room. Clothes on wire hangers were hooked over the edge of some of the treads. The fire hissed, and James could hear the wind in the wide chimney as it wafted another cloud of smoke into the room. Iain returned with the drinks, which he placed on the table.

Before he sat down on the bed he put more wood on to the fire, giving it several kicks with his desert boot. A flame started to flicker and then died out. It was cold and very damp.

"Well, cheers then!" James said. "It's good to meet you. We're nearly neighbours."

"Cheers! So you know Kenya, too. Did you spend much time there?"

"No, no. Just a lot of superb holidays. In fact, once a year for three or four weeks over the last twenty years. I might have missed one or, perhaps, two years, but not more. It really is God's own country... Or it used to be."

"Which parts did you like the most?" Iain asked. "It's a big country, as you know."

"Well, that depends upon whether one is thinking in terms of the bush and game-viewing, or looking back at lazy, often boozy, times enjoying the sea and the sun. I suppose one of our game-viewing highlights has to be when we bounced our way across the lava rocks up to Lake Rudolf in the days before any road existed. On another occasion we came across a family of bongo in the Aberdares."

"Heavens!" Iain exclaimed. "You were lucky! There are people, who have lived all their lives out there and never seen a bongo. They're very rare indeed. Magnificent beasts, aren't they?"

"Yes," James nodded, sipping his drink, "and very shy."

James wondered briefly how old Iain might be, judging him to be in his late fifties.

"And what else?" Iain asked, inviting him to continue.

"Well then, I suppose I would have to single out a large herd of elephant at a waterhole in one of those extinct craters in Marsabit. We were on foot then, before the area was designated a Game Reserve. We came across a lovely, old Turkana, complete with his spear and *debi* still full of water. He was up a thorn tree where he had scrambled to escape an angry rhino, which was browsing nearby. We managed to rescue him! I'll never forget that old boy; he had the largest feet I've ever seen!" He paused briefly, and then continued, "Oh, yes! Then there's always the migration of the wildebeest crossing the Mara river. You know, Iain, I thought I would never have the privilege of such game-viewing again, but I believe Zambia is even better in that respect. The Luangwa Valley is just paradise... Except that there is not one rhino left — they've all been poached, every single one of them. That is one of the big differences between the two countries. The Zambian Game Department was absolutely useless, underfunded, and corrupt. It was a very sad state of affairs, unlike in Kenya, or Zimbabwe for that matter."

He lit another cigarette, a wistful look on his face, and finished his drink.

"Anyway," he continued, "after I managed to get my private pilot's licence, we used to fly regularly into a small bush strip up there. Wonderful place! Diana adored it."

"That's interesting to know. So you've got a PPL," Iain said. "So have my two sons, who are still in Kenya. Did you ever get to the camp on Lake Turkana?"

"Sadly, no. But we heard a lot about it from a very nice young man we met once on Lamu Island. Diana is still in regular contact by letter with the boy's lovely old grandmother, a most unforgettable character, who still lives out there. They are quite the most extraordinary family we've ever come across!"

"Tell me more," said Iain, leaning forward from the edge of the bed, a bemused look on his tanned face. "Go on, but let's first get another drink."

James checked the time, while Iain disappeared into the adjoining room. The mongrel, wagging her tail lazily, came into the room and lay down across his shoes. Iain returned, raised his glass and smiled pleasantly.

"*À la vôtre, mon vieux! Continuez!*" His accent reminded James of the proprietor of one of his favourite *auberges* in Normandy.

"It's quite a story, and every bit of it is true," James said, as he took his glass. "*Tchin, tchin!* Thanks. But I do hope I'm not boring you."

"No, no. Not yet."

But for the mischievous twinkle in Iain's eyes, James might have interpreted his last remark as a somewhat laconic put-down.

"Well, stop me if I do bore you. You know Lamu Island, of course?" Iain nodded. "Well, one evening at Peponi's, we were having a bit of a session, drinking what was called 'Rocket Fuel', a champagne-based concoction, almost guaranteed to floor most people. We were all quite high, including this young chap who was telling us about the beach safaris which he had been running for tourists. They would walk along the beach, looking for ambergris, and the dhows would either follow on behind, bringing up the food and drink, or go on ahead to pitch camp for the night. I remember he had a superb, large spaniel, which he had trained to sniff out this ambergris. He joked about the feasibility of training the tourists to do the same! Any pieces the dog found, he would store in a leather pouch which he always kept on his person. It's apparently quite valuable stuff, you know."

"Yes, I do know," Iain nodded. "The Arabs buy it for huge sums of money as a perfume ingredient."

James nodded, coughed as he stubbed out his cigarette, and wished that he had never smoked it.

"Well... Where was I? Oh, yes... Anyway, this young chap had given all that up, and he had come to Lamu to visit his grandmother. He was then hoping to get a job at a place which, if I remember correctly, was up somewhere near Rudolf, or rather Turkana as it's now called. It was some kind of a game camp, with an emphasis on bird-watching. At about eleven o'clock that evening, or maybe even later, this guy picks up two big, black, plastic sacks. They were filled with bread, melons, fruit, or whatever. He strips off his clothes and stuffs them into one of the sacks, tying it to the collar of his dog. The other sack he fixes around his own waist. He was quite drunk by then. We wondered what on earth was going on, but not for long. He explained to us, as coherently as he could in his condition, that he had to swim the channel to Manda Island and take the sacks to his grandmother, who lives there all alone,"

"Yes," Iain commented. "There's one hell of a tidal race between those two islands. If you're not careful, none but the strongest of swimmers can take that on."

Iain's drinks were strong, and James, having eaten neither breakfast nor lunch, found that he was having to concentrate on what he was saying.

"You can say that again!" James agreed before continuing his account. "We were all quite concerned. Anyway, off he went with his dog down the beach and into the sea. Fortunately, it was nearly full moon, and we watched him safely reach the other side. The dog was the first to arrive. We saw them both running along the beach towards the point. He must have been a really powerful swimmer, you know. We all went to bed quite relieved that night."

"And then what?" Iain asked, as if he was waiting for the next instalment of a thriller.

"Well, nothing much. The next day, we decided to take the speedboat across to Manda Island to investigate. You see, I had always believed Manda to be uninhabited, because it's all coral rock and therefore there's no fresh water there. We crossed the channel, and walked towards the point where we had seen the young man running the night before. We came across these two simple *shambas*, an arrangement of two small *makuti* huts just back a bit off the beach. And there we found this little, old lady and her grandson. He had a bit of a thick head, but he was otherwise none the worse for his midnight escapade. She was just incredible! We became very good friends. I remember the boy very well, a really nice, young man, with a lot of character. I would really like to meet him again one day, and find out what he's doing."

"Do you remember his name, by any chance?"

"No, I don't," James confessed, shaking his head. "I'm terrible with names. It was something like Simon, or Stephen... A name like that. But we know the old lady's name very well, because she and Diana still write to each other each month. In fact, there was a letter from her yesterday. It had been waiting for us to arrive here. She's called Nellie."

Iain fell back, laughing on the bed. He struggled to sit up again, spilling some of his drink into the dog basket, a broad grin on his face.

"You know, James," Iain boomed. "That's a most extraordinary story and an even more curious coincidence. You've just been telling me about one of my sons and my mother-in-law! Bloody good!"

They both started laughing and their laughter echoed around the cliff tops of Saint Juste for a long time, while they had another drink.

"How incredible!" Iain fought to get the words out, as he held the stitch in his side. "We don't know each other from Adam! We both come from Africa, and we pop up here on the same day in Saint Juste, one of the smallest communes in the Lot! You know my mother-in-law, who lives in the Indian Ocean on a remote island nobody has ever heard of before! And you've met Stewart, one of my sons! That last time you saw him, he was coming to help me build my camp on that island on Turkana which I've just left! That's the job he was after! And just guess who is coming here next week to help me rebuild this place! Bloody fantastic!"

"Stewart! That's right! His name was Stewart Drummond-Delaire. It's a very unusual name."

"That's because I'm half-French, from Normandy, on my mother's side of the family."

"Just you wait till I tell Diana about this!" James said, shaking his head in disbelief. "She's never going to believe it!"

James checked the time again and, to his horror, he realized that he had spent more than an hour with Iain.

"*Merde!* Look at the time!" he announced. "I really must get back. We haven't even started to unpack yet."

They started walking up towards where James had parked the jeep.

"Where's your wife, then?" James enquired.

"She's still in Kenya. We've moved apart, you could say. Laetizia, my girl friend, has had to go back to Poland to get her passport, visa, or whatever, organized. She'll be back, I expect, in a day or two."

"Well, Iain. I'm sure we'll all be seeing each other quite often. If Diana can manage it in all our chaos, you must come for a meal... Or at least a drink."

He explained how to get to Bon Porteau and, after exchanging telephone numbers, he drove away up the slippery track. Iain was still holding his side as he watched the jeep disappear into the straggly woods at the top of the incline.

"Well, I'll be buggered!" he snorted. "*Quelle connerie!* How crazy!" He waved briefly and walked back into his smoke-filled cottage.

*

Driving back up the waterlogged track, James was still feeling the unreality of his meeting with Iain. However, his detached frame of mind was short-lived. Everywhere he looked, as he went up the drive to Bon Porteau, he could see that there was work to do and plenty of it. He entered the house, and noticed immediately that the fire was almost out. He collected some more logs and spent a few minutes reviving it. He could not hear Diana anywhere in the house.

"I'm back, my love!" he shouted down the steps. "Is all well here?"

She came up the miller's ladder looking harassed and worried, and fell into his arms. She held him tightly, pressing her face into the side of his neck, and then burst into uncontrollable tears.

"Hey! Darling! What's up? What's the matter?" he asked gently.

"I'm sorry, my love," she sobbed. "You know I'm not a wet. But I just can't get anything to work. Neither of the two cookers Félicie has left us work properly. The bloody things are either red hot, or else they're practically cold. I made you some nice soup for lunch. I turned my back for two seconds and the whole lot boiled over, leaving a burnt-out saucepan. I've just spent half-an-hour trying to clean it all up..."

Tears were running down her cheeks. Her whole body was trembling, and he was surprised at the strength with which she was holding on to him.

He was about to say something to try to console her, when she continued a little incoherently.

"The damned dishwasher doesn't work either. It's just a useless piece of junk! Félicie has swindled us! Her old fridge is just as bad. It leaks like a sieve. It'll never work properly — the door won't close tight. The cats have been driving me crazy, trying to get out all the time. Jacob, in particular, is being a very naughty boy. He really ought to know by now that he's not allowed out at all during the first week in a new place. And then..." She made a wailing sound, and looked up at him, her eyes full of tears. "And then... And then, I looked at my watch, and saw that it was after two and you hadn't come back... And I thought you must have had an accident, otherwise you would have rung me... And I can't speak French properly, and how was I going to deal with the police? Then the phone went, and I didn't want to answer it. I was frightened, and there's this bloody Frenchman gibbering at me down the phone, and I was thinking what on earth am I going to do in this cold, wet dump all by myself, and... And... Oh! My darling! I'm just missing my beloved Africa so very, very much! I feel just awful, and useless, and unhappy... My darling, I'm sorry! Thank God you're safe! And I really do love you!"

"I'm here now, my love. Calm down. Here, stop crying, and come and sit down."

He dabbed her eyes with his handkerchief and kissed her, holding her close to him. Gradually she stopped shaking, and her body quivered as she let out a long, deep sigh.

"Don't worry about all the equipment. If it's junk, we'll replace it. It doesn't matter. But I'm sorry you're feeling homesick for Zambia. Here, have you had a drink?" She shook her head. "I'll get you one now. And stop trying to do too much too quickly. We've got all the time in the world to get straight."

He gave her a squeeze, went over to the sideboard, and mixed a strong gin and tonic.

"Voila! Try this, my love. Cheer up now! It's not all bad. We've got this far in one piece, although I'm not quite sure how. Come on, darling. Give me one of your big, sexy smiles!"

She wiped her eyes, managing a smile as she sighed again and sipped her drink.

"What do you want for lunch?" she asked. "I'll get it for you when I've finished this."

"Nothing, my love. And I've decided that we're going out for supper tonight, and tomorrow night, and every night if needs be. So to hell with the bloody cookers! We'll chuck them into Félicie's *folie!* They'll help to fill up the hole. *Et voilà!"*

"Did you manage to get the new jeep?" she asked.

"Yes. No problems, and the people at Toulouse hope to be able to deliver our freight sometime after four this afternoon. That's probably who was trying to phone us. I'll get them to put it all in the barn, where it can stay until we're ready to unpack it. That is, if I can ever get the tops off those crates. Did you see the size of those Zambian nails? And the way they banged them in!"

She laughed, and picked up Fosbury to cuddle him. Jacob rubbed himself hard up against her legs, and let out a long, loud Burmese wail.

*

He noticed that Diana had found the electric kettle, and decided to make himself some tea. It tasted very strange, and he was about to throw it away when he heard the sound of a car in the drive. He looked out of the window to see Félicie arrive. She came bustling into the house, carrying a cardboard box, which she almost dropped on to the table.

"Bonjour à tous!" she greeted them with a chuckle. *"Tout va bien, hein?* Is everything all right? I've brought you my house-warming presents!" She pointed at the box on the table, indicating that Diana should open it. "I see you've been busy, James," she said, while Diana examined the box on the table. "You've bought a second-hand car already! *Quelle énergie!* Is he always in such a hurry?"

"No! No! It's a *new* car," he replied. "Or rather, it *was* new this morning. It's just got a bit of mud on it, that's all."

Diana looked out of the window and peered in horror at the mud-coated jeep.

"Good grief! It looks as if it's been raced in a cross-country rally!" she exclaimed. "Are you sure it's new? What colour is it supposed to be? It looks a bit of a wreck to me! Where on earth have you been in it?"

"I haven't had a chance to tell you yet. It just needs a good hose on it."

Lying on top of the box, wrapped in brown paper, were four large, old, framed photographs of the original house at Bon Porteau. They had been taken before the addition of the bedrooms and the roof *terrasse*.

"Oh, how lovely, Félicie!" Diana cried out with delight. "They're beautiful! What a really nice thought! We'll have to find somewhere very special to hang them."

Tucked into the bottom of the box were a bottle of *Guyot-Chopin* champagne and a sample of Félicie's own homemade *pruneaux*.

"*The pruneaux* is five years old," she proclaimed proudly, "and is ready to drink as a *digestif*. Now I must rush on, because I'm very late. Don't forget that we are going to the Mayor's house for an *apéritif* tomorrow afternoon. And then, I suggest you come to my apartment for dinner afterwards."

James just managed to stop her as she was half walking, half running for the door.

"Félicie?" he asked. "Have any electricity bills arrived in our name since January? I need one for the car's *immatriculation*. The car insurance agent is demanding one."

"Yes," she nodded. "I have all your bills in the car with me, but I can't stop to explain them today. I'll give them to you now, and then we'll go through them all tomorrow afternoon. I'll come here at about four. I'm sure there are several electricity bills among them."

"The other quick question," he said, as Félicie was opening the door to leave, "is about the water. Is it really safe to drink? It's very calcified, and it tastes awful, particularly in tea. It ruins it completely! And it's left a thick scum all over the inside of our kettle."

"Oh, it's perfectly safe," she replied. "But that reminds me. If you haven't switched taps, then you're still on the town water. You must change over to the *source du château*. And I've asked the water company to come and read their meter today, and Tillet will come some time during the week to do the same with the meter for the *château source*. Until that is done, I'm still paying for your water."

"*Why* do we need an electricity bill?" Diana asked, as Félicie drove away at high speed.

He felt tired as he tried to explain the system to her.

*

It was six o'clock when the representative of the water company arrived in a small van. After he had prised open the heavy manhole cover with a small spade, he stooped to read the meter. Before he replaced the cover, he asked James whether he understood the functions of the various taps.

"*Mais oui, Monsieur,*" James replied. "There's no problem with the taps. It's your bloody water that is the problem! It's awful! *Merde!* I don't know how you have the nerve to sell it like that! Are you sure it's safe to drink? Come and have a look at my kettle — the inside is coated with scum! And that's after less than one day!"

James showed him the kettle and pointed out the film of *calcaire* which had already started to form on the element. The Frenchman was not impressed, viewing *ce truc électrique* with distaste and suspicion.

"*Ouais! Ça c'est tout à fait normal,*" he said with a disinterested shrug. "That's quite normal. This water is very good for you. Why, you only have to look at how healthy everyone is around these parts. All you have to do is to decalcify it and your other equipment regularly."

"What do you mean by regularly?"

"*Eh baah, bien! Disons tous les quinze jours, M'sieur,*" he answered gruffly. "Oh, let's say every fortnight,"

"But that's intolerable! We've just come from Africa. This water is worse than in Lusaka, except that I suppose it's not riddled with cholera! I think it's disgraceful! We shall use our *château source* in future, which will save you the trouble of reading our meter too often."

The water engineer retreated to his van, muttering about the ignorance and bad temper of all Englishmen, particularly those who are stupid enough to have lived in Africa.

"Decalcify every fortnight!" James grumbled. "What bloody nonsense!"

"Well, I thought you were being really quite unkind to that little man," Diana said. "He was only doing his job and trying to help. Anyway, come on. We need to make up a bed before we go out to supper." He followed her down the miller's ladder, ducking low through all the doorways.

"You're right," he said, when they reached the bedroom.

"Right about what?"

"He *was* a little man, wasn't he? You must feel quite strange being here."

"What on earth are you getting at?"

"Well, I mean... Well, for the first time in your life you tower above most of the natives!"

Chapter Eighteen

It was pitch dark. With the tall, double shutters closed and Félicie's old, heavy velvet curtains drawn tightly across the French windows, no daylight could penetrate the bedroom. He had no idea of the time, nor what had disturbed his sleep. He then realized that Diana, a light sleeper was sitting up in bed. She was shaking him into full consciousness.

"James, there's some kind of a lorry trying to get up the corner of the drive"

He turned the light on, and saw that the time was nine-thirty.

"Merde!" he cursed, opening one of the windows and its shutters. "Look at the time!"

Looking through the rain across to the left towards the walnut trees, he could see a large vehicle. It appeared to be stuck on the steep corner of the drive, its wheels spinning uselessly in the wet gravel. Their nine large crates were roped on to the long flatbed of the truck. As its engine raced, he could see the juddering wheels shaking their precious cargo.

He dressed hurriedly and sprinted over to the vehicle, waving his arms at the driver, who was in the process of making a further determined, but futile, attempt to navigate the steep gradient. The driver either did not see him or was choosing to ignore him. All he achieved was to gouge out two deeper ruts in the gravel, the wheels churning up the hard core base of the drive. James could think of only one way to prevent further damage. Taking his life in his hands, he stood in front of the huge cab with his arms up and hands outstretched, hoping that his gesture to halt proceedings would be understood and implemented. The driver banged his fist on the steering wheel, switched off the engine, and climbed out of his cab.

"Bonjour, Monsieur," James greeted him, trying to show no concern over the damage. "I think you've got a problem there."

"Vous charriez, M'sieu! Et votre chemin est un vrai bordel!" the driver growled at him. "You've got to be joking. And your track's a real mess!"

"Leave it there for the moment," James suggested, waving at the huge machine. "I'll show you first where all that lot has got to go. Then we'll go inside, have a cup of coffee or something, and make a plan." He tried to see inside the cab, but it was too high. "And bring your *copain* with you."

"There is no mate. Two years ago the bloody union made a daft one-man-in-the-cab agreement with sodding management. So I have to bust my gut out on my own."

Although the driver was short in height, he was quite fat and had powerful arms. Looking at the man's paunch, James thought that there was plenty of gut to bust there.

He led the Frenchman up to the barn, opened the wide double doors, and they went inside.

"I want it all in here, out of the rain. But at the moment, I don't know how you're going to do it. Some of those boxes weigh nearly five hundred kilos, you know."

"Merde! C'est de la connerie!" the driver swore, as he followed him down to the house through the icy rain, which looked as if it might change to sleet at any moment.

"Have something to warm yourself up," James offered the driver, who accepted a glass of *Calvados*, swallowing it in one gulp.

"Ce foutu temps est déprimant! Ce n'est pas normal!" he said. "This bloody weather is depressing. It's not normal. I don't think I can make that bend. I'll have to reverse back to the bottom. The best I can suggest is to stack your crates under those large trees, and you'll just have to unpack there, if and when the bloody weather gets a bit better."

"Now it's you who are joking," James said firmly. "Those boxes are definitely not staying out in this rain. No way! The problem is that the track is too steep, and your load is far too heavy. We can't change the gradient of the drive, but we can lighten your load. You've got that little crane thing on the back of your cab. We can swing six of the nine crates over the side and put them temporarily on the grass. Then you take what's left on board up to the barn, and come back for the next load. I should think three, maybe four trips might do it. It's worth a try, anyway. *Je vous donnerai un coup de main.* I'll give you a hand."

The Frenchman looked doubtful. He accepted another tot of

Calvados, and then lumbered to his feet.

"Allez!" he said. "Let's go! Before the bloody truck gets washed away!" This time, loaded with three of the lightest crates, he had little difficulty with the corner of the drive. It was the slippery, wet grass leading up to the barn, which was the problem. Eventually, with the aid of a crowbar and a two-pronged, lifting device designed for use on the smooth floor of a warehouse, they managed to lever and manhandle the boxes one by one into the barn. At the end of two hours, the task was finished, leaving them both exhausted and soaked with sweat and rain.

"Merde!" the driver grinned. "I never thought we would make it!"

"That," said James, giving him a slap on the back, "is what the bishop is supposed to have said to the actress!"

The attempted joke went over the Frenchman's head.

The two men stood in the barn and surveyed the collection of crates which had survived, thus far, a journey of several thousand miles and the Customs authorities of both Zambia and France, all within a period of less than a week. James could hardly believe his eyes.

"You might find that we've just done the easiest bit," the driver panted. "By the look of some of those nails, it's not going to be too much fun opening that lot. What on earth have you got in them?"

"Oh, just junk from Africa," he joked, making light of his aching back. "There's a life-size, wooden carving of a hippopotamus in that one, and I'm hoping that two of our African staff are in box number seven. Come to think of it, we should have opened that one first! They would have had no difficulty carrying the boxes up here!" He stopped his bantering, feeling the cold rain reach his skin.

"Have you got any dry clothes?" The Frenchman shook his head. "Come on, then. We'll see what we can do for you, otherwise you're going to catch pneumonia. By the way, what's your name?"

"Je m'appelle Jean-Pierre."

They went together round the side of the house and entered the cellar, which had the appearance of a disorganized, second-hand auction room. There were boxes and tea-chests everywhere. The oil-fired boiler was booming away in the next room, which was also filled with boxes and suitcases.

186

"Wait here a minute, Jean-Pierre," he said. "Diana!" he shouted into the passage. "Get us a towel and any old blanket, darling. Otherwise there's going to be a little, overweight Frenchman running naked round the house!" He turned back to be driver, who was beginning to look perplexed.

"You'll never get into any of my clothes," he explained. "So, give me a hand with lifting this drying machine, and we'll plug it in over there." The driver picked up the tumble-drier by himself, and carefully positioned it in a corner of the cellar. Diana appeared, carrying a towel and a blanket. Nobody spoke for a few seconds — it was as if each was waiting for one of the others to offer an explanation for this bizarre intrusion.

It was Diana who broke the short, uncomfortable silence. She shook the Frenchman's hand and then swung round to face James.

"What's going on here?" she asked, looking surprised and amused.

"This is Jean-Pierre. He's soaking wet," he said, as if that was sufficient information.

"I can see that! So are you, my love!"

"We're going to put all his wet clothes into the tumble-drier and then he's going to take a shower. By the time he is out, his stuff will be dry, won't it?"

"I doubt it," she replied, smiling at the small, fat man. "Maybe in an hour's time."

Jean-Pierre took his shower, emerging with the towel and blanket wrapped around him. His hair was wet and tousled. He was beaming, as if he had just been saved from a shipwreck.

"Ça va mieux maintenant?" James asked him. "Feeling better now?"

"Eh baah, ouais! Impeccable, M'sieu!" he replied, as he reached across the table for the bottle of *Calvados*.

When the Frenchman finally left, his clothes adequately dry, Diana looked up at James, a question forming on her lips.

"What's the matter, love?" he asked.

"The matter is that that's the third strange man who has taken a shower in our bathroom, and I haven't even had one yet! I'm beginning to wonder how much longer this is going to continue! Anyway, I'm not going to use that dreadful, plastic, shower curtain. It reminds me too much of Janet Leigh in the "Psycho" murder scene!"

"We'll get a proper cubicle put in there. I'll stick it on the list."

"I suggest you stick those wet clothes somewhere and have a shower yourself, before the whole of France uses up all our hot water!"

*

As James showered, he started to make a mental list of all the things he had to do. New kitchen... New utility... Shower cubicle (as the slimy, plastic curtain brushed against his back)... Fix fireplace... Planning permission to build on a new bathroom... Finish unpacking stuff from England... Hang pictures before I tread on them... Power drill and wall plugs... Break open crates in barn... Fill up the wine racks with good Cahors wine... List all equipment to be bought: radio which will pick up BBC, refrigerator, deep-freezer, washing machine... Garden machinery, if this weather ever improves: tractor mower for lawns, probably a small trailer, hover mower for banks, some kind of brush-cutter for jungle-bashing the brambles and nettles, safety glasses, jerrycans, oil, chain saw... More logs for fire... Ladder...

He resolved to list in writing as many of these items as he could remember, otherwise priorities would not be met, with a severe risk that something important would be overlooked or, perhaps, even forgotten. It had happened before on several occasions. Fortunately, Diana would also have her list.

"Don't you have to take that electricity bill to the garage today?" she asked, putting her head round the door of the bathroom, as he stepped out of the shower.

"*Merde!* Thanks for reminding me. I had completely forgotten that! I'll go and do it now."

"And don't forget that Félicie is coming at four to explain bills. We may as well confront her with her junk equipment which doesn't work properly, and at the same time deal with pricing the other things, like the curtains and lights, which she's left behind for us."

He dressed quickly and went upstairs to find a cup of coffee and a notepad.

"Right," he said, sounding as if he was now about to do some serious long-term planning. "You can help me with two things. Start making your own list of things we need to do, and—"

"I've already done that. It's about a page long, I'm afraid."

"And have a think about anything really urgent you want me to get out of the Zambian crates. I don't really want to start opening all of them yet, unless it's something urgent."

"Since you mention it, there are two things I want. I must have my English measuring jug. I can't fathom out these litres and grams with the jug Félicie has left here. And we took most of our linen to Africa, so that had better come down to the house at the same time, although I don't know where I'm going to put it. There's no linen or airing cupboard in the house.

"Put it on the list then, darling."

*

He arrived at the garage to find that Fifine was the only person on the premises. She was in her office reading a book which, she explained, claimed that meditation was an essential route to reducing the stress of modern life. He noticed that the author had an Indian name and that he had been educated at Bombay University.

"Still slimming, then?" he asked.

"Yes," she replied, coming forward to greet him. She stood for a moment in front of him and then, in one quick movement, she kissed him. Her lips were moist and sensuous. She took his hand, pressing it on the outside of her thigh.

"Yes. Feel me there. I have to lose twelve kilos in the next three weeks — particularly here, off my hips and thighs. And I was waiting for you, hoping you would come while everyone else is at lunch, so that we could be alone."

Her blonde hair was tied back in a pony-tail, which reached down to the collar of her maroon blazer.

"Your name is James, isn't it? It's a nice name, a royal name. I've never had a lover called James. I was told by a friend that a strong, vigorous massage would help me. It's also supposed to be a good way to turn on a real man. *Tu ne veux pas venir voir mes estampes japonaises?* Don't you want to come and see my etchings? We could go now, if you like." He laughed, gave her a light kiss on her cheek, and placed the electricity bill on her desk.

"Thanks for the offer, little one," he said kindly. "I really mean it, but the answer is no. And I really mean that as well!"

"Well," she smiled cheerfully, "if you don't ask, you don't get. Right?"

"True," he said seriously, and made good his escape.

*

On his way to the outskirts of the town, he had noticed a large store which looked like a Do-it-Yourself emporium, and he parked outside it. The notice on the door announced that it was open every day of the week, including lunchtime. He never enjoyed shopping at the best of times, and he was bewildered by the variety of power tools from which he had to make a choice. After being used to coping with the shortages of Zambia, this was to be one of the most difficult elements in the cultural shock to both his and Diana's systems during their first few months in Europe. Eventually he bought a powerful, Bosch electric drill and a box of wallplugs in assorted sizes. The store was promoting garden hoses as a special offer, their price reduced by two-thirds. Despite the continuing rain, he decided to take full advantage of the bargain, and purchased three of them, each twenty-five metres long. Thinking of the crates in the barn, he also found a good, strong jemmy which, he hoped, would help him to draw the nails out of the boxes. He was not looking forward to tackling that task, wondering at the same time how long all the unpacking would take.

While he had been away from the house, Diana had been very active, making good progress with the task of unpacking tea-chests, cleaning, and putting things away. Seventeen empty tea-chests were out in the porch.

"I've cleaned all the pictures which were in store, and stacked some of them in there," she announced, indicating the room which they had decided would become their future drawing-room. "I've also sorted out those, which we'll have in the passage and bedrooms, and they are downstairs. If we could put them up, then they'll be out of the way."

"Great minds think alike," he said, putting the electric drill on the table. "But don't forget the ones in the crates, otherwise we won't know exactly where to hang all of them."

"And I've found the old stereo system. If you could connect it up, then at least I can have some music to cheer me up. It would be nice if you could bring my tapes down from the barn. According to the inventory, they should be in the same box as the books."

"I've no idea whether that old thing still works, but I'll give it a go."

*

He took the inventory, checked which crates he would have to open, and made his way up to the barn. To his dismay, in order to recover the house linen, Diana's tape cassettes of music, the pictures, and the measuring jug, he found that he would have to open four different boxes. As he set to work with the jemmy and a heavy hammer, he recalled the scene in Nalikwanda Road, when the crew of twelve Zambians arrived to build the crates and pack their air freight. Many items had been sold, including all their electrical appliances. Others had been given away, particularly to Fackson and Phebian, their house steward and gardener. It was hard to believe that it had all taken place during the previous week several thousand miles away.

He remembered how they had been both surprised and disturbed by the remaining mass of possessions, which they had accumulated over the duration of their stay abroad. They lay, sorted into heaps, on the floor of the large, L-shaped room under the watchful eyes of their staff — china, glass, ornaments, pictures, saucepans and cutlery, linen, books and photograph albums, the journals which Diana had written almost every day, Persian rugs, woodcarvings, a collection of earthenware pots of different tribal designs, baskets and trays in wickerwork, a small dining table, and a sideboard.

The packers and carpenters arrived in a pantechnicon, which was far too big to get in through the gate. He had visions of a crowd of people quickly gathering in the road, among whom would be some who were genuinely curious, but most would be looking for handouts and, no doubt, there would be some thieves.

"You can't leave your van out in the street," he told the supervisor. "I don't want to let half of Lusaka know that we're moving out. You'll have to take out the gate and remove a section of the fence, so that you can get it in here beside the house." The task of demolishing the gate and two panels of dry grass fencing caused great amusement and it was noisily completed, the men laughing and joking among themselves.

"Careful!" James warned them. "It's got to be put back before you leave."

The driver edged the huge truck tentatively into the drive, trying to heed at least six different sets of loud, conflicting instructions. On his first attempt, he managed to wedge the vehicle's fixed canopy under a large, overhanging branch of a flame tree. He reversed gently to try again, this time running over the remains of the gate, which had been thrown down in the drive. At the fourth attempt, with much frenzied gear-changing and shunting backwards and forwards, he at last positioned the rear of the large van near the house. An excessive quantity of packaging materials and wood were unloaded on to the lawn, and immediately the three carpenters started sawing the tough *mukwa* wood into planks of different sizes.

As soon as the unloading was completed, the driver started his engine and the removal van rolled slowly towards where the gate had been. It now lay in a twisted mess in the middle of the driveway, blocking the exit.

"And where's he off to now?" James asked the supervisor

"Ah, *Bwana*. There is no diesel in Lusaka. The tank, it is near to empty. The driver has heard from his brothers that there is some, maybe little bitty, diesel in Kabwe, so he go there now-now to join the queue, but very quickly."

It was perfectly true that there was no fuel in the capital. This was part of the normal pattern of life in a country which was lurching from one distribution crisis to the next. However, it was also a well-known trick, frequently employed if circumstances were favourable. Away from the control of the depot manager, either the vehicle would be hired out privately for the day to earn the crew more money or, worse still as far as James was concerned, a number of items could already have been smuggled out of the house and into the truck, ready to be sold in any one of the many African markets in the vicinity of the city.

James stopped the driver and climbed up into the cab to check the fuel gauge. The needle was on empty.

"The gauge doesn't work?" he asked the driver.

"Ah, yes *Bwana*. It is boogard."

"Then how do you know you are low on fuel?"

"I take this little bitty stick to the fuel tank, *Bwana*," the driver replied seriously. "If it becomes a little wet, then I have no problem, *Bwana*." The man gave a broad smile. "But if it might come out quite a lot dry, then I know it is as empty as a bottle of *chibuku*." He roared with laughter at his reference to the local, home-brewed beer, which they drank copiously at every available opportunity.

"And is it dry now?"

"Yes, *Bwana*. It is now very dry indeed. It is so dry, it is almost like my mouth."

James checked the inside of the truck and satisfied himself that it too was empty.

"But Kabwe is sixty miles away!" James reminded the supervisor. "The driver hasn't got enough fuel to get there, has he? And even then, there's no guarantee that he will find fuel. The rumour might be untrue, or the queue might be several miles long. He could be there all day and night!"

"Don't worry, *Bwana*. One of his many brothers on the road will give him assistance if he runs out of fuel. But this man, he is very clever. He will find a full tank of diesel in just three, or maybe even a little five hours."

The packers were standing in a group watching the carpenters at work. They were making good-natured fun of one of them, telling him that he was not good enough to be a skilled carpenter.

"This one, *Bwana*," said the tallest man in the group, "he use five nails and break all of them before he get even one in straight!"

"And that one," retaliated the carpenter, laughing and pointing his saw at the big man, "you watch him good, *Bwana*! He can't pack a pillow without busting it into feathers. Don't give him anything to pack. Go home, Godfrey, and play with your big titty, ugly girlfriend you have made with child. You will just be in the way of all us experts."

They all started laughing joyously, falling down and rolling about together on the lawn.

The foreman shouted at them, and they all trooped obediently into the house. This was always an awkward moment for Diana, watching them survey the possessions, which represented to them untold wealth. There was no envy written on their faces; nor did they covet the trappings of another civilization. It was more a look of childlike awe, disbelief that anyone could wish for so much, let alone make the effort to collect it all together. If they stole anything, the reason would be one of necessity — the goods would be sold to buy food for their large, extended families. For most of them, all they possessed in the world were the clothes they were wearing beneath the ill-fitting overalls issued by their company.

With uncanny skill, the supervisor estimated the number and sizes of the boxes which would be required, delivering his instructions in a deep voice to the carpenters. The packers worked diligently in pairs. James remembered particularly the man called Godfrey who, despite his huge hands and immense strength, had wrapped gently, almost lovingly, the collection of earthenware pots.

"This one, Mummy," he said to Diana, "is from my tribe. I am a Lovale."

"And that big one is Tonga," said his companion.

The other packers stopped working and approached to see if examples of work from their tribes were represented in the collection.

"But you have no Bemba pots, my Mummy," one of the group protested. "They are the most strong and the very best of all."

"If you are a Bemba," joked another, "then why are you not a Prime Minister in a Mercedes, instead of just a stupid packer?"

Great roars of laughter filled the room, gradually dying down as they resumed their appointed tasks.

The carpenters finished making the boxes, and one by one they were carried into the house to be packed, while the foreman noted the contents of each and started to create an inventory. The general principle appeared to be to fill each box, so that its contents, whether fragile or not, protruded some two inches above the lip of each box.

Then, more packing material and a plastic lining would be forced in as a supplementary top layer, before the lid was placed in position. At this point, two, and sometimes three, men would stand on the lid, their combined weight forcing it down, so that the carpenters could hammer home the six-inch nails which they had brought for this purpose. When the lid was fixed to the box containing the pottery, James gritted his teeth, imagining that none could possibly survive such rough treatment. When he queried their methodology, the supervisor explained that nothing would break in transit, provided that the contents were packed so tightly that they could not move. James refrained from commenting that it was not the transit phase which concerned him, fully convinced that he was about to export nothing more than a load of shards.

When the final box was being filled, they found that a significant amount of empty space was left. The supervisor asked Diana if there were any other items which might be used to fill it.

"I don't think we could fit Fackson in there!" quipped Diana, bringing all further work to a standstill while guffaws of noisy laughter filled the room. James considered bringing some of his shoes, but then decided against the idea. He would, after all, have to be able to wear them in Europe and he did not want them to suffer the same crushing fate as the pottery.

"Maybe," Diana suggested, "we could fit Exhilda in there."

She pointed to the life-size bust of a naked woman, beautifully carved and polished, now standing forlornly in the corner of the room. They had decided reluctantly to leave her behind on account of her weight. The entire team of packers gathered to admire her shining, black face and proud, young breasts. It was Godfrey who stooped to pick her up gently.

"You must not leave her behind, my Mummy," he said, looking very seriously at Diana. "She is a beautiful Lovale bride from Zambezi. I am going to pack her for you."

Godfrey checked the size of the remaining space in the box and then wrapped the figure, first with shredded packaging material, then with several layers of thick, brown paper, and finally taped up the package. He worked as carefully as if he was handling a piece of finest porcelain. For good measure, a bath towel was removed from the box of linen to provide a fourth layer of protection. Reverently he placed the carving in the box. It fitted the space perfectly.

"There, my Princess," he said softly. "You will now be very rich and famous in a land far away. Everyone will love and honour your great beauty, and you will be happy for ever and ever." He looked up; there were tears in his eyes as he quietly left the room, only to return with a small, plastic bag. "You will need food for your journey, my little one," he whispered, as he leaned over the box. "Here is my *nshima. Pitani bwino-bwino!* Here's my food. Go now, and remain well!" He then picked up the lid, collected a hammer and nails from one of the carpenters, and carefully sealed the box. Nobody spoke, until he handed the hammer back to the carpenter.

"Chabwino! Well done, Godfrey," Diana said quietly, shaking his hand.

"Now you will submit triplicate for job as bloody carpenter!" the Bemba packer shouted with a broad grin.

The whole group bellowed their approval. Everyone was shaking hands and smiling happily.

It had only taken some three hours to build and fill all the boxes. Twelve expectant faces then turned to look at Diana. Nobody said a word.

"Bread and jam and tea and sugar for everyone?" she asked.

The roar of approval and the clapping which ensued would have done justice to the winning goal scored in a Cup Final. It was repeated again when Fackson appeared with plates piled high with bread cut into thick slices, each liberally covered with homemade tomato jam. Mugs of tea followed, together with a large bowl of sugar. Another hush fell on the group of men as they enjoyed the unaccustomed luxury of fresh bread, which they could seldom afford for their families.

"Can we have some more sugar, my Mummy?" The question came from Godfrey, who had just emptied four tablespoonfuls into his mug of tea.

"Zikomo kwambiri, Mama!" he thanked her, when Fackson reappeared.

"You will all lose your teeth," Diana scolded them, "if you continue to eat so much sugar!"

Twelve shining, black faces grinned back at her, their teeth gleaming white, even, and healthy.

The meal over, the only remaining activity was to load the removal van. It had not yet returned. One by one, the crew rose from the stoep and strolled over to the shade of the avocado trees at the end of the garden, where they chatted among themselves until sleep overcame them. It was twilight when the pantechnicon arrived. This time the driver did not attempt to navigate the drive. Three long blasts on his horn were enough to wake the group of sleeping Africans, as well as most of the immediate neighbourhood. Under the glare of the security lights, they grunted, then chanted in unison under the weight of the boxes, loading them carefully into the van.

"So, you found some diesel, then?" James asked the driver.

"Ah yes, *Bwana*," he replied with a sheepish smile. "Just as I am about to be leaving here this morning, I see the tanker at the filling station around this very corner. I am the very first transport in the line. It was my *very* lucky day indeed."

James forbore from laughing out loud at the blatantly dishonest trick.

"*Chabwino!* Well done!" he said to the driver. "And well done, all the rest of you. See you tomorrow at the depot."

He remembered how he had felt when he went back into the almost empty house, wondering if or when they would ever see their belongings again. Now, as he surveyed the nine large boxes, which almost filled the barn, he wished he had a dozen men like Godrey to make light of the heavy work which confronted him.

Chapter Nineteen

It was very cold in the barn, but the task of drawing the six ...
nails from the lids of the boxes was strenuous. Some refused to be
removed, and he had to split the tough wood and prise open the tops.
He soon discovered that the numbers painted on the sides of the boxes
did not correspond with those shown in the inventory. The first to be
opened, which should have revealed books and the music cassettes,
contained the pottery collection. There was no pressing need to unpack
it, but he was curious to know whether any of the pots had survived
intact. He dragged the heavy lid to one side and started to remove
them. When he had emptied the box, he could scarcely believe his
eyes. All seventeen pots had arrived unscathed and now stood in a
proud row against the wall of the barn.

"Bloody good!" he said aloud. "*Chabwino sana,* Godfrey! Very
well done!"

He was faced now with the choice of which to open next, and
realized that it would have to be by guesswork. The door of the barn
opened, and Diana entered, carrying a tray of tea.

"I thought you might need something to warm you up," she said,
noticing his shirt, which was damp with sweat. "It must be very hard
work. Do be careful of your back! Who were you talking to just now?
I thought I heard you saying something as I was coming over."

"Godfrey, the Lovale packer," he replied, waving the jemmy at the
row of earthenware pots. "Bloody miracle, that is. Not one is
broken!"

"Great! But we don't need them yet. Why did you unpack them
first?"

"Because the box numbers in the inventory do not agree with the
numbers painted on the boxes. Number six, which I've just unpacked,
is down as books, but those pots were in it. Now you tell me which is
which, if you can."

"Well, my love, I should have thought that the books and my
music must surely be in one of the heaviest crates."

The weight of each box was clearly marked on the outside. He
wondered why he had not arrived at the same logical solution.

As he worked, he quickly found that he was becoming more proficient at extracting the big nails, despite the blisters forming on his hands. Soon, more than two hundred bent nails lay scattered on the floor, and six of the nine boxes had been opened at random. He swept up the nails and fetched the wheelbarrow from the *prunerie*. Then began the task of wheeling load after load of their belongings down to the house through the rain.

"Where do you want this lot?" he shouted from outside the house. "Up or down?"

"What is it?"

"Linen!"

"Down, of course!"

The house was beginning to fill up, and Diana was unable to find places to put things, before the next load arrived. He found the large, wooden bust which Godfrey had wrapped so carefully. Next to it was the small plastic bag of *nshima*, the supply of food which Godfrey had donated. He noticed that the bag was now empty. It took him more than ten minutes to extract the carving from the layers of packaging.

"*Muli bwanji,* Exhilda," he breathed, stroking her hair. "Welcome to France!"

They had nicknamed the carving after an attractive and intelligent Zambian woman who had made some clothes for Diana. Subsequently she had become a close friend. With difficulty he managed to lift her into the wheelbarrow.

"Rugs and Exhilda, this time!" he bellowed.

"In here then, but I don't know where I'm going to put it all."

At that point the telephone rang for the first time that day, startling both of them. They had forgotten about the confusion over telephone numbers, and the administrative chore of informing all who might need to know the correct one.

"I wonder who that can be?" Diana asked, going to answer the call.

"*Bonjour, Madame.*" It was a man's voice.

"*Bonjour, Monsieur.*"

"*Est-ce que vous avez perdu un chat jaune avec un collier rouge?*" the man queried. "Have you lost a yellow cat with a red collar? The identity disc says that he is Jacob."

"Jacob! You have my Jacob? Where?" she cried.

"My name is Guy Raynal. I am one of your neighbours. Jacob is safely in our old bakery. He was very wet, but he let me dry him. I will bring him over. You are the new owner of Bon Porteau, yes? *Un vrai paradis, n'est-ce pas?* A really nice spot, isn't it?"

"Yes," she replied. "But don't you bother to bring him. He might escape again! I'll come to you. Which is your house?"

Monsieur Raynal gave her directions, offered again to deliver Jacob to Bon Porteau, which Diana politely refused for the second time, and then he rang off. She gathered her car keys, snatched up a towel, and ran to the car.

"Jacob's been walkabout! He must have somehow got out," she shouted over the noise of the jeep's engine. "The poor boy's got very wet, and he'll catch a terrible cold! He's holed up in the old bakery of that house across the fields up there. I'm going to get him. You had better stop unpacking now. Félicie is due at four."

"But that's over two miles away!" James yelled after her.

Monsieur Raynal came out of one of his outbuildings. He was smiling cheerfully as he greeted her.

"I heard this noise," he explained. "It was coming from that big field over there. I thought perhaps it was an injured bird, so I went to investigate. Instead, I found your cat. *Il est mignon.* He's nice. He let me pick him up. He's safely in there, and I've dried him as well as I can. It's a good thing he wears a collar and an identity disc. But the telephone number on it is not yours — it's Félicie Gautier's. So I rang her, and she told me you had cats and gave me your number."

"Thank you, *Monsieur* Raynal," Diana said, as they walked towards the old bakery. "It's very good of you to have phoned me straightaway."

Jacob caught the sound of her voice, and his loud wails could be heard clearly. As the door opened, the bewildered cat took a flying leap from one of the beams, where he had been crouching safely out of reach. He landed on her shoulders, and immediately started purring contentedly. "You very naughty boy!" she scolded him, giving him a big hug.

"I'll go and find a box for him."

"No, don't worry, *Monsieur*. He'll be fine in the car. Thank you so much for your kind help."

"Mais c'est normal!" the Frenchman replied, shrugging his shoulders. "I've never heard a cat make a noise like that before. What is he?"

"He's a Burmese. But he's what is called 'red', not yellow. I also have a blue one."

"Très étrange! Un rouge et un bleu! C'est con, hein?"

She carried Jacob to the jeep, shut him inside, and turned to shake hands with Monsieur Raynal.

"We must meet properly next time," the Frenchman said. "I believe Félicie is going to bring you and your husband over for an *apéritif* some time soon."

"Thank you, *Monsieur*. And we'll look forward to that"

When she returned to Bon Porteau, Jacob was lovingly carried inside, towelled down, and installed in front of the big fire, where the memory of his disorientation in the cold, wet fields soon faded. Half-an-hour later he was still sleeping contentedly, when Félicie arrived.

*

Félicie was clearly still upset over the incessant telephone calls which she had been receiving from their friends. To calm her down, James put a glass of *pruneaux* in front of her, but he forgot to remove the bottle, which she had brought as a present the previous day.

"Are all the British people so abrupt on the telephone?" she asked.

"Félicie, I must teach you English," James suggested. "At the least, you could learn how to say the eight figures of our telephone number, and then you can pass it on. You would then be the perfect telephone answering service!"

"Aïe! Aïe! Aïe!" she protested, not finding his bantering the least bit amusing. She helped herself quickly to a second glass of *pruneaux*. "But then you must write to them!" she insisted. "Or, better still, you must ring them! They must be very stupid people! Why can they not simply ask for International Directory? They will give out the correct number."

There was not much time left, before they would be due at the

Mayor's house in Saint Juste. The various bills were explained, Félicie taking pains to demonstrate that she was paying for her share up to the end of her occupancy of the house. Diana broached the subject of paying or not paying for the things which Félicie had left behind. Agreement was reached amicably on such items as the two large, wrought-iron lanterns on the roof *terrasse* and other light fittings around the house. The problem came when they started to discuss the two cookers, the dishwasher, and the refrigerator.

"I'm sorry, Félicie," Diana insisted politely but firmly, "they are simply *not* in good working order."

"But they were all working when I left," Félicie claimed.

"Well, I'm absolutely certain that the thermostats on the cookers have all had it," Diana argued. "The fridge door doesn't shut properly. And the dishwasher is old and clapped out."

They were in danger of falling out, when James decided that it was time he intervened.

"How much money did you have in mind if we pay you *en espèces*, in cash, for all of it, including the carpets, the curtains, and the big table out on the *terrasse*, which you agreed to leave behind?"

"Oh!" she said magnanimously. "All that junk. I was going to give you that for nothing. They're part of the house. But don't get the curtains cleaned! They'll all fall to pieces!"

She then answered his question, mentioning a ridiculously large sum of money.

"Bagshot! Sounds painful!" Diana muttered loud enough for him to hear her disapproval.

He reluctantly wrote out a cheque for the figure Félicie was demanding. "Thank you, Félicie," he smiled grimly, handing her the cheque. "That will be just fine."

*

The friendly gesture on the part of *Monsieur le Maire* and his wife to welcome them to the commune of Saint Juste took place in a solid Quercy farmhouse with grey shutters and a small *pigeonnier,* the latter still being used for its original purpose. The house was less than fifty metres from the *Mairie*, standing in a pretty garden, through which a narrow path led past a wooden shed to the front door. James noticed at the side of the house a carefully tended vegetable garden, in the middle of which stood a large, red rotovator. With a degree of formality, which she saw fit to bring to the occasion, Félicie introduced them to Monsieur and Madame Larguille. The eighty-year-old Mayor spoke in a deep, gravelly voice with a thick accent, as he welcomed them.

"Bonjour, M'sieur Wyllis, Madame Wyllis! Enchanté!" He pronounced their name *"Willie"* and his words came out almost as a growl, but his smile was warm and his handshake firm. *"Bienvenue à Saint Juste!"* Everything else he said during their meeting was almost entirely incomprehensible. Either Félicie or Madame Larguille, who was older than her husband and spoke rarely, had to act as interpreters.

They were shown into a room which was long and dark, with small windows and an open fireplace which was even wider than that at Bon Porteau. There was no visible concession to comfort, and the room looked as if it had not been decorated for several decades. A heavy, oak table took up the centre of the room, which was lit by a solitary bulb in a green lampshade made of glass, over which a cream-coloured piece of attractively embroidered lace was draped. There was only one picture, a photograph hanging slightly askew over the sideboard. It was a portrait of a young soldier in uniform and, when he had an opportunity to took more closely at it, James realized that it was Monsieur Larguille. Six oak chairs, with plain, tall backs and wickerwork seats, were arranged around the table, on which there were two unlabelled bottles which had been chilled and some small, thick glasses on a tray. Three bowls, containing olives, prunes and walnuts, had been put on the sideboard.

"Installez-vous, je vous en prie," said Madame Larguille as she sat down, her voice barely louder than a whisper.

Her husband took the chair at the opposite end of the table, nearest to where the drinks had been placed. He drew the stopper from one of the bottles and poured out some of the amber liquid.

"Santé!"

It sounded as if he was calling a platoon to attention.

"À la bonne vôtre!" they replied.

James took a discreet sip, unable to place the slight aroma rising from his glass. Although the drink was ice cold, it was strong and fiery, and he enjoyed it.

"Do you know what it is?" asked the Mayor, who had been watching his reaction.

"Je n'ai aucune idée, Monsieur," James replied. "I have no idea, but it's very good. One thing is for sure — you can't buy it in Africa!"

"You can't buy it anywhere," the old man said, refilling their glasses. "We call it *"Rataffia"*. It's like a *Pinot,* but stronger, and made from a recipe my grandfather gave me. It's two-thirds *raisins* and one-third *eau-de-vie*, with just a suggestion of homemade *pruneaux*. Thirty-two percent alcohol. It must be kept *dans le frigo* once it's opened, and it's delicious with melon."

They stayed for more than an hour, and the conversation ranged over different parts of Africa, the immigrant population in France, how the nation's bureaucracy had changed during his forty-two unopposed years as Mayor of Saint Juste, last year's excellent wine harvest, the abnormal weather currently in the Lot, the British royal family, and the completion date for the construction of Félicie's new house behind the library in Montcarmel. Both bottles were empty when the Mayor stood up, giving a hearty tug at his elastic cloth braces.

"Ouais, bien! Je peux voir que vous aimez le ving," he burred. "I can see you like your wine. One day I'll introduce you to some of the *vignerons* around here. Don't buy the rubbish in the supermarket. That's strictly for tourists!" He laughed loudly at his quip. *"Enfing, nous sommes trés heureux de vous faire un acceuil chaleureux.* Anyway, we're very happy to welcome you most warmly to our growing *commune dans le Lot!"*

"But what do you mean?" shrieked Félicie, who was by then a little tipsy and finding it difficult to walk steadily down the path to the gate. "Has the birthrate of Saint Juste suddenly increased?"

"You could put it like that, but the truth is that the arrivals of *Monsieur* and *Madame Willie,* together with that of *Monsieur* Drummond-Delaire and his lady friend, have put the number of inhabitants up to seventy-three."

"O-là-là, là-là!" Madame Larguille cried. *"C'est encore une fois l'invasion Britannique!"*

As they were about to leave, the Mayor opened the door of his wooden shed and emerged with two dusty bottles, one of which he gave to Félicie and the other to Diana, whose hand he held for several moments.

"M'sieur et Madame Willie," their host growled, looking up at the sky. "This will help you beat this foul weather."

"Mais, ce n'est pas du tout normal," Félicie added, slurring her words, as she struggled with the door of her car. "Come in about an hour's time, Diana," she added, as she slumped into the driving seat and fumbled with her keys.

"I honestly didn't understand a word of the Mayor's French," Diana said, climbing into the jeep and waving goodbye to the smiling old couple.

"I didn't do much better," James agreed. "I understood his *'bonjour et bienvenue'* when we arrived, but that's about all."

"I wonder how Félicie will cope with having us to supper. I think she was a bit pissed."

"I think we're probably going to be known as the *'Willies de Pisenhaut'* from now on."

*

Standing on the roof *terrasse* back at Bon Porteau, James noticed that something was different. The wind had dropped. It had stopped raining and, low in the western sky, the thick layer of cloud ended in a well-defined line, giving them their first glimpse of the sun since leaving Africa.

"Perhaps it will now get hot, like last year," he observed. "That looks like a new weather system coming towards us."

"Let's hope so. Then we can let that damned fire out, and perhaps the cats could have a supervised run outside tomorrow."

"And I'm going to have to do some gardening. Bon Porteau must be tidied up, before autumn sets in properly. Over supper this evening, I'll have a word with Félicie about finding someone to help me. I'm sure she can get something organized quickly. I seem to remember her saying last year that there is plenty of cheap, local labour to help. All I want is a reliable, hardworking, peasant to help me with the worst of the jungle-bashing. That's all."

They spent a pleasant evening at Félicie's rented apartment. She was more or less sober again by the time they arrived. Pascale was there, and they met Félicie's younger sister and her husband, Monique and Guillaume. They were an attractive couple, who had recently remarried after a twelve-year interval of divorce. Guillaume was acknowledged to be an expert in wine-tasting and the owner of an extensive cellar. He also offered to introduce James to some of the better vineyards of the region.

"There's something I've always wanted to do," Diana said enthusiastically. "I would love to tread the grapes with my feet. Do you think you could try and fix that for me, Guillaume?

"O-là-là, Diana!" he replied. "I wish I could, but almost every aspect of harvesting is mechanized nowadays. Long gone are the wonderful, romantic days of 'Marguerita, press the grapes with me'. But don't let that spoil your enjoyment of some of the finest wine in France, which is grown here in the Lot."

James took the opportunity to follow up his growing concern over the state of the grounds, and he told them that he now urgently needed to find someone who could work diligently for about a month, cutting the long grass and cleaning out the nettles and brambles which had invaded the property during the summer. When he discovered that no garden maintenance had been done since May, he became even more agitated.

"But Félicie, I'm sure I remember you saying," he persisted, "that there was plenty of cheap, local labour around here. I need someone *now*! Surely there is *some* able-bodied individual who wants to earn a few francs and is available to make a start, preferably this week? If it's all left untouched until the spring, it will be a really huge task. The hedge badly needs cutting as well, and there's masses of rubbish to burn. It's all over the place. As soon as it's dry enough, I shall have a good bonfire."

Guillaume picked up the last point. Whilst conceding that bonfires were permitted at this time of the year, he advised James that much of the vegetation was still dangerously dry, in spite of the recent rain, and that he should take every precaution if the fine weather returned, as was now forecast. On the matter of help in the garden, he promised to make appropriate enquiries in the nearby garden machinery shop and at the *Tabac,* the latter generally considered to be one of the best sources of local gossip and information.

"But," Guillaume added, "don't imagine that you can find cheap labour. Nothing is cheap nowadays in France. I don't know who put that strange idea into your head."

James and Diana looked over towards Félicie, the colour of whose face was turning from her normal ruddy complexion to bright crimson.

"If you ever find that you want to buy or sell anything," Félicie pronounced, quickly changing the subject, "even if it's second-hand, then you must tell *Monsieur* Aminot in the *Tabac.* He and his wife know all that goes on around here: whose husband has walked out, how much was won by whom in the latest lottery, what the tax investigator was doing in town last Tuesday, who is sleeping with whom, and, quite possibly, who might be interested in doing some part-time work. They know it all. I'll speak to him tomorrow."

"Anyway, James, I can solve one of your problems," Guillaume offered pleasantly. "You can borrow my hedge-cutter. I'll bring it over to you tomorrow. It will make light work of that privet."

"And Diana," urged Félicie, as they were preparing to leave, "you must come with Pascale and me to tomorrow's market at Libos. It's the best in the area. We'll go in my car, and I'll collect you at eight in the morning. I'm sure James can manage without you for one morning." They all laughed, except James.

Later, during the drive back to Bon Porteau, they briefly discussed the things each of them would have to do.

"We're going to get into a terrible muddle," he observed, "if we don't make a list and put some sort of a priority against certain tasks."

"I think my first two priorities are clear," Diana replied. "I'm going to need a cupboard for the linen, and we'll have to buy something to cook on, even if it's only a temporary arrangement. I can't have all that linen lying about everywhere. And we don't want to go out to eat all the time — it will be far too expensive."

"The weather is an important factor," he resumed, "with all the things I have to get done. I think I'll draw up two lists: one as a wet weather programme, and the other for when it's fine. Look, darling! You can actually see the stars now. It must be going to be fine, as

Guillaume said. But be wind is quite strong and damn cold. Still, perhaps it will blow this depression away. I'm going to call in at that local garden machinery centre tomorrow and see what equipment they have in stock. "

"Well, don't go mad and buy everything at once, otherwise we'll run short of francs. "

*

It was late, and they were about to go down to the bedroom, when Fosbury stalked mournfully into the living-room. He sat at Diana's feet, looking up at her with a meaningful stare. It was, James thought, a kind of intimate telepathy, which frequently led to curious happenings.

"Fosbury's looking more than a little lonely," Diana said. "He's trying to tell me something. Have you seen Jacob recently?"

"No, I haven't, come to think of it. Not since that water man was here. I remember seeing him curled up over there by the fire before we went out. "

They both leaped to their feet, and a frantic search ensued. The main problem was where to look first. More than an hour passed, and they found no sign of him.

"He must have escaped outside when we left," she said, a note of concern in her voice. "He'll be completely disorientated out there in strange surroundings and in this bitterly cold wind. I just hope and pray that he hasn't been taken by a fox. "

"He has already been out of bounds once today. He can't have got out again," he said firmly, trying to sound reassuring. "We've been so careful about the doors. But just in case, I'll see if I can put my hands on the whistle. It should be somewhere in my Zambian suitcase. Then I'll turn on all the outside lights, and he'll come in. Don't worry. "

It was a much travelled whistle, which had gained itself a well-earned reputation and some notoriety on the Wiltshire Downs, in the Shires of England, in suburban Surrey, and in the bush of Africa. While he searched for it, he recalled how he had acquired it many years previously in the gunshop in Marlborough.

"I want to buy one of those silent whistles," he told the old man behind the counter, who was arranging a display of collars for dogs and cats. "You can vary the pitch by screwing it up tight or loose."

The old man regarded him with a quizzical look.

"How old be your dog then, Zur?"

"Dogs," James corrected him. "Five of them. All Jack Russells. They're between thirteen and two years."

The old man finished arranging his display and then walked slowly round to face James from behind his counter.

"You'm wasting your money, Zur, except maybe for the pup." The old man wagged his grey-haired head. "Doubt it, though. He be hardly a pup at two year. Pack o' dogs like that, they got no mind for discipline."

"Yes, that's why I want one," James insisted. "To call them in off the Downs."

"You'm still throwing your money away, Zur. I said the very same thing to a gentleman only this last week, but he weren't of a mind for to heed the advice of a silly old bugger like I. Three-year-old Labrador, he had. Nice looking bitch, t'was. But he had to have his whistle, too, just like you, Zur. I told him he'd be back inside a week to buy a good dog lead instead." He chuckled. "He were in here yester' morn!"

"I'm sure you're probably right, but I would like to try one."

That evening, when the terriers had scattered across the fields, he blew and blew the whistle, now and then adjusting the pitch. The only notice the dogs had paid to his considerable physical effort was to interpret the high-pitched sound as more direct encouragement to stray further and further afield. At the time, he had noticed with fascination that some young badgers had reacted out of curiosity, popping their heads briefly out of their sets, before disappearing quickly back into safety. The dogs, he remembered, were absent until after breakfast on the following day. The experiment had demonstrably failed.

A few days later, he was back in the gun shop, and the elderly proprietor recognized him.

"No good, Zur?" he asked, holding out his hand. "I'll give you your money back this time. Them things only work with the very young, when they can be trained."

James had placed the whistle in the shopkeeper's hand and sheepishly accepted his refund. But he was not to be deterred; he had read somewhere that the manufacturer had introduced an upgraded model. There would be no harm in investigating it.

"I believe they make a more powerful job," he persisted. "Have you got one in stock by any chance?"

"Aargh! You'm meaning the 'Zilent Thunderer', I suppose," replied the old man. "Zame difference. You'm throwing good money after bad, Zur."

"I would still like to take one and to try again," he said, handing back the refunded money.

"I'm afraid this 'ere one's a mite more expensive. It'll cost you another one pound, two-and-sixpence, Zur."

Satisfied that he had not succumbed to any form of subtle salesmanship, he had left the shop with the old man's words ringing in his ears.

"Now, there be no refund on that model you've chosen, Zur. I got to make my living zumways."

The old man was proved correct, but James never threw away the whistle, thinking that perhaps one day it might prove to be valuable.

One day, some years later, when they were living in the Chilterns, he found the discarded whistle and, sitting in their small garden, he told Diana about the old man in the gun shop, the dogs, and the young badgers in Wiltshire.

"Silly of me, really," he concluded. "I just didn't want to be defeated by that crafty old man."

He screwed the whistle up to its highest pitch setting, and blew on it as hard as he could. Almost immediately the three Burmese cats came tumbling through the flowerbeds in response to the new sound.

"Look at that! Well I'll be damned!" Diana exclaimed. "All three came to it, just like that! Let's take them for a walk across the fields and see if they respond to it reliably."

This time the whistle passed its user trials with flying colours.

He had always intended to write to the manufacturer about this development, but somehow he had never followed through his good intentions. Instead, the whistle was put to good use in Surrey, where it proved a godsend. Their neighbours had commented frequently on the nocturnal sight of an eccentric figure, clad in pyjamas, a glass of whisky in one hand, with a cigarette and whistle in his mouth, leading the three cats back up the street like a latter-day Pied Piper of Hamlyn. There were only two occasions, when the whistle failed. The first was over a long weekend, when Jacob was locked accidentally by a neighbour inside his garage. That was hardly a fair test. The second was in the depth of one night in the Luangwa Valley, when a serious experiment was conducted to lure an aardvark out of its hole. This was the only animal in the African wild which they had never managed to see.

He continued rummaging in his suitcase, convinced that he would find it. In the meantime, he could hear Diana calling the cat as she went from room to room.

"Now where the hell is the damn thing?" he muttered. He found it two minutes later, safely tucked into one of his desert boots.

"Has he come in yet?" he shouted, climbing up the steps.

"No, he hasn't, and he won't now." Diana was distressed. "He will have gone off exploring and marking his new territory, which he hasn't seen in daylight and doesn't know. There are no fences, so he'll just wander and get lost."

He could see the prospect of a full night's sleep receding rapidly over the horizon. He was beginning to regret that they had gone out for supper.

"This will find him, darling," he said full of confidence as he waved the whistle, making for the door and the cold night air. "Don't worry! Just send out a search party if I'm not back by morning."

Before opening the door, he blew gently into the whistle to check its pitch. From one of the tea-chests there came a rustling of newspaper and, with a long, low wail, Jacob climbed out, blinked twice, then yawned, and stretched himself languorously in front of the fire.

"Voilà, ma chérie!" he laughed. "It never fails!"

As a precaution against any future feline walkabouts, he hung the whistle on a nail in the beam over the fireplace. He looked at his watch. It was almost three o'clock. He yawned and took her hand.

"Shall we go and get some sleep now, my love?"

Chapter Twenty

He awoke the next morning to find a glorious day dawning. The sun was rising just above the level of the roof of the barn, bathing the house in welcome warmth and light. The elongated shadow of the *pigeonnier* stretched across and beyond the lawn into the field on the other side of the valley. He quickly decided that it would have to be the dry weather programme, confirming his intention to investigate French garden machinery. He was in Montcarmel shortly after the shop opened and introduced himself to the proprietor, a stocky man with smiling eyes and several days' stubble on his face. He showed James his workshop and proudly emphasized the after-sales service he provided.

"My name is Casarin, but everybody calls me Miguel," he announced. "I am of Spanish origin. I myself maintain all the equipment I sell here. If you buy from me and anything breaks down, then I lend you a replacement at no cost while the repairs are being done."

Miguel claimed that he knew Bon Porteau well, having always serviced the machines owned by Madame Gautier. He had also received a telephone call from Guillaume just before James arrived at the shop.

"I gave him the name of a man," he continued, "who I'm sure will be able to help you to bring the grounds under control. His name is Robert, a good worker with his own equipment. I'll give you his number and you'll catch him in at lunchtime. There's a lot of work at that place. *Il vous faut du courage, M'sieu!* And you will need good, strong machinery to cope with it all."

James remembered the hotelier making almost the same remark about *du courage* earlier in the week.

"Well then, since you know Bon Porteau," James said expectantly, "perhaps you can suggest what I should buy. There are lawns, banks, brambles and nettles, and woods, where I'll want to cut my own firewood."

It took about an hour to select and agree exactly what was

required. His purchases were moved out of the shop on to the forecourt: a tractor mower, a trailer, a sturdy electric hover mower with two fifty-metre extension leads, an electric chainsaw, a *débroussailleuse* — a powerful two-stroke brush-cutter, two jerrycans, some oil, and safety glasses. Miguel offered a discount, and was both surprised and pleased to hear James's reaction.

"Miguel, I don't have money to throw about but, in matters like this, I am not concerned to screw a discount off your profit margin. I am much more interested in a first-class service from you whenever I need it and that includes weekend, high days, and holidays. Agreed?"

"D'accord, M'sieu Willie," Miguel replied, shaking hands on the deal. James gave Miguel his cheque and then recalled Diana's cautionary remark from the previous evening.

"Miguel, would you mind," he asked, "if you held on to that cheque until the beginning of next week? That will give me time to get some more money transferred out from London."

"Pas de problème, M'sieu," he agreed. "But I would like to deliver these to you in about an hour, because I have to call in to *M'sieu* Bouyou-Carendier, one of your neighbours in Pisenhaut. With this sun and drying wind, there's no reason why you should not make a start on your gardens today."

When Miguel arrived at Bon Porteau, he showed James how to use the *débroussailleuse*. He delivered a stern warning on its lethal power.

"This machine can be very dangerous in the wrong hands. Always work from right to left, so that it does not kick back at you. And never use it without wearing strong boots, long trousers, and the safety glasses." James struggled into the harness and soon conceded that the machine was potentially deadly, at the same time admiring its fast rate of work. Just before Miguel left, James pointed to a rusty, old, diesel tank standing against the wall on the other side of the barn.

"I won't have any use for that *truc* over there," he said. "Do you think you could take it away in your van and dump it for me?"

"I'll do better than that," Miguel proposed. "With a lick of paint, that'll be worth five or six hundred francs. I'll put it on my forecourt with a price on it. Someone will buy it for their central heating oil." He examined the tank, and looked inside it.

"Merde! There's still a fair amount of diesel in there. Anyway, I can't take it now — it's far too heavy for us two to lift. I'll bring the

other truck and come back for it later in the week."

Within two hours, James was loading the small trailer with discarded packaging material, sheets of corrugated cardboard, empty cartons, piles of newspaper, and any other rubbish he found. He decided to clear the debris, first from the house, and then from the barn itself. He chose a spot in the field behind the barn in preparation for a good bonfire. This is much better than a wheelbarrow, he thought, as the small tractor and trailer shuttled to and fro between the house and the field. It would give Diana a nice surprise to find that most of the rubbish was out of the house when she returned from the market at Libos. It was hot work, but he enjoyed it. By the time he was satisfied that there was nothing else which he could usefully remove from the house, seven full loads had been deposited in the field.

The sunshine was hot and there was little or no breeze. Soon a good bonfire was ablaze. He remembered seeing a pile of dead branches down by the millstone at the end of the grass track, and he set off to fetch them. He managed to fit them into one load, and ten minutes later he was driving back up to the barn. It was as he regained the track that it dawned upon him that something was wrong. A column of grey-black smoke was rising from behind the barn. Then he saw the vicious, orange lick of flames above the level of the ridge of the barn's roof. Pushing wide open the throttle of the tractor, his first thought was that somehow the barn must be on fire.

Panic gripped his throat as he approached to see what was happening. There was now a slight breeze and, during his absence from the bonfire, it had changed direction towards the barn and the thick, dry undergrowth beneath the trees. The upsurge of heated air from the bonfire had caught two large pieces of blazing corrugated cardboard — one had landed under the trees, and the other had come to rest in the weeds beside the wall of the barn. The bonfire itself was in danger of becoming beyond control. Several fires had started below the trees, and small flames were travelling menacingly towards the corner of the barn through the dry, dead weeds.

"Merde!" he shouted aloud. "They will soon reach the barn door!"

He leaped from the tractor and started sprinting for the house, his first instinct being to reach a telephone and call out the *sapeurs pompiers,* the local volunteer fire brigade. He stopped and doubled back to the tractor and trailer, believing that he might have left them too close to the blaze. He moved it quickly to safety and ran towards the barn door. Then he saw the diesel tank. He had forgotten it and failed to notice that it would be in the path of one of the fires. Small flames were now no more than three feet from its base. His heart was racing as he picked up a shovel. Frantically he beat at the closest flames, managing to extinguish some, but not all.

It was difficult to breathe in the black smoke. His eyes were streaming. He felt his left eyebrow as it was singed. Glowing red embers were falling out of the air, landing on his shirt and in his hair. The heat was intense, and the fire was now spreading at an alarming rate. He had visions of the diesel tank igniting, and the whole barn burning down, together with the contents of the boxes of freight, three of which were still unopened, and most of the remainder only partially unpacked. Trying to remain calm, he continued to work desperately with the shovel while he decided what to do. He was not winning the battle. The fires under the trees were gaining a strong hold, fanned by the seemingly increasing breeze. Soon, it would not be merely a matter of a bonfire out of control; it could easily develop into a forest fire.

He recalled with terrifying clarity his conversation with Guillaume the previous evening. The Lot's proud record of very few, serious forest fires had been discussed, as had also the swingeing penalties which would fall on anyone who behaved negligently and caused a fire. Bonfires, he was informed, were strictly forbidden for this very reason from mid-May until mid-September, the latter date being moveable and under the control of the *Préfecture,* dependent upon the dryness of the summer months and, hence, the fire risk. Even then, Guillaume had advised, great care must be taken, since the grasses and brushwood are tinder-dry after long, hot summers. If the *sapeurs pompiers* were called out, there was invariably a large bill to pay for their services, which would be followed up in every case by a visit from the *gendarmes.* Unlike the many problems experienced in Provence, where thousands of trees are lost each year, frequently as a result of fire-raising, the *Préfecture du Lot* was determined to maintain rigid control.

He was on the point of responding to the urge to call for help from the professionals, when he remembered that he had bought three long garden hoses. As he snuffed out another flame which was threatening the diesel tank, he calculated that they should be long enough to reach the area of the fire if they were joined together. Throwing down the shovel, he ran as fast as he could down to the house and round to the outside door of the cellar. It was locked. He slipped and fell, as he raced up the bank to reach the porch. Bursting into the house, he took the miller's ladder in a flying leap down it. He found the hoses and connectors in the cellar, and rushed out to the garden tap outside the lower entrance to the house. Panting and sweating, his shaking hands ripped at the strong, plastic packaging around the hoses, and he cursed his stupidity. As he worked, he saw that one trouser leg had been scorched up to his knee and the soles of his shoes were badly burned. He swore at the thin, nylon straps, which fastened the hoses, unable to break them with his bare hands. More precious moments were lost while he searched for a strong knife. He looked quickly towards the barn. It was still there, but the pall of smoke was ominously large, reaching high into the sky. Perhaps, he thought, someone would see it, and come to his assistance.

At last he had the hoses unpacked and connected together, and, in order to avoid having to run back to the tap, he turned it on, increasing the weight of the seventy-five metres of hose. As it filled up with water, he dragged it, half running, half stumbling, up the slope towards the barn. It was sufficiently long, and he gave a rasping sigh of relief, standing ready to douse the strongest of the flames. He found that he could not approach the worst areas, driven back by the heat. He used his thumb to pinch the end of the hose in an attempt to create an effective jet of water. The water pressure was too low.

"Con!" he yelled out in frustration. "I'll have to change over from the *château source* to the mains supply!" He dropped the hose and swung round to race for the two manholes down by the house. Then he saw that he could not leave the hose where it lay in the smouldering grass — it would soon be charred and useless. He pulled it clear and then staggered away towards the house.

The manhole covers were very heavy. He managed to lift the first one, tearing his nails in the process. Reaching down, he turned off the private water supply and bounded up the bank to the second manhole. The cover would not move. Then he remembered how the man from the water company had used a small spade to lever the lid upwards. The spade was in the *prunerie*, and yet more vital seconds were wasted as he retrieved it. The lid came up easily, and he felt a surge of relief as his hand felt down for the tap. He quickly turned it on, pausing only for a few seconds to verify that the meter was turning. He sprinted back to the fire, and this time the water pressure was more than sufficient to enable him to direct a long, heavy jet of water at the flames.

The highest flames were now in the bushes under the trees, but he was more frightened of the diesel tank. Once he had rendered that area safe, he was able to turn his attention to preventing the fire from spreading further into the trees, working his way along the edge of the scrub. He sensed that he was gaining on the fire and felt elated, ignoring the heat that was coming up through the soles of his shoes. As he progressed, he continued to check from time to time that no flames were reappearing in the vicinity of the diesel tank. Gradually, among the steaming clumps of grass and the black, charred undergrowth which he had thoroughly soaked, the flames died back. He watered the entire area affected by the fire for another half-an-hour, before he was satisfied that he had won a remarkable, if unlikely, victory. Exhausted and red-eyed, he put down the hose and walked over to rest by the tractor. Sitting down on the grass to recover his breath, he surveyed the damage, remembering the last time he had been involved in a fire.

*

The dinner party in Nalikwanda Road was being enjoyed by all the guests. He could not remember whether it had been given in honour of some particular occasion. He did, however, recall that the wines could not do justice to the exquisite meal which Diana had prepared. This was quite normal for Lusaka. The bottles had probably been left for days outside the warehouse in the blazing sun. Their eight friends were relaxing in the warm night air on the outside stoep, a large verandah off the sitting-room. Lively conversation continued unabated, and James always wondered how it was that people needed to talk so much on these occasions. It was probably due to Priscilla's presence, since she lived on a beautiful but remote farm, three hundred miles away in Southern Province. Lonely, an avid reader, she truly believed that she knew everything about everything, and when any good opportunity arose, incessant debating and arguing were a natural outlet for her inquisitive mind.

Because it was a Sunday, Fackson had not been on duty in the kitchen or at the table. Diana and James had cleared the dishes earlier and, since he very rarely drank any coffee at night, James had volunteered uncharacteristically to make it. Entering the kitchen, he immediately saw the tall flames which were moving with devastating speed along the thatched fencing behind and perilously close to Fackson's cottage, in which the parents and nine children would be asleep. He rushed back to his guests.

"Fire! Fire!" he yelled at them. "The fence is on fire behind Fackson's quarters! Priscilla, call the fire brigade! Diana and Sue, get Fackson's family out of their beds before they are roasted! Be careful! Austin, take the men and form a bucket chain fast! Use buckets, bowls, saucepans, anything! I'll get the guard, the gate, and the hose!"

Priscilla was already on the telephone by the time he had finished issuing orders, and Diana was sprinting with Sue to the cottage to rescue her charges.

James ran for the gate to get Moses, the night-guard, to man the electric water pump and open the gate for the arrival of the fire-engine. Moses, muffled in what remained of his ex-Army greatcoat, his woollen hat pulled down over his eyes and ears, was fast asleep.

"Moses! Moses! Wake up, man!" he screamed at the prone figure, which continued to snore peacefully. "Shit! You're bloody drunk again, or else high on *daka*!"

James fumbled in the dark for the light in the guard's shelter, and quickly located the switch for the water pump. He heard the high-pitched wail of the alarm on Lusaka's only fire-engine, as it raced up Independence Avenue. Less than a minute later, the machine drew up outside the locked gate, its blue lamps flashing. At such close quarters, the strident din of the alarm was earsplitting. The firemen were shaking the gate vigorously. Moses had still not stirred.

"Open the gate, *Bwana!* Open the gate!" the Captain of the fire crew was bawling urgently from the other side. "Open the gate to let my men in!"

Moses, sleeping through the cacophony of noise, rolled over, but did not wake. James grabbed a broom handle, poking it hard into the inert form of the sleeping guard.

"Moses! Wake up!" he bellowed, continuing to prod the shapeless bundle on the ground. "There's a big fire by Fackson's house! Quickly, man! Open this bloody gate! Where's the key?"

Moses emerged, bleary-eyed and sweating profusely. He staggered to his feet and stood up unsteadily, his lean body racked with paroxysms of coughing. He tried to give James a toothless grin, as he pushed his woollen hat off his face.

"You lazy blighter! Fine time to be asleep! Open this damned gate! Quick, man!"

"Ah, *Bwana*! Sorry-sorry! I was not asleep, *Bwana*! Only just a little bit. It is the malaria," Moses protested, slurring his words as he fumbled with the padlock and chain, at the same time searching for the key.

The gate at last swung open, and the firemen raced towards the blazing fence, unrolling their hoses with practised skill. James dragged the garden hose behind him, moving as fast as he could towards the two cars in the carport. The efforts of the human chain, throwing buckets and bowls of water at the flames, had made little impact on the progress of the fire, which had now reached the corner of the fence and was advancing inexorably towards the carport.

"Austin!" James cried out, panic in his voice. "The Avgas will go up if the fire reaches the carport! Here, take the hose, and soak that section of the fence to stop it coming any further."

The firemen were now directing their two powerful hoses at different sectors of the fence, the heavy jets of water working efficiently towards each other.

Within minutes the blaze was under control, and half-an-hour later only steam was rising from the charred remains of the fence.

"*Chabwino,* Captain! That was bloody good!" James congratulated the senior fireman. "You got here damn quickly. I'm going to send a commendation to your Chief tomorrow. That was an excellent piece of work and very well done!"

"*Zikomo, Bwana.* Thank you," said the fireman, as they watched the rest of his crew joking and laughing with Fackson, who was wearing a pair of James's cast-off, striped pyjamas, which Diana had given him. "But *Bwana,* you must not keep your Avgas here, even a little bit. It is very dangerous. Regulations say underground. You must store it underground. I will not put it in my report."

"Fackson!" James called. "Get your family back to bed. You're back on duty for thirty minutes. Tea, bread, and jam for all these brave people. Hurry now! And tell your children to be more careful where they throw their charcoals next time."

James went back into the house, returned with his camera, and took photographs of the nine smiling firemen at the scene of their latest triumph. When finally they had rolled up the hoses and left to return to the fire station, it was James who shut and locked the gate. He hung the key to the heavy padlock on its hook in the guard's shelter and then bent down to shake Moses, who was already asleep again.

"Moses," he said quietly, "you must take this *mankwala.* Two pills now, two in the morning, and two again tomorrow when it is just dark. And don't report for duty tomorrow night, unless you are fit again."

"*Ah! Zikomo kwambiri, Bwana.* Thank you very much. I will do as you say. I will not be selling them in the market this time."

Three weeks later, when James called in at the fire station, the men were practising their fire drills, but they stopped when they saw him.

"Do you have striped pyjamas for me *Bwana*?" one of them shouted.

The crew started laughing and joking, until a crisp order obliged them to return to their duties. James entered the small block of offices and placed on the Captain's desk a packet of colour prints, together with a framed enlargement, showing his happy crew standing proudly beside their gleaming fire engine.

"I passed your house some nights ago," said the Captain in his deep, dry tone. "I see you are still employing my brother, Moses, as your night guard."

*

The sound of Félicie's car returning from the market brought him out of his reverie. He heard the three women talking and laughing together, but remained lying on the grass by the tractor, too exhausted to go and help unload the car. It was not long after Félicie and Pascale had left, when Diana came looking for him.

"James, where are you?" she called out. "Have you seen Fosbury?" She came round the corner of the barn and, seeing him lying down on the ground, she hurried over to him.

"Good Lord!" she laughed, realizing that he was neither dead nor injured. "You're the first black man I've seen around here since we left Africa. You look like a chimney sweep! Quick, blow me a kiss! What on *earth* has been going on here?"

He gave her a detailed account of the morning's drama, ensuring that the description of his heroic action in the face of so many dangers left no room for any suggestion of negligence or stupidity.

"Thank heavens I bought those three hoses, otherwise the whole lot would have gone up in smoke by now. Good thing, too, that I did my survival course in the Regiment, otherwise I might have panicked."

She looked at his blackened, torn clothing and the remains of his shoes.

"My poor, brave man! Come on down to the house and have an *apéritif.*"

"Did I hear you say something about Fosbury?" he asked, limping towards the house.

"Yes. Have you seen him? When we got back, the front door was wide open. Jacob is in his bed, but there's no sign of Fosbury."

"*Merde!* That's my fault. I must have left the door open when I fetched the hoses. Hell! That must have been *well* over an hour ago. We had better start looking for him now. I'll get the whistle."

The whistle, usually infallible, failed to induce Fosbury to respond this time. After searching for a long time, they were about to give up.

"He must be a hell of a long way off," James observed sombrely, "if he hasn't heard the whistle by now. He always comes back to it."

Then Diana heard a faint, distressed wail. It sounded weak, almost strangled, and unlike the normal, demanding tone of the Burmese cat.

"It sounded as if it came from over there, below the barn," Diana called, running towards the area affected by the fire. "God! I hope he wasn't trapped in your fire! He must be hurt!"

They stood by the barn on the edge of the burnt grass beside the trees overhanging the steep bank. He blew the whistle again.

"Shh! Listen!" Diana whispered. A plaintive cry came from somewhere below the overgrown bank. She scrambled down, looking towards the water in the *bassin*. Something was moving through the bright green algae which covered the surface of the water.

"James! Quick!" she shouted. "Down here! Look!"

Then she saw the cat, his eyes and nose covered in green slime, swimming manfully from one side of the *bassin* to the other, unable to claw his way up to the top of the concrete edging.

"Get a good, long plank of wood!" she screamed. "He can't get out! He's getting very tired! Hurry!"

As Fosbury clung to the piece of wood, Diana carefully pulled him in to the side, where she could reach down and lift him out of the water. He was panting from his strenuous efforts, wide-eyed with fear and shock, his fur matted with a thick layer of the slippery, green slime.

"My poor, poor baby!" she breathed into his sodden ear, hugging him and removing particles of algae from around his face.

"He looks just like a baby crocodile!"

"He's terribly cold, in shock, and exhausted. Your Mummy's got you now, Mr Man."

"He must have thought that all that green muck on the surface of the water was grass and so he jumped straight in. Félicie said it was dangerous for little people. I'll get it pumped out, before Jacob does the same thing."

"Jacob is *much* too wise to do such a stupid thing," she retorted. "Silly, old Foz! How long were you in there, I wonder?"

She took him into the house and, after cleaning and drying him with loving care, she installed him on a blanket in an armchair, where a patch of hot sunlight was streaming in through the window.

"I think we both need that *apéritif* now," Diana said with a sigh of relief.

Fosbury looked up at her, blinked, and then started to purr gently.

*

Sitting out on the roof *terrasse* in the hot, mid-afternoon sunshine, they had a belated snack lunch, during which they were briefly interrupted by Guillaume, who delivered his hedge-trimmer. He explained how the machine worked, joined them for a glass of wine, and then excused himself, since he was due in Cahors to listen to some plans to boost tourism in the Lot. After he had left, James decided to take a short rest to recover from his exertions during the morning and to sleep off the effects of drinking his share of the two bottles of red wine which stood empty on the table. He had just closed his eyes and was drifting off to sleep when he heard a moped coming up the drive. He raised his head from the pillow, and saw the diminutive figure of Gérard Tillet, protected by his distinctive, bright red crash helmet with the smoke-coloured visor.

"I think it's the Mayor's Secretary!" Diana called down from the small kitchen in the *pigeonnier*.

"Damn! I wonder what he wants."

Gérard dismounted in the middle of the drive, and was walking across the lawn towards the manhole for the *source du château*, the cover of which was still raised.

"Bonjour, Monsieur Willie!" he said pleasantly. "I always leave my *mobylette* down here. That steep corner by the trees is too much for me."

"Bonjour, Gérard! Are you here on mayoral business, or is this a social call? Either way, come into the house. Have an *apéritif,* if you would like one."

"Non, non merci! I've just come to read the *source* meter so that *Monsieur* Bouyou-Carendier can send *Madame* Gautier her account. I see you have the cover up, which is lucky. It's sometimes a swine to lift, that one is."

"I know," James agreed. "I had to lift it this morning."

While Gérard noted the meter reading, James told him about the fire, and the problem with the water pressure. They walked together up to the barn.

"*O-là-là, là-là, là-là!*" exclaimed Gérard, as he surveyed the extent of the fire damage. "*Eh bien, bon! Bon Dieu! Vous avez eu de la chance, hein?* Good God! But you were lucky, eh? To burn down your barn within four days of your arrival would have been seen as very suspicious by your insurers, not to mention *les flics*. You must be more careful next time."

Gérard refused a second offer of refreshment, excusing himself because he had two more meters to read that afternoon. He was about to mount his moped when be suddenly stopped. He raised his visor, an irritated took on his face.

"*Merde!* I nearly forgot," he muttered, taking out of his pocket a piece of paper with some handwriting on it. "There is a meeting of the *château source* association in the *Mairie* at three o'clock on Sunday afternoon. We hope you and your wife will be able to come. Pierre Bouyou will read the accounts, and we will agree the price of water for the next six months. By the way, have you met *Monsieur* Bouyou yet?"

"No, not yet," James replied, shaking his head. "Although Miguel Casarin mentioned to me that someone called Bouyou-Carendier lives in Pisenhaut. Which is his house then?"

Before he replied, Gérard waved his hand down the valley and then pointed towards the north of Bon Porteau's woods.

"It's the very large place with pale green shutters and a beautiful garden at the bottom of the hill," he explained. "*Monsieur* Bouyou was an important industrialist from Lyon, before he came to live here. Rumour has it that he owns several sugar plantations in Réunion. Anyway, he's always flying off somewhere, and he seems to spend a few months each year in Paris." He hesitated, lowering the tone of his voice. "He lives in that enormous place with another man, Jules Carendier, a painter and sculptor. *Ils font ménage à deux.* They live together, calling themselves Bouyou-Carendier... With a hyphen. *Et voilà!* You will like them, I'm sure. And, by the way, never refuse a dinner invitation there; I'm told they're quite something! Anyway, both of them should be at the meeting."

"Ah, bon! Merci bien, Gérard! There's now't so queer as folk! And thanks for the tip! *Au revoir!*"

Although he was not aware of it, James was smiling to himself when he rejoined Diana.

"What was that all about and why are you looking so cheerful?" she asked, while she continued to wash the cats' bowls in the sink.

"Oh, nothing much. Gérard came to read the *source* meter for Félicie's final account. He also told me that there's a meeting of the *Association* at three this Sunday. We're both expected. Then he filled me in on the owners of that big house at the bottom of the hill... You know, the one with pale green shutters and that huge walnut tree in the middle of the lawn. Apparently two guys, who rejoice in the name of Bouyou-Carendier, live together there. One's called Pierre, but I don't know the other's name."

"Well, that's no big deal nowadays. It happens all the time. They're probably also very sophisticated, charming, and present no threat to anyone. Look at some of our closest friends. It'll be nice to meet them some time."

"Anyway, Gérard interrupted my nap, *con!* I think I'll just take a few more nods before I get on with the next chores."

As he went downstairs, his mind worked on something to do with the gender of French nouns but, once in the bedroom, he gave up trying to recall his elusive train of thought. He was soon snoring contentedly.

*

He was woken up by the telephone bleeping on his bedside table. Checking his watch, he could not believe that he had slept for more than two hours. *"Allô, oui! Bonjour!"* he mumbled.

It was Miguel, who had already found a buyer for the diesel tank.

"Bon Dieu! You don't waste any time, do you, Miguel!"

"De la chance, M'sieu," was the reply. "Just luck. This chap wanders into the shop and starts complaining about all the *bricolage* he had taken on at home. He's installing his own central heating system. So I asked him if he had yet bought an oil tank. He hadn't. *Et bien, voilà!* But he has now! I'm coming up to fetch it if it's convenient."

When Miguel saw the fire damage, he became very serious, explaining that he was himself a volunteer *sapeur pompier*. For the third time in just twenty-four hours, James then received a stem lecture on the hazards of bonfires and the folly of fire-raising.

"Still, I put it out successfully all by myself," James parried. "I think I ought to apply to be a *sapeur pompier.*"

"Don't even bother, *Monsieur*," Miguel said politely. "If you're over thirty, they won't take you on as a trainee. And don't let the *gendarmes* see this mess."

Miguel drained the remaining diesel from the tank, swung a small hoist over the side of his lorry, and lifted the tank on board. He then secured it with the skill of an experienced long-distance lorry driver.

"I assumed," Miguel ventured, as he tied the last rope down, "that you had come here to retire and enjoy yourself, *Monsieur*. I mean, you realize that keeping Bon Porteau looking tidy is a full-time job in itself."

Feeling his age and aching muscles, James wandered slowly back to the house, his thoughts turning to the list of financially viable projects which had been gestating in his mind ever since they had acquired Bon Porteau.

"*Merde!*" he rasped. "I can't retire yet! I'm only fifty-one! I'll have to generate some francs somehow."

Chapter Twenty-One

It was hard to imagine that such tranquility could replace the turmoil and panic of the earlier part of the day. It had turned into a perfect evening, still, warm, cloudless, and unbelievably silent. It was a setting, ideal either for relaxation or for thought. Every corner of the roof *terrasse* basked in the pleasantly cooler sunshine. They were sitting quietly, drinking their first *apéritif* under the shade of the Virginia creeper. Earlier, three young *biches* trotted out of the trees into the field. Then the trio of does stepped serenely down the drive, not threatened as yet by the imminent start of the shooting season. From their vantage point on the parapet, the two cats were patiently contemplating the garden and the valley, where they would soon be allowed to roam at will.

James was relating the extraordinary sequence of coincidences which he had experienced with Iain earlier in the week.

"Stewart," he finally announced, "is Iain's second son, and Nellie is his mother-in-law!"

"You must be joking, James! I don't believe you!" Diana laughed, until he shook his head and swore that he was telling the truth.

"So it was Iain and Laetizia," she exclaimed, surprise and pleasure showing on her face, "who were with the dog at Toulouse Airport! And they're going to be living here in Saint Juste! Well, that's the second amazing coincidence since we arrived here! I wonder if we've brought some weird African spell with us to the Lot! It will be good to see Stewart again, and I must write and tell Nellie as soon as possible. That reminds me, we must buy a good typewriter to replace the one we sold in Zambia."

He repeated some advice which, he recalled, he had given her some months ago.

"If you're going to continue writing your journal and newsletters," he urged her, "you would do better with a simple word processor. They're not so expensive nowadays, I believe."

"Garden machinery is," she retorted. "I was horrified at how much you spent this morning, when we've got so many other urgent things to buy."

"But Miguel, the garden machinery man, has already sold that old, diesel tank," he said defensively.

"That's just a drop in the ocean," was her reply. "You'll have to ring the bank tomorrow."

"How much do you think we should transfer?"

"Oh, I should think about a quarter of a million," she said nonchalantly. "Pounds, that is, not francs. We'll need *that* much, at the rate you're going at present."

He never enjoyed talking about money at the best of times, and he switched their conversation to listing those items, which they needed to buy immediately: a decent mini-oven, which would permit cooking without burning everything; a refrigerator, which doesn't leak — these first two items would be a temporary arrangement, while they decided what to do about a sensible kitchen; a second-hand cupboard, large enough to take all the linen, which they would put in the boiler room; a good stereo system, to replace the twenty-year-old Sony, so that she could listen to her favourite music, collected painstakingly over many years; a radio, able to decipher the BBC, instead of the wailing mullah, who was constantly summoning them to prayers on their battered portable; and a second cat flap.

"And don't forget the typewriter," Diana reminded him. "And some time soon, I'm going to have to find someone to alter the curtains, which are in a real mess. They all have different headings. Most of them don't even cover the windows when they're drawn. Some have one or two wooden rings, others have five. The lengths are all over the place. And practically every fixture is different from the next."

Diana pressed her point on the urgency of some of the items, and they soon agreed that it would be sensible to spend the whole of the next day in Cahors.

"Let's see how much we can knock off the list," he said supportively. "But I don't think we'll have enough time to choose a reliable, second-hand car, capable of towing a big trailer."

"*What* car?" she demanded, taken aback by this entirely new suggestion. "Why do we need *two* cars? And what's this about a trailer? What are we going to use for money? You've spent it all this morning!"

"No I have not," he parried. "Miguel agreed to hold the cheque until next week. And it's obvious we're going to need two cars. I can't leave you stranded out here, while I get busy and lift some of my projects off the ground. I'll have to be mobile as well if I'm to start earning some francs, instead of transferring our precious pounds out here. I'll tell you what I have in mind in a minute, but let's have another drink first."

He returned with fresh glasses and a carafe of red wine, and then began pacing up and down the *terrasse*, while he tried to collect his thoughts and put them in a logical sequence. He took a deep breath and decided that now was the time to share with her the burgeoning plans which he had been carefully mulling over in his mind for some time.

"I want to see Louisor, the estate agent—"

"Why? You're not already thinking of selling Bon Porteau, are you?"

"Don't be facetious, darling. This is serious stuff. It's my plan of action! This is all about our future here, our survival in fact. Anyway, as I was saying before I was interrupted, I want to see Louisor. I remember suggesting to him that he really needs someone part-time to handle his English-speaking clients. You know, to take them around, answer all their daft questions, and make sure they don't fall into the more obvious traps. I also mentioned to him that I speak fluent German, but he wasn't very impressed with that. They don't seem to like selling properties around here to Germans..."

Diana was giggling helplessly, and he waited quietly for her full attention to return to what he was about to say. She, however, was still in a mood to banter.

"Did you by any chance tell him," she quipped again, "that you are also a private pilot?"

"Diana! Stop making a joke of it!" he protested once more. "This is serious stuff. Now... Where was I? Right then. In short, I told Louisor that I'll provide a trilingual service to ensure that buyers find what they want, just as smoothly and cost-effectively as we managed to do ourselves. He'll pay me a commission, of course, but I can't do it without a car." He paused for a few moments, expecting her to challenge his plan and he was pleasantly surprised when she remained silent.

"Still thinking about languages, I'll get some translating work, do some lecturing and, as a result, pick up some well-paid consultancy work along the way."

Diana was watching him as he paced earnestly to and fro on the other side of the table, his expression showing that he was intent upon a serious discussion.

"Do sit down, darling, if you're going to have a sensible chat," she suggested. "I'm getting a crick in my neck watching you wandering about all over the place."

He pulled up a chair and sat down facing her.

"I also want to build up a programme of tutoring girls and boys," he resumed. "Perhaps they should be around eighteen years old and preparing for their *baccalauréat,* which is their 'A' level. I've got my language learning system to market as well. You know, we've enough space here to start a language school. It would have to begin as a day school, of course. Later, it could develop and expand quite logically into a residential crammer, a bit like how Millfield was created by Jack Meyer. But that will depend upon what we decide to do with the bedrooms in the roof, the barn, and the old bakery. I'll come back to possible plans for the outbuildings later. If, or rather when, all that starts generating enough francs, I thought I would take my pilot instructor course and teach student pilots. There's a flying school at Lalbenque, the Cahors commercial airfield."

He tried to judge Diana's reaction from her expression. She appeared to be deep in thought. He decided that he may as well continue, surprised and a little dismayed that she was not being more supportive.

"Then, I must get our land and woods productive and self-sufficient. We're both *far* too young — you more so than I — to sit on our bums doing nothing. And so I'm going to investigate the feasibility of bottling the water from our private *sources*; that means getting it properly tested in Cahors. I know exactly what I'm going to do. I'll take three plain bottles to the water analysis laboratory. I'll mark them with a secret code. Two of them will contain different proprietary brands of still water. The third will be our water, which will prove itself to be the purest! *Et voilà! Hop!* That will put the test to the test as well, if you see what I mean. And then we'll be in business!"

"Is that all?" Diana enquired, picking up Jacob and giving him a kiss.

He helped himself to another glass of red wine before he answered her question.

"Good heavens, no! I want to get the nearest field back from Griffoul, the farmer. I'll have to handle it delicately, but that won't be a real problem for someone as diplomatic as I am. That field is south-facing. It looks to me like the right kind of soil for a vineyard, and it's large enough to produce about three thousand bottles of wine a year. That should keep us going: on average, about eight bottles a day if we drank all of it ourselves! No, I'm joking, of course. We'll apply for A.C.C. — *Appellation Cahors Controllée.* A good, five-year-old Cahors wine, like ours will be, retails direct from the *vigneron,* the grower, at between thirty and fifty francs a bottle. If we kept a thousand bottles for our own consumption and... um, for our many visiting friends of course, then... " He made a quick calculation. "Then the balance at, say, thirty-five francs each, would generate seventy grand a year. I will design and sketch our own label. We'll call it *'La Domaine de Bon Porteau'* and sell it all over the world! We'll exhibit in Paris, Macon, and all the other international fairs. Once they elect me a *Seigneur des Vins*, we can also organize, for a suitable fee of course, a few wine-buying tours for our lovely, rich American tourists."

"James! Have another drink! You know that's all pie in the sky!"

He was beginning to feel worried about her apparently negative attitude thus far towards his outline plans, and he reacted accordingly.

"I really don't see why you should say that," he snapped with ill-concealed irritation. "I've given it all a great deal of thought. What's more, if you want to make a contribution to the success of this enterprise, I don't see why we shouldn't breed golden pheasants. You never see one in the supermarkets, and hardly ever in a *boucherie.* I'll build suitable pens for them and get a few lucrative contracts going. It's simple — money for old rope, I should think! All *we* have to do is feed them, and they'll grow fat. When they're ready, *you* can kill them. Then, all that remains to be done is to persuade the great French nation to eat them."

"I thought for a moment that I heard the royal 'We' changing to 'You'. If *you* think *I'm* going to kill the babies *I'm* rearing, then *you've* got another think coming! *No way!*"

Exasperation was not far away, but he was determined not to be discouraged.

"Now you're just being wet," he persevered. "Another profitable idea is to grow lavender. You could look after that, but I would have to help you at harvest time. If you wanted to do something else, you could start a cattery and breed Burmese cats. You never know. You might end up as Madam President of the Burmese Cat Club of France, which includes Martinique and Réunion. Come to think of it, when you visit the islands on Cat Club duty, you could take me on holiday with you!"

"You should be so lucky!" Diana laughed. "I'll take a tall, handsome, male secretary, who is well-endowed and can give me plenty of what I haven't had enough of since we arrived here!"

Her laughter reassured him a little, and he felt that they might now be able to develop his remaining thoughts more seriously.

"That leaves the old bakery and the stone barn," he resumed, ignoring her gibe at his libido. "I remember when we first saw this place, Félicie said something about converting the old bakery into a TV room for her grandchildren, or perhaps it was a guest bedroom. Well, I think it would make a superbly romantic honeymoon suite. It's completely private and it could have its own little garden, tucked away at the back there by those maple trees. Admittedly, a little work needs to be done on it, but then it would be up and running, with a shower, basin, loo, bidet, and a huge bed. We could advertise it in *The Times*. The barn is a more serious affair. Very little needs to be done to make it into the perfect classroom for the language school. The investment there would have more to do with equipment. The other alternative is a guest cottage, or a *gîte*. I should think that two good bedrooms are possible. But I would need a strong trailer for the second car to carry cement, sand, tiles, wood, and so on, during its conversion. As a *gîte*, it would make a steady income. Both the old bakery and the barn as *gîtes* could be extremely tax effective as well for very little effort. I would think that, after—"

He was not expecting the rapid reaction with which Diana chopped off the financial estimates he was about to reveal to her.

"Except on my part," she bridled swiftly. "I would be forever either making sandwiches or buffet lunches for your crazy idea of a language school, or else washing and ironing holidaymakers' dirty sheets and towels. It would be a terrible tie. We would never be able to get away on holiday to see other parts of France and Europe, let alone visit our friends in Africa. And it would be far too much hard work. I'll have quite enough to do here in the house without all that."

"No, no!" he went on a little wildly. "You're not thinking big enough. Given that they're successfully converted, that is to say the honeymoon suite and the *gîte,* we'll form a company, which will employ a housemaid, a cook, a gardener, a woodsman, or whatever. When the maid is not involved with the *gîtes,* she will become your *femme de ménage.* She will work in the house. The gardener, of course, will be a proper full-time job. Ideally, he would be a woodsman and a mechanic as well, so that the cars are properly maintained. He would be a kind of *Lotois* Phebian, washing the cars and doing all sorts of odd jobs, such as making sure that the cats' tray is always full of dry sand at night. If he were also a good handyman, that would be an additional bonus. I would take charge of him, of course."

He paused again, hoping at last that the look on her face was encouraging him to expand on his business plan.

"And then," he announced confidently, "the company accounts would be presented in such a way that you would end up having free help in the house, more or less whenever you wanted it, and I would have permanent help with the estate in general. And, what's more, you can always put your friends up in the *gîtes!* You would never be lonely, while I am busy making it all happen smoothly! We might even find that we do not need a second bathroom in the main house although, on second thoughts, I think we will, because we will have to get a proper bath, instead of that yellow hip monstrosity. *Voilà!* Finally, if I'm not boring you, I thought, as a wet weather activity, that I should really write a book about some of our African experiences. A good title, I feel, would be *'The Z Factor'* and it will be mostly about our Zambian escapades, which is why the letter 'Z' is in the title. Any sensible, commercially-minded publisher would take it on, since I write so concisely."

"And which of these little projects are you going to start first?"

He wondered briefly if it was a serious question. He decided that there was nothing to be lost and everything to be gained if he spoke his mind.

"Oh, Lord!" he admitted with a sigh. "I haven't the faintest idea. "We must get this place sorted out a bit." He stood up and then continued vaguely, "Sooner or later we must get down to asking for some quotations from the local builders and tradesmen. The new kitchen... utility room... stairs... bathroom... fireplace... and then, um..."

Before he could continue, the telephone rang, and they both stood up.

"I'll get it," Diana volunteered. "But I think that's quite enough wild speculation for one day," she called over her shoulder as she went to answer the call.

"Humph! If you don't speculate," he mused, "then you don't accumulate. Damn! I forgot to ring Robert at lunchtime."

*

The telephone call was from Iain, who told Diana that Laetizia was now back from Poland and that Stewart had arrived a few days earlier than he had expected.

"They've asked us to go round for drinks and a snack supper."

"What! This evening?" James asked.

"Yes. He said to come as we are, as soon as we are ready"

"These people brought up in the bush!" he grumbled. "They don't change. There's no order, no planning in their lives. They just drift with the mood. I really didn't want to go out this evening. I'm bushed."

"Oh, come on, James. Don't be such a wet blanket. I haven't planned anything special for supper anyway. I can't, with these bloody cookers! And it will be fun seeing Stewart again after all this time. I wonder what Laetizia is like. I'll just go and quickly get changed."

"Well, I'm not going to... He said to come as we are."

The track to Iain's house had not dried out very much, and the jeep slithered and splashed through the woods and across the two large fields down to the house. Iain had erected some electric fencing, on which was hanging a crudely painted notice with the words: *'Danger! 10,000 Volts!'* Two horses, a grey mare and a chestnut gelding, were standing placidly outside the open barn, inside which they could see a bed with a mosquito net over it.

"Hey! *Jambo, Mzee! Habari?*" Iain's voice boomed out. He pointed past the bed into the barn. "Stewart is somewhere in there, putting in some temporary lighting. He'll join us when he's finished. Hullo, Diana. We sort of met on the plane, didn't we? Come and meet Laetizia."

Laetizia was in her small, narrow kitchen, surrounded by vegetables and saucepans. There were dishes and glasses on every available work surface.

"Hullo," she said. "I'm Laetizia, and please excuse the debris."

Her voice was positive, almost authoritative, with a faint accent. "Iain, take Diana and James into the other room. I must just finish preparing these vegetables, and then I'll join you." Iain took a stone bottle out of the refrigerator and picked up some liqueur glasses.

"Laetizia brought this fiendish stuff back with her," he explained, pouring out the clear, icy liquid. "It's vodka, like you've never tasted it before. You take it in one bold swig. *Voilà!* Cheers everyone!"

He was still wearing the same bush shirt and boots, but he had exchanged his trousers for a Somali kikoi, which now hung casually from his waist and almost touched the floor.

He took Diana and gently guided her towards one of the only two chairs in the room.

"Isn't it extraordinary," he said pleasantly, "that you know Nellie so well?" They discussed the old lady of Manda Island, and it soon became apparent that, through her frequent letters, Diana was in much closer contact with his mother-in-law than was Iain. Laetizia joined them, taking off her apron as she entered the room. Petite, with blonde hair, her complexion also tanned through years of living in East Africa, she fell into easy conversation with Diana, discussing their respective first impressions of the Lot. Iain was telling James about a visit from the *gendarmes* the previous day.

"You know," he said seriously, "you have to be careful with these blighters. Someone down there in Saint Juste must have reported seeing the smoke from a bonfire which I lit to get rid of some rubbish before Laetizia returned. They came to check on me and they asked to see my *Carte de Séjour*. Of course, I haven't got one yet. We have six months' grace in which to organize all that."

James was on the point of starting to relate the dramatic episode of his fire, when Stewart returned from the barn. Noisy greetings followed, and they worked out that it was eight years since they had first met on Lamu Island.

"Bloody strange, isn't it?" Stewart sounded like his father, speaking in a deep, booming tone. "Dad told me about your first meeting here. It's funny that you should remember me through ambergris, my dog, and swimming the channel with those black plastic sacks. I still have Mistral, the dog. But in my mind is the memory of you and Diana telling us about your treasure hunt on the long beach. You walked off the beach into the bar, just as we were concocting that dreadful drink. I expect they're all still down there talking about it even now. Do you remember?"

"Yes, I do now. Diana and I used to walk miles up that long beach every day, but we never managed to reach the end of it On that occasion we took with us Wolf, the alsatian from the hotel. It was a very hot day, and we swam every ten minutes or so to cool down."

Iain prevented him from continuing for a few moments while he filled up any glasses that were empty.

"Go on, James," Laetizia said, excitement showing in her eyes "I want to hear about this treasure."

"Well, it was Wolf who spotted the object lying in the sand right up by the high tide mark. His hackles went up and he circled it suspiciously. He growled, and even barked at it. I picked it up. It was almost round, surprisingly heavy, wrapped with what looked like a kind of grease-proof paper similar to parchment, and tied up with strong string. We could see Arabic writing on the paper. I remember Diana didn't want me to touch it. She suggested that it might be something to do with their religion, or contain some foetal remains which might have been buried at sea, or even a severed hand. She was quite agitated about it. Of course, I knew that it was nothing of the kind. It had obviously fallen overboard from one of those big dhows which sail from the Gulf down to Mombasa. There was a good chance that it was a cache of jewels or, maybe, even gold, which would account for its unexpected weight. Whatever was inside, it was bound to be of value. Why else would the string be tied so carefully and securely?"

His rhetorical question produced an almost childlike cry of awe from Laetizia, who was now leaning towards him with impatient curiosity.

"I had no knife with me," he continued. "So I used some small, sharp seashells to cut away at the string. It was hard work out in the full sun, and sweat was pouring off me. At last I managed to remove the outer layer of thick paper, only to find more string and more paper. In fact, there were five or six such layers, and all the pieces of paper had this Arabic script on them. It took more than half-an-hour to undo the whole thing. Wolf lost interest and strayed back along the beach, heading towards the hotel."

"Well, what did you find in it?" demanded Iain, who had also been listening intently to the tale.

James, never a good raconteur, could not resist the opportunity to make what he believed to be a required dramatic pause. Nobody spoke; only Stewart was smiling.

"Well, that's the whole point," James replied slowly with a rueful smile. "There was *nothing* inside, absolutely nothing at all!"

An embarrassed silence fell on the party, until Iain prompted James to put forward some final explanation of the event.

"There really isn't much more to say," James resumed. "Diana was convinced that we had interfered with something sacred and, as we walked back, we agreed that it would be prudent to say nothing about it to anybody. That was before the dreaded "rocket fuel" loosened my tongue. Then I was telling these guys about it. We felt a bit stupid when we found out what we had discovered. It was that character with the Union Jack swimming trunks who told us... Diana, what was his name?"

"Mohammed British," she reminded him.

"Yes, that's right. It was that strange character whom everyone knew as Mohammed British. It was he who told us what it was."

"And *what* was it?" Iain insisted.

James looked at Stewart, inviting him to provide the dénouement for the so-called treasure hunt.

"Go on, Stewart. You tell them. I'm sure you remember."

"No, no," he protested. "After all, it was you who found it."

"Well," James said quietly, playing with their anticipation. "In fact, it was nothing more than a homemade, native football!"

"It had been kicked into the water, probably three miles away in Lamu town," Stewart added. "The tide carried it out to sea, and eventually it was washed up round the corner of the point and on to the long beach, where Wolf found it. He knew full well that it was an African, makeshift football, because he didn't like them, or rather the feet which kick them. That was why he was growling."

"But a football made out of paper and string can't be all that heavy, can it?" queried Laetizia, looking perplexed by the whole episode.

"Because it had been in the sea, probably for some time," Stewart explained, "it had become waterlogged. That would account for its weight."

"It was a shame you didn't find some nice jewels for Diana," was Laetizia's final comment.

*

Over a very late supper they continued to exchange tales from Africa. Stewart was also a qualified private pilot, and he and James were soon enthusiastically discussing their hobby.

"Are you going to continue flying in France?" asked Laetizia, who had been listening quietly to them.

"I'd love to, Laetizia," James replied. "But I'll have to earn a lot of francs. It's a very much more expensive pastime here, unlike Africa."

"How are you going to earn enough francs?" Iain asked politely.

"Oh, I have a few little projects in mind," James confided. "But they are only at an embryonic stage."

"Iain, please don't get James on to the subject of his projects," Diana begged. "Otherwise, we'll be here until dawn the day after tomorrow, and we must be going soon."

"No, I was just curious," Iain said. "I'll have the same problem, once I've finished this place. I'm thinking of organizing safaris on horseback, going *from château* to *château* around the Lot, ending up each evening with a good dinner and living in a style to which I could rapidly become accustomed. That's what a friend of mine is doing, except that he uses camels, and there aren't any *châteaux* in Northern Kenya!"

"Bloody good idea!" James said, helping himself to a whisky. "Tell us a bit about what you plan to do to this place."

Iain outlined some of his ideas for enlarging their cottage, one of which would involve raising the height of the roof by about one metre and putting in windows.

"Then we'll be able to put proper bedrooms and bathrooms up there in the roof space," he explained. "At the moment it's all just useless space. Even the shortest Frenchman could not stand upright in it!"

"Have you found, or do you know, a good builder?" James asked. "You'll need a competent stonemason to take on that kind of work. We'll be needing one as well."

"No. I'm going to do it all myself," Iain replied. "I'm not going to waste money on tradesmen, and anyway I can't afford European labour rates. It shouldn't be too difficult. You might be able to give me a hand when there's anything really heavy to lift, and I'll do the same for you."

"I'm afraid I'm not too good at weight lifting," James mumbled quietly into his empty glass. "Bugger that for a fast route to a fortnight's bed rest!"

Iain stood up, went into the kitchen, and returned with a full bottle of whisky. Diana looked across at James, who nodded his recognition that she thought it was time to be leaving.

"The trickiest part," Iain continued enthusiastically, "will be forming the openings for the windows and the new doorways to the outside. Those big blocks of stone and the lintels are damned heavy, and it will be block-and-tackle work — but I've done it before. Admittedly, we weren't working in stone. We were using large, heavy trees, with twenty or so lovely, strong Africans doing the lifting. Anyway, we should have the new roof on by the end of winter. I'm also going to replace all the tiles with those nice, old ones. They're cheaper than the new ones, and much more attractive."

"Well, that really does make all our projects pale into insignificance!"

"Whose projects?" Diana interjected.

"Okay, darling. I was referring to *my* projects. Best of luck, Iain, but I don't think I would take the roof off during the winter months, any more than I would like to sleep in a barn with no doors! They'll all catch pneumonia!"

"No they won't," Iain retorted firmly. "They're tough youngsters, not like you and me!"

His laugh was reverberating round the room as he put another large whisky in front of James.

"By the way, James, you were in the cavalry, weren't you?"

"Only for about eight years, and in a very amateur role. Most of the time I was either skiing, playing cricket, or else on leave. I only ever fired a few shots in anger. That was in the Radfan, and they all missed! Why do you ask?"

"Well, you must know a lot about horses. My grey, Mermaid, is being a bit of a problem. I can't get her to move faster than a reluctant trot. Perhaps I'm too big for her, do you think?"

"Hell, no! Not from what I saw of her when we came past your barn. What you need is the convenient hot potato trick. You bake one in its skin, wrap it in tinfoil to retain the heat and keep it in your jacket pocket. When you want Mermaid to take off, remove the potato from the foil, lean backwards, and lift her tail. Then, in one swift, easy movement, pop the spud up her arse, at the same time letting go of her tail, which she'll use to clamp it in place. Then she'll go like shit off a shovel, as she tries to get away from it. The only problem will be stopping her! You'll need good braking power!"

They were all laughing at this unlikely solution to the problem, as Iain picked up a big torch and led them up towards the jeep by the barn.

"No, no! It's quite true!" James protested, slipping on the muddy track in the dark. "That's what our fierce Sergeant-Major used to bawl at us in our riding school. 'Don't sit there, like a fucking sack of old potatoes, Captain Wyllis, Sir! If you don't get that horse of yours into a canter, I'll ram a red-hot, baked potato up your jacksy, Sir!' Anyway, he obviously believed it. If I heard those words once, I heard them a hundred times!"

"But he wasn't referring to the horse, you fool!" Iain roared at him. "He was threatening to tamper intimately with *your* person!"

Then, in the beam of light from Iain's powerful torch they saw the damage which had occurred while they had been eating, drinking, and telling stories and jokes. The jeep, a gleaming example of modern manufacturing technology earlier in the week, looked as if it had been attacked by vandals. Two of the doors had been stove in by something, and angry, deep scratches criss-crossed the bonnet.

"Merde! Quel con! Quel con!! Qu'est-ce qui s'est passé ici?" James demanded, taking Iain's torch to have a closer look. "What the hell has been going on here? Our poor, new jeep! It looks as if it's come out of Beirut!"

"I didn't want to worry you, Dad," Stewart said quietly, "so I haven't mentioned it before, but I think it's the horses..."

"Horses? No, no! It can't possibly be the horses!" Iain bellowed in protest. "Never!"

"Well, come and have a look at my car," Stewart replied.

They all walked over to the furthest corner of Iain's barn, where Stewart pulled back a thick tarpaulin to reveal his lovingly restored, vintage Volkswagen Cabriolet. Its bodywork had suffered a similar fate, and the fabric of the roof had been shredded.

"Shit!" cursed Iain. "Hell, what a mess! But it can't be the horses! There must be a gang of hoodlums around somewhere. When did you notice all this, Stewart?"

"It had been done within three hours of my arrival. I hadn't even finished unloading the car."

"Maybe you should check yours, Iain," Diana said jokingly. "Accidents always happen in threes, you know."

Iain shone his torch over to where his car was parked, and walked slowly towards it. They could see him carefully running his hand over the paintwork of the bonnet. He said nothing, until he rejoined the group.

"Mine is the only French car here," he announced, grinning at them. "It has only been licked. They obviously don't like foreign cars! It's *got* to be these fucking French horses! Typical!"

"It's *got* to be these fucking French horses! Typical!" they all mimicked him in unison, laughing at his sudden volte-face.

"Stewart has come off worst," Iain said seriously, as their laughter died. "I'm terribly sorry about this. But don't worry. In France it's compulsory to insure your horse against claims from a third party. Fortunately, my policy arrived with yesterday's mail. It will give me the greatest pleasure to tell my insurance to pay up. The bloody premium is high enough anyway. Get a *devis*, James, a quotation for renewing the bonnet and the doors, and let me have it with a formal letter. Same applies to you, Stewart. You know, James, Mermaid must have heard you talking about that baked potato, but don't put that in your letter!"

Iain's good humour was contagious, and everyone was laughing again. Laetizia ran into the house to fetch her camera, and they stood beside the two wrecked cars in a happy group, smiling for posterity.

"Hey! Bloody good to have you as neighbours!" James shouted, as he wrenched open the battered door of the jeep. "I think I'll buy a French banger for our next visit! Funnily enough, I was just saying to Diana earlier this evening that we will be needing a second car. *Lala salama!* Sleep well!"

"*Kwaheri!*" Diana shouted over the noise of the diesel engine. "Goodbye!"

Chapter Twenty-Two

The plan was to spend one whole day shopping in Cahors. It would be 'simple', James had said confidently. Most of their immediate needs were electrical appliances, and the big stores with the widest choice were all located in a commercial complex outside the city centre. However, although they set off early, the plan was to be thwarted for a variety of reasons. The first unexpected factor was that they had not allowed for the time it would take to go twenty kilometres in the opposite direction to Cahors in order to call at the garage from which they had bought the jeep. Fifine was there, but this time she was on her best behaviour in the presence of Diana.

"O-là-là! she exclaimed, when she saw the scratched and dented vehicle with its coating of mud. "Have you driven it to Zambia and back already? Or perhaps you have been in the East African Rally?"

The foreman insisted that the jeep was washed, before he could make a realistic assessment and prepare a quotation. As a result it was not until after eleven o'clock that they were able to proceed with their shopping expedition.

"We've got about forty minutes left before everything shuts at midday," James grumbled as they approached Cahors.

"In that case," Diana decided, "that will just give me time to do the food shopping."

After some difficulties working out how to procure two shopping trolleys with ten franc coins, they decided to go their separate ways. James disappeared in the direction of the Wines and Spirits section of the store.

The first obstacle confronting Diana was the problem of choice, a luxury which hardly existed in Lusaka. Faced with almost permanent shortages, the most usual option had been to learn to do without. It was not so much the variety of cheeses, displayed on a counter almost thirty yards long, which shocked her; many of the brands were unknown to her anyway. It was rather more the multiplicity of different shapes and sizes of loaves of bread which brought her to a numbed halt, blocking the passage between the counters and shelves. She stood transfixed, her mind obsessed with the thought of how an ordinary Zambian family, such as that of Fackson or Phebian, would react to such obscene abundance and luxury.

She recalled how, at the height of one of the more prolonged periods of shortages, when there was not a grain of flour legitimately available in the capital, she would make a rendezvous on the Great East Road with a black marketeer, a cunning, twelve-year-old boy. He would watch and wait for the distinctive, white Suzuki jeep. When he saw it approaching, he would reach down into a large, concrete pipe, carefully positioned for this purpose in the roadside ditch, and extract six or, sometimes, even ten loaves. The bread would be transferred quickly to the car in exchange for a price more than four times the normal level. A friend, attempting the same clandestine operation, once returned triumphantly to her house to discover that she had bought a dozen loaves, the outer crusts of which covered nothing more than old newspapers. She had chosen the wrong youngster.

A diminutive Frenchman, grumbling impatiently that he wished to position his over-loaded trolley where Diana was standing, brought her back from her day-dream to the reality of the teeming superstore. She walked penitently past the shelves of bread, her trolley still empty. She accepted stoically the challenges of shopping in a completely new and bewildering environment, although it was not easy. The language barrier alone might have been enough for someone beginning to learn French, although her progress was remarkably swift. The problem of converting kilos, grams, and litres into pounds or fluid ounces was an additional burden. A tiresome, physical aspect during her quest for information on products was that frequently she had to stand on tiptoe to reach the top of some of the shelves. Surely, she thought to herself, these must be out of reach for most French people. Several times a minor avalanche of cartons of soap powder or rolls of paper towelling cascaded to the floor from the tightly packed racks.

The most difficult task, however, was the simple act of being able to read comfortably, in order to decipher the printed instructions on those products which she needed to buy. This was not because the lighting in the store was inadequate — it was on account of the extraordinary pair of glasses which had been prescribed for her by the only allegedly competent optician in Lusaka. The Indian proprietor tested her eyesight in a desultory manner, told her blandly that he had only three pairs of glasses in stock, one of which he removed from the otherwise empty shelf, and then mournfully demanded an exorbitant price. They now hung round her neck on a cord but, when she put them on to read the small print on the packaging, the words leaped into vision, badly out of focus and twice their normal size. Conversely, when she took them off, she could see nothing for a few moments, while her eyesight readjusted itself.

Doubts and questions rushed in and out of her mind, as she progressed slowly through the store. Was this self-raising or ordinary? What kind of salt is that one? What's the French for descaling a kettle? I wonder if that is real beef, or is it just horsemeat? Does this softener work in a washing machine? Why does it state that a possible side-effect of these herbal-based pills is diarrhoea, with a warning that they are not to be taken by people suffering from depression or schizophrenia? With a sigh of relief, she found the cats' favourite brands of food. She started tentatively to select the flavours which they preferred. She began filling her trolley with sufficient tins to last one week. She then moved on in search of cat litter.

In the meantime, James was progressing at a leisurely pace along the racks of wines, examining labels and comparing vintage, colour and price. A small stall was offering *dégustation gratuite*. No other customers were taking advantage of the offer to sample the wines free of charge, and he felt concerned for the pretty, well-dressed, young woman standing behind the opened bottles and empty glasses. She looked lost, or perhaps downhearted, he thought; in fact, she was bored, depressed since she was only paid on sales commission, and longing to escape from the noise and crush of shoppers who were ignoring her. He tried five of the different vintages on offer and bought a case of 1985 which, he judged, should complement the cheeses Diana would be buying. Although he was mindful of the warning given by the elderly Mayor of Saint Juste, he had no difficulty filling the trolley, mostly with a good selection of Cahors red wine. He found a few samples of *rosé,* about which he knew very little. For good measure, he added to the load in his protesting trolley some bottles of gin, whisky, an interesting *Calvados*, and two bottles

of *Ricard*. There would be time enough later, he thought, to visit
vineyards, buy his wine in bulk, and bottle it himself. Guillaume
would no doubt advise and assist in the process. He was looking
forward to organizing the cellar properly, but he reluctantly thought it
wise, perhaps even tactful, to relegate that task to a lower priority —
at any rate for the moment.

Diana found him at the checkout as the store was about to close.
Behind him a queue of people waited impatiently, feeling the approach
of lunchtime.

"I can't get my *Banque Lotoise* card to work!" he shouted across to
her. "I think I've forgotten my zap code, or whatever it's called."

Diana struggled to manoeuvre her trolley through the jostling
shoppers in an effort to join him at the front of the queue.

"Je m'excuse, mais c'est mon mari. Il a un petit problème!" she
offered a sea of protesting faces. "Please excuse me. It's my husband.
He's got a little problem!"

Reluctantly the longsuffering shoppers politely reversed their heavy
trolleys, colliding with each other and creating a bottleneck in that
area of the store. It was left to a long-haired Scotsman standing in the
queue to sum up the situation.

"Look at tha-a-t!" he rasped at the middle-aged woman wearing an
anorak and tight jeans who was standing beside him. "Yon daft
bugger, wi' his dandy check cap, he couldn'ay organize hissel' a pee
at a distillery Open Day wi'oot wettin' hissel. Reminds me o' tha'
Conservative Minister who owns big estate near Galla', allus makin' a
bloody crisis fra' noot."

"Och, Angus! Show a wee bit o' patience, mon!" his companion
whined.

"Gi' on wi' it, laddie!" Angus finally shouted, ignoring her advice.

James ignored the display of boorish behaviour and waited
impassively to be rescued from his unplanned demise.

Diana finally reached the front of the queue and smiled sweetly at
the young cashier, who finished filing a fingernail before she looked
up.

"I'll pay for both of us," she told the girl, who looked as if she had
just left school.

"Is that all you bought?" he demanded, as he peered into her trolley, which contained only a few tins of cat food, two bags of cat litter, and a packet of six rolls of paper towelling for the kitchen."

"Yes," she admitted quietly. "I don't feel very well. The sight of all those goodies made me feel quite sick, and they've got nothing at the other end in Zambia."

The bill for the wines and spirits was almost thirty times the cost of the rest of the items.

Once in the fresh air and sunshine, Diana started to feel better and began laughing.

"That was *un bon plan*, wasn't it?" she joked, as he loaded the bottles into the back of the jeep.

"What do you mean?" he asked innocently.

"Pretending that you couldn't work that card machine. It was your not-very-subtle way to get me to the front of the queue, otherwise we would still be in there." She looked at the receipt for the wines and refrained from any comment on how much he had spent. "You're a cunning liar!" she went on. "I don't know whether you had really forgotten your code, or whether you just wanted me to pick up the bill!"

"You're right on both counts," he admitted. "Actually, it was quite embarrassing. Did you hear that uncouth Jock? And I had visions of having to put all those bottles back on the shelves. So thanks for rescuing me. *Allez! Tout est fermé.* Most places shut for two hours now, so I'll buy you a decent lunch."

*

It was after three o'clock when they finally emerged from an excellent lunch at *La Taverne* off the Boulevard Gambetta. James unashamedly used the restaurant's comprehensive list of wines to increase his knowledge of the names of local vineyards, making notes in the back of his pocket diary. Over the meal he explained to Diana how, when he eventually found the time, he was planning to create a series of collages out of the labels of all the wines they would drink in future years. Each label was to be marked with the date of consumption, and a quality rating up to a maximum of fifty points. He planned to hang them under picture lights on the walls of the cellar. They had probably eaten too much; they had certainly drunk enough.

Neither of them now relished the prospect of prolonging their shopping expedition. The warm sunshine added to the soporific effect of the *menu gastronomique*. They decided to sit on a bench in the Place Chapou while they considered their options.

"There's one thing that isn't on our list," Diana said ominously.

"Oh? What's that?" he asked, stifling a yawn.

"Some time very soon, I really must get my eyes tested properly."

He said nothing, slowly arriving at the connection between a time-consuming eye test and the opportunity to take a quiet siesta in a silent, darkened waiting-room.

"Yes," he agreed suddenly. "You really must look after your lovely green eyes. I had forgotten about that problem. Let's keep it simple. We'll find an optician, and we'll do it now. You can get tested this afternoon. Splendid idea!"

It did not prove entirely simple. The first optician they found explained to them that she needed a prescription from a qualified eye specialist.

"In this country the *opticien lunetier*, like myself, only supplies you with suitable glasses," he said apologetically, and directed them to a surgery where he was sure there would be no need for an appointment in advance. James dozed contentedly while the specialist completed his examination and tests. They stopped for a cup of coffee before returning to the first optician, who wisely nodded his head as he studied the hieroglyphics on the prescription.

"Now, all you need to do is to choose which of these frames you would like," the Frenchman said.

He took some measurements and then led her over to a display of several hundred frames in every shape, design, and colour.

James headed for a comfortable chair at the other end of the shop, and drifted into his second siesta of the afternoon.

"You need large lenses," the optician went on, offering her one of the samples. "Your prescription is for multi-focals, which is better. Then you need only one pair, instead of a pair each for reading, shopping, driving, and watching television."

"Bloody choices!" she muttered to herself. "Everywhere I'm confronted with choices!"

It seemed to her that she must have tried on most of the entire stock. The process of selection was made all the more difficult since the price of each model was marked on minuscule labels, which she could not read — the very reason for entering the shop in the first place. On principle, she never bought anything without knowing its cost.

At last, she chose a green frame and looked over towards James, seeking his approval.

"Look, darling," she said, believing James to be taking a close interest in the proceedings. "These ones match the colour of my eyes, don't they, darling?"

James awoke abruptly, yawned, and rose to examine the final choice.

"Bloody good!" he said approvingly. *"Très, très chic, ma chérie.* When will they be ready? Today, I hope. *Aujourd'hui, j'espère."*

The optician consulted his notes again and disappeared into an office to use the telephone.

"You can collect them shortly before seven o'clock this evening when we close," he announced on his return.

"Bugger that," James grunted. "We'll collect them tomorrow morning. I think we've had enough hanging about for one day."

"Comme vous voulez, Monsieur," the optician said deferentially. "As you wish."

Returning to the jeep, he looked at the formidable list of items which they had intended to buy that day.

"Well, that wasn't very productive," he said dryly. "We haven't managed to get any of this lot. I think we'll do the rest of our shopping tomorrow. At least you'll be able to see, which should make it a bit easier to choose the right electrical equipment."

"As long as the instruction manuals are in English," she said, not very confidently, shuddering at the prospect of all that technology.

"Anyway," he concluded, "we've had a really good lunch and seen a bit more of Cahors. It seems a really pretty place. Let's go back to Bon Porteau a different way. I suggest we go over the Pont Valentré, that lovely old bridge reputed to be one of the finest in France, and follow the Lot down towards Puy-l'Evêque, and then wander slowly back home through the vineyards of Vire and Floressas."

It was late in the evening when he finally found time to make a number of telephone calls. He was about to pick up the handset, when it suddenly rang beside him.

"*Allô! Oui, bonsoir!*"

"Do... you... speak... English?"

He could not recognize the female voice, which was speaking slowly and deliberately, as if addressing a moron. He put the handset to his other ear.

"Yes, strangely enough, I do. I am English. Who is calling?" His question was ignored. The line crackled as the voice started to shout stridently.

"Well, why do you answer the phone in French?"

"Because, my dear whoever-you-are, this *is* France. People speak French here," he said impatiently. "Would you prefer me to answer in Swahili? Who are you?"

"I've had a hell of a job getting your number," the voice went on, again refusing to reveal its identity. "You sent me the wrong one..."

The interference on the line prevented him from catching the rest of the sentence. He held the handset away from his ear and put his hand over the mouthpiece.

"There's some stupid bitch on the line," he called to Diana. "She won't say who she is, silly cow!"

He tried listening again. The voice continued volubly, not pausing for breath.

"And I don't know how you expect your friends to make contact with you. Three times I've rung the number you sent me, and all I get is some mad Frenchwoman. Is she your housekeeper, or something? You really must teach her to answer the phone in English. In English, do you hear me? Is Diana there?"

"Yes, she is. Hang on, the line isn't too good." With an ill-concealed sigh of relief he passed the handset to Diana. "It's for you," he said with a shrug.

"Hullo. Diana speaking... Oh! Hi, Sarah!"

James left the room and poured himself a whisky. If it was the Sarah he remembered from before their departure for Africa, he could not tolerate her.

"Stupid bitch!" he muttered aloud to himself.

He paced impatiently round the Persian rug in the drawing-room while the two women talked to each other. Almost an hour elapsed before he rejoined Diana in the living-room.

"Merde!" he shouted in frustration. "If that woman had not rung, I might have been able to get some of these calls off my list. It's too late to try now. They will just have to wait until the morning. Come on, let's go to bed."

"That was Sarah," Diana said in a matter-of-fact tone. "She's run off with some guy and is getting divorced."

"I'm not bloody surprised," he retorted, recalling Sarah's husband, who seemed a pleasant enough fellow. "I don't know how *anyone* can talk for so long on the telephone! What the hell did *she* want anyway?"

"To bring her new toy boy here on holiday for ten days."

"Bloody hell! *Ten* days!" he gasped. "Guests and fish stink after three days. Three hours with Sarah would be quite enough! What did you arrange?"

"Oh, I put her off, don't worry. I said that we've only just moved in, that we're all at sixes and sevens, and that it wouldn't be convenient just yet. Anyway, I haven't seen her for years. It annoys me when people you know lose touch, and then they ring up out of the blue when they want something. Still, pity about the marriage — they've got three lovely, talented daughters."

*

That night he dreamed. Whether the images of his subconscious mind were enhanced by the large portions of cheese and wine at supper or, perhaps, fuelled by the frustrations of shopping, he would never know. His whole being was back in Zambia, vividly experiencing the enjoyable, but nevertheless tiresome, fourteen months during which he learned to fly light aircraft. Enjoyable, because it was something he had always wanted to achieve; tiresome, due to the many factors outside his control which frustrated many a flying lesson. One evening he and Diana, who had patiently tolerated his new obsession, calculated that, for every hour in the sky, there were seven hours of administration and waiting time. By contrast, study of textbooks and preparation for the written examinations added less than thirty minutes to their calculation.

The obstacles to his progress came in many guises and seldom, if ever, had anything to do with the weather: the aircraft was grounded, waiting for spare parts to be smuggled into the country; there was either no aviation fuel or no aero-engine oil; the instructor had failed to note the date and time of his student's meticulous booking of the aircraft; the airport was closed, because some dignitary was arriving at an unspecified time that day; likewise, the airport was closed due to the departure of His Excellency, the President; yet again, the airport was closed, because the national airline had taken delivery of a new, leased aircraft, which was in the circuit with the crew completing flight training; finally, on at least two occasions, nobody knew the location of the Club's Cessna 150, which had vanished somewhere into Zambian airspace and had not yet returned to base! During these trying episodes, and regardless of whether or not he actually achieved a few precious airborne minutes, James adhered rigorously to the pilot's rule of twelve hours between bottle and throttle, although several times he was tempted to get blind drunk as he waited... And waited... And waited.

As he dreamed, he could feel the intense October heat burning through the perspex of the cockpit. He turned over with a loud sigh. He had just been licensed to fly, and was at last allowed to carry passengers. He was practising his take-offs and landings at Lusaka International Airport. Diana was there in the passenger seat beside him. Kim, her daughter, had come out for a holiday. Since she wanted to reassure herself that he was fully competent to fly her mother around Africa, she too had come along for the ride and was sitting nervously in the rear seat. He had been cleared to final approach, ahead of a British Airways Boeing 747. And then suddenly he realized that the Control Tower was calling him. He adjusted his headset to listen carefully.

"Romeo-Hotel-November, where are you? We cannot see you. You are cleared to touch-and-go Number One."

It was a beautiful, clear morning with perfect visibility.

"Left, downwind, at six hundred feet," he reported, resisting the temptation to add that he was no more than three hundred metres away from them.

"Ah! Good!" continued the Air Traffic Controller, whom James had met on several occasions at the small Flying Club.

"Romeo-Hotel-November, we have you visual now. I am wondering if you can give us today's newspaper. Also, I have one of my brothers here, who would like a lift into the city when you may be going."

This exchange was cut short abruptly by the tired voice of the British Airways captain, who was now starting his second circuit of the airport.

"Hotel-November! Come on, Biggles, Romeo, or whoever you are! Get down, or clear off! I can't continue to burn expensive fuel like this, while you sort out newspaper deliveries and transport arrangements for our friends in the Tower."

He remembered thinking that the captain of the Boeing might be getting a little irate. He reached his final approach as quickly as he could, thinking that he had done enough for one morning and that he should land and stop.

"Tower, this is Romeo-Hotel-November," he reported. "Turning short finals now. Request permission to land and stop."

"Hotel-November, you are cleared to land. Expedite!"

The Tower then referred to the circuiting 747 which, as far as James was concerned, might have been anywhere in the sky. He just hoped that he saw it first.

"Hotel-November," the voice in the Control Tower crackled in his headsets. "After landing, clear runway at first exit. 747 is now on long final and closing fast."

In reality he was still learning the skills of becoming a pilot, regardless of the licence he proudly carried in his shirt pocket. He had no idea what might be the rate at which a Boeing 747 could overtake the two-hundred-and-forty-horsepower Piper Cherokee in which he had acquired a half share and which he was now flying. However, he knew that he had no time to waste. He also knew that jet aircraft of any size had to be avoided, and that flying a light aircraft into or near the vortex, the turbulent air, in the wake of a large jet airliner is an extremely hazardous activity. This was the kind of pressure he did not need while he was trying to sort out his speed and approach for landing.

Fortunately for them, neither Diana nor Kim were aware of the drama, since they were not wearing headsets. Then he realized something was drastically wrong. It was dead ahead, and not very far away.

"Tower! This is Romeo-Hotel-November on short finals. There's an old 707, which appears to be parked right across the threshold of the runway."

"Ah! Hotel-November. I am very happy you have seen it. It is boogard. The tow-bar, it is broken. You must land over the top. Please not to hit it."

The outcome of a collision between an airborne Piper Cherokee and a stationary Boeing 707, the latter at least a dozen times the larger of the two aircraft, did not bear thinking about. He had no intention of hitting it and followed the Control Tower's instructions, completing what his instructor usually described as 'a somewhat unorthodox, but controlled, crash-landing'.

As he took the first available exit off the runway, he could hear the heated exchange between the Control Tower and the captain of the British airliner, who was condemning the large obstacle, which was stranded like a whale on the end of the only serviceable runway. In the end, they managed to locate another tow-bar and dragged it out of the way just in time. When he parked in front of the Club, he transmitted his usual final message.

"Tower. Hotel-November. Closing down now. Thank you, sir, for your co-operation. Good day!"

Just before he switched off the radio he heard a crackle in his headset, and an anonymous voice softly uttered the words, 'You creep!', a procedure which he did not think would be listed in an Airline Captain's training manual. Next, as the noise of the engine died away and the propeller stopped, a small voice called out from the rear seat.

"Mum? Why couldn't you marry someone normal?"

He had forgotten that Kim was on board. He looked over his shoulder to give her a reassuring look and then fell out of bed, realizing that he was in a muck sweat but, nevertheless, with a contented smile on his face.

Chapter Twenty-Three

Despite the Saturday crowds in the shops, they met with unexpected successes the following day. This was only in part due to the new glasses, which they collected as soon as they arrived in the town. Their progress was the more enhanced by the fact that James was neither impatient nor bad-tempered. Nor did they spend three hours over lunch, as on the previous day — in fact, they did not stop at all, since several of the larger stores remained open throughout the day. However, the main reason was that Diana announced after breakfast that all the electrical equipment should originate from the same manufacturer. She justified this by claiming that such a policy would greatly simplify any subsequent maintenance contracts and after-sales service. If any one appliance broke down, then the expert would repair it and, while on the premises at Bon Porteau, he would be asked to check that everything else was functioning properly.

In this way, Diana reasoned, the whole arrangement would be much more cost-effective, since there was also a good chance that they could negotiate an exceptionally significant discount on the grounds of total product loyalty. This seemed logical to James, who gave her plan his full support. The only remaining question was the choice of manufacturer.

"Well, we have a Philips tumble-dryer and a Philips electric kettle," she observed. "And all the manuals will be available in English." Thus, at a stroke, the intellectual challenges of choice, language, and technology were swept aside confidently and, by mid-afternoon, every item except one on the list had a bold tick against it.

The exception was the linen cupboard. It did not need to be an object of great beauty, merely functional — it was, after all, destined only for the boiler room. He borrowed a telephone book in one of the superstores, and the Yellow Pages revealed a second-hand furniture warehouse which was only about ten kilometres outside Cahors. James found a suitable, large cupboard there which, he calculated, would fit through the doorways. When the proprietor explained that he would take it to pieces and deliver it on the same day, James was in favour of buying it on the spot.

"It's very ugly and a bit on the large side," Diana commented.

"No problem," James said confidently. "Look, it's in kit form. You just have to put the parts together with these wooden dowels. Simple! It'll only take about thirty minutes at the most to re-assemble it. I've got the roof-rack in the back of the jeep. We'll take it with us."

He confronted the proprietor and demanded a lower price, since no delivery costs would be incurred. The cupboard was dismantled rapidly and loaded on to the jeep. Some of the sections were surprisingly heavy.

Opposite the furniture warehouse there was a large establishment which manufactured and sold new furniture. On one of the show windows, a notice claimed that they were also one of the leading designers of kitchens in the Lot.

"Do you fancy looking at kitchens now?" James asked.

"May as well, since we're here," she replied tentatively. "I might get a few ideas."

A young, well-dressed man led them between displays of outrageously expensive, hideous sofas and highly polished coffee tables to a separate showroom, which was dedicated to different designs and styles of kitchens.

The immediate effect was impressive — the layout exuded quality, efficiency, and high cost. They strolled through the showroom, feeling that they might almost be on a film set. Modern, traditional, futuristic, large, small, a corner arrangement — they were all there. Diana liked best the simple, spacious farmhouse kitchen, with its long, oak, refectory table as the main work surface. They looked at hobs, conventional and microwave ovens, sinks, taps, tiles, cupboards finished in a range of different materials, and built-in refrigerators.

As a result, they became thoroughly confused, looking at each other in bewilderment.

"Did you see anything you particularly want?" the salesman asked, coming straight to the point when they were in his office.

They offered no response to his question.

"In that case," he continued, looking at his desk diary, "I'll come to your place next Tuesday, if that's convenient. It will be during the afternoon. Once I've seen how much space you intend to devote to your new kitchen, I'll try to help you with some ideas without obligation at all on your part." He smiled boyishly, and then added, "I am the chief designer here. I created all these designs. Here are some photos of my work for clients." He presented an album, which portrayed the transformation he was capable of achieving in kitchens, the original state of which was, in many cases, worse than that at Bon Porteau. It had the desired effect on both of them.

"We'll see you next Tuesday, then," James said.

"You won't regret it," was the young man's reply.

"I bloody hope not!" said Diana, as she climbed into the jeep.

*

Morale is a curious condition of the mind. It has to do with achievement, pride, recognition, and praise where it is due. The day before, he had started to feel depressed by the fact that, as fast as he was able to reduce the list of things to do or items to be bought, other requirements and priorities were inexorably added to it. It was like a soggy punch ball — you hit it hard on one side, only to find it sag on the other. That evening his spirits were boosted by the successes of the day, and he resolved to consolidate his lead over the hitherto expanding inventory. He therefore decided that he would complete before supper three more tasks: securing the new mini-oven at eye level on the wall of the small, upstairs kitchen; assembling the second-hand linen cupboard; and fitting an internal cat flap in the door to the boiler room which, they had agreed, was the best place for the cats at night. The mini-oven was soon firmly in place, with a chicken turning on the spit, causing Diana to sing happily for the first time since their arrival.

"I'll just fix the linen cupboard and the cat flap now," he told Diana confidently, taking his *apéritif* with him. "It shouldn't take more than about half-an-hour."

He assumed that there would be some straight-forward instructions on how to rebuild the cupboard. He was wrong. He had to cast his mind back to his early days as a junior management consultant, when he had applied the technique of method study to similar, simple problems. It was obvious that the three sliding doors could only be fitted last. Then he began to doubt his analysis. If fitting the doors was not the final activity, then it must surely be fixing in place the top of the cupboard. Most of the sections of wood were the same size but, after a period of trial and error, he correctly identified the doors and the top, placing them to one side. The base was in one solid, heavy section. He positioned it in the corner of the boiler room, taking care to allow sufficient space to enable him to reach into the narrow gap between the wall and the side of the cupboard, which would have to be attached with the use of a soft hammer and the wooden dowels. He propped the back of the cupboard against the wall and then secured the two sides.

So far, so good, he thought. Then he noticed the two vertical grooves on each side of the back board.

"Merde!" he cursed, as he realized that the back should have been assembled before attaching the two sides. The boiler fired, and the room started to get warm. He removed his pullover and dismantled the two sides. Twice he had to turn his attention away from the cupboard. Jacob, curious as ever, had taken a liking to the small wooden dowels, and was busy nudging them into inaccessible places, such as under the roaring boiler. Once the back was solidly in position, he made rapid progress. One after the other, he fitted the two sides, the central support at the front, then the top, and finally the sliding doors, making sure that he hammered home firmly the dowels, which held together the entire structure. He stepped back to admire the solid, sturdy handiwork which he had created, and he was about to summon Diana to approve the finished article when he tripped over a wooden plank. He looked down at it and at seven other similar, but smaller, pieces of wood.

"Merde! Merde! Et merde encore!" he shouted.

The noise he was making brought Diana downstairs, and she put her head cautiously round the corner of the door to the boiler room.

"What's the problem?" she asked.

"It's taken me over an hour to erect this fucking thing," he moaned.

"Mais, c'est normal, chéri. Tell me something new. I was beginning to think that you must have chopped off your hand. Have

another *apéritif.*"

"Look at this bloody cupboard!" he shouted. "Just look at it!"

"It looks just fine to me," she said placatingly. "Except that I don't want it in that corner. I won't be able to reach the top shelf from there."

"That's the whole point," he growled. "There are no bloody shelves. I've forgotten to put the bloody things in. Now I'll have to take off the doors, the top, the centre support, and one of the sides to get them in."

"Anyway, I don't want it in that corner. It's too near that concrete step and I'll fall over backwards every time I want to put anything away."

"That's the only place in the room it can go," he protested, raising his voice to be heard over the roar of the boiler. "The beams are too low over there." She beat a hasty retreat, recognising the probable approach of a childlike tantrum.

He now began to rue the force with which he had secured the wooden dowels, three of which snapped during the laborious task of dismantling his earlier work. A stream of oaths in English, French, German, and Swahili provided a running commentary on his progress, or lack of it. When, at last, he was ready to attempt to fit the shelving, the outer frame of the cupboard developed a mind of its own, swaying precariously from side to side. Four times he thought he was going to succeed, only to find that the shelves collapsed before he could secure one particular dowel which appeared to be crucial to the stability of the entire structure. He finally managed to lock the side into position by using as wedges a mop handle and a broom, which left both his hands free. The shelves remained in position, and he hammered home the offending peg.

Hardly daring to breathe, he silently set about completing the rebuild.

"Tout va bien?" Diana called down to him, alerted by the sudden silence.

"Et baah, oui! Oui enfin! Yes, we're getting there slowly at last! *On arrive doucement."*

She decided to give him some encouragement, and entered the boiler room just as he was gingerly pushing the cupboard, so that it was flush with the wall. It creaked and swayed slightly but, with one more determined push, it seemed to settle, firmly locked into position in the corner.

"There! What a monstrosity!" he sighed, inspecting his efforts. "There are three pegs missing from the top, but that will just have to do. Never again! *Ce bordel-là,* if we ever move from here, can bloody well stay there!"

"Brilliant, my love! I never knew you were so patient." She gave him a big hug. "And I knew you would find it quite simple, once you worked out exactly what to do. Anyway, there's a nice supper waiting upstairs. It's been ready for over an hour, so you can fit the cat flap later or, better still, leave it until tomorrow morning. You're always telling me not to try to do everything at once."

"Ah, but this is different. And anyway, don't do as I do — do as I say."

*

The aroma from the roast chicken with all its trimmings was an entirely new smell in the house. Diana was ecstatic over her latest acquisition.

"Look, I can also use it as a grill," she explained happily.

They both agreed that it would go a long way to solving any further culinary problems, until a new kitchen was installed. Having had no lunch, James was hungry. He was enjoying the meal, at the same time feeling both relief and satisfaction that the linen cupboard was at last in place. Halfway through the meal, the telephone rang.

"Damned thing," he grumbled, as he tried to finish his mouthful. He listened for a few seconds, and then a smile appeared on his face.

"Hullo, Hans-Peter! How very nice to hear from you," he shouted into the handset. "How are you and Renate? When did you get back from Petauke?"

"Mein lieber Mann, du! We're fine, my dear chap! About one month ago. Thanks to send us your address, but you know the phone number is not okay. Renate is again pregnant since seven months. We still have no house here in Germany, but the mobile camper will for the moment do. Look, I ring you because we think we make you a visit! It will be good again to meet. *Wahnsinnig gut, nichtwahr?* Bloody good, eh?..."

"It's that young German doctor from Zambia," James whispered to Diana. "They want to come and stay..."

He put the handset to his ear again, concentrating on the guttural voice at the other end of the line.

"For about four weeks," Hans-Peter was saying, "before Renate more heavy is. We like to come at the end of next week, if that will be suiting you."

"*Aber Hans-Peter, hör mal!* But, listen a moment! *Das wäre völlig unmöglich.* That might be completely impossible. We've only just arrived and moved in here. *Wir haben kein Schlafzimmer bereit für Euch.* We have no bedroom ready for you. *Du musst ein Bisschen warten... Vielleicht im Sommer.* You'll have to wait a bit... Perhaps in the summer."

"*Nein! Nein!* We come, James, with the camper in the garden. We, how you say?... We rough it up! The twins will be in the tent to enjoy theirself. All we need is to be eating and drinking with you. *Ach ja!* I forget. We also bring the two dogs always. You remember our Rotweilers, *ja*? You like those big fuckers, *nicht*?"

"Hans-Peter, I don't want to sound rude, but I've got some workmen here at the moment who need to talk to me. Give me your number and I'll ring you at the same time tomorrow evening."

"I speak from the Hotel Schmalzkopf in Lindau. It is by my friend owned. You anytime can ring, and they us from the car park fetch. We speak tomorrow. Renate, she give you... How you say? She to you send a big slap and tickle! *Also Tchüss! Auf wiederhören!*"

He put down the receiver and carefully placed beside it the scrap of paper on which he had noted the Lindau number.

"Thank God, practically everybody has got the wrong number!" James sighed, looking at Diana, "They want to come for four weeks at the end of next week. Renate is seven months pregnant. They'll have the terrible twins and those two Rotweilers, and they propose to camp in the garden."

"We'll just have to work out a bombproof excuse to put them off," she said firmly. "I'm not having those two killer dogs anywhere near the place. They're a nice couple, though. Do you remember when we stayed with them in Petauke, and he came back to his house from the operating theatre? He'd been delivering babies, amputating arms and legs, and taking bandits' bullets out of patients all morning. I can see him now, his white coat all covered in blood, and he looked quite exhausted. Then he sat down at his piano, just as he was, still wearing his gory, rubber operating boots, and played Mendelssohn exquisitely. He told me later that he didn't know whether he wanted to be a doctor or a concert pianist."

"She's clever, too," he added. "Damn good-looking girl, that one!"

*

Immediately after helping Diana to clear away the dishes, he felt the urge to return to the boiler room.

"That was just lovely, darling," he said. "I'm just going to fix the cat flap now. If I don't get it off my list, I won't sleep tonight."

"Oh, James! Must you try and do it now? Leave it until the morning," she urged. "It's already quite late enough, and..."

"No, my love, I would rather do it now. Remember, tomorrow is the cats' first day of controlled freedom outside."

He went cheerfully down the miller's ladder, and carefully opened the carton. He knew precisely how to insert a cat flap. Earlier in the week, he had fitted the external one in the door from the cellar to the garden. The task was not as difficult as he had imagined it would be. The external flap operated perfectly, although they had kept it firmly shut for the period of the cats' confinement indoors. He wondered why he always felt nervous when confronted by any form of carpentry. This should be straightforward, he thought, as he removed the layers of packaging to reveal the plastic device and the instructions in six different languages which accompanied it.

The internal cat flap, they had jointly decided, would serve two purposes. It would not only control the movements of the cats inside the house, most especially at night, but also allow the boiler room door to be closed during the day. James was particularly in favour of this second apparent benefit, since it would eliminate an uncomfortable draught from the cellar into the passage and thence into the bedroom, which he intended to convert to his office-cum-dressing-room. However, he soon became aware of one unforeseen complication. Normal cat flaps of British origin, such as the external one in the cellar door, are relatively simple devices. The flap itself is either locked firmly shut to prevent cats entering or escaping, or else it hangs loose, allowing freedom of entry or exit. The model he was now examining was altogether a more beautiful affair — it was French. As he checked the fitting instructions, he came to the conclusion that it was unnecessarily complicated. It provided four possible settings on the flap: entry only, exit only, both entry and exit, and locked shut. Any one of these four programmes could be selected by an intelligent human being by sliding a button to a given position, illustrated by miniature traffic signs representing a one-way street, no entry, two-way traffic, or no thoroughfare. He wondered briefly how this could possibly benefit the well-being of feline society, but thought no more about it.

The manufacturer had provided a template and, having created the required size of opening, he screwed the mechanism into position. He was tightening the final screw when Jacob started to become interested, watching his master as he tested his workmanship. All four options appeared to be working perfectly. He closed the door to the boiler room, and left the flap swinging freely in the two-way traffic mode.

"Go on, Jacob," he called. "Jump through it, big man!"

The fifteen-year-old aristocrat did as he was told, and then sauntered away with a twitch of his tail and a bored expression on his face.

Later, when it was time to go to bed, Jacob and Fosbury, together with their electrically-heated bed, were installed for the first time in the boiler room.

"There you are, my babies," Diana whispered gently. "This is your new bedroom. Now that all the flaps are fitted, you can go walkies outside tomorrow!"

James pushed the button to set the flap to no thoroughfare, and checked that it was firmly locked in place. He then programmed the boiler, so that it would not fire during the night. Diana shut the door, and hung on the doorknob a notice which read, 'Cat Nap in Progress', ensuring that her charges would not to be disturbed unless there was a dire emergency.

"Goodnight, my babies!" she called through the door from the passage. "Be good boys and sleep tight!"

"Goodnight, my love," James replied as he climbed into bed, thinking she was speaking to him.

As soon as the light went out they both heard a faint noise, as if someone was tapping gently on a water pipe in the house.

"What's that sound?" she asked.

"It must be the boiler cooling down," he ventured.

The sound continued, the tap-tapping becoming more persistent and regular. He turned over and was on the point of drifting into sleep when there was a quite different, unmistakable noise. It was the sound of the cat flap swinging open and then shutting. Seconds later, with a triumphant wail, Jacob bounded on to the bed, purring loudly. James switched on his light.

"How the bloody hell did you get out?" he demanded angrily.

Jacob sat on the end of the bed with his back to them, the smug expression on his face revealing nothing of his innermost thoughts.

They both climbed out of bed and went to inspect the door to the boiler room, staring in disbelief at the cat flap. The button had been moved from the no thoroughfare position, where James had fastened it firmly. It was now set to provide unimpeded two-way traffic throughout the night. He shut the door and, as if to prove his point, Jacob jumped through the flap and strolled nonchalantly over to his bed, from which Fosbury gazed with a blank look on his face.

"Jacob! You wicked, crafty bugger!" he scolded.

"The problem, my love, is that you've put the flap in the wrong way round. That control lever should be on the other side of the door, where Jacob can't get at it during the night."

"But that's no use, either," he argued. "If Jacob can change the settings from the inside during the night, then he'll do the same from the other side during the day. I can't spend my whole life changing the flap round each morning! Whether it's on the inside or not, he will be able to lock Fosbury in or out whenever the mood takes him. No! It's a dead loss, I'm afraid."

He paused to think through how he might defeat Jacob, who was now sitting benignly in his bed listening to them.

"I know how to do it," he decided. "You go back to bed. Open one of the bedroom windows, and I'll join you in a minute or so."

He knelt down, locked the flap for the second time, and then picked up a folding bed, placing it against the boiler room door to prevent any tampering paws from reaching the control lever.

"Not this time, Jake," he growled at the cat. "This'll fix you!"

For good measure, he then used the broom handle to wedge the barricade firmly in position.

"Goodnight, big men," he called. He went out through the cellar door into the cold night air and entered the bedroom through the French window.

"That should fix him," he said, shivering as he climbed back into bed. He explained to Diana the precautions he had taken, and they settled down to their second attempt at passing a peaceful night.

Rather less than ten minutes later, there came the sound of a loud crash from the boiler room, followed briefly by rapid and skilled tapping.

"I think Jacob is busy demolishing either your barricade, or the cupboard, or both," Diana whispered. "He'll be here in a minute."

She was right. In the morning, the linen cupboard was leaning away from the corner of the wall at an angle of almost forty-five degrees. Fosbury, looking mournful, was crouching uncomfortably on the top right-hand corner. James reluctantly removed the cat flap and repaired the door, while Jacob looked on triumphantly.

"Because of *you*," he grumbled at Jacob, while scowling at the traffic signs on the redundant flap, "we'll just have to put up with the howling draught all day!" He buttoned up his pyjama jacket. "I suppose you'll be taking your driving test next!" he added, as Jacob winked one eye in Fosbury's direction.

Chapter Twenty-Four

Driving up the hill towards the town, James reminded Diana that this was the second time they had visited the Sunday morning market in Montcarmel. He remembered the lack of available parking space in the centre, so they walked the last few hundred yards. It was another warm, sunny day and, although it was not yet ten o'clock, the *place* was bustling with activity. Diana announced that she was going to inspect each stall before deciding where she would buy the produce on her list. She suggested to James that he should wait for her in the *Café de la Terrasse*.

"Have a café au lait, while you recover from Jacob's carpentry lesson!" she joked. "You can help me carry the bags later."

He sat at one of the tables on the pavement, dunking his *croissant* in a large bowl of coffee, and watched the people strolling in the sunshine. He spotted Félicie and Pascale, and then Guillaume joined him and sat down with a small cup of black coffee. Miguel and his wife waved to him as they passed. The same *gendarme* was on duty, but he thought the young girl to whom he was talking was not the same one as last year — perhaps she just looked different because she was heavily pregnant. *Monsieur le Maître* recognized him and bade him a formal *'Bonjour'*, enquiring how they were settling in at Bon Porteau. He saw Diana twice, moving busily between the stalls on the far side of the square. He waved to her, but she was too preoccupied with her tour of the stalls, taking seriously the task of finding the best quality and prices.

His attention was caught by a small, very old lady who was carrying a wicker basket. Her frail body stooped almost at right angles, as she shuffled forward in her carpet slippers. She paused at one stall, picking out two carrots, a leek, one turnip, and a sprig of parsley. She handed her purse to the vendor, who returned it unopened. At the next stall, she selected a *baguette* and again proffered her purse, which the baker waved away with a smile. As she moved slowly past a table with wines displayed on it, the grower stepped out to place a half bottle of red wine in her basket. James pointed out the old lady to Guillaume, who explained that she was the mother of a young pilot who had been killed over Dien Bien Phu. To this day, when the Mirage jet fighters of the French Air Force make their low-level passes over the cemetery, they roll their wings in noisy salute. Guillaume finished his coffee and left, promising to be in touch about their planned tour of a few vineyards.

Suddenly he felt a hand on his shoulder. It was Iain with Laetizia, and a youngish couple whom he had not seen before.

"James!" Iain's voice boomed. "Meet Airlie and Vincent, who arrived last night. They've come to stay with us while they look for a house to rent and some work. May we join you?"

Airlie was pretty in a petite way. She had a young, fresh face, smiling beneath a floppy, maroon hat, which was set at a jaunty angle. Vincent, a serious expression on his swarthy face, was tall and gangling, looking like a public schoolboy standing casually at ease in front of matron at school.

"I know Airlie's father from Nairobi," Iain explained, pulling up a plastic chair. "And Vincent came out once or twice to my Lake Camp."

"There was a Wyllis at Marlborough in the same house as me," Vincent announced. "You're an Old Marlburian, aren't you?"

The young man's voice was pleasant, his long-fingered hands constantly moving to emphasize each carefully chosen phrase. James wondered if he was a 'resting' actor. He had read English, or probably Greek, at Oxford, he thought.

"Yes," James replied with a nod. "I was there, and my son, too."

"He wouldn't be Piers, by any chance?" asked Vincent. "Hey! Come to think of it," Vincent continued, when James nodded a second time, "he looks just like you. He was a friend of our best man, a chap called Harry-John Fotheringay."

"I can remember H-J very well indeed," James exclaimed. "In my previous incarnation, that is to say my first marriage, we took Piers and H-J on holiday to Belle-Île-en-Mer. He collected butterflies. I got to know his father quite well."

Diana found them talking animatedly an hour later. James explained that Vincent was an exact contemporary of Piers at school.

"The Lot is really weird, man!" she said in disbelief. "That's the third coincidence in just over a week!" She turned to face Airlie and said jokingly, "And I suppose Airlie is from Africa as well."

"Yes, I am. Born and bred in Kenya," was her reply. "We were married last year in Nairobi."

She had a clear, attractive laugh, raising her chin in a way which James found almost provocative.

"And with a name like Vincent," Diana quipped, feeling for his left ear, "you're now going to tell me you're a painter."

"Actually," Vincent replied slowly, "I'm planning to hold an exhibition in London next year. I've come here to create beautiful paintings of dead sunflowers."

"Oh really?" James heard himself saying rather vaguely. "Now that really *is* fascinating!"

"This is for real," Airlie added. "Otherwise, with no money we'll starve."

James had not seen Stewart in the group, and he asked Iain whether he was somewhere in the market.

"In the woods," Iain replied. "He's logging for me at the moment. I've told him I want a cubic metre of logs for each week he stays. He's behind his schedule, so he said he hadn't the time to come to market. And his girlfriend arrives tomorrow — that'll bring him to a grinding halt! She was born in Zambia."

"I don't believe this can be true!" Diana gasped.

"Where on earth are all you guys sleeping?" James asked.

"In the luxury end of the dormitory," Vincent moaned, and then added with a note of sarcasm, "I mean, in the lovely barn which Iain is going to finish converting next week, after he's completed the rebuild of the house."

"I've got a chap called Greg coming out here next week with a mate," Iain interjected. "He's a boat-builder from Mombasa and works really well with wood. They're going to replace all the joists and rafters in the roof. We've got the tiles off already. By the way, James, you haven't got any camp beds, have you?"

"In fact, we have two," James replied. "Why don't you all come and have a drink before lunch, and then you can take them with you."

As he and Diana stood up to leave, he remembered that all the people in Iain's house party came from Africa. Punctuality would not be their strong suit.

"But don't make it later than midday," he added as a precaution. "I've got an important meeting this afternoon."

"What a circus!" Diana remarked dubiously, as they walked away. "That means Stewart and his girlfriend, Vincent and Airlie, and then Greg and his mate, will all be living in that draughty barn alongside the horses. I don't know how Laetizia puts up with feeding them all. And did you see the bites on Airlie's legs?"

"No, I didn't," lied James. "But they're very shapely."

"If they're not careful, they'll run out of dormitory space if any more are squeezed in there!"

"Well, if that happens, and if they ask us to help, then we're bloody well not going to house them! " he parried.

"Something tells me," Diana was frowning as she spoke, "that Iain is used to having a lot of people about him. There's no problem with that, I suppose... Except the cost of food and drink!"

*

Iain and his house guests arrived for their *apéritif* two hours late. James was furious. They swarmed on to the roof *terrasse* in the brilliant sunshine. As the small gathering became more animated, with every sign that a lively party would develop, he grew increasingly agitated.

"Why can't these Kenya cowboys arrive and leave roughly on time?" he asked Diana angrily, while the empty bottles accumulated in the kitchen. "I didn't have time for breakfast this morning, and now it looks like I'll have to go to the *château source* meeting on an empty stomach! I'm due at the *Mairie* in ten minutes."

"Well, my love," Diana insisted quietly, "it was you, not I, who invited them to come."

He was the last to arrive at the meeting in the *Mairie*. Gérard Tillet was sitting behind his small table, a semicircle of chairs arranged in front of him. Two of the chairs remained vacant. Bottles of wine and glasses stood on a tray which had been placed on top of the photocopier.

"Bonjour à tous!" James said, shaking hands with Gérard. He had

met the farmer, Monsieur Griffoul, but the other faces were new to him. Gérard guided James through the small group, introducing him as *'Monsieur Willie, qui vient de l'Afrique'* to the other members of the association.

"My cousin, Marcel Briand, who lives between here and the next hamlet and owns a large digging machine; *Monsieur* Griffoul, Gilles, whom I think you have met through *Madame* Gautier; *Monsieur* de Maufort, who is buying the *château* and is going to have it restored it to its former splendour; *Monsieur* Roussy, Henri, the butcher in Montcarmel, who says he has the best meat in the region." Everyone laughed heartily at his aside. "And this is *Monsieur* Jules Carendier, one of your two nearest neighbours, who lives in the big house below you at the bottom of the hill."

They all sat down. The noise of chairs scraping on the bare floorboards ceased and, for a few moments, there was an expectant hush. One chair still remained empty, and Gérard was looking at it quizzically.

"*Monsieur*, is your companion unable to be present?" he addressed Jules Carendier. "He has the accounts, no?"

If a pin had dropped, all present would have heard it. Someone coughed, and feet shuffled in ill-concealed embarrassment.

"No, *Monsieur* Tillet," Jules Carendier replied calmly. He spoke with an exquisitely clear Parisian accent. "Pierre has had to go to Paris on business, but he's given me the accounts to present to the meeting. Shall we begin?"

The finances of the association were sound, with a surprisingly large sum of money on deposit in the bank, almost as much again invested in a savings plan administered by *La Poste,* and a small current account. Consumption of water had been lower during the year under review. Therefore revenue had fallen but, fortunately, so had costs. The accounts were passed around the group and were unanimously approved. There followed a brief debate on the price to be levied on water during the next six months, and the meeting agreed rapidly to make a reduction of seven centimes on each cubic metre. The decision was received with loud applause, followed by sighs of satisfaction.

"*Messieurs,*" James ventured, "in these days of high interest rates, continuing inflation, and constant tampering by governments with farming policy and prices, don't you think we should invite *Monsieur* Jacques Delors to our next meeting? He could learn a thing or two, no?" They sat in silence, stunned by the effect which his unexpectedly fluent French had on them, and then as one they dissolved into laughter and emotion.

The next item on the agenda was the election of officials. With due solemnity, the names of the existing committee were read out by Gérard.

"Briand, Marcel; Tillet, Gérard," he paused for a split second, adding unnecessarily, *"Ça, c'est moi.* That's me." He looked quickly around the group, as if to check that the remaining members were present, and then reverted to his notes. "Griffoul, Gilles; Roussy, Henri; Carendier, Jules." He hesitated, and then went on, "And, of course, Bouyou, Pierre, who is unable to be with us today... Unfortunately." He finished the roll-call, and then announced, "And now, it is my pleasant duty and honour to propose that we welcome to the committee both *Monsieur* de Maufort, Phillipe, and *Monsieur Willie*, James. All agreed?" There was spontaneous applause. Everyone stood up and started edging towards the photocopier, shaking hands, and congratulating each other on the spirit of *fraternité* which always prevailed on this important occasion. James was thinking how very curious it was that everyone in the room had just elected everybody else, when Gérard tapped on the table with his pencil, and they all sat down again.

"Ce n'est pas du tout comme 'Jean de Florette', hein?" James said in the brief, ensuing silence, causing more laughter.

"Ni 'Manon des Sources' non plus!" added Phillipe de Maufort.

"The formal business of the association being completed," Gérard shouted over their noisy guffaws, "I now declare the fifty-third meeting closed. Marcel, if you would open the wine?"

They were all on their feet, crowding round the photocopier to collect their glasses of wine. James had a brief discussion with Marcel Briand about his excavator, telling him that at some time he would like some work done beside the barn. Phillipe de Maufort talked about his plans to restore the impressive *château*, expressing the view that it would take at least a year to complete all the work.

"There are quite a few serious architectural problems, you know," he explained. "At some time in the past, someone tampered with the main entrance. And, of course, the twin towers, are *en ruine* anyway."

"James, when Pierre returns from Paris," Jules Carendier interrupted quietly, "you and your wife must come to dinner with us and meet some of our friends. I'll be in touch."

Before Jules left, James asked him if he could recommend a good craftsman, capable of designing and constructing a wooden staircase. Jules replied that they had employed an excellent *ébéniste* for all the woodwork in their house. He assured James that the cabinet-maker's skill was of a very high standard, and promised to let him have the man's telephone number.

The small talk continued until all the bottles were empty and then, one by one, the members of the newly-appointed committee drifted away, exhausted by the intellectual demands of the afternoon's business. They would have six months in which to recover before the next arduous meeting. James was about to leave, when Gérard called to him.

"I have something to show you, James," he confided, opening a copy of *La Dépêche* at the pages which cover local news items. *"Voilà!"* he announced proudly. "I submitted this small article on behalf of the commune."

James put on his glasses and read the words which Gérard had marked with his pen:

> 'Recently arrived with their wives in the *Commune de Saint Juste* are *Monsieur* Iain Drummond-Delaire, *gentleman-farmer* from Kenya, and *Monsieur* James Wyllis, *haut fonctionnaire* from Zambia."

"So, Gérard," James said in an admiring tone. "You are indeed a man of many parts. You are not only the *Secrétaire de Mairie* and the *Secrétaire de l'Association*. You are also our very own local newspaper correspondent!"

"Ouais! I am the official photographer and historian as well. Here, take this photocopy, and show it to your beautiful wife."

Back at Bon Porteau, a little the worse for drinking rough red wine on an empty stomach, he passed the photocopy to Diana.

"O-là-là!" she laughed. "It might have been worded rather more carefully! It sounds as if two harems have just descended upon Saint Juste. How many wives do they think you and Iain have between you? Anyway, it's inaccurate — I notice that Iain always refers to Laetizia as his *concubine.*"

*

A distant, solitary church bell was ringing out its weekly invitation to Vespers. It was strange how the sound seemed to him to be coming from two quite different directions, now from across the valley, and then from the other side of the woods at the back of the house. He was trying to identify the village where the church might be, when the telephone rang.

"Monsieur Wyllis?" James recognized the cultured accent of Jules Carendier.

"Oui, Jules! C'est moi, James, à l'appareil."

"I have the name of the *ébéniste* for you. He is *Monsieur* Dusseau, Georges. If you ring him now on a Sunday evening, you will probably find him at home. He doesn't live far away."

James thanked him and promptly dialled the number he had been given. The voice which answered his call sounded like that of a youngish man, which took James a little by surprise. Perhaps illogically, he was expecting to speak to an older, seasoned craftsman. After he had explained the recommendation of Bouyou-Carendier and outlined the reason for his call, Monsieur Dusseau suggested that he should come immediately to make a preliminary assessment of what might be involved.

"If I don't come now," he confided, "it will have to wait a few weeks, because I am overloaded with work at present. I know your house. *À tout à l'heure!* I'll be with you shortly."

Monsieur Georges Dusseau was wearing a jacket and tie, and he carried a small drawing board with graph paper pinned to it. His appearance was more that of a junior management consultant than an experienced cabinet-maker working in the depths of the *Lotois* countryside.

"C'est vraiment dommage," James admitted freely, as he led the

way through to the small kitchen and pointed to the two miller's ladders. "It's a great shame to have to rip them out. I suppose they've been there for two hundred years, but I don't find them all that beautiful, and frankly they are totally impractical."

"There are those who would say it is a crime to replace them," Monsieur Dusseau remarked tactfully, his hand caressing the wooden banisters.

"An ideal solution," James suggested, "would be *un escalier en colimaçon*, a spiral staircase, climbing from ground level down there right up to the top room, with a landing midway, perhaps even there in that corner. It should be constructed in well-seasoned oak."

The Frenchman did not react immediately, as he looked around him and continued to stroke the rickety banister. When it came, his quietly spoken reply took James by surprise.

"I don't make spirals," the young cabinet-maker explained. "I can only construct conventional staircases. The floor will have to be broken here and up there, and some beams will have to come out. Also, all the electrics and pipework appear to converge here. You would have to arrange all that and take charge of all the other tradesmen. I am just a simple cabinet-maker, *Monsieur*. Many will tell you that I am one of the best around here."

James was beginning to comprehend the scope of the problem and the structural changes which would be involved.

"Well, I need to find someone," he said firmly, "who is prepared to accept responsibility for the entire project, including the co-ordination of all the different tradesmen. I really need an experienced foreman or, if you prefer, a gang boss."

"Then, *Monsieur*, I'm definitely *not* your man," Monsieur Dusseau replied politely. "But I can tell you who could be. I don't know whether or not he is free, but this job is made for him. And, what is more, he can make a good spiral staircase which, in case you don't realize it, is a job for a specialist. His name is Serge Chambon, and he works with his son, André." He took a notebook from his pocket. "If it will help you, I'll call him now."

James waved at the telephone and there followed a discussion, which was conducted in such rapid and heavily accented patois that

James was quite unable to understand even the gist of it.

"Serge will come tomorrow. He was unable to say at what time, but this is his number."

"And you're quite sure that he's good at his job?" James queried. "I want first-class work. No botch-ups!"

"*Je vous assure, Monsieur,*" the Frenchman, replied, "that Serge is one of the best. After all, it was he who taught me everything I know about working with wood. Anyway, I would not have been able to start for another ten months. Serge told me that he will be free, *en principe*, after Christmas."

"This year or next?"

"You'll have to check that with him," Monsieur Dusseau said with a shrug, shook hands, and then hurried out of the house.

*

Diana had been sitting in the living-room, listening to the discussion between the two men. She had been able to follow most of it, only losing the gist when technical words had intruded.

"It sounds to me," she said, after the Frenchman had gone, "as if new stairs are going to let us in for a major structural change from top to bottom of the *pigeonnier*. We haven't allowed for that, if the work proves to be expensive.

"Don't worry about it. Let's see what Chambon makes of it all tomorrow. I think I'll put up some more of these pictures, before I fall over them."

He looked at the several piles which Diana had cleaned and stacked carefully, and decided to hang the collection of framed photographs and portraits of their families.

"Where do you want the rogues' gallery?" he asked.

"I haven't given it much thought. The only sensible place I can see might be over there," she suggested, indicating the wall space on the right-hand side of the French windows in the living-room. "They would look good there, I think."

"Where did you put the photo albums?"

"Why? And which one do you want?"

"The one with the picture you took in Zambia of the rogues' gallery, after Fackson had dusted them. I know every picture is askew, but at least I can replicate the same layout. The grandfathers must be at the top, with Piers and Kim at the bottom."

While she went in search of the album, he collected together his power drill, the wall plugs, screws, and a dustpan. He arranged the pictures on the table, and spent some time checking the precise layout. He then started drilling into the hard stone wall. Fine white dust not only penetrated his nostrils and drifted down to the tiled floor, it also covered most of the other objects in the room, including the pictures he was about to hang and the quiche which Diana had made for supper.

"Don't say anything, my love!" he shouted over the noise of the electric drill. "I'll clear everything up afterwards!"

"I only wanted to say that the drill sounds very different from yesterday. Are you sure it's working properly?"

He switched it off to check that nothing had come loose. Then he, too, heard the strange sound.

"There you are," she said. "That's what I heard, and I thought it was coming from the drill."

He listened. It was a clanking sound, which squeaked and grated, reminding him of a Centurion tank with its tracks incorrectly tensioned.

"It's coming from outside!" she cried in alarm. "Whatever can it be?"

James switched on the two large outside lanterns, and they went out on to the roof *terrasse*, peering through the dark towards the sound. Four large, powerful headlights, preceded by a long, yellow arm, were lumbering noisily between the two millstones at the end of the drive. The strange apparition slowly ground and scraped its way forward, lurching from side to side and jerking spasmodically, as it advanced to a point on the driveway opposite and below the *terrasse*.

The growl of the motor suddenly stopped, and silence returned to the valley. In the darkness the monstrous machine looked like a stranded, mechanical dinosaur, its arc-lights bathing the drive in brilliant white light.

"It's come from outer space!" Diana gasped. "Or else it's the army! What on earth can it be?"

He offered no suggestion.

"What have you done now, James?"

"I think it might well be Marcel Briand and his digging machine," he replied sheepishly. "I told him at the *source* meeting that at some time in the future I would want a *terrasse* excavated on the other side of the barn. You know, where the fire started. But I wasn't expecting him yet!" A young woman, clad in overalls and wearing a baseball cap, climbed out of the machine and stood in the glare of its eerie lights.

"*Bonsoir, M'sieu, 'dame!*" she called up to them. "Papa asked me to bring it down this evening, because it's going to be fine tomorrow. We can begin excavating in the morning. I'll make a start at about six o'clock, if you show me what has to be done."

"*Attends, M'mselle! J'arrive tout de suite!*" he shouted down to her. "Hang on, I'm coming now! I'll show you where to go."

When he returned to the house, he picked up the drill to finish the task of hanging the pictures.

"What was that all about?" Diana asked

"It's the barn project, which we discussed yesterday," he yelled over the whirr of the drill. "We're applying for a *Permis de Construire*, so that we can put in a couple more windows and double doors in the far wall of the barn. The doors will open on to a *terrasse*, which Briand's daughter is going to excavate tomorrow. She is called, appropriately, Micheline, about twenty-five years old, I should think. She'd make a damn good front-row forward, that one! Toulouse would jump at the chance of having her in their first team, particularly in the showers after a match!"

Diana said nothing and continued preparing the supper, while he hung the last of their family portraits.

"There! That's another one off the list," he said, looking with satisfaction at the wall. "It's all beginning to happen now, my love." He started sweeping the film of dust on the floor into a corner of the room. "You know," he went on, "I'm beginning to change my mind about these people. It's damn good that they react so quickly and always do what you ask them to do. I mean, look at the willingness of Louisor, the estate agent, and the excellent service from the jeep dealer. Then there's Miguel Casarin, with the garden machinery and the speed with which he sold that rusty, old, oil tank; Gérard Tillet with the *Certificat de Domicile* and his *petite annonce* of our arrival here in *La Dépêche*. And now, today, we've had Dusseau and Marcel Briand, and then tomorrow Chambon will be here about the stairs, with that young kitchen chap due the day after tomorrow. It's great, isn't it? They've all done pretty well so far, haven't they?"

"You can say that again," she retorted in sarcastic tone. "It's hardly surprising. They can all see you coming from a mile off, like an overloaded Christmas tree!"

*

It seemed to him that a Sunday evening was as good a time as any to make contact with individual *entrepreneurs*, a term used loosely in France to describe independent contractors or operators who provide a wide range of services, the rewards for which frequently, but by no means always, fall outside the taxation system. Three needs were rapidly rising to the top of their list of priorities: the first two were clearly in Diana's sphere of activity, namely someone to alter curtains, and a part-time cleaning lady; the third concerned the state of the grounds, for which he accepted full responsibility. Accordingly, James decided to solve all three problems that evening, and selfishly tackled the external requirement first. The lawns remained untended. The brambles and nettles were still growing in profusion. Autumn leaves were starting to fall. He listened to the weather forecast which, if he understood it correctly, promised that the warm, dry spell was set to continue.

Having failed to make contact on several occasions earlier in the week, he again dialled the man called Robert to secure his assistance with bringing the gardens under control. This time he succeeded and, in response to his plea for immediate help, Robert agreed to bring all his equipment the following morning, adding that it would not be before ten o'clock, because he had a previous commitment to pluck some ducks for a client of long standing.

"Je ne veux pas que vous me déceviez, Monsieur," James warned him. "I don't want you to let me down."

"Eh baah, bien sûr! Vous pouvez compter sur moi, M'sieu!" came the reassuring reply. "But, of course! You can rely on me! I'll come as soon as I can."

He put down the telephone and looked towards Diana, who was busy cutting to size new flea collars for the cats, in preparation for their release outdoors during the next day.

"Tomorrow," he announced, "since it's going to be fine, and apart from discussing stairs with Chambon, I shall be spending the whole day in the garden. Robert is coming to help.

"Well, be careful this time, particularly if you have any bonfires."

It was not until much later that he was able to give his full attention to the question of curtain alterations. Miguel's wife, Pénélope, had given Diana the name of a woman who, allegedly, was a competent seamstress.

"I'll ring *Madame* Menot now," he told Diana. "Is there any day this week when you cannot see her?"

"Sometime soon, I want to explore the shops in Cahors properly. I was thinking of Wednesday, because it's also market day. I was not impressed by the prices on the stalls in Montcarmel market this morning. They were almost double those of Libos. It will be interesting to see how Cahors compares."

After trying two different numbers unsuccessfully and then checking with Directory Enquiries, he at last made contact with Madame Menot. Knowing that he now had the correct number, he left the telephone ringing for an unconscionable time. She sounded as if the call had woken her up. He looked at his watch and, to his surprise and horror, he saw that it was already after ten o'clock.

"Mais, Madame, je m'excuse. J'espère que, je ne vous dérange pas," he apologized. "I hope I'm not disturbing you." He explained what they wanted and asked if she was interested in the work. She agreed to come to the house, but could not suggest any particular day.

"It will depend upon when my husband can bring me. He is your postman, so he knows your home. I'll ring your wife later in the week to let her know."

"Well, that's good," Diana said purposefully, when he told her the plan. "I can get on with that next week, I hope."

They had just undressed and were ready to go to bed, when they heard the bleep of the telephone coming from the room which was not yet his office. With an impatient sigh, he went down the passage to answer it. *"Allô, oui! Bonsoir!"*

"Hullo, Dad! Hope I'm not too late for you." It was his son, Piers, calling from the Channel Islands. "How was your trip? How are Diana and the cats? Have you settled in okay? We've got a lot of catching up to do." They chatted until well after midnight. He felt excited at the prospect of seeing his only son. He would be arriving on Thursday, in time for Diana's birthday, for which he had been quietly planning a series of surprises. In the morning he would have to tell Diana a white lie. He would say that Piers felt overworked and needed a short holiday; that he would be arriving at the weekend and planned to stay for three days. Thursday, he hoped, was going to be a great occasion.

Before he returned to the bedroom, he made a note that he would have to speak to Kim in the morning and then concentrate his mind on putting his final plan together for the Big Day! Diana was fast asleep when he at last crept into bed, wondering whether he would manage to get all the details organized in time. He started to make a mental list, trying not to forget those items which were crucial for success. Three minutes later, however, he was snoring contentedly.

"Please don't lie on your back, darling," Diana said sleepily. "You really must see a doctor about your sinus."

"Merde!" he swore gently. "I'm sorry I woke you. Sleep tight, my love!"

"I will, if you will just stop that terrible racket!"

Chapter Twenty-Five

Promptly at six o'clock the next morning, Marcel Briand and Micheline raced up the drive. He was driving a rusty, yellow 2CV van, and his daughter a large, high-sided, tipping lorry. They did not call at the house, and a few minutes later James heard the angry growl of the excavator's powerful engine. He slipped out of bed, put on his dressing-gown, and went upstairs to switch on the kettle. He found his gumboots in the porch and walked through the heavy dew up to the barn. Micheline, wearing clean, blue overalls and her baseball cap, was sitting in the cab of the excavator, warming up the engine and directing its battery of headlights towards her father, who was hammering wooden pegs into the hard ground. They shook hands and agreed that the pegs were near enough in the right places.

Marcel took off his beret and waved it in a circular motion at his daughter. The huge machine lurched forward, a cloud of black smoke belching from its vertical exhaust pipe. The yellow arm swung round with a hiss of hydraulics, and the vicious teeth on the leading edge of the bucket soon scraped away the thin layer of top soil in the area to be excavated.

"On va garder tout ça," Marcel bellowed over the din. "We'll keep all that. Top soil is hard to find around here. I'll dump it over there. You might need it for your vegetable garden." A vegetable garden, thought James, will never become one of my projects.

As soon as the excavator started biting into the compacted limestone rock, the noise became almost intolerable. Both father and daughter were wearing ear-protectors, but James had to clasp his hands over his ears. Marcel laughed and nodded his head. Each time the bucket descended, it was as if a bomb exploded beside him. Then, as it clawed and tore at the rock, metal on stone screeched and grated, setting his teeth on edge. Micheline was pumping at the controls, swinging each load round and up. As the loaded bucket swayed free, rock and debris cascaded into the back of the truck, throwing up a cloud of white dust, like a salvo of heavy artillery fire.

Micheline handled the complicated machinery with delicate expertise. James wondered how it was that a young girl should choose to do such noisy, dirty work. The rhythm was fascinatingly painful and had an hypnotic effect — the roar of the engine, the whine as the hydraulics surged, the thud of the bucket as it hit the ground, followed by its hideous screeching and rasping, another hiss of air as the arm swivelled round, and then the final boom as the lorry shuddered and accepted each load, its metal sides amplifying the deafening explosion, which then reverberated across the valley. He watched until the tipper was full. Marcel drove it away, and Micheline switched off the excavator's motor, while she waited for her father to return from the dump. The silence which followed was blissful. The sun was just rising.

"C'est très, très dur, con!" Micheline's words sounded like those of a boy whose voice is about to break. He waved to her and walked back down to the house, looking forward to his pot of tea, and wondering if the Parisian duo would lodge any complaint about the early morning bombardment.

*

He knew that an energetic and physical day lay ahead of him and he was thankful that the sky was, for the moment, slightly overcast. The heavy dew precluded any mowing until the long, wet grass dried; it would clog in seconds both the heavy rotary blade and the grass-catcher mounted on the rear of the tractor. There was nothing, however, to prevent him from making a start on the lengthy task of tidying the banks and cutting down the brambles and nettles. Robert would be arriving, he hoped, soon after ten o'clock. He first checked that the excavation work was progressing well, relieved that he was able to distance himself from the immediate vicinity of the continuing din, which seemed to him to have become louder as the machine dug deeper into the side of the rock.

Mindful of Miguel's stern safety instructions, he was wearing a long-sleeved shirt, thick trousers, and gumboots. He checked the fuel tank of the *débroussailleuse*, and donned the safety glasses. The small Japanese two-stroke engine fired with his first pull on the starter toggle. He wriggled into the harness and secured the motor unit on his back, making a few adjustments to the shoulder straps, until it rested like a light rucksack in the small of his back. He worked methodically and without a break along the banks, the noise of the tiny engine masking the crashing and booming of the excavator. He was astounded at the efficiency of the brush-cutter, operating it like a mechanical scythe. Once he had mastered how best to swing its long arm, he made rapid progress. On two occasions, when his concentration lapsed, it bounced back at him viciously, and he had to jump away from the uncontrolled path of the circular blade. He resolved to take greater care. "Most accidents happen through carelessness," he muttered to himself.

He cleared all the banks in just over an hour. It was becoming difficult to see clearly through the safety goggles and he decided to cut the motor and have a rest. The sky had cleared, and he was sweating. His gumboots, the front of his shirt, and his trousers were caked in shredded grass and debris, which the small blade had spewed back at him like a miniature forage harvester. He pulled out his shirt and wiped at the dirt and grass on the glasses. Less than a quarter of the fuel in the tank had been used. Walking back over the area he had cleared, he admired the rapid transformation.

I'll soon have it all under control, he mused, as he strolled down to the porch. "I'm taking a break now!" he called to Diana. "Any chance of some coffee? I can't come into the house like this, so I'll have it out here."

"Look at the state of you!" she laughed, as she came out with his mug. "Like a green man from outer space! It's all in your hair as well. Why don't you wear a cap?"

"It's a bit late now," he panted.

Fosbury wandered in from the garden, took one look at him, and then ran off, his tail as bushy as the brush of a fox.

"No sign of Robert yet," he moaned, looking at his watch. "I hope the blighter is coming. He hasn't rung, I suppose?"

Diana shook her head. He sipped his coffee and noticed that he had two minor cuts on the back of his left hand, one of which seemed to be swelling like a small bruise.

"That machine is amazing," he said, still a little breathless. "It'll take on practically anything."

"Well, don't let it take off your ankle!"

"You're right. It's very dangerous, and you must never try to use it."

"Don't worry! I have *no* intention of doing so, my love."

"Anyway, I'll have to stop cutting for a bit. Clearing up always takes longer than one thinks, and I want to set a good example for Robert. I ought to do some raking next and then start a bonfire."

"Well, don't overdo it. Be careful of your back," she urged, and then added, "Don't go away just yet."

She went into the house and returned with the portable telephone handset.

"While you're sitting there," she said, "try and get hold of this *femme de ménage*. Her name is Chantal Chaumeil, and I was told you should be able to get her before lunch at the library. Apparently, she works there as an assistant."

He spoke to Chantal, who sounded very affable, and she agreed to call at the house shortly after midday on her way home to lunch.

"I'll leave you to negotiate with her," he called out. "I must go and find that rake and pitchfork."

Diana did not notice that he had tucked the handset into his shirt as he walked away. He disappeared from view behind the *prunerie* and took the handset out from under his shirt.. He knew by heart the two numbers he wanted to call in England and quickly dialled the first. He spoke rapidly, giving a detailed list of instructions.

"I'll ring John now," he concluded. "Would you please tell the others? Thanks a lot, Kim. That's a bloody good idea, and I'll tell Piers to pick you up at Toulouse airport. I think it's going to be the best birthday party this side of Suez! In fact, I *know* it is! See you on Thursday then."

He tapped out the second number, spoke briefly, and then sauntered nonchalantly back to the porch, where he placed the handset quietly on the bench. He did not think that he had been seen or heard.

"Do you want anything from the town, Diana?" he shouted through the front door.

"I thought everywhere was shut on Mondays."

"Oh, I only have to get some more fuel for the brush-cutter, that's all," he lied. "I'm going now."

"If the baker is open, just get a *baguette* for lunch, and take the rubbish to the *poubelle*. Wait a minute, though. Where do you want Robert to start, if he arrives while you're out."

"Oh, I won't be *that* long. Tell him to cut the long grass around the fruit trees."

He was quite oblivious of his unkempt appearance as he drove towards the town, and it was not until he dumped the rubbish sack that he looked in the mirror. He was still covered in pieces of shredded, wet grass, and nettles.

"*Merde!*" he said to himself. "Never mind. It's not as if I've got an appointment with the Chairman of Courtaulds."

He tidied himself as best he could, and then continued with his errands. He was back within an hour, having called at two of the three local hotels and at the Citroën dealer outside Montcarmel. Marcel and Micheline had almost finished excavating the *terrasse* for the barn, and were confident that they would complete it before lunchtime.

Robert had still not arrived, so he hitched the trailer to the garden tractor and drove it across to the area which he had been clearing earlier. He transported four trailer loads of cuttings up to the field beyond the barn. Marcel came across and emptied some old sump oil on to the heap. Soon the bonfire was smouldering reliably.

"*Evidemment, vous avez déjà eu une incendie là en bas!*" he said. "I can see you've already had a fire down there. You must be careful, you know. It gets dry very quickly as soon as the sun comes out."

James fetched the hoses, and placed them ready for any emergency.

"*C'est bon,*" Marcel beamed at him in approval. "*Vous avez bien fait, Monsieur!* Well done! *Il faut toujours faire attention!*"

He picked up the *débroussailleuse* and continued working, stopping at intervals to rake up and burn the cuttings. It was hard work, and the long arm of the machine seemed to become heavier as the morning went by. It was with relief that he heard Diana ringing the bell for lunch, which she had set outside. Before he joined her he went up to the barn. The excavator and lorry were no longer there, having finished the work. He had not heard them leaving.

"Still no sign of Robert," he muttered, as he sat down.

"Nor *Madame* Chaumeil, Chantal. Perhaps last night you spoke too soon about the reliability of these people." She paused. "By the way, I couldn't find the handset just after you rang Chantal. I wanted to get hold of Kim."

"Oh?" he replied innocently. "I thought I left it on the cushion on the bench in the porch."

She went to look for it and put it down on the table. Neither of them spoke for a few moments.

"That's very strange," she said with a frown. "I must be going blind. I'm sure it wasn't there earlier."

She gave him a challenging look and then thought no more about the incident.

He was feeling tired after lunch. As he finished the remains of his glass of red wine, he realized that his back was aching.

"Before I get started again I think I'll just lie down for a few minutes on the lawn over there in the sun."

He was woken by the sound of female voices. From where he lay on the grass he could see Diana in front of the porch. She was talking to a woman, who might be in her late thirties. She had long, blonde hair, bright red lipstick, and was wearing a black leather miniskirt over long, black boots. The shape of her breasts was suggested under a mohair pullover, and sunlight glinted on a gold necklace. He blinked, guessing that this must be Chantal — it was certainly not Robert. He heard her car start and go down the drive and jumped to his feet. He went to the telephone and dialled Robert's number. A woman answered and, in reply to his query, she told him that her husband had not come home for lunch, and that he must have been delayed plucking ducks.

"*Ce type est un emmerdeur!*" he cursed, putting down the handset. "He's a pain in the ass, this guy."

Throughout the afternoon he mowed. He finished all the lawns, and then plunged into the rougher grass. Diana told him later that she could not see the tractor at all in some places — only his head and shoulders were visible, bobbing through the long grass. The mower performed well, and he was surprised how the blade withstood coming into contact with some of the larger stones in its path. Robert arrived eventually, as James was having a cup of tea. He was a lean, dark-haired man, who spoke with a lisp. Apologizing for being so late, he dragged a brush-cutter from his trailer. It was almost twice the size and weight of the model which James had been using.

"Et bien! Où dois-je commencer?" he asked. "Where should I start?"

"Un moment, Robert. J'ai des choses importantes à vous dire," James stopped him. "Hang on, Robert, I've something to say to you you." He then gave the young Frenchman a short lecture on the merits of tidying up his own work. "You must rake up your own cuttings, and then give me a shout. I'll cart them off in my trailer to the bonfire. I don't want you to leave me with a fortnight's extra work clearing up behind you!"

Robert reluctantly picked up the pitchfork, gave him a broad grin, and then disappeared towards the tangle of brambles and nettles which James had indicated. He could hear the snarl of Robert's brush-cutter working until it was almost dark, but when he went out to pay him, his car and trailer had vanished. A brief inspection of the area assigned to Robert revealed that his instructions to keep the work tidy had been totally ignored. The debris of tangled brambles and nettles lay everywhere. In some places they had been kicked aside to form a layer over two feet deep.

"That man, Robert, is a brush-cutting maniac," he said to Diana, as he prepared for a shower. "The good news is that he's cut down roughly twice as much as I expected him to do."

"And the bad news?"

"None of it has been cleared up. Absolutely nothing!"

"Well, don't *you* clear it up! And don't pay him until he's done the work properly!"

"Don't worry about that!" he retorted, as he emptied his pockets. "I had no intention of paying him!"

"You fibber!" she protested, looking at the money he had just placed on the top of his chest of drawers. "Anyway, when is he coming back? You said you might need him for several weeks."

"I've no idea. He left without seeing me."

*

Diana was putting the finishing touches to what promised to be a good meal, fussing over a small saucepan of sauce to which she was adding tiny pieces of chopped mushrooms.

"About thirty minutes, my love. You must be hungry, after all that work and fresh air," she said.

"Averagely," he replied, opening a bottle of his favourite Cahors wine, a *Château Nozières, '85*. "*Monsieur* Chambon hasn't turned up. I can't stand unreliability!"

He had just sat down with his *apéritif* and was looking forward to looking at his mail, when the telephone rang.

"Will you get it, my love?" he asked. "I'm absolutely bushed!"

"*Allô, oui! Bonsoir!*" Her concentration was visible, as she strained to overcome the additional difficulty of understanding a foreign language over the telephone. "*Un moment, Félicie. Ne quittez pas!*"

"Félicie has just opened a bottle of champagne," she told him. "She wants us to go round there now!"

"Tell her I'm too tired," he suggested, and then went on a little wildly, "Tell her I've been working all day in the garden, clearing up the mess she's left behind. Tell her any bloody thing! I'm not going out at this hour! Anyway, supper's nearly ready, isn't it? It smells bloody good to me. I think I am quite hungry after all."

"*Félicie, tu es très gentille, mais...*"

He could hear Félicie's vociferous protests from where he was sitting on the other side of the room. Diana continued to insist that they were unable to accept her kind offer, and then the conversation ended abruptly.

"Oh dear! She sounded quite put out."

"I can't think why," he bridled, looking up at the ceiling. "Don't worry about it. We can't go charging about the countryside at eight o'clock in the evening, just because someone like Félicie decides to open a bottle of champagne! Who the hell does she think she is?"

"Eat in twenty minutes?" she laughed, putting a cassette into her new hi-fi system.

"Bloody good, my love," he replied, as Grace Jones started to sing.

*

Suddenly there was someone knocking insistently on the front door. Diana had just finished warming the plates, and she was about to serve two succulent *filets charollais* in a *sauce chasseur*.

"Sugar!" she cursed. "Who on earth can that be? We're not expecting anyone, are we?"

"I bet it's the Kenya cowboys," he muttered as he crossed the room to open the door. "They never have the remotest idea of the time of day!"

Three men and a woman stood in a sinister group in the light from the lantern in the porch. He could see behind them an old Renault van and a dusty truck parked in the drive. The unexpected quartet gave him the immediate impression that they were poised, ready to enter the house. He remained boldly in the doorway, wondering if this could be the normal way the French attempted burglary in isolated spots. The nearest man was big, heavily built, and looked as if he meant business. The thought flashed through his mind that the woman must be the gangsters' moll. The heavy brass poker lay on the hearth, about six feet behind him and to his left. He was prepared for the worst.

He remained firmly blocking the entrance, while he decided what to do or say to preserve body, soul, and property.

"*Qui êtes-vous? Qu'est-ce que vous voulez?*" he demanded abruptly. "Who are you, and what do you want?"

"*Bonsoir, M'sieu,*" rasped the heavyweight. His voice was deep, with an atrocious accent. "*Chambon, votre entrepreneur,*" he added, offering a hand the size of a plate. James winced as he shook it.

"*Ah! Monsieur Chambon! C'est vous!*" he said loudly, so that Diana could hear him over the climax of '*La vie en rose*'. "It's *Monsieur* Chambon, the stairs man, darling."

The music stopped, and he could hear behind him the unmistakable sound of plates being wrapped in in foil.

"*Merde!*" he said to himself. "That's fucked supper good and proper."

He stepped aside, allowing his untimely visitors to enter.

"*Bonsoir à tous! Entrez, s'il vous plaît,*" he greeted. "*Mais, je m'excuse! J'ai cru que vous étiez des cambrioleurs!*" he added. "I'm sorry! I thought you were burglars!"

If Monsieur Chambon noticed that he and his companions had

frustrated the start of a good meal, he showed no sign of it. He stood four-square in the middle of the room and introduced his wife and his son, André. The third man, who looked as if he might be a boxer or a rugby scrum-half (or, perhaps, both), waited expectantly, shifting his weight from one foot to the other, giving the impression that he was exercising with an invisible skipping rope. He stood no more than five feet high, but his physique suggested immense strength and fitness.

"Et voici Monsieur Quecher, Guy. Il est maçon," Monsieur Chambon concluded his introductions. "He's my stonemason,"

"Ah! Bon!" James replied, confused as to the role a stonemason might play in the design and construction of a spiral staircase made from seasoned oak, and unsure why he should be represented at the briefing which he was about to begin.

"Installez-vous, je vous en prie," James waved his hand at the chairs around the dining table. "Do please sit down."

There was a moment's embarrassed silence as the six of them looked at the four chairs, not knowing where to sit.

"Ah! Une petite erreur!" James said, blowing out the candles on the table. He pointed to the stone bench in the corner of the room.

"Why don't you entertain *Madame* Chambon over there?" he suggested to Diana, noticing that the Frenchwoman was staring with ill-concealed distaste at 'Exhilda', the bust of the nude Zambezi tribeswoman. "Then we men can sit at the table."

"Madame, je vous en prie," Diana said, ushering her unwanted guest to the corner bench.

As the four men sat down, Monsieur Chambon produced a gnarled pipe from his jacket pocket and sucked at it noisily. As if by magic, it was suddenly alight, and he sat back contentedly in his chair.

"Alors, Monsieur! On m'a dit que vous aviez envie d'un escalier en colimaçon!" he grunted. "I'm told you want a spiral staircase."

"Je crois que oui," James replied. *"Mais un petit moment, Monsieur Chambon. Je peux vous offrir quelque chose à boire?* I think so. But first, can I offer you something to drink?"

"Et bahh, ouais," he nodded. *"Je m'appelle Serge."*

Father and son accepted whisky, and Guy Quecher requested an orange juice. André lit an American cigarette, and soon a pall of blue smoke floated beneath the lamp over the table. Serge swallowed a large mouthful and sniffed hard, before offering a loud belch, which he made no attempt to suppress.

"*A la vôtre!*" André said politely, raising his glass.

James helped himself to a whisky, which he normally only drank after supper, and left the decanter on the table.

Diana crossed the room. He heard her switch on the kettle and then go downstairs. She returned with an armful of photograph albums. The two women settled in the corner, and James felt sure that they would amuse themselves for as long as it took him to explain to Serge the outline of his proposed project.

"*Vous venez de l'Afrique?*" he overheard Madame Chambon ask, as Diana opened the first album and started flicking through the pictures of Zambian wildlife.

He looked back at the men sitting at the table, who were still waiting for him to expand on his last comment.

"Ah, yes. Now, where was I? Yes... A spiral staircase could well be the best answer. I'll show you the problem."

They followed him into the small kitchen. There was barely enough standing room for the four of them. He waved at the two miller's ladders.

"*Ça y est!* There you go! They're the problem. They've got to come out. Now, gentleman, before I explain anything else, you must understand that we're going to redesign this kitchen, probably into a utility room. Everything must be ripped out, including all this dreadful, red plaster. I want exposed stonework, like in the other room. Briefly, the new sink, dishwasher, and some cupboards will go there along that wall, and more cupboard space and a fridge against that other wall. The kitchen designer is coming tomorrow."

He walked back into the living-room, and the trio followed. Chairs scraped, and all except James sat down.

"The cooking area," he resumed, "will go there, in this corner, we think. But that's a separate project, which I'll refer to as Phase One. We can proceed with Phase One in here, quite independently of the timing for the various stages of Phases Two and Three."

He paused to check that they were following his simple logic.

"*Ouerk!!*" shrieked Madame Chambon from the corner of the

room. James looked towards the two women. Diana was explaining the development of the children in Fackson's family as they had grown up.

"You don't mean to say you *love* them?" Madame Chambon cried, wrinkling her nose at the photographs. *"O-là-là! Tintin!* I don't know how you can bring yourself to... You couldn't... Could you! *Aïe! Aïe! Aïe!"*

Diana was making heavy weather with her uninvited companion, and it looked as if she might need rescuing soon.

James dragged his attention back to the Frenchmen at the table and resumed the task of defining his proposed projects.

"It's Phase Three which I now want to explain," James began.

"What's happened to Phase Two?" André asked, looking bewildered.

"I'll come back to Phase Two in a moment, if you don't mind, André," he replied, sounding like a schoolmaster admonishing a backward pupil. He ushered them back into the kitchen. "We cannot proceed with Phase Three, Stage One — which is the sink and so on over there — nor with Phase Three, Stage Two — that's the fridge and cupboards there — until the problem of the stairs has been resolved. So there's the answer to your question, André." André looked vacantly at him; so did his father and the stonemason.

"The stairs, André," he said slowly and patiently, "have to go in first, ahead of Stages One and Two of Phase Three."

Three blank faces continued to stare back at him. He would have to persevere and try again.

"The stairs are Phase Two," he sighed in exasperation. "Now, Serge, what I suggest is this. You three all go and have a good look around up there, in here, and down there. Then come back and tell me your plan and what might be involved."

Serge took out a crumpled notebook, the stub of a flat pencil, and a folding ruler.

"Allons-y, con!" he growled at his colleagues, and they clattered down the ladder to the lower level. He heard them all start talking at once, until Serge barked something unintelligible. James peered down the ladder and observed them casually taking some measurements. He did not know why, but he felt uneasy about the accuracy of that

folding ruler.

He strolled over to the two women in the corner of the room and asked them if they would like to drink anything stronger than coffee. Madame Chambon chose a small glass of *Armagnac*. He poured himself a second whisky, passed Madame Chambon her drink, and gave Diana a gin and tonic.

"Here, darling. You look as if you might need this."

It was no easier to understand Madame Chambon than her husband. The conversation soon faltered and then ceased. In desperation, Diana gave the Frenchwoman a recent copy of *Cosmopolitan*, which she found much more interesting than the photographs from Africa. Serge and André had progressed up the *pigeonnier* and were talking quietly in the top room. Guy was silently measuring one of the walls of the kitchen, pausing from time to time to carefully record his calculations.

James looked at his watch and saw that it was approaching ten o'clock. The fine wine still stood untouched on the sideboard, and the red light of the mini-oven continued to blink its invitation to dine. Serge at last finished his survey. He placed his open notebook on the table and slumped into one of the chairs. James glanced at the page full of measurements, but they were scrawled so illegibly that he could not tell whether they were in arabic or roman numerals.

"There's a hell of a lot of work there," Serge began ominously. "The inside of the entire *pigeonnier* will have to be completely gutted. Top to bottom! That means all the floors will have to be broken, and all the beams will have to come out. I'll show you where we can put your spiral." He walked into the kitchen and pointed to the far corner. "There! We'll give you two flights, with a landing here. The lower flight will have fourteen treads, with another twelve to reach the room at the top. It will take up one and a half square metres of floor space, so the end of the banisters will reach about here." He waved his wooden ruler vaguely at the floor. "You'll have to employ plumbers and electricians for any replacement work, new lighting, and so on."

"And you want all the stonework made good and cleaned?" Guy asked, and when James nodded, he quoted from his carefully prepared notes. "I make it approximately sixty square metres of wall to clean and all the pointing to renew. The room above is okay. Below, in the *sous-sol,* I'll have to take back all the tiling in the area of the basin and hip bath which you want removed. Finally, it's my job to renew the floor tiling."

James was numbed into temporary silence by the catalogue of tasks which appeared to lie ahead.

"Serge, let's be clear about one thing," he said firmly. "*I'm* not going to employ any craftsmen. It's *you* I want to employ them, including Guy here. Apart from anything else, I don't have your technical knowledge and experience. I want *you* to procure, co-ordinate, and supervise the entire project, and that will include liaison with the kitchen people. I want *you* to be responsible for everything. That means, if anything goes wrong, then it is *you* who will be held fully responsible. My wife and I will choose the design of the staircase, but that's the only thing we will do. It must be built from seasoned oak." He paused, and then asked, "Now, can you do the job properly?"

"*Baah, ouais! Bien sûr!*" Serge replied. "I'll bring round a plumber and an electrician sometime, and then I'll prepare a *devis,* an estimate for you."

Serge glanced across at his wife, picked up his notebook, and made as if he was about to leave.

"*Un moment, s'il vous plaît, Monsieur,*" James said, looking straight into the burly Frenchman's eyes. "When you say 'sometime', what *exactly* is that supposed to mean?" James demanded. "We want to get on with the job, you know. *On veut faire du progrès.* I can't risk my wife breaking her leg on those ladders!"

"*Alors, Monsieur. Disons la semaine prochaine, en principe,*" Serge replied a little vaguely. "Let's say next week, in theory."

"But we don't know what's under these floor tiles, *con!*" André protested, stamping his boot on the floor of the kitchen. "From our measurements, we suspect that you have a double layer of flooring and beams under here. So the estimate will only be an *approximi,* a rough one."

"And if I accept your *devis,* when can you start?" James asked, addressing his question to the father.

"In about three months. Let's aim for the first week of January."

They all sat down, helping themselves to his decanter, which they left empty when they departed. It was ten minutes before midnight.

*

Diana collected together the photograph albums, returned to the drawing-room the magazines which Madame Chambon had been reading, and went over to the mini-oven.

"I don't suppose you want any supper," Diana said.

"No, my darling. I'm sorry, but it's far too late now. Let's go to bed."

"What a terrible waste! I'll just go and get Jacob in."

She took the silent whistle off its hook and went out into the porch, leaving the front door open. Almost immediately he heard her sharp intake of breath.

"Oh, my God! Oh, my God!" she wailed. It sounded to James as if she was in acute pain, as if she had hurt herself. "James! Come quickly!" she cried. "Something's happened to Jacob!"

He rushed out to join her. Jacob was lying on his side on the stone step. He was breathing, but only just, and with great difficulty. Both his eyes were half closed. He did not move, his vision impaired by his prominent third eyelids, which were lowered. She picked him up gently, holding him into her neck and face.

"He's terribly cold and very sick," she said hoarsely, choking back the tears welling in her eyes, "Oh, my baby boy! Where have you been? What have you been doing, my man? He must have been just strong enough to crawl back from wherever this has happened."

She examined him carefully all over, her fingers moving slowly and tenderly through his fur.

"There are no marks on him, but he's dying, James. Don't die, my love! Please don't die on me!" Tears were now rolling freely down her cheeks. "Jacob! Jacob, you've got to live!" she sobbed. "You're the best cat ever! Don't die, my baby!" An ear flicked, and then, through her tears, she thought she saw a very slight eye movement. "He's trying to purr, but he's too weak. We must get him to a vet quickly! Do you think we can reach one at this hour? I wrote the numbers down on the emergency list by the phone."

"I'll try," he said, and quickly tapped out the vet's emergency number. "Try not to worry, my love. He's such a strong cat. He'll pull through."

The number was not engaged, and he let it continue ringing. Diana was becoming visibly more agitated, cradling the elderly cat in her arms, as he waited for someone to reply.

"If you manage to get through," she said quickly, "tell him that Jacob is still very dehydrated from the flight. He must bring strong antibiotics, rehydration jabs, and put him on a drip. Tell him he's dying, and that he's damned well *got* to turn out. Don't take no for an answer. Tell him that it looks to me like poisoning, and that he'll have to take a blood sample for analysis."

There was a click on the line, and a tired voice answered. James spoke quickly in a clipped, military tone which she had never before heard him use, as he rapidly relayed her instructions to the person on the other end of the line.

"Yes, he's fifteen... I know that's quite old for a Burmese, *mais il est très cousteau,* he's very strong and fit. He's a champion of champions, if you know what that means... Yes, but now, and quickly!... That's right. It used to belong to *Madame* Gautier... Bon Porteau. I'll put on all the outside lights for you. You can't miss it... On the left. *Mille fois merci, Monsieur! À tout à l'heure!"* He breathed a sigh of relief. "He's coming straightaway" he told Diana. "I'll go and put on the lights."

Monsieur Flouret, the vet, took one look at Jacob and ran back to his car, calling out to James as he went.

"Come, *Monsieur.* Help me carry some things. And tell your wife to find a good box or something for the cat."

"Ask him if the cats' cage will be okay?" Diana shouted to James.

"Even better," the vet replied. "We can secure the drip to it."

He worked quickly, efficiently and, it seemed to James, with great concern.

"Mais, qu'il est beau! How handsome he is! *Superbe!"* were the only words he spoke for a while.

He pumped three long syringes of rehydration salts into the scruff of Jacob's neck. Two different injections quickly followed, and then he took a blood sample from the cat's limp, left paw, on which he neatly tied a small bandage. He examined the cage, went out to his car again, and returned with a metal rod, on one end of which there was a hook. He deftly tied the rod to a corner of the cage and then devoted his attention to his patient He opened one of Jacob's eyes, clicking his tongue with concern, and then placed him gently inside the cage, finally inserting the drip. Less than ten minutes had elapsed since his arrival.

"Et Voilà!" he said with a smile for Diana as he stood up. "That's all we can do for the moment."

He started to pack his syringes into his bag, as if he was about to leave, but then turned to Diana.

"Have you had any veterinary training?" Diana shook her head. "Well, your diagnosis was only too correct. It's that bloody, so-called environmentally friendly poison which people are using nowadays, *con!* The rat, or mouse, or whatever, eats it but then takes two or three days to die. If, during that period, either a dog or a cat, perhaps a bird of prey, or even a fox finds and eats the rodent, then of course it too ingests the poison. If action is not taken very quickly, it will also die. It's not a painful death, but it's a sure one. I know, because I've seen it too many times before."

Diana's face had turned a ghostly white, and her eyes were staring in horror, appalled at what the vet had just related.

"Is he going to die?" she asked. "I can't imagine life after Jacob!"

"How long had he been out of doors, do you know?"

"Not more than an hour, at the most. This was the first day I have let them out."

"I don't want to raise your hopes. He's very ill indeed." Monsieur Flouret looked down at Jacob and then went on, "He's obviously eaten a whole mouse, or... "

"Non! Monsieur! Non!" Diana interrupted him. "I've trained both my cats not to eat mice or birds! They just catch them and then, either they let them go outside, or else they bring them into the house and put them on my foot as a little present for me. They never harm them, and there's never a mark on them. Jacob, in particular, has a very soft mouth, just like a well-trained labrador. So, even if one of Jacob's teeth did puncture something poisoned, then he can only have taken very little poison, can't he?"

"Now, this drip," the vet resumed, giving her an indulgent look, "should last the rest of the night. Just in case it doesn't, I've left you a spare one. You just clip it on like this. It's important that it doesn't come out by accident, do you understand? I have sedated him, but you will still have to take it in turns to watch over him tonight, in case he tries to stand up. Bring him to my surgery at half-past eight."

James was expecting him to add the words, "*If* he's still alive".

Monsieur Flouret picked up his bag and was on the point of leaving, when Diana stopped him.

"Thank you for coming out," she said simply and then kissed him on each cheek. "Please save him for me! He's so very, very precious to me. He was born in England. He's been to Zambia and back. And now here he is in France." She looked at Jacob. "He's the best cat *anyone* has ever had!"

"*Bon courage, Madame!*" he said, smiling sympathetically. "*Cette nuit, touchons du bois!* Chin up! Tonight, let's keep our fingers crossed! Phone me again if you get worried tonight. Otherwise, I'll see all three of you tomorrow. *À demain!*"

Chapter Twenty-Six

Diana refused his offer to share the vigil over Jacob, saying that she could not bring herself to sleep and, since there was no real benefit to be gained by both of them staying up for the rest of the night, James went to bed. He did not sleep well, and was up before dawn, knowing that it was going to be a long and busy Tuesday.

"How is the big man?" he asked, trying to sound optimistic when he joined Diana in the living-room, where she had sat beside Jacob throughout the night.

"I think he may be coming through the worst," she replied. "His eyes are now open, but he can't hold his head up for long. He's been like that for most of the night, with his nose down on his blanket."

Jacob was in Monsieur Flouret's surgery twice that day. At the first appointment, the vet expressed his surprise and satisfaction at the cat's determination to recover.

"*Bon Dieu!*" he exclaimed. "Would you believe it? He's even trying to stand up! He's a tough chap, this one."

More medication followed, and Monsieur Flouret announced that he expected to receive the results of the blood analysis by mid-afternoon.

"It would be altogether better," he advised, "if you leave your cat here, where we can keep an eye on him. Come back at four this afternoon." Diana looked at James, shook her head vigorously, and reached out to lift up the cage. James could see clearly that she was not going to comply with the vet's suggestion.

"No disrespect to you, *Monsieur*," James said quickly, "but my wife will be much happier to have him at home. Jacob will only pine if we leave him here alone. It may even impede his recovery."

"*D'accord! Comme vous voulez, Madame,*" Monsieur Flouret conceded. "Okay, if that's what you want to do."

When they returned to Bon Porteau, James carried Jacob in his cage into the house and placed it gently on the stone corner bench in the living-room.

"You must get on with whatever you have to do today," Diana told him. "I can manage Jacob by myself, and I'll take him back at four o'clock without you."

She stayed beside the cat throughout the day, stroking him and whispering words of love and encouragement to him. Now and then, Jacob tried to purr, each attempt becoming more sustained and regular. By the time she arrived for her second visit to the surgery, Jacob had rallied sufficiently to drink a little water, and he was standing up, albeit unsteadily.

"I have the computer printout of his analysis," the vet reported to her. "It was indeed a poison but, fortunately, not too much of it. He'll be all right now, although for the next few days he will feel weak. However, the analysis indicates that his kidneys are his biggest problem. It also shows anaemia, and his blood count is low. Does he drink a lot of milk?"

"No. He has never had milk," she replied. "Nor does my other Burmese. As a breed, generally they only drink water, but I have noticed recently that he's been at his water bowl more frequently than usual. He seems to be drinking as much as four or five times a day.

"Oui. Il est tout comme les Français, con!"

The vet opened the cage and gave Jacob a thorough examination. He pursed his lips in thought, while he formulated the advice he was going to offer his new English client, whom he found charming and attractive.

"Bon!" he said, putting his patient back in the cage. "We will put him on a strictly controlled diet from now on. What does he normally eat?"

"Back in Zambia, that is until just over a week ago, his food was either boiled chicken or dried food. I suppose that could have something to do with it."

"I'm afraid you must cut out the dried food, and you will have to give him this vitamin course for the next four weeks. Does he let you put drops down him?"

"Monsieur," she retorted archly. "Jacob will allow me to do anything with him!"

Monsieur Flouret flashed a smile. He did not think it would be necessary to see Jacob anymore. On the other hand, he felt a desire to meet his English client again.

"I think, *Madame*, that you should now go home and get some sleep," he said pleasantly. "When he has fully recovered, you must bring him back, and I'll clean his teeth. But before that, you and your husband must come and take an *apéritif* with me and my girlfriend. Sabine speaks pretty good English, and I know she could help you with learning how to live in France. I'm not referring just to improving your French; understanding our culture and customs is most important, since I'm very pleased to hear that you're going to be living here permanently. I'll call you soon to arrange it." He smiled again at her. "And well done, last night. It was really you, not I, who saved Jacob's life."

As they shook hands, it was his turn to place a kiss on each of her cheeks.

She drove back to Bon Porteau feeling light-headed with relief.

*

When Diana suggested that he should make progress with his own tasks, he decided that he should concentrate on his preparations for the Big Day. All administration and preliminaries, he resolved, must be completed by the following evening. That would leave him free to spend all Thursday enjoying the company of his wife. He was determined that it was going to be a sensational success. He decided that there would have to be a dry weather programme, utilizing the roof *terrasse,* and a contingency plan, which would involve using the barn in case it rained. He added to his list of tasks: breaking open the remaining crates, sweeping out the barn, and preparing the fireplace, since it might be needed. He checked his shopping list and set off for Montcarmel. On his way, he stopped to invite Iain's house party, swearing them all to secrecy, since he insisted that every element of Thursday's programme had to be a surprise for Diana. Before he left, Stewart agreed to fabricate two charcoal braziers before Thursday lunchtime. James did not see Vincent or Airlie there, but met briefly Vanessa, Stewart's girlfriend who, he thought, was very attractive.

Outside Montcarmel, his first call was at the Citroën dealer. Monsieur Thiebaud was beaming when he greeted his strange English customer from Africa. Not only was he confident that he was going to make a good profit but also he was enjoying the subterfuge. In thirty-eight years of dealing, he had never before sold a car in this curious way.

"I've succeeded," he whispered conspiratorially, although nobody was within earshot. "Come and have a look at her. I haven't told a soul. I haven't even told my wife. You can't be *too* careful with women, you know; they talk too much, *con!*" He led James into the workshop and pointed. "*Voilà!* That's what you wanted, isn't it? Cute, isn't she? *Est-elle mignonne, hein?*"

An almost new 2CV was parked inside the double doors of the large workshop. James glanced inside it; it had been driven less than two thousand kilometres, if the reading was genuine.

"Excellent, *Monsieur* Thiebaud! How much?"

They bargained briefly, and then James noticed the clock on the workshop wall.

"Right, I'll take it and settle up with you next week. Now this is what I want you to do... I'll be back inside an hour, and you can follow me. We'll put it in the barn, where it won't be seen."

The rest of his shopping was straightforward and much less expensive. He was able to tick most of the items off his list: champagne, some reasonable wines, the stationer, the florist, the supermarket, charcoal, two metres of scarlet ribbon, and then back up the hill to the gift shop for a knick-knack which, he insisted, must be decorative but otherwise completely useless. He liked to keep things simple. Every birthday and anniversary he gave her an enamel or porcelain box to add to her collection. Finally, he returned to the garage. Monsieur Thiebaud, driving the 2CV, followed him up the hill to Bon Porteau, where they turned down a track which was not visible from the house. The small Citroën was parked safely inside the barn. He did not think that they had been seen. It's a stroke of luck this is all still here, he mused, recalling how the fire had almost destroyed the barn.

"That was very well done, *Monsieur*," he told the car dealer, whom he then returned to his premises outside the town.

During the return journey to Pisenhaut, he saw Jules Carendier standing with another man in the beautifully landscaped garden which surrounded the house at the bottom of the hill. Jules recognized James, as he slowed down to take the corner. He ran to the gate to stop him.

"Bonjour, James," he said. "Come and meet Pierre, and you're just in time for an *apéritif* before lunch."

Pierre Bouyou was about ten years older than Jules and, even in his gardening clothes, he looked elegant. He was also much travelled, sophisticated, and extremely charming. Thinking of earlier times and other places, James felt it a lucky omen that their nearest neighbours were so *sympa*. He accepted a glass of chilled white wine, and the three of them sat out in the sunshine beyond the shadow cast by a huge walnut tree.

Pierre's quiet, dry sense of humour and worldliness were in stark contrast to the sensitive imagery which Jules wove into his conversation. Perhaps, after all, James thought, opposites really do attract each other.

"You have a superb place there, James," Pierre was saying, looking up the valley towards Bon Porteau. "Whatever you paid for it, it will be a good investment, because such properties, with all the surrounding land still intact, are very rare nowadays. I've always thought of it as a man's place, and it never felt right to me that Félicie Gautier should have stayed on all those years after the death of her husband."

"I see you have started to restore the gardens," Jules observed. "In their way, yours are even more sensational than ours, which is totally man-made. Yours were fashioned by Nature herself. They sprang up between the layers of rock years and years ago with their different levels and superb views. In my mind, you have *en effet* seven discrete gardens, each one leading into the next, gently changing emphasis and character. You have everything there, and your trees at this time of the year are *tout à fait épatants*, quite stunning. And then, of course, you have three magnificent *sources,* and the big well under the walnut trees. *Superbe!* You were lucky to find Bon Porteau."

He was instantly enjoying their company, and he felt sure that Diana would also warm to them. He therefore decided on the spur of the moment to invite them to the Big Day.

"Pierre and Jules," he began, a little unsure of himself. "I know we don't know each other well, although I'm sure we will as time goes by, and of course you haven't yet met my wife, Diana—"

"She has blonde hair, cut in a very French style, no?" Jules interjected. "I saw this attractive woman passing the house twice yesterday. I thought she must be *la belle Anglaise* from Bon Porteau."

"Also, I know it's very short notice," James resumed, "but I'm giving a party for Diana on Thursday evening. She knows nothing about it, so it's a kind of a surprise birthday party. I wonder if you would both like to come."

"Mais quelle drôle d'idée! Incroyable!" Pierre reacted immediately. "What a lovely idea! Amazing!" Turning towards Jules, he continued, *"Ça y est! C'est l'Anglais typique! Ils ne s'étonnent de rien!* There! Typically English! Nothing surprises them! Of course, James, it would be an honour, and we would love to come."

Jules went into the house and returned with a bottle of champagne, which he opened with nonchalant ease.

"May I ask you what you have bought her as a present?" Jules enquired.

"A *deux chevaux,* a 2CV," he replied, feeling that he might be giving them a false impression of himself.

"Superbe!" exclaimed Pierre.

"Fabuleux!" Jules added, and then asked, "Have you got it yet?"

"Yes. *Monsieur* Thiebaud and I smuggled it into the barn this morning. I'll give it to her on Thursday morning."

"Et bien," Pierre ventured, "but you cannot put even a 2CV into a surprise parcel with its gift wrapping! You must let Jules tie a big bow on the bonnet. He makes the most exquisite bows!"

"Volontiers," offered Jules.

"That's very kind of you, Jules," James said, accepting the glass of champagne which was being offered to him. "By chance, just this morning, I bought two metres of scarlet ribbon. I think Diana may be planning to go into Cahors tomorrow. I don't know whether it will be during the morning or in the afternoon, but I'll let you know. We can do it then."

When Pierre rose to refill their glasses, James noticed that he removed an upturned spoon with a long, thin handle from the neck of the champagne bottle.

"Pierre, why do you put a spoon in there?" James asked.

"You don't know this old trick? It's the cheapest and most effective way to retain the fizz in champagne, once a bottle has been opened. You can buy all sorts of pretty and expensive gadgets if you want. However, this is the best way, even if it is a trifle inelegant. May I ask how many people you are expecting for your party?"

"Oh, I'm not sure exactly. It might be about forty. I was thinking of a buffet supper with some music and dancing afterwards."

"*O-là-là, là-là, là-là!*" Jules exclaimed. "Do you cook? I mean, if the party is to be a surprise, how can you possibly prepare the food yourself without immediately creating suspicion? *Ça va gâcher la surprise!* It'll give the game away!"

"No. I can't cook at all. It's funny you should ask that," James admitted. "It's about the only problem I have yet to solve."

The two Frenchmen looked at each other, and a suggestion of a smile appeared on Pierre's face.

"Please excuse us for a few minutes or so," Pierre said, waving at the drinks trolley. "Help yourself to whatever you want."

The two men walked towards the house. James could not follow their rapid conversation as they went out of earshot. From the way they were gesticulating, he thought that they might be having an argument. Well, he mused, even men disagree between themselves occasionally. When they returned, he was relieved to see that they were laughing happily.

The two Parisians rejoined him and sat down again. They looked at each other conspiratorially, and Jules gestured to Pierre that he should take the lead.

"James," Pierre began. *"Nous aimerions bien vous faire une petite proposition.* We would like to suggest something to you. We think you will like our little plan. Let us try to solve your little problem."

"What little problem?"

"Let *us* do the food for the party. It's our hobby. We'll thoroughly enjoy doing it."

"Yes," Jules joined in supportively. "I think the menu could be... To start with, a hot fish soup, perhaps a nice bouillabaisse; then move on to a course of *charcuterie,* different cold meats. The main course must not be too fussy, so we could offer your guests a choice of either *jambon persillé*, a ham set in a parsley jelly with mixed salad, or else *thonine ligurienne*, which is a Mediterranean variety of tuna fish, with tomatoes, risotto, and duchesse potatoes. We will finish with one of our favourite creations: *pêches Bourdaloue,* a peach tart with frangipane cream, followed by the *plateau de fromages. Voilà! C'est tout simple!"*

"I can't let you do all that!" James protested.

"Au contraire. C'est un fait établi," Pierre insisted in a way that would brook no argument. "But nothing could be more simple!"

"I don't know what to say, gentlemen... Except... Well, how fantastic! I will probably be able to give you exact numbers tomorrow. Thanks to you two, I now *know* it's going to be a sensational party."

The two Frenchmen were beaming with pleasure at each other as he drove away up the hill.

*

An old, battered Mini estate car was parked in the drive, and he could hear voices coming from the living-room as he went up the stone steps to the porch. Vincent and Airlie were drinking coffee, telling Diana about the changes in their immediate plans.

"It was the postmistress who tipped us off," Airlie explained. "The people who own *Château Maulieu* are frequently away. They're New Zealanders and very rich. Well, they were looking for someone reliable to live in their annexe, a converted barn, to babysit the place, do a little bit of gardening, and feed the six dogs. Oh, and there are some horses as well. And guess what! We got the job yesterday. We've just moved out of Iain's place. *Voilà!* We get a small wage and a free roof over our head!"

"Yes," Vincent added. "And when they're away, we can take over the *château* and watch their television. The Five Nations rugby starts soon!"

James was listening to their account while he mixed a glass of *Kir* to complement the drinks which he had enjoyed with the two Parisians.

"Hey! But that's great news," he said supportively. "It's only about five kilometres away. But is there enough space there, Vincent, for your studio?"

"Not really, but we'll manage somehow," he replied, and then added, "By the way, you'll never guess who is coming to stay tomorrow! It's H-J! He'll be with us until the weekend."

"That will be nice, because Piers is also coming," James commented, stopping himself just in time from adding, "For the Big Day." He walked with the young couple to their car and told them about his surprise plan.

"And bring H-J, of course," he whispered.

"How *simply* delicious," Airlie replied enthusiastically.

*

After lunch he decided that he must complete the task of issuing the remaining invitations. During the short drive back to Bon Porteau from his visit to Pierre and Jules, he had suddenly had an inspired idea. Diana was going to be forty-six years old. The number by which the Lot is identified is forty-six. Therefore, he decided, it would be quite logical to have forty-six people at the party. He took the telephone handset and the local telephone book up to the barn, and wrote down the names of all the guests, some of whom might not be able to come. He began by noting those who already knew and were coming: Kim and Piers; Iain's house party, comprising Laetizia, Stewart, Vanessa, Greg, and his mate (Find out his name!); Vincent, Airlie, and H-J; Pierre and Jules Bouyou-Carendier." He put a tick against all their names.

He then continued, listing the local people who had been kind and helpful on their arrival: Félicie and Pascale Gautier; Guillaume and Monique; Gérard Tillet; Marcel and Micheline Briand, and her younger sister, Sophie, whom he had not yet met; Miguel and Pénélope; the vet, Monsieur Flouret, and his girlfriend, Sabine; the Mayor and Madame Larguille; Gilles Griffoul and his young wife (Find out her name!); and the Louisor couple from Cahors. His thoughts turned to good friends in England. It was some time since they had last seen them. Jim, a successful Scottish entrepreneur, and Carol, his attractive wife, would be able to come. He was not so sure about Barbara and Bill — Bill was always working too hard, but Barbara would certainly add to the glamour of the event. He wrote down their four names. Finally, for the sake of completeness, he added the group of friends, known as 'the Windlesham Mob', who were coming out from England: John and Dorothy; Kate and Jim; Ron and Bernie.

He twice counted the names on the list. With Diana and himself, the total was three short of his target. He made a note that he would have to find one more couple and someone on their own, as he started telephoning England and the remaining French guests. When he finished, he had established that all except three could come: the Mayor and his wife, who excused themselves on the grounds that they were too old for such fun, and Sophie Briand, who would be at school in Montauban. He thought for a few seconds, and rang Guy Raynal, their bachelor neighbour, who had rescued Jacob. He then remembered Fifine at the garage, and called her.

"But of course I'll be there, *chéri!*" was her reaction.

As he returned to the house, he was wondering where he might find four more suitable guests to make up his target of forty-six, which had now become a symbolic objective.

*

He had intended to spend the rest of the day working in the garden. As he was going back down to the house, he was surprised and delighted to see Robert's car and trailer coming up the drive. When Robert had left the previous day without saying anything about returning, he had assumed that it was because he had plenty of other jobs to do. They would now be able, he decided, to work together and clear another area of undergrowth. Before they started, he reminded the young Frenchman that an untidy gardener was a poor gardener.

"So, before you do any more jungle-bashing, you must first clear up that lot from yesterday. I'll go and get changed, and then I'll bring the tractor and trailer to take it up to the bonfire."

His plan was promptly frustrated. Before he reached the house, a smart van swung into the drive. Its sole occupant was the young kitchen designer.

"*Merde!*" he swore softly. "I had forgotten he was coming today."

Seconds later he heard the whine of Robert's *débroussailleuse* starting, evidence that his instructions were being ignored. He showed the young Frenchman into the house.

"We don't know your name," James said, as they sat down with Diana at the table in the living-room.

"I am Jean-Pierre de Vauban," the young man replied, opening his brown leather briefcase, from which he removed drawing pens and a sketch pad. James noticed that the case was filled with shiny brochures.

"Would you please now show me, as precisely as possible, the area you are prepared to devote to your new kitchen? I will then do some sketches to give you some ideas. While I take measurements, perhaps *Madame* would like to look at some of these."

James described the outline plan and explained the proposal for the spiral staircase.

"It will take up about this much space," he indicated. "So we think the most sensible thing is to have the utility room here, with the cooking area in the corner by the French window in the other room."

He went on to recite the need for phases and stages of work, and was relieved when Jean-Pierre, unlike Chambon father and son, understood immediately the need for careful planning and co-ordination. The designer produced a workmanlike tape measure and in neat, precise handwriting, he quietly noted heights, lengths, widths, and corner angles.

They watched him in fascination, as he started to create his sketches. With a few strokes of his pen, a corner kitchen appeared on his pad. He removed the sheet of paper and, with similar economy of effort, there was a *plan travail* for the utility room with sink, mixer tap, dishwasher, and work surfaces. The third sketch depicted an arrangement of storage space, which flanked a built-in refrigerator. He returned to his first two sketches, and added some shading here and there. Finally, he brushed a colour wash over the kitchen furniture and sat back in his chair. He had been in the house for no more than thirty minutes.

"Voilà!" he announced. "That's what I can do for you."

He explained where the appliances would fit, flicking in a practised way through the brochures to reinforce his recommendations.

"The furniture will all be of the highest quality, and the equipment I have suggested is the most reliable. All you have to do is to choose the door design, the tiles you want, and buy a good quality tap. Don't be tempted to get a cheap one — they're more trouble than they're worth." Closing his briefcase, he stood up, leaving two brochures on the table.

"The day after tomorrow," he resumed, "you will receive in the post your final drawings to scale. I now have seven more clients to see this afternoon. *Monsieur, Madame, Au revoir!*"

"Well, he knows his onions!" James said in admiration, as the young man's back disappeared out of the front door.

"It all looks like it'll cost a bomb," Diana murmured in a sombre tone.

*

The noise of the *débroussailleuse* died, and a few minutes later Robert was knocking on the door.

"Il faut que je parte maintenant. J'en ai plus de mélange," he told James. "I must go now. No two-stroke fuel left." He then hinted that he wanted to be paid. "That's seven hours you owe me."

"Hang on, Robert," James said. "I'll have to go and find some money."

"Has he cleared up the mess he's created?" Diana asked. "If not, don't pay him, James. Don't let him get away with it."

When James discovered that Robert had devoted his labours solely to cutting, he was suitably stern.

"Robert, I've asked you twice to rake it all up as you go," he reminded him. "Now there's at least half a day's work left behind. I'm not going to pay you, unless the job is done properly. *Pas un sou!* Not one penny!"

The Frenchman looked as if he was about to burst into tears. He turned his trouser pockets inside out.

"But I have no money," he whined. "I told my wife I would be paid today, and we were planning to go out to dinner tonight." He shrugged and then went on, "She won't have prepared any food at home, and I worked through my break for lunch so that I could give you three hours today. A man's got to eat, you know."

James had no idea whether or not he was telling the truth. He was inclined to take Robert for a simple soul, with insufficient guile or intelligence to concoct such a plausible lie. He decided to relent a little.

"If you promise to come back tomorrow and clear it all up, then

I'll give you now half the amount I owe you. That should be enough for a good meal for two."

"I promise, *Monsieur*, to do it next time," Robert replied sheepishly, putting the money in his pocket. "I promise faithfully that I will be here at ten in the morning, and my very first task will be to clear up all the trash."

During the early part of the evening, Diana returned to the subject of Robert and his unreliability.

"I bet you bloody paid Robert," she accused him, while he started to mix their evening *apéritif*.

"No, I did not," he retorted sharply. "I only gave him half his earnings." He repeated to her Robert's promise. "He'll return tomorrow and keep his word. I'm sure he won't let me down."

Their discussion was cut short as the front door opened quietly behind James. Diana's eyes widened with surprise.

"Someone else has arrived," she whispered to him, looking over his shoulder.

He turned his head to see Marcel Briand, bare-headed and clutching his beret in his hand. With him was a young, pretty girl in a jumper and blue jeans.

"I've brought your account for the excavation work," he explained. *"Le voici, Monsieur!* I have had to add tax to it, I'm afraid, because everyone in the village knows that we were working here. You cannot operate secretly with an excavator... Unfortunately! But, as you can see, I've given you a *prix d'ami,* as we call it — a special price for a friend."

Marcel pushed the girl forward gently. Her dark hair reached down to her shoulders, and her eyes were bright blue.

"This is my second daughter, Sophie. She is at school in Montauban."

"Enchanté, Sophie. Quel âge as-tu?" he asked. "How old are you?"

"Eighteen, at Christmas," she replied shyly. She bore no resemblance to Micheline, her heavyweight, elder sister.

"She takes her *bac* in two years," Marcel announced. "Will you teach her English?"

"Très volontiers! Mais je suis pas prof," he replied. "I'd love to

help, but I'm not a teacher."

Marcel did not appear to be the least concerned with James's teaching qualifications. They agreed that Wednesday afternoons and Saturday mornings would be the most convenient times, and that they would start the following week.

They stood facing each other, the Frenchman remaining silent. James looked down at the bill in his hand, waiting for Marcel to tell him how much he was prepared to pay for the individual tuition of his daughter. In fact, he was expecting him to say that his fees should be set against the bill for his excavation work. However, before he could broach the subject and strike a tax-effective deal, Marcel had put on his beret, shaken hands, and both father and daughter were out of the door.

"Allez! Bonne fin de soirée!" Marcel called, as they disappeared into the darkness. "Enjoy the rest of the evening!

"What very peculiar behaviour, and at this hour, too!" James remarked, looking at his watch. "Do you know, he didn't even knock on the door, or say please or thank you — just like a Zambian!"

"The word must be getting about," Diana observed wryly. "They all want to get in on the act! I noticed you didn't mention any tuition fee. You'll never learn, James. It was just the same in Zambia. Look at how many times you were taken for a ride."

"Oh, I don't know. On the whole, I thought I did pretty well out there."

He put her glass in her hand. He did not want to get into an argument. He was feeling tired after the events of the day, and looking forward to a nice, relaxing evening.

"Well, just think back," she persisted. "Time and time again you were had. Anyone with any nous can see you coming from a mile off: that gang of men, who were supposed to rebuild the grass fence after the fire; Felix Sitole and that expensive electric guitar; the exorbitant, fictitious landing fee at Livingstone airport; the loan to the Permanent Secretary, who said he needed to buy fertilizer for his smallholding; the con man, who told you he was from the Secret Service, or Special Branch, or whatever it's called, who fooled you into believing he had been assigned to see to it that you settled in without being bothered by people just like him!"

"That's all water under the bridge, my love," he said, trying not to take her criticism personally. "You're making too much of a thing of it. Teaching little Sophie will be no big deal... "

He felt that the discussion was heading towards an unproductive conclusion. He turned his back on her and walked through to the drawing-room.

"But others were," she chided him, following him into the adjoining room. "And some of them, you can't deny it, were not exactly chicken feed. The property in Lusaka, which we almost bought from that Greek chap; the bogus puncture trick you fell for, when you had your pouch stolen with everything in it, plus the cash for two return air tickets to Mauritius; and then the building materials for Fackson's house. By the time..."

"Now that's *not* a fair one," he argued. "How was I to know that he would take over three years to build his house and that, during that time, there would be more than six hundred percent inflation?"

"Okay. I take back the last one," she conceded. "it was a very Christian act to provide him with the means to build himself a house. But there were many, many others."

She picked up the rough sketches of the kitchen, looking at them and shaking her head.

"I just want to say one more thing. Watch out for this lot! I mean Serge Chambon's staircase, and Jean-Pierre's grandiose ideas for the kitchen. It's you, not I, who keep saying the French think just like the Africans. They all know they're on to a bloody good thing. You must not go on behaving as if you are the World Bank, or the International Monetary Fund, or British Overseas Aid!"

"Or Oxfam!" he added, feeling that this was the nearest that they had come to having a meaningless row since their arrival.

"You look just lovely, my darling. Let's stop arguing and drink up. Come on! I'm taking you out for supper."

"But what about the duck that's roasting?"

"Fuck the duck! We'll have it cold for lunch tomorrow."

Chapter Twenty-Seven

Silence is a curious phenomenon. It can be blissful, weird, brutal, or simply depressing. It can play tricks on the mind. Total silence, with the absence of all background sound — near or far — disturbs the balance of the senses, as if they are in the grip of a sudden onset of deafness. With the loss of one sense, the others work harder to compensate for the deficiency. Awareness of movement is heightened and, even as the eye detects a falling leaf, the ear strains illogically to catch the imperceptible whisper as it brushes the ground.

The inner voice is more intrusive, even at times garrulous, as the two sides of the brain compete to dominate the thought processes, one moment pragmatic, mechanical, numerate, and the next romantic, fanciful, and sensitive to surrounding shapes and images. The effect of silence on animals is visible. A cat will prick and turn its ears in quest of a sound; a dog may rest awake, eyes open, nose alert, its hackles shifting as it senses real or imaginary dangers; horses quiver, head up with pointed ears and dilated nostrils, stamping their hooves to reassure themselves and warn others. When unexpected noise erupts under such circumstances, it bursts on the scene like a sudden explosion.

James was lying awake, not moving, listening to the silent valley outside the bedroom, reviewing the past ten days, and listing in his head the tasks ahead of him. Wednesday is market day in Cahors, he remembered. Diana, peacefully asleep by his side, intended to go there at some time during the day. He thought that there would be an opportunity, a day ahead of the Big Day, to contact Jules Carendier about tying the bow on the bonnet of the car. He hoped he would be able to tell him how many people were coming to the party, worrying that he was still four short of his target of forty-six. He remembered that this was the day the *femme de ménage,* Chantal Chaumeil, was coming to start work, but he could not recall whether she was due in the morning or in the afternoon. He made a resolution to exercise more control over Robert and then wondered, as an afterthought, whether he would come again. If he wanted the other half of his pay, he would have to return. At some time during the day, he reminded himself, he must not forget to telephone Piers, who would be driving from the Channel Islands. His son could collect Kim from the airport at Toulouse. And the barn must be cleaned and prepared, in case the weather changed on the evening of the Big Day.

Planning for the Big Day prompted a thoughtful smile. He had always regarded birthdays as more important, more significant, than any New Year's Day which he could ever remember. A birthday is entirely personal to the family. It commemorates the day when a mother pushes a baby into the world through a mist of pain, danger and, hopefully also, joyfulness. It heralds the start of a life which may be good or evil, contented or miserable, with its hopes, dreams, and ambitions, a future of frustrations, achievements and failures which may or may not follow, and the sorrows and regrets which lie ahead, like the opening phrases of an unplanned book. It marks the finish of one year, one's very own year, and the beginning of the next. Being born is the first step towards death.

He closed his eyes, and his face creased into a happy, reminiscent smile. He was back among the silence, the sounds, and the smells in the heat and dust of early October in the Luangwa valley. They were the only guests in the small game camp on the river bank at Nsefu, which lies beyond Mfuwe. He knew it was his birthday the moment he awoke and, for some unaccountable reason, he sensed that it was going to be a truly magical day. Being by themselves, alone with a trail leader, or together with their friends who managed the camp, was a situation which they cherished, since it was a guarantee for good game-viewing, a pre-requisite for which is silent patience.

Other people in the bush were a liability and, frequently, an annoying distraction. They wore brightly coloured clothes, or coughed at a critical moment; they wriggled in their seats of the open vehicle or, worse still, they started to talk aloud. An attractive Danish woman, whose figure was much better than her intellect, shrieked in fright when they were trailing a fully grown leopard in broad daylight. She received her just deserts some minutes later, when she was bitten by tsetse flies. He recalled the German tourist who suffered from chronic, early-morning flatulence, habitually setting out to view the animals with his sophisticated camera near the end of a reel of film. On several occasions, a glorious moment was ruined by the click and whirr of his film rewinding itself. In the end, they refused to go out in the same vehicle with him, but not before James had told him that he was *'ein blödes Arschloch'*, and almost created a diplomatic incident.

On this occasion, however, the early morning game drive provided his first birthday presents. In the second ebony grove, not far from either the camp or the river, they watched in disbelief as wild dogs chased a small pride of lions off a buffalo kill, which they had heard during the night. The lions were obliged to spend the rest of the morning up the trees, until the magnificent dogs had satisfied their hunger. Further upstream, the biggest crocodiles he had ever seen had assembled to twist and tear at the rotting flesh of a hippopotamus, which had died of anthrax. Diana had stopped counting when she reached three hundred, as the menacing reptiles waited for their turn, their hideous jaws opening slowly and then, with horrifying speed and power, snapping shut to lock on their prey with a sound like the crack of a high-powered rifle. They thrashed with rapid, corkscrew movements, whipping the water with their long tails, as they wrestled for their share and gorged themselves on the unexpected banquet in the seething, muddy water.

On that day, it was Howard Sanders, the youngest of the three trail leaders, who was in charge. His skill, knowledge, and enthusiasm enhanced their every experience in the bush. Returning towards camp for a welcome breakfast, Howard suddenly stopped the open Toyota vehicle.

"There's an abandoned jeep over there," he whispered.

Being the driver, he did not enjoy as good a field of vision as did his clients from the vantage point of the high bench-seat behind him. Yet it was he who usually spotted first anything of interest.

"We had better go over and have a look," James urged. "Whoever it is might have broken down, or they might have had an accident."

"Or it might be poachers!" Howard added, concealing the smile on his face.

They pushed forward slowly through the long, dry grass, twisting and turning between the trees and nosing their way through light bushes towards the clump, where they had last seen the other vehicle. They turned past a large thornbush, climbed a steep bank, and emerged on to a grassy clearing where, in the shade of a mahogany tree, a table was set with a white tablecloth and chairs beside the river.

"Breakfast in the bush for the birthday boy," Howard announced with a big grin on his face. "Happy birthday, James!"

"Happy birthday, *Bwana!*" a voice came like an echo from behind the tree, and then appeared the smiling, black face of Brighton, the cook-cum-waiter whom they had nicknamed, 'Bognor Regis'.

"Bugger Bognor!" James exclaimed.

Brighton responded with his inimitable cackle of laughter, preening himself over the compliment that a *musungu*, a white man, should do him the honour of giving him a nickname.

They greeted each other in the African way, supporting the right elbow with the left hand while they shook hands, followed by two squeezes around their thumbs, and finally shaking hands again. Brighton then began tapping softly on his bongo drums the call which announced that food was ready, and they were served with a cooked breakfast. Using only his fingertips and the palms of his hands, he changed rhythm during the meal, and when James asked him what the beat signified, he stopped to explain.

"I am telling the animals not to worry even one little bit. I tell them that you, my brothers and my sister, friends of my family, even of my tribe, have come again to your second home in the bush. The big ones know that today they are as safe as the Bank of Zambia!"

Brighton was not the only onlooker. Four noble giraffes stepped gracefully into the clearing. They approached serenely to within twenty feet, their limpid, brown eyes shining with curiosity over the strange spectacle below them. The sound of Brighton's drums fell away to a softer beat. Satisfied that these humans were no threat to them, the giraffes began to browse the nearby trees, their necks arching upwards as they tailored the lower branches at the extremity of their reach, creating the illusion of skilled topiary on the underside of the luxuriant foliage. James walked slowly up to the nearest giraffe and, as a wet nose, long eyelashes, and stunted horns filled his viewfinder, the towering beast wheeled round.

"Be careful, James!" Howard called. "They've got a hell of a kick."

As he raised the camera again, the giraffe defecated noisily, and the shutter clicked.

"That's what he thinks of your birthday!" Diana laughed.

"Ah! Shit!" was Brighton's amused reaction to the event.

*

A sound similar to that of an alpine horn, followed by three loud shots in rapid succession, broke into his reverie and shattered the silence of the valley. Then two more shots were fired as he opened his eyes in shock.

"Poachers!" he yelled, leaping out of bed.

"What is it?" Diana cried, rudely awoken by the commotion.

"Guns! Bloody guns! And dogs! Lots of them, by the sound of it!"

He opened the shutters and looked towards the orchard, where a group of five stocky men with their dogs were walking up between the plum trees, heading for the drive.

"Fucking hunters!" he cursed. "The season must open today. Damned cheek, coming on to our property! Anyway, they're not allowed to shoot so close to a dwelling. I'll soon fix that lot!"

He ran upstairs, picked up the large conch shell which he had found on Lamu Island, and went out on to the roof *terrasse*. The hunters were now almost level with the house and were advancing up the drive, their dogs baying and running hither and thither, apparently out of control as they picked up the scent of the cats.

"They've got a bloody nerve!" he said to himself.

He filled his lungs and sounded three long blasts on the horn-like shell, each note fading into a ghostly vibrato. The eerie sound echoed across the valley, and the group of men halted, looking about them in confusion over the nature and origin of the noise. They had not seen him, still dressed in his pyjamas, standing on top of the parapet of the roof *terrasse*.

"Ne bougez pas!" he bellowed down to the group. "Don't move! *C'est une violation de propriété privée! Je descends.* You're trespassing on private land! I'm coming down."

He struggled into his gumboots and ran down the stone steps to confront the intruders. Diana had reached them first. Clad in her short nightdress, she had run in her bare feet through the dew and was now standing defiantly in their way. He did not recognize any of the men.

"Qui êtes-vous? Vous n'êtes pas d'ici?" he demanded angrily. "Who are you? You're not from around here, are you?"

No reply was offered. The men looked about guiltily, giving James the courage to press home his advantage of surprise.

"Vous n'avez que deux petites minutes pour maîtriser vos sales cabots!" he threatened. "You've got just two minutes to control your rotten dogs!" It was an empty threat, and he knew it as soon as he had uttered it. If they spent the rest of the morning trying to collect their hounds, there was not very much he would be able to do about it, except perhaps to summon the *gendarmes.*

Three of the men obeyed his command and, more by chance than as a result of any effective gun-dog training, one by one the hounds were grabbed, restrained, and safely put on their leashes.

"Vous êtes tous auteurs d'une violation de propriété! Si jamais vous revenez ici, vous serez passible d'amende!" he growled at them. "You are all trespassers! If you ever come back, you will be prosecuted! *Et la chasse est.formellement interdite sur nos terres!* And hunting is strictly forbidden on our land!"

"If one hair of my cats is harmed," Diana screamed like a fishwife at them in English, "then I'll bloody well kill the person responsible!"

The men stood rooted to the spot, mouths agape, without comprehending her vicious tirade, but the tone of her voice was sufficient to scare them into retreat.

"Allez vous faire foutre, bande de voyous!" he shouted at their backs. "Go on! Piss off, you hooligans!" He took her hand, and they climbed the bank up to the bedroom.

"Merde!" he swore. "What a way to start a Wednesday!"

Diana sat pensively on the bed, while she dried the dew on her feet. James found her in the same position when he took her a cup of coffee.

"We had better keep the cats in today," she muttered. "Just in case another lot tries the same game. Now I want you to do an urgent job for me. After breakfast, you must go to town and buy enough of those red *'Chasse Interdite'* notices. I've seen them in the *Co-op Agricole*. Then, as soon as you get back, and before you do anything else, will you please put them up on the trees all around our boundary?"

"But that will cost a fortune!" he protested. "I'll have to buy at least a hundred to do that!"

"Don't talk to me about spending vast sums of money! To hell with the cost! I'm not going to risk it. Do we know their shooting days?"

"Wednesdays and Sundays, *en principe*, I'm afraid."

He could see from the look on her face that she was about to say something which either or both of them would later regret.

"And I thought we were going to buy a house," she said in an irritated tone, "with cat security and no hunters, without too much garden and land, and which needed no structural alterations! All four requirements have been bust wide open already!"

He was about to protest that the decision to buy Bon Porteau had been a joint one, when she relented.

"I'm sorry, my love," she said contritely. "I didn't sleep too well last night. Your snoring is getting much worse. Chantal is due at two o'clock, so I'll tell her what I want her to clean and then I'll go to Cahors. I may be back late, I want to get my hair cut."

"Good idea," he agreed, hoping his comment would not be misinterpreted.

*

The *Co-op Agricole* in Montcarmel could provide only thirty-five red notices forbidding entry to the hunting fraternity. Some were circular, plastic plaques, and others were oblong signs made of metal. He bought their stock, which he knew would be insufficient. As he was leaving the shop, he toyed briefly with the idea of cutting and painting the rest of the notices himself, but he soon discarded the idea — he was no sign-writer and, furthermore, the task would take weeks, if not months, to complete. He realized that he was now obliged to drive to Cahors to make up the deficiency, and he cursed at the extra time and work involved in his already busy schedule for the day.

After combing seven different shops, buying in each their stock of notices, he finally managed to find a box of twenty red, triangular signs, bringing his total up to eighty-two which, he suspected, would still not be enough to do the job properly. It was of no consequence, he felt, that their shapes and sizes were not uniform, although he had to admit to himself that it irritated his tidy mind. The morning was almost over, and he exceeded the speed limit during most of the journey back to Bon Porteau. Fortunately for him, he saw no sign of any *flics*, and there was no speed trap.

It was just before midday when he parked in front of the barn. He hurried down to the house, anxious to get started on the lengthy task along the boundaries of the property.

"Don't worry about any lunch for me today," he called to Diana. "I'm off to finish this job. Have you seen any more hunters?"

"No, but I've heard plenty of them," she replied from the bottom of the miller's ladder. "I'll warn Chantal not to let the cats out. Keep an eye on her from time to time. She'll be here at two for four hours. See you this evening when I get back."

"Oh, by the way, I forgot to tell you, darling," he called down to her in what he hoped sounded a suitably casual tone, "I've booked a table at the *Auberge de la Tour* for tomorrow night. They've got some kind of a dance on as well, which might be fun. So you'll be able to get dressed up in your party clothes. *À bientôt!*"

It took him over two hours to carefully position all the notices where they would be seen easily, and then to fix them securely to selected trees. However, his supply of signs was exhausted when he had covered only about two-thirds of the perimeter of the property. He walked along the remaining section of the boundary, counting as he went. He calculated that he needed an additional thirty-seven signs, two of which would have to be nailed to stakes in the ground on a stretch where there were no trees.

"That will have to do for now," he said to himself, standing at the top end of the property. "I'll try to get the rest done before Sunday." Walking back to the house, he decided to telephone Piers as soon as he could, and then to contact Jules before he started cleaning the barn.

*

The first thing he noticed was that the jeep had gone. Diana had left for Cahors. A small, bright blue Renault stood in the drive. That must belong to Chantal, he thought. Then he saw the front door. It was wide open. He started running towards the house.

"*Merde!*" he cursed "She'll let out the fucking cats!"

Then he stopped, a baffled look on his face. He knelt down to make a closer examination.

"What the hell is going on around here?" he shouted out.

Lying in a heap on the grass where they had been thrown were two of his finest Persian rugs, part of a collection assembled diligently over many years. They were soaking wet. He slowly entered the front door and peered around the corner, wondering what he might find. The floor of the living-room was awash with soapy water. An upturned bucket and the floor mop were sufficient evidence of what had happened. Of Chantal, there was no sign. More importantly, as far as he was concerned, neither Jacob nor Fosbury were in their bed beside the French windows. He heard behind him the creak of the miller's ladder, as if one of the cats was climbing stealthily up the steps. Looking over his shoulder, he noticed the soapy water had reached the edge of the stairway. He could hear it trickling down to the lower level of the house.

Then Chantal's head appeared at the top of the ladder. Her long, blonde hair had fallen across her face. She stepped up into the kitchen. She was naked, except for her knickers, which were drenched. He gulped, speechless; his first, fleeting impression was the beauty of her body and the tantalizing perfection of her breasts, which tilted firmly upwards. He could see the triangle of her pubic hair, which was dark. She is beautiful, he thought, but not a natural blonde! Then he realized that she had been crying. They moved towards each other and she fell against him. She was no taller than his shoulders, and he could smell her perfume as she turned her face up to look at him with dark brown eyes.

"*M'sieu, je m'appelle Chantal. Je m'excuse...*"

"*Enchanté, Chantal,*" he replied, forcing himself not to be distracted by her nudity and to remain as calm as possible under the circumstances. "*Mais, qu'est-ce qui vous est arrivé?*" he asked gently, putting his arm around her shoulders. "But what's happened to you?"

"*Merde! C'était le gris!* It was the grey one. I put the mop and bucket up there. *Euh! Baah, je lui ai dit d'arrêter de faire l'idiot.* I

told him to stop fooling around. *Bof!* He took fright and knocked the
whole lot for six, all over my clothes. *Et puis, il s'est enfui.* And then
he ran away out of the door."

She stepped back from him, pulling her long hair off her face. She
was shivering, her arms clasped to her stomach. She was not
embarrassed by her nudity; she was feeling cold.

"Come, Chantal," he said, taking one of her hands. "We'll find
you a towel and one of my wife's housecoats."

He went ahead down the soaking steps and turned to help her.
From his position on the lowest step, he admired her boyish hips,
which gave the illusion that her slim legs reached up to her narrow
waist. She followed him demurely into the bedroom without saying
another word.

"Wait here, while I find you a towel."

He went to the linen cupboard and returned to the bedroom. She
pulled down her knickers, stepped out of them, and dried her crotch
and under her breasts. Her nipples dilated and then went hard again.
He found a long, cream-coloured, cotton wrap, and handed it to her.

"*Ça va mieux? T'as plus froid?*" he asked her, using the familiar
form of address. "Is that better? You're not feeling cold any more?"

"*Eh baehh, oui! Oui, j'ai assez froid!*" she repeated, leaving the
front of the housecoat hanging open. "Yes! Yes, I'm quite cold!" She
looked at the wide bed. "*T'es un mec cool! Chiche! Un petit bisou?*"
she whispered. "You're a cool guy! Go on, I dare you! A little cuddle,
eh?" She sat down on the bed, the wrap falling free of her shoulders,
and looked him up and down. He could feel his desire mounting
rapidly. It had not escaped her notice.

"*Aïe! Là-là! Que t'es vachement bien monté! Viens voir ta petite
cocotte!*" she breathed invitingly. "Hey! That's a good one you've got
there! Come to your little chick!"

He smiled down at her and pulled the wrap up around her. As she
stood up, he tied the belt firmly around her slim waist.

"*Viens, Chantal,*" he said kindly. "*Il y a beaucoup de boulot à
faire.* Come, there's lots of work to do."

They went into the cellar and put her wet clothes into the
tumble-dryer, watching silently for a few moments as it started its

programme.

"Only a week ago," he said, remembering the stocky lorry driver from Toulouse, "there was a nude Frenchman standing where you are now. He was also waiting for his clothes to dry."

"Buerk! Baah, tu marches pas à voile et à vapeur, toi?" she cried, with a disgusted took on her face. "Yuk! You're not AC-DC, are you?"

"You're a much better sight than he was, I can assure you," he laughed. As they went upstairs, he told her what had happened on that rainy morning when their boxes arrived from the airport.

"I'll help you clear up this mess," he offered. "And then we'll have some coffee. But first, let's mop up the rugs and spread them to dry out there over the parapet."

Later, while they drank their coffee, she answered his questions, one slim thigh seductively positioned outside the wrap. She was, as she put it, 'not yet forty years old', and married to François, the manager of a building materials firm working in Villeneuve. She had five children: a seventeen-year-old son, Matthieu; a daughter, Rosalie, who was nearly sixteen; Jean-Pascal, a boy of only five years; and baby twins, Daniel and Véronique. James's only reaction to her evident fertility was an ill-concealed *'Phew!'*, which spluttered out of his mouth with most of the contents of his small cup of black coffee.

"François has two lovers, you know," she announced suddenly. "I have seen him with the fat one. *C'est une vraie pouffiasse!* She's a real scrubber! So, you see, if he has two, I don't see why I shouldn't have just one, do you? I mean, a strong, healthy girl like me needs it, and I only get it twice a month if I'm lucky. Don't you want to be my lover? Don't you want to screw me?" She loosened the belt of the housecoat, and it felt open again.

"You don't have a lover at the moment?" he queried, avoiding her last two questions.

"Non! Pas du tout!" She shook her head and smiled demurely.

"Well, that should not be too difficult for a nice, good-looking girl like you," he confided in a matter-of-fact tone.

She leaned forward across the table, allowing him an uninterrupted view of her breasts. He thought that she was going to try yet again to seduce him, but she changed the subject.

"Matthieu takes his *bac* next year," she said, and then asked, "Will you teach him English? And Rosalie, too?"

Since Chantal was charging them an hourly rate, he did not hesitate this time to discuss a tuition fee.

"What we'll do is this," he suggested. "For every two hours you work here, I will repay you with one hour's tuition. So, if you do four hours a week, then that means Matthieu and Rosalie will each get an hour of English each week. In that way, money won't change hands, and the taxman can lump it. Agreed?"

"D'ac! T'es très sympa, James!" she replied coyly "Done! You're really nice! I wish we could get to know each other better."

"I must go and find the cats," he muttered, and left her to continue with her work.

He found Jacob and Fosbury in the barn. They had cornered a vole and they were both playing gently with it. Closing the door, he decided that he may as well allow them to stay there, while he broke open the three remaining crates, cleaned the floor, prepared the fire, and burned the rubbish. When he finished, he carried the cats down to the house and let them in through one of the bedroom windows, checking that all the doors on the lower level of the house were firmly shut. The tumble-dryer was whirring and squeaking towards the end of its programme. He shut the door to the cellar. Then he heard the shower. He walked slowly down the passage to the bathroom. The housecoat and her knickers lay on the bathroom floor. Chantal, he thought, was taking a shower.

"Ça va, Chantal?" he called to her.

"Et baah, ouais! Ça va très bien, merci," she replied, drawing aside the shower curtain which Diana disliked so intensely. *"Excuse ma tenue. Baah, pour nettoyer ici, c'est plus facile toute nue.* Excuse my dress, but it's easier to clean in here in the nude. You want to come in with me? *T'as envie d'entrer avec moi, hein?"*

"T'es drôlement bien foutue, et tu le sais, non?" he replied. "You've got a great body there, and you know it, don't you, eh?"

They both laughed. He gave her slim bottom a light slap and then quickly closed the curtain on her, grimly denying himself the pleasure of contemplating her beautiful body.

When Chantal announced that she had finished her work, he offered her an *apéritif*. She had never before tasted gin and tonic, so he mixed her a weak one. The last thing he wanted on his hands was having to deal with a tipsy Frenchwoman who was looking for the nearest, convenient lover. Nevertheless, he liked her for her lively spirit and her sense of humour; he also enjoyed her good looks. For a while, they talked and smoked over their drinks, and then he had an idea. He told her about the Big Day.

"Why don't you and François come to the party tomorrow?" he asked. "And bring Matthieu and Rosalie as well."

"*Quelle bonne idée!*" she exclaimed. "What a good idea! Of course we would all love to come."

When he shut the front door behind her, he remembered as a teenager his father's sound advice.

"Never shit on your own doorstep, my boy!"

*

He was pleased with himself. He had reached his target of forty-six guests for the Big Day and, with little effort on his part, he now had his first three language students. He ignored the fact that tutoring Sophie Briand would be an unpaid activity. Perhaps, he thought, he could in due course persuade Marcel to repay him in kind, such as logging in their woods. As soon as Chantal had left, he telephoned Jules Carendier.

"There will be forty-six people tomorrow night," he told the sculptor. "I believe they will all be present."

"And when can I come round to make a bow for the you-know-what?" Jules enquired, choosing his words judiciously in case Diana might be listening to their conversation.

"Well, Diana is in Cahors, so if you like to come over, we could do it now."

The result of his work was an exquisite creation. It was tied, not on the bonnet, but across the windscreen, and held in place by the car's two doors. Jules stepped back to admire it.

"*Et voilà!*" he cooed softly. "Now that really *is* a bow fit for a fairy!"

Chapter Twenty-Eight

The Big Day did not begin well. In fact, it would be difficult to imagine how it could have started any worse. Each morning over the past week, James had intercepted the post before Diana had any opportunity to open the letterbox under the walnut trees. He secretly removed all her birthday cards and three small parcels, hiding them carefully under the pullovers in his chest of drawers. Now, clad in his pyjamas, he pushed the 2CV silently out of the barn and parked it by the porch. He then repeated his clandestine raid on the mail, while Diana was struggling with the yellow hip bath. There were a few more cards, a pile of brochures, and an income tax demand. He opened the latter, and was both appalled and depressed by the sum of money which he might be required to pay. This, he thought, could never have happened in Italy.

As he returned to the house and went downstairs, Diana called to him on her way to the bedroom to get dressed.

"Ugh! You have to be a contortionist to get in and out of that bath. I really do want that shower curtain replaced before I use it. We need one of those proper cubicles with a door you can close. Please, James, put it on the top of your list for next week, will you?"

"We won't be putting anything much on the list if I really owe Great Britain Limited this much," he moaned, showing her the tax demand.

"You've always said that it's better to pay too much tax than too little, but this is crazy!" she protested. "You've been too honest with them. That's the trouble."

"They must have made a mistake. I'll appeal, of course," he countered, and then added nonchalantly, "Anyway, there are one or two things in today's mail for you. They're upstairs, waiting for you."

"Let me get dressed and I'll come up," she replied. "It looks as if I won't be getting many cards this year."

She opened a drawer, found the shirt she wanted to wear, and, before she could close it, Jacob jumped in and settled down for his morning nap.

"All my friends seem to have forgotten me," she said in a resigned tone, "including Kim. It'll be more than a bit off, if my only daughter forgets my birthday!"

He smiled and walked away down the passage towards the bottom of the miller's ladder, thinking that perhaps now matters could only improve with all the surprises he had in store for her.

"Ouch! *Merde alors!* Shit!" he cried out, having forgotten to duck through the low doorway.

"Oh, you haven't done it again, have you?" Diana shouted. "I heard that thump. Are you all right?"

He staggered back down the passage, clutching his forehead with both hands.

"Damn! I think I've really cut my head this time," he groaned, examining his bloodstained fingers.

"Don't come in here if you're bleeding," she said quickly. "Go into the bathroom. I'll bring a bandage."

He looked in the mirror and examined the result of her first aid. Watching the small patch of blood seeping through the bandage on his head, he thought it looked as if someone had put a bullet through the centre of his forehead. He felt weak at the knees. Then he realized that his ashen colour had more to do with the fact that he had not yet shaved the grey stubble from his face.

"Feeling better now, darling?" she asked solicitously.

"Bloody doorway!" he cursed. "Yes, I'll be fine, my love."

The cards and parcels lay carefully arranged on the table in the living-room. On top, as usual, were his own card and one from the cats, together with the gift-wrapped porcelain box. He felt sure that she would guess its contents, even before opening it.

"Oh! How lovely! What a surprise!" she exclaimed excitedly. "Look at all these cards!"

He stood beside the table, anticipating her usual ritual. She would open his card first, next the one from the cats, and then shuffle through the envelopes to find those written by her mother and by Kim. After putting these four important cards on the mantelpiece, she would open his small present, to be followed by a kiss and then, and only then, would he wish her a very happy birthday, swear his undying love for her, and promise her a magical day.

He was perplexed, therefore, when she ignored the cards and parcels, turning instead to the simple *petit déjeuner* of hot *croissants* and café au lait which he had prepared for her.

"What's up?" she asked. "Why are you staring at me as if I were a ghost? Are you sure you're feeling okay? That bang on your head..."

"Nothing, my love," he replied, his nonplussed frown concealed by the bandage. "Let's have breakfast first."

The remainder of the short meal passed in total silence, while he searched his mind and soul for some explanation of her bizarre conduct. Well, at least it's a lovely day for it, he thought, looking out at the cloudless sky.

When Fosbury sauntered into the room, she pushed back her chair and crossed to the front door.

"Go on, my big man," she told him quietly. "Out you go, but don't go far away."

She opened the front door, and Fosbury walked slowly out to the porch.

Then she saw it.

"James! What's *that* in the drive?"

"It's a car."

"I can see that, you idiot! But why is it there?"

"It's a 2CV, a baby Citroën, one of your birthday presents, my darling. Very happy birthday, my love." He kissed her tenderly. *"Je t'aime aujourd'hui plus qu'hier, mais moins que demain!* I love you today more than yesterday, but less than tomorrow! Come on, open your cards and other presents. It's going to be a day of magic! I can promise you that, as well!"

She looked at him, surprise and bewilderment on her pretty face, and then slowly sat down again.

"Oh James, darling," she sighed. "You're just impossible!"

He looked down at her and then, quite suddenly, at the same moment as she burst into silent tears, he realized that something was terribly wrong.

"Blimey! What on earth's the matter, darling?" he asked, putting his arms around her. "What's the big problem?"

"My birthday," she choked the words out between sobs, "is not today, my love. *It's tomorrow!*"

"Merde!" he cursed quietly, his mind racing in numbed panic. "What have I done now?"

"You're only a day out," she replied sombrely, drying her tears. "That's all you've done, isn't it? I know you too well by now. Don't tell me you've made other..."

Even if he had wanted to scream, or to own up to his other secretive preparations, he did not have time to answer her question, because at that moment Piers arrived, noisily sounding the horn of his large car.

"It's Piers," he announced, going out to greet his son. "He's made bloody good time. He must have driven much too fast."

"I thought he wasn't supposed to be coming until Saturday," she called after him. "The bed's not even made yet."

Out in the drive, he told Piers in a few words about his mistake and warned him that Diana was not very amused by it.

"All the surprises will misfire. It's all my fault. The day will be ruined. Just because I've got the wrong fucking day!" he concluded with a groan.

"Hell, Dad! It doesn't matter," Piers reacted calmly to his father's tale of woe. "Think positive! That's what you used to tell me. It'll be her birthday at midnight, and I'm sure the party will have only just started swinging by then, if you've got anything to do with it. We'll just have to forewarn your guests as they arrive, that's all. Don't worry about it. What have you done to your head?"

He told him about the low doorway and started to feel better immediately. It's amazing, he thought, how bloody confident and flexible the young are nowadays. Then he felt another spasm of concern.

"Where's Kim?" he asked. "You were supposed to..." He hesitated, and then went on quickly, panic sounding in his throat. *"Aïe! Merde!* I completely forgot to ring you yesterday! That Chantal, prancing around in the nude, put it right out of my head. I was going to ask you if you would kindly collect her from Toulouse airport on your way here. She lands in..." He looked at his watch. "She lands in fifty minutes."

"Okay, Dad. No problem. You ring the airport and leave a message for her. I'll go and fetch her now. See you in about two hours' time. You can tell me then all about Chantal and your bout of amnesia when I get back!"

James went back into the house as his son sped away down the drive, scattering gravel on to the grass. It would take him about fifty minutes to reach the airport.

"Where is he off to in such a hurry," Diana asked. "He didn't even come in to say hullo? Is everyone barking mad, or is it just me?"

"Just something I forgot to do, my love," he replied. "He'll be back soon. I'll go down and make up his bed now."

"There are times, James, when I think you're going prematurely gaga. These last few days your mind seems to have been on another planet!"

While Piers was collecting Kim from the airport, there were no other incidents. Stewart arrived unseen, driving down the track which led to the barn. He brought with him the two braziers which he had promised to make.

"Great! There's just one more thing, Stewart. Now that Airlie and Vincent have moved out, are you still using those folding beds? If not, do you think you could remember to bring them with you when you come this evening? I have a feeling that we might be needing them."

Later, during the morning, Guillaume telephoned to say that he was free on Saturday and he invited both of them to accompany him to three local vineyards.

"I think the ones which will interest you the most are: *Château Nozières* at Vire, near Puy-l'Evêque; *Domaine de Boulbènes,* in Saux; and *Château Laur* at Floressas. All of them are good friends of mine — you'll be sure of a good welcome. The wines, of course, are all quite different. Oh, and see you this evening! We're very much looking forward to it." They arranged that they would set off at about three o'clock on Saturday afternoon and, because Diana was in the room, he said nothing about the probability that Kim, Piers, and ten of their friends from England would also like to come.

Piers returned from Toulouse before midday and this time he had Kim with him. She was looking superbly fit, her long, auburn hair a delight to see.

"You're looking absolutely blooming!" James greeted her with a hug.

The three of them crept quietly into the house. They could hear Diana singing happily in one of the bedrooms below.

"Shh! Both of you go into the drawing-room," he whispered. "We'll give her a treat, as well as a surprise. Piers, take the champagne glasses with you."

He took a bottle out of the refrigerator and called down to Diana.

"Someone to see you. Can you be interrupted, or shall I tell him to go away?"

He heard a snigger from the other room.

"I'm coming up!" she shouted. "Who is it?"

He did not reply. He loosened the wire and the cork exploded, flying into the living-room, just as Diana emerged from the steps.

"What's going on now? Who is it, James? You should have kept the champagne for tomorrow." She almost tripped over the cork as she crossed the room. "We don't want to celebrate my..."

She stopped and stared in disbelief at Kim, who was sitting in one of the armchairs.

"Oh, Kim!" she shrieked.

"Mum!" shouted Kim at the same time.

Then mother and daughter rushed to each other's arms. For the second time that day, Diana started to weep. This time they were tears of joy.

They had not seen each other for about six months, and the bond between them was very close and loving. They were very good for each other.

"Darling, how wonderful! But what a lovely surprise!" Diana said, excitement and happiness in her voice. "How did you get here?" Before Kim could reply, she went on, "But where is Andrew?"

"Piers collected me from the airport. I can only stay for a week. My virile, rugby-playing husband's fine and sends his love, but he couldn't get away. He's in charge of the school's Sports Day at the weekend."

"Hullo, Diana," Piers broke in, giving her a hug. "I hope you don't mind me turning up two days early. I wanted to be here for your birthday."

"Don't be silly, Piers darling. You know your wicked stepmother loves you dearly. You're welcome here at anytime."

"And that goes for both of you," James added.

Piers took the champagne bottle and filled their glasses. Both Jacob and Fosbury came into the room to investigate the cause for the impromptu celebrations.

"Cheers everyone!" James said. "And Kim, Piers! A big welcome to Bon Porteau! We thought we would all have a little birthday reunion. Just the four of us, I mean."

"What a lovely surprise!" Diana said for the second time, her tears now turning to laughter.

"And don't forget to be ready at eight in your party clothes," James reminded them. "It's supper and dancing at the *Auberge de la Tour*. I've booked a table for four."

"Oh James," Diana said. "I don't want to be a spoilsport or throw a wet blanket on something you've planned, but can't we go out for lunch instead? Then we won't have to dine out this evening. It's lovely to have Kim and Piers here, but obviously I didn't know they were coming. It would be so much more convenient to go out now. Anyway, not having seen Kim for ages, we would much prefer to sit and chat quietly this evening, instead of a whole lot of noise and dreadful French music."

He felt immediately threatened. On what was supposed to be the perfect day, nearly everything so far had gone awry, or at least not exactly as he had planned. Starting to panic again, he wondered how he was going to manipulate events so that she would be dressed and ready for the party, unless he used the ruse of a fictitious date for dinner and dancing.

"It's going to be a bit tactless to duck out of my booking," he retorted without thinking where his off-the-cuff comments might be leading him. "I mean, it's obviously limited numbers and ticket-holders only tonight... And I did book almost a week ago... I really don't think it would be very fair to cancel at this short notice, my love... Unless, of course, you insist..."

He left his words hanging, hoping that the power of silence would provide a solution. It was Kim who came to his rescue She winked at James and asked for another glass of champagne.

"Mum, I'd really like to go out tonight," she began decisively. "I mean, there's something else to celebrate. I've got another surprise for you." She paused, a broad smile on her attractive face. "But I think you had better sit down before I tell you."

They sat together on the sofa, looking into each other's eyes. Kim took her mother's hand. There was a moment's hush.

"We can have a good chat this afternoon, Mum." She took a sip of champagne and then announced, "You're going to be the world's best grandmother! I'm pregnant, Mum!"

"Oh! My little baby!" Diana squealed with delight. "Oh, my darling Kim! That's marvellous news! You pregnant, and Jacob fully recovered are the best of all possible birthday presents!"

They hugged each other tightly, both of them looking up at the ceiling with glistening eyes.

"Oh dear! I think I'm going to cry again!" Diana said weakly. "It's all too much! I'm going to be a granny at forty-six!"

"Hey! Well done! Great news, Kim!" said James, joining in the hugging. "How did it happen? I mean, how much pregnant are you?"

They all laughed, and Diana dried her eyes for the third time that morning.

"How the hell do you think it happened?" Kim replied, rolling with laughter on the sofa. "I'm either going to have a baby, or I'm not. One can't be just a little bit pregnant, you know!"

"Congratulations!" Piers said, grinning happily. "What does that make me? Some kind of half a step-uncle! I'm very happy for you and Andrew."

"When are you due?" Diana asked, looking at her daughter's flat stomach.

"Yes," Piers added. "I thought you were supposed to have a bump. That's normal, isn't it?"

"They — that is, my doctor — said it should be towards the end of March. But Andrew and I think it will be the third week."

"Either Pisces or Aries," Diana said quickly.

"No, no!" James insisted. "The baby can't have a name like that, darling. If a girl, she must be Charlotte or Lottie; and if a boy, then he will be Lancelot. *Voilà!* And it's high time that you got married, Piers. There are not too many of us left now."

*

While he was fetching a second bottle of champagne, he

remembered the last time he had heard the words, 'Just a little bit pregnant'. Exhilda was visiting Diana at the house in Nalikwanda Road. They were sitting outside on the stoep, both women looking very pretty. Diana was wearing the kanga, which they had bought in Lamu. The caftan-like, long dress suited her figure perfectly. Exhilda had made her own traditional Zambian costume, giving the impression that at any moment she was going to sway gracefully into a fashion show. A strong bond of friendship existed between the two women, each enjoying the other's quick sense of humour. He had left them talking animatedly for more than two hours, and from time to time he heard their peals of laughter.

The sun was setting, and he decided to serve drinks before joining them. Before he sat down he looked up as always in wonder at the magnificent bougainvillaea hedge which enclosed the garden. It was at least twenty feet in height and in full bloom.

"You two have been having a good laugh," he said as he handed them their glasses. "Any good, new jokes?"

"We were just laughing at silly things," Diana replied.

"It's not so very silly for me to want to get married," Exhilda insisted with a giggle. "James, surely you can find me a rich, white husband, can't you? I need one so badly, and then I can leave here for good. It's my only hope."

"You don't want to leave, do you? Why?"

"Everything here is so very expensive. It's getting worse and worse every day. Our money is worth nothing, and most of our men are lazy fools. They are so incompetent, they can't even organize a successful coup!" They laughed at her, as she continued. "Most of them are thinking of only three things: free handouts, how to succeed at corruption, and sex."

"Sounds like a lot of other places in this mad world," Diana observed seriously.

Exhilda smoothed her skirt, pouting her lips as her large dark eyes looked at James.

"I suppose the only answer," she resumed, "is for me to go to bed with one of these young Swedish Aid men and get a little bit pregnant. Then he'll have to marry me."

"But you would die of cold in Sweden," he protested. "No, we'll find you a handsome *Marquis*, with a beautiful *château* in the South of France."

They laughed at his suggestion.

"If you were not already married, *I* would marry you, James."

"You wouldn't like his snoring, I can tell you," Diana warned her.

"But you can't snore when you're making love, can you James?" Exhilda pouted again, and then gave a flirtatious smile. "So there would be no time for snoring if *I* was your woman!"

*

Diana was teasing him, while she was dressing for the evening. She was radiantly happy and he had hoped that she might have put his earlier gaffe out of her mind.

"You and your surprises, James!" she gibed at him. "One of these days you'll get your come-uppance! I hope there are no more lurking around the corner. I've had enough today to last me for a lifetime!"

He did not reply immediately, but her remarks gave him a queasy feeling and prompted him to reflect. Surprises are supposed to be pleasurable — that is what most people are brought up to believe. A parent or a relative says to a small child, "I've got a lovely surprise for you!", and the child becomes excited. The question is then asked, "And which hand is it in?", and the excitement grows. The hand is opened, revealing a sweet, or a Dinky toy. The outcome is one of delight. Yet adults, he mused, are generally wary of surprises. Like a telegram, they represent an unexpected event. Surprises induce feelings of loss of personal control, a disruption of order and normality, as if life can no longer plod along its planned course.

"Don't worry, my love," he called to her, avoiding her implied question. "Not all surprises are nasty ones. Kim's news is exciting, isn't it? It's going to be a great evening, I'm sure. You know you like the *Auberge de la Tour*. The food is always fabulous, and I expect they'll have some good music. We haven't danced for ages."

He went upstairs to make a final check on the few remaining details. While Diana and Kim had gone out for an afternoon walk, the florist had delivered to the barn as instructed. He now carried the flower arrangements carefully down to the house, and hid them in one of the bedrooms in the roof space. Earlier in the day, Piers had produced an idea which delighted him.

"Why don't I go and buy forty-six big, red candles?" he had asked. "We can light them just before midnight and then give one to each guest. Diana will have to go round and blow them all out one by one. And then the birthday party spirit will get off to a good start with a lot of kissing!"

"Bloody good idea, Piers!" he agreed enthusiastically. "And I must introduce you to Pierre and Jules, because I want you to make sure that they are given some help when they bring in the food this evening." He now checked that the candles were in the sideboard. They were still in their original wrappers.

"Bloody modern packaging!" he cursed, as he fumbled to undo them. It would have taken him much longer if Piers had not arrived to help.

"Thank God it's going to be a fine night," he said. "Now, all we've got to do is to move the braziers and the four Tilley lamps out to the *terrasse*, light them, and bring the flowers down from the roof. Is there anything else? Oh, yes! Just one more thing. Help yourself to a drink, Piers. I'll be back shortly."

He crept silently down to Kim's bedroom to remind her of her essential role during the next ten minutes or so.

"It's your job to distract Mum," he told her. "Keep her down here, until you hear me blasting away on the conch shell. I'm going to turn on all the outside lights now. The British contingent should be here in about five minutes." He paused, a frown on his face. "Ah! That's it! I forgot to ask you to do one more thing. You know best your Mum's favourite music. Will you please take charge of all that?"

"Stop flapping, James," she whispered and then kissed him.

"Clever girl!" he murmured. "And wonderful news about the baby! Well done! We're going to have a great party now."

He went back upstairs to join Piers and started playing Barbra Streisand's "Love Songs" a little loudly, in the hope that she would help to dispel any lingering doubts about the night ahead. He checked the refrigerator.

"I hope we've got enough champagne, *con!*" he said aloud, and poured himself a large gin and tonic.

Chapter Twenty-Nine

He had told John, one of their closest friends, that it was important that 'the Windlesham Mob' should be the first to arrive at the party.

"I've ordered a ten-seater minibus to collect you from the hotel. It will be there at half past seven. You'll have to ask Jim to be firm with Kate, since she's likely to spend three hours getting herself ready. So, if you don't mind, I'm putting you in charge of the bus. I'll be expecting you at eight for drinks and supper, and then the birthday party will begin at midnight."

"I've always wanted to be a bus conductor," John said with his dry sense of humour. "But it's too late for me now. They're all one-man crews."

He now stood with Piers by the parapet of the roof *terrasse*, waiting for a glimpse of the minibus. The conch shell was ready beside him.

"It really is a superb spot here, Dad. You've done bloody well. How on earth did you manage to find it?"

"Oh, that's a long story. I'll tell you sometime. You can have a good look round tomorrow morning, before we all go on our wine-tasting trip in the afternoon. But you're right. I'm very pleased and happy about it. Good neighbours, and it's so..."

He stopped talking, looked at his watch, and then peered across to the end of the drive, into which a white minibus had just turned.

"Merde!" he said. "I don't believe it. Good old John! They're bang on time. It's a blooming miracle! I wonder what Jim had to say to Kate to achieve the impossible!"

As the bus passed the front of the house, he was waving happily, trumpeting as hard as he could on the shell. He could hear the noise of laughter and shouting coming from the minibus, as it climbed the steep bend at the end of the drive.

"I don't think you know this wild bunch," he told Piers. "Don't forget to grab the driver. His next job is to help Pierre and Jules bring the food."

The bus drew up, disgorged its passengers, and noisy greetings were exchanged. Then, in the deepening twilight, beyond the pool of light from the porch, they formed themselves into a ragged line. Signalling the beginning of a conga dance, they started chanting, just as Diana and Kim appeared, framed in the front doorway.

"James!" Diana yelled, straining to see out into the gathering dark. "What on earth is going on? Who are all these people?"

She stepped aside, speechless, as ten of her closest friends danced into the light coming from the porch. Without pausing, they passed her noisily up the stone steps into the house, the conga winding its way through the living-room, into the drawing-room, and then out on to the roof *terrasse*. There was a momentary lull in the bedlam and Diana, with Kim at her side, stepped out into the floodlit scene. Their friends, men and women alike, were all dressed as Breton fishermen, with rope-soled shoes, baggy trousers, black berets, their blue-and-white striped T-shirts under dark blue Guernsey pullovers.

"Welcome to Bon Porteau everybody!" James shouted. "Here she is! Out of Africa! Her birthday party starts at midnight, so until then, let's have a bloody good house-warming party! It's wonderful that you have all made the effort to come out here. Now that you know where we live, both Diana and I hope that you will come again. *Allons-y, nos amis!*"

Then everyone was hugging and kissing Diana, who was laughing and shouting excitedly.

"I hope she's not going to burst into tears for the fourth time today," James whispered to Kim.

"Of course she isn't. Look! She's loving every minute of it. By the way, Piers told me about your little mistake this morning. Mum's right, you know. You are going a bit gaga, but we do love you. I'll go and organize some music now."

"And I the champers."

When he gave Diana her glass, she hugged him tightly and kissed his ear.

"You're just impossible, James. But I really do love you, and this is all a wonderful surprise. When are we all going to move on to the *Auberge de la Tour*?"

"We're not," he replied with a grin. "You said you didn't want to eat out tonight with, as you put it, a whole lot of noise and dreadful

French music. So we will be eating here and then we'll dance to your own nice music. I hadn't booked the *Auberge* anyway. *Voilà!"*

"But the food...?"

"Don't worry about it. *Tout est en ordre, ma chérie.* Every little detail is arranged, my darling. You just enjoy yourself. You're still only a young forty-five-year-old."

Félicie and Pascale were the first of the French guests to arrive, followed closely by Guillaume and Monique.

"O-là-là, là-là, Diana!" Félicie shrieked. "It's just as I told you when you bought the house. It was built for magnificent parties and lots of guests! *Superbe!"*

Guillaume was ceremoniously carrying in a crate of rare, still champagne.

"C'est doux," he explained. "Delicious with the sweet course."

Then Guy Raynal came into the house and kissed Diana.

"And how is your errant Jacob? He has not visited me recently."

Amid the increasingly animated gathering, James missed the arrival of Monsieur and Madame Louisor, and it was not until he saw the back of the svelte, chic Frenchwoman, that he realized who she was. She turned towards him as he approached.

"Bonsoir, Madame Louisor! It's so nice to see you again. You're looking fabulous, if I may be permitted to say so."

"Please call me Martine. But you have not come to see me in Cahors," she said, offering her cheek for a kiss. It was not all she offered — as she leaned forward, her expensive, black silk, low-cut evening dress presented more than just a glimpse of her cleavage. She knew that James was enjoying the view, and offered her other cheek, moving her shoulders sideways sensuously.

While she sifted through a pile of cassettes and compact discs, Kim was talking to Fifine, who was wearing the kind of tight dress which does nothing to conceal overweight thighs below heavy buttocks.

"Hullo, Fifine," James greeted her with a light kiss on each cheek. "I see you've met Kim. Are you still slimming?"

"You haven't come to the garage recently," she laughed, returning his kisses a little less formally. "I leave for the States at the weekend. You must come to my farewell party on Saturday. Kim tells me your son is here. His name is Piers, yes? Which one is he?"

He pointed her towards the area where the champagne was being opened. "The one with blond hair and a blue and yellow, striped shirt. Go and have some fun!"

"See you later then, Kim," Fifine said over her shoulder.

*

A car's horn sounded as it parked near the porch. It was the minibus, from which Pierre and Jules were struggling to lift a large box.

"I'll get some more pairs of hands!" James called down to them. "Don't try and lift that! You'll rupture yourselves!"

Willing helpers descended on the bus and, supervised by Pierre, box after box was carried into the house. The two Parisians were dressed in identical, white linen suits, over which they were wearing pink aprons and tall, white, chef's hats. Diana had yet to meet them but, for the moment, she and the rest of the already boisterous party fell silent and watched in awe as the meal was revealed.

"And we have brought some champagne," Jules announced. "Just in case your cellar runs dry!"

"Diana," James said, taking her hand. "These are our amazing neighbours, Pierre and Jules Bouyou-Carendier."

"Enchanté, Diana," the French couple said in unison, and then Jules added, *"Voilà, Pierre!* I told you she is stunning, isn't she?"

"Fabuleuse!" crooned Pierre, as he gently held on to her hand for a few seconds. *"Nous nous réjouissons de votre venue dans le Lot!* We rejoice at your coming to the Lot!"

"You are too kind," Diana protested to them and then turned to face James. "But you should never have allowed them to go to all this trouble. Look! They've even brought an entire dinner service and cutlery!"

"Diana, we explained to James," Pierre confided, "that this is our hobby. God does not subtract from our allotted span of life on earth the hours one spends preparing food! Now, if you will excuse us, we must attend to one or two little things."

The Parisian couple moved away to rummage among the boxes and were beginning to fuss over the display of magnificent food, just as Miguel and Pénélope appeared in the doorway. Vincent and Airlie, dressed in harlequin outfits, danced into the house, and there followed a noisy reunion between Piers and H-J who, like every well-prepared ex-public schoolboy on holiday, was wearing a slightly crumpled dinner jacket. James overheard the first question with which Piers greeted his schoolfriend.

"And what the hell are you doing with yourself nowadays, Hairy-John?"

"I've just finished my reference book on butterflies of Eastern Europe and Asia. Got to find a publisher now. It's very comprehensive... Unique, in fact. It shouldn't be too difficult. And you..?"

"*Merde!* The confidence of the young!" James said under his breath, thinking of the young man's brilliant father.

He was distracted as he noticed the farmer, Gilles Griffoul and his young wife coming up the steps, together with Marcel Briand and Micheline. He chided Marcel, when he produced a bottle of rare *Armagnac*.

"I've brought you six chickens," Gilles announced, pointing to a coop which he had dumped unceremoniously in the porch. "You'll find they're good layers."

In the meantime, Diana was greeting Monsieur Flouret and a petite, dark-skinned woman.

"I'm delighted to be able to tell you that Jacob is fully recovered, *Monsieur*," she told the vet. "I am so grateful to you for coming out so quickly in the middle of the night." She turned to the good-looking woman by his side. "Being a vet's wife, you must put up with a lot."

"*Ah non, Madame! Je ne suis pas sa femme! Je m'appelle Sabine, sa concubine.*" Her lilting words sounded like poetry. Then she broke into fluent English. "I could never get married and live with him! I believe in liberty and all that!" She spoke with hardly a trace of an accent.

Chantal swayed into the room behind the vet, and James was introduced, first to the children, and then to her husband. Matthieu appeared to be very nervous, in contrast to Rosalie who was a taller and even more attractive version of Chantal.

"I shall be teaching you two English on Sunday mornings," he said, looking from Matthieu to Rosalie.

"Good," replied Rosalie in English, while she looked him up and down. "I don't like *le prof* who teaches us English at school."

François peered suitably sternly through the thick lenses of his spectacles at his daughter, already six inches taller than him. James recalled Chantal's comment that her diminutive husband had two lovers and wondered how it could be true.

"I wonder what he's got that I don't have," he said to himself. "He looks like a normal, serious father."

The party was now in full swing, and everyone was enjoying themselves. Most people had finished eating and were now dancing to the latest compact disc release from Dire Straits. He tried to spot Jules and Pierre to thank them for a memorable meal, but they were nowhere to be seen.

"Someone has still not arrived," he said to Diana.

"It's the Kenya cowboys," she replied. "I presume you invited them."

As Diana was speaking, Fifine took her third helping to finish the *pêche Bourdaloue*, together with the last of the frangipane cream.

"Typical white Africans!" he muttered. "If they don't turn up soon, they'll miss all the food."

Chantal, with a strange, almost contemptuous look on her face, was watching Fifine.

"Having a nice time, Chantal?" he asked. "Come and dance."

"Look at her!" Chantal spat out the words, as they moved together. "How did she get here? That's her, the slut! She's the fat one I told you about. And look how François ogles her all the time. It's disgusting! I would like to give her a damn good thrashing here and now!"

"Not tonight, Chantal. Not here. I'm sorry," he said sympathetically. "She's due to leave for the United States at the weekend, if that's any consolation."

"I won't make a scene, James. I promise," she sighed, and he felt her pelvis move against him as they started dancing more closely. She had the same perfume which she had been wearing in the shower. He enjoyed it, as well as her proximity to him.

Iain's house party announced themselves noisily, sounding the horn of their car all the way up the drive. Laetizia and Vanessa were both in authentic Arab costumes, with yashmaks covering their faces. Stewart, Greg, and Boet, his friend from Namibia, were all wearing Somali kikois wrapped around their waists.

"We had a bit of a delay," Laetizia explained. "I hope we're not too late." Then she noticed the remains of the feast being cleared away. "Oh dear! I didn't know you were providing food..."

"Well, there's plenty of liquid left," James interrupted her. "I'm sorry you missed an amazing supper. Jules and Pierre prepared everything." He checked the time. "The birthday celebrations start in twenty-five minutes." He looked out beyond them into the porch and then asked, "But where's Iain?"

"He's coming as soon as he can," Stewart replied, picking pieces of hay and straw off the front of his shirt. "And I've brought back your two folding beds."

A short while later, he spotted Diana with the vet. She was moving like an African girl to the rhythm of *'Malaika, na kupenda, malaika'*, the Swahili love song sung by Myriam Makeba. Piers was dancing with Chantal. They were talking and laughing. He worked his way through the dancing couples to join them by the parapet.

"What are you two finding so amusing?" he asked them.

"Chantal has just explained to me why she was wandering about in the nude, which you told me was the reason why you forgot to ring me yesterday. Honestly, Dad!"

"Your father thinks I've got a beautiful body!" Chantal shouted just as the music paused, causing several startled faces to turn in their direction. "Well, so do I, Chantal," Piers murmured, holding her firmly against him.

"Piers, I'm sorry to interrupt your fun. I think you had better prepare to light the candles. I'm sure Chantal and Kim will help you. The night is young."

"I don't want candles, James," Chantal whispered. "I just want cuddles. I want *you*!"

He looked out over the parapet and thought he saw two figures in pale clothing moving about in the grass on the other side of the drive. Then they were gone. Next came an unfamiliar sound from somewhere down to his right. He looked out across the lawns towards the millstones. A lantern was waving from the end of a shepherd's crook. As it came abreast with the house, he realized that it was Iain, riding his chestnut gelding, his kikoi pulled up about his waist, exposing his bare legs and his feet in pink, rubber flip-flops.

"Jambo, Mzee!" Iain shouted his greeting up to James, at the same time raising what appeared to be a bowler hat. "Sorry I'm a bit late. It took me rather longer to get here than I expected. I forgot to bring my hot potato! I'll put Thunderballs up in the barn, if that's okay with you... Just in case there are any edible car bonnets about. I don't want any more insurance claims just yet!"

*

The party was becoming increasingly noisy. It was five minutes before midnight. Kim gradually faded the music and, one by one, the dancing couples stopped moving.

"Kim and Piers are now coming round to give each of you a candle," he announced in the lull which followed. "In a few minutes, Diana will be a year older and just as beautiful as ever..."

He was interrupted by shouts of approval from their English friends.

"Unlike you, James!" John heckled.

"Will you all please make sure your glasses have got something in them?" he resumed when the laughter died down.

He asked Iain to turn down the Tilley lamps, and Chantal switched off the big outside lanterns. In the darkness, forty-six candles were held high, flickering in a circle which formed around Diana. James kissed her, and suddenly *'Joyeux Anniversaire'* was competing raggedly with 'Happy Birthday to You'.

"Very happy birthday, my dearest love," he whispered softly in her ear and then announced, "Now Diana must blow out all your candles!"

James offered his candle first, followed by Jules and Pierre, who withdrew discreetly from the immediate circle of friends and guests. When she had blown out the last candle, everyone applauded and then, suddenly, fireworks started to stream up into the clear night sky, rockets exploding, coloured balls with silver and golden rain cascading into the valley, where three catherine wheels whirred, banged, and then spluttered, finally petering oui.

"Kim!" Diana yelled out, as soon as she realized what was happening. "Kim! Quickly! Help me to find the cats and shut them in the cellar!"

Jules and Pierre could be seen darting to and fro, maintaining the momentum of the display. At one stage, seven rockets were competing for attention and air space at the same time. Whenever a particularly loud explosion resounded or a spectacular pattern appeared, it was accompanied by childlike cries of delight, more applause, and people shouting 'Ooh!' and 'Aah!'. Diana and Kim returned in time to see the final noisy rocket soar above the heads of the gathered guests and streak safely over the roof of the house, where it separated with three simultaneous, dramatic detonations, one of which curved away to jettison its cargo of coloured stars against the window of the barn. One and all were whooping and whistling at this grand finale.

As the noise died away and the smoke cleared, another sound intruded upon the happy, festive scene. It seemed like loud, viciously determined, hammering. Wood was splintering and cracking. Then there came a shattering crash. The next moment, a terrified horse galloped in a crazed state away from the barn, hooves clattering down the drive.

"Merde!" James swore. "That's all we needed! Hey, Iain! There goes Thunderballs! You had better get after him and retrieve that hot potato, before he gets all the way to Toulouse!"

The four men in Iain's party rushed out into the night, their torches lighting up their flapping kikois as they sprinted after the runaway horse. Before they disappeared from view, both Iain and Stewart had lost their kikois and were running on boldly in their underpants.

"They canna' be real Jocks dressed like tha-a-t!" Jim shouted after them.

"And they had better not be caught by *les flics* either!" laughed Martine Louisor.

"I hope the fireworks display wasn't your idea," Diana muttered quietly to James. "You know I don't like them. The cats were petrified, like Iain's horse."

"No, I think that was a surprise present from our two splendid

Parisians. Misfired a bit, didn't it? Still, the horse won't go far."

The party regained momentum, and the merry-making continued until the first soft signs of dawn emerged through the light swathes of mist in the valley. The French guests were bemused when confronted with fried eggs, omelettes delicately flavoured *aux truffes,* mushrooms, and bacon, which Airlie and Vincent had surreptitiously prepared to mark the end of the celebrations.

"I could get a job as a *commis chef* anywhere," Vincent said proudly, as he scraped the remains of an omelette out of the pan.

James thanked them for their timely gesture and congratulated them on their skill, thinking to himself that it would be interesting to get to know them better. He then quickly turned away from the chaotic scene which they had created in the kitchen, and went in search of Jules and Pierre. He found them, together with Monsieur Flouret in the drawing-room, discussing the pregnancy of their miniature poodle.

"Jules et Pierre," he interrupted them. *"Qu'est-ce que je peux vous dire?* What can I say to you? That was an exquisite meal and the fireworks were superb! Thank you both for helping to make it a great party... And for being such wonderful neighbours! *Vous êtes, tous les deux, très, très sympa!"*

"We have enjoyed ourselves enormously," Jules laughed.

"Une fête réussie doit se terminer par le bouquet final!" Pierre added with a smile. "Every good party must go off with a bang!"

The music was playing more softly, and only those with sufficient stamina continued to dance slowly, among them Piers with Chantal, and Kim with Matthieu. All their English friends were talking animatedly, enjoying the excellent champagne which the Parisians had brought with them as a reserve supply.

"You haven't come here to retire, James, have you?" John asked. "What are you going to do to keep yourself out of mischief?"

"Good Lord, no! I'm only fifty-one," he replied to the first question and then began to expound on his projects, some of which he planned to start very shortly. "I begin English lessons on Sunday with Matthieu over there and Rosalie, his pretty little sister. Sophie, who isn't here tonight, begins her tuition next Wednesday. She's eighteen at Christmas, I think. Then-"

"I see," Jim interrupted, winking at Kate. "So that's what you call keeping out of mischief, is it?"

James ignored the innuendo and helped himself to a glass of Guillaume's still champagne.

"By the way, you're all invited on a wine-tasting trip this afternoon. Guillaume has selected three vineyards and he's agreed to delay our departure from here until five o'clock. That should give Kate enough time for beauty sleep and washing her hair." They all laughed as Kate blushed with embarrassment. "I can't wait to get my vineyard project started," he concluded.

The guests started to leave, and soon they were the only couple on the *terrasse*. One bottle of champagne remained. He opened it and filled their glasses.

"Well, that's the lot!" he said quietly, not feeling in the least bit tired. "Another year coming up for you, my love. Let's make it a damn good one!"

"As long as it's not like the last ten days," she sighed. "It seems as if we've been here a year already!" He squeezed her hand and raised his glass.

"*Tchin, tchin! Le Lot! Une surprise à chaque pas!* Never a truer word. Anyway, *ma chouette*, all that really matters is that you and I are happy with our Lot!"

He turned out the lights, and once more the special, soft silence of the valley wrapped itself around Bon Porteau as they crept into bed.

(La Fin du Début!)